'A strikingly restrained novel about a
woman awakening from grief and discovering
her own space, her own will'
WASHINGTON POST

'A moving masterpiece. Tóibín really
plumbs the heart of his characters and I
relished Tóibín's powerful writing'
WOMAN & HOME

'Urgent and sophisticated . . . it leaves
you with much to ponder'
INDEPENDENT ON SUNDAY

'Haunting, triumphant . . . will remain with
the reader long after the story has ended'
THE LADY

'Beautifully told'
GOOD HOUSEKEEPING

'So expertly crafted that it achieves a luminous
intensity, which lingers long in the memory'
MAIL ON SUNDAY

Nora Webster

COLM TÓIBÍN

PENGUIN BOOKS

PENGUIN BOOKS

UK | USA | Canada | Ireland | Australia
India | New Zealand | South Africa

Penguin Books is part of the Penguin Random House group of companies
whose addresses can be found at global.penguinrandomhouse.com.

First published by Viking 2014
Published in Penguin Books 2015

014

Copyright © The Heather Blazing Ltd, 2014

The moral right of the author has been asserted

Set in Dante MT Std
Typeset by Palimpsest Book Production Ltd, Falkirk, Stirlingshire
Printed in Great Britain by Clays Ltd, St Ives plc

A CIP catalogue record for this book is available from the British Library

ISBN: 978-0-141-04175-9

Bríd Tóibín (1921–2000)
Niall Tóibín (1959–2004)

Chapter One

'You must be fed up of them. Will they never stop coming?' Tom O'Connor, her neighbour, stood at his front door and looked at her, waiting for a response.

'I know,' she said.

'Just don't answer the door. That's what I'd do.'

Nora closed the garden gate.

'They mean well. People mean well,' she said.

'Night after night,' he said. 'I don't know how you put up with it.'

She wondered if she could get back into the house without having to answer him again. He was using a new tone with her, a tone he would never have tried before. He was speaking as though he had some authority over her.

'People mean well,' she said again, but saying it this time made her feel sad, made her bite her lip to keep the tears back. When she caught Tom O'Connor's eye, she knew that she must have appeared put down, defeated. She went into the house.

That night a knock came at almost eight o'clock. There was a fire lighting in the back room and the two boys were doing their homework at the table.

'You answer it,' Donal said to Conor.

'No, you do.'

'One of you answer it,' she said.

Conor, the younger one, went out to the hall. She could hear a voice when he opened the door, a woman's voice, but not one that she recognized. Conor ushered the visitor into the front room.

'It's the little woman who lives in Court Street,' he whispered to her when he came into the back room.

'Which little woman?' she asked.

'I don't know.'

May Lacey shook her head sadly when Nora came into the front room.

'Nora, I waited until now. I can't tell you how sorry I am about Maurice.'

She reached out and held Nora's hand.

'And he was so young. I knew him when he was a little boy. We knew them all in Friary Street.'

'Take off your coat and come into the back room,' Nora said. 'The boys are doing their exercise, but they can move in here and turn on the electric fire. They'll be going to bed soon anyway.'

May Lacey, wisps of thin grey hair appearing from under her hat, her scarf still around her neck, sat opposite Nora in the back room and began to talk. After a while, the boys went upstairs; Conor, when Nora called him, was too shy to come down and say good-night, but soon Donal came and sat in the room with them, carefully studying May Lacey, saying nothing.

It was clear now that no one else would call. Nora was relieved that she would not have to entertain people who did not know each other, or people who did not like each other.

'So anyway,' May Lacey went on, 'Tony was in the hospital bed in Brooklyn, and didn't this man arrive into the bed beside his, and they got talking, and Tony knew he was Irish, and he told him his wife was from the County Wexford.'

She stopped and pursed her lips, as though she were trying to remember something. Suddenly, she began to imitate a man's voice: 'Oh, and that's where I'm from, the man said, and then Tony said she was from Enniscorthy; oh, and that's where I'm from too, the man said. And he asked Tony what part of Enniscorthy she was from, and Tony said she was from Friary Street.'

May Lacey kept her eyes fixed on Nora's face, forcing her to express interest and surprise.

'And the man said that's where I'm from too. Isn't that extra-ordinary!'

She stopped, waiting for a reply.

'And he told Tony that before he left the town he made that iron thing – what would you call it? – a grille or a guard on the windowsill there at Gerry Crane's. And I went down to look at it and it's there all right. Gerry didn't know how it got there or when. But the man beside Tony in the bed in Brooklyn, he said that he made it, he was a welder. Isn't that a coincidence? To happen in Brooklyn.'

Nora made tea as Donal went to bed. She brought it into the back room on a tray with biscuits and cake. When they had fussed over the tea things, May Lacey sipped her tea and began to talk again.

'Of course, all of mine thought the world of Maurice. They always asked for him in their letters. He was friends with Jack before Jack left. And of course Maurice was a great teacher. The boys looked up to him. I always heard that said.'

Looking into the fire, Nora tried to think back, wondering if May Lacey had ever been in this house before. She thought not. She had known her all her life, like so many in the town, to greet and exchange pleasantries with, or to stop and talk to if there was news. She knew the story of her life down to her maiden name and the plot in the graveyard where she would be buried. Nora had heard her singing once at a concert, she remembered her reedy soprano – it was 'Home, Sweet Home' or 'Oft in the Stilly Night', one of those songs.

She did not think that May Lacey went out much except to the shops, or to Mass on Sundays.

They were silent now, and Nora thought that maybe May would go soon.

'It's nice of you to come up and see me,' she said.

'Oh, Nora, I was very sorry for you, but I felt I'd wait, I didn't want to be crowding in on you.'

She refused more tea, and when Nora went to the kitchen with the tray she thought that May might stand up and put on her coat, but she did not move from the chair. Nora went upstairs and checked that the boys were asleep. She smiled to herself at the thought of going to bed herself now, falling asleep and leaving May Lacey down below, staring into the fire, waiting for her in vain.

'Where are the girls?' May asked as soon as Nora sat down. 'I never see them now, they used to pass up and down all the time.'

'Aine is in school in Bunclody. She's settling in there now,' Nora said. 'And Fiona is doing her teacher training in Dublin.'

'You'd miss them when they go away,' May Lacey said. 'I miss them all, I do, but it's funny, of all of them, it's Eily I think about most, although I miss Jack too. There was something, I don't know, I just didn't want to lose Eily. I thought after Rose died – you know all this, Nora – that she would come home and stay and she'd find some sort of job here, and then one day when she was just back a week or two I noticed her all quiet and it wasn't like her, and she started to cry at the table, and that's when we heard the news that her fellow in New York wouldn't let her come home unless she married him. And she had married him there without telling any of us. "Well, that's that, Eily, then," I said. "You'll have to go back to him, so." And I couldn't face her or speak to her, and she sent me photographs of him and her together in New York, but I couldn't look at them. They were the last thing in the world I wanted to see. But I was always sorry she didn't stay.'

'Yes, I was sorry to hear that she went back, but maybe she's happy there,' Nora said and immediately wondered, as May Lacey looked down sadly, a hurt expression on her face, if that was a wrong thing to say.

May Lacey began to rummage in her handbag. She put on a pair of reading glasses.

'I thought I'd brought Jack's letter but I must have left it behind,' she said.

She examined a piece of paper and then another.

'No, I haven't got it. I wanted to show it to you. There was something he wanted to ask you.'

Nora said nothing. She had not seen Jack Lacey for more than twenty years.

'Maybe I'll find the letter and send it to you,' May said.

She stood up to go.

'I don't think he's going to come home now,' she said as she put on her coat. 'What would he do here? They have their life there in Birmingham, and they've invited me over and everything, but I told Jack I'd be happy to go to my reward without seeing England. I think though he'd like to have something here, a place he could visit and maybe Eily's children or some of the others.'

'Well, he has you to visit,' Nora said.

'He thought you'd be selling Cush,' May said, settling her scarf. She spoke as though it were nothing, but now, as she looked at Nora, her gaze was hard and concentrated and her chin began to tremble.

'He asked me if you'd be selling it,' she said and closed her mouth firmly.

'I've made no plans,' Nora said.

May pursed her lips again. She did not move.

'I wish I'd brought the letter,' she said. 'Jack always loved Cush and Ballyconnigar. He used to go with Maurice and the others, and he always remembered it. And it hasn't changed much, everyone there would know him. The last time he came home he didn't know half the people in the town.'

Nora said nothing. She wanted May to leave.

'I'll tell him I mentioned it to you anyway. That's all I can do.'

When Nora did not reply, May looked at her, clearly annoyed at her silence. They walked out and stood in the hall.

'Time is the great healer, Nora. That's all I can tell you. And I can tell you that from experience.'

She sighed as Nora opened the front door.

'Thank you for calling up, May,' Nora said.

'Goodnight now, Nora, and look after yourself.'

Nora watched her as she made her way slowly down along the footpath towards home.

She drove to Cush in the old Austin A40 one Saturday that October, leaving the boys playing with friends and telling no one where she was going. Her aim in those months, autumn leading to winter, was to manage for the boys' sake and maybe her own sake too to hold back tears. Her crying as though for no reason frightened the boys and disturbed them as they gradually became used to their father not being there. She realized now that they had come to behave as if everything were normal, as if nothing were really missing. They had learned to disguise how they felt. She, in turn, had learned to recognize danger signs, thoughts that would lead to other thoughts.

She measured her success with the boys by how much she could control her feelings.

As she drove down the hill outside The Ballagh and caught her first glimpse of the sea, it occurred to her that she had never been alone before on this road. In all the years, one of the boys, or the girls when they were younger, would shout out, 'I can see the sea!' just here and she would have to make them sit down and quieten.

In Blackwater, she thought of stopping for cigarettes or chocolate or anything to postpone her arrival at Cush. But she was sure that someone she knew would see her and want to sympathize with her. The words came easily: 'I'm sorry' or 'I'm sorry for your trouble.' They all said the same thing, but there was no formula for replying. 'I know' or 'Thank you' sounded cold, almost hollow. And they would stand looking at her until she could not wait to get away from them. There was something hungry in the way they held her hand or looked into her eyes. She wondered if she had ever done this to anybody, and thought that she had not. As she turned right towards Ballyconnigar she realized that she would feel much worse if people began to avoid her. It struck her that they were probably doing so, but she had not noticed.

The sky had darkened now and drops of rain hit the windscreen. It seemed much barer here, more wintry than the countryside on the road to Blackwater. She turned left at the handball alley for Cush and she allowed herself the brief respite of imagining that this was some time in the recent past, a dark summer's day with a threatening sky and she had gone into Blackwater for meat and bread and a newspaper. She had thrown them lightly on the back seat, and the family were all in the house beside the marl-pond, Maurice and the children, and maybe one or two friends with them, and the children had slept late, and they would be disappointed now that the sun was not shining, but it wouldn't stop them playing rounders or messing in front of the house or going to the strand. But if the rain was down for the day, of course, they'd stay in and play cards until the two boys would grow irritable and come to her to complain.

She let herself imagine all of this for as long as she liked. But as soon as she caught a view of the sea and the horizon beyond Corrigans' roof, such imaginings were no use to her, she was back in the hard world again.

She drove the car down the lane and unlocked the large galvanized gates. She parked in front of the house and closed the gates again so that no one could see the car. She would have loved it had one of her old friends been here, Carmel Redmond or Lily Devereux, who could talk to her sensibly not about what she had lost or how sorry they were, but about the children, money, part-time work, how to live now. They would have listened to her. But Carmel lived in Dublin and came only in the summer and Lily just came from time to time to see her mother.

Nora sat back into the car as the wind from the sea howled around her. The house would be cold. She should have taken a heavier coat with her. She knew that wishing friends were here or allowing herself to shiver in the car like this were ways of postponing the moment when she would have to open the door and walk into the empty house.

And then an even fiercer whistling wind blew up and seemed as though it would lift the car. Something she had not allowed herself to think before but had known for some days now came into her mind and she made a promise to herself. She would not come here again. This was the last time she would visit this house. She would go in now and walk through these few rooms. She would take with her whatever was personal and could not be left behind, and then she would close this door and drive back to the town, and, in future, she would never take that turn at the handball alley on the road between Blackwater and Ballyconnigar.

What surprised her was the hardness of her resolve, how easy it seemed to turn her back on what she had loved, leave this house on the lane to the cliff for others to know, for others to come to in the summer and fill with different noises. As she sat looking out at the bruised sky over the sea, she sighed. Finally, she let herself feel how much she had lost, how much she would miss. She got out of the car, steadying herself against the wind.

The front door opened on to a tiny hall. There were two rooms on each side, the rooms on the left with bunk beds, a living room on the right with a tiny kitchen and bathroom behind it, and their room beside it, peaceful, away from the children.

Each year in early June they came here, all of them, on a Saturday and Sunday, even if the weather was not good. They brought scrubbing brushes and mops and detergent and cloths for cleaning windows. They brought mattresses that had been well aired. It was a turning point, a mark on the calendar that meant the beginning of summer, even if summer was going to be grey and misty. The children, in the years she wanted to remember now, were noisy and excited at the start, as though they were an American family from *The Donna Reed Show*. They imitated American accents and gave each other instructions, but they soon grew tired and bored and she let them play or go down to the strand or walk into the village. And this was when the serious work began. When the children were out of the way, Maurice could do things like paint the woodwork, use distemper on the cement; the lino on a floor could be covered in the places where there were holes and she could patch the wallpaper where there was mould or too many stains, and for this she would need silence and concentration. She enjoyed measuring down to the last fraction of an inch, making the paste to the right consistency, and cutting up bright new patches of wallpaper in floral patterns.

Fiona hated spiders. That was something Nora remembered now. And cleaning the house meant, more than anything, displacing spiders and clocks and all types of creepy-crawlies. The boys loved Fiona screaming, and Fiona herself enjoyed screaming too, especially as her father would protect her with elaborate gestures. 'Where is it?' he would shout, mimicking the giant in 'Jack and the Beanstalk', and Fiona would run to him and hold him.

That was the past, then, she thought as she walked into the living room, and it cannot be rescued. The smallness and coldness of the room gave her an odd satisfaction now. There was clearly a leak in the galvanized tin roof because there was a fresh stain on the ceiling. The house rattled as a gust of wind brought a hard sheet of rain against the glass. The windows would have to be repaired soon, and the wood had begun to rot. And who knew how long it would take for the cliff to be eaten away as far back as here and their house to be dismantled on the orders of the County Council? Someone else could worry now. Someone else could repair the leaks and treat the walls for damp. Someone else could rewire and repaint this house, or abandon it to the elements when the time came.

She would sell it to Jack Lacey. Nobody who lived locally would want to buy it; they knew what a bad investment it would be, compared to houses in Bentley or Curracloe or Morriscastle. No one from Dublin who saw the house in this state would make an offer for it. She looked around the room and shuddered.

She walked into the children's bedrooms and into their own bedroom, and she knew that for Jack Lacey in Birmingham owning this would be a dream, part of a memory of scorching hot Sundays, and boys and girls on bicycles, and bright, open possibilities. On the other hand, she imagined him coming into the house in a year or two, when he was back for a fortnight in Ireland, with the ceiling half fallen in and cobwebs everywhere and the wallpaper peeling and the windows broken and the electricity cut off. And the summer's day all drizzly and dark.

She looked through drawers, but there was nothing that she wanted. Only yellow newspaper and bits of twine. Even the crockery and kitchen utensils seemed not worth taking home. In the bedroom, she found some photographs and some books in a locker and she gathered these to take with her. Nothing else. The furniture was worthless, the lightshades were already dingy and worn. She remembered buying them in Woolworth's in Wexford only a few years earlier. Everything rotted and faded in this house.

The rain began to pour down. She took a mirror from the bedroom wall, noting how clean the space it covered had remained, compared to the discoloured, dirty wallpaper all around.

At first she thought the knocking she heard was something banging against the door or the window in the wind. But when it persisted and she heard a voice, she realized that she had a visitor. She was surprised because she had thought that no one had noticed her approach and no one could see the car. Her first instinct was to hide, but she knew that she had already been seen.

As she opened the latch, the front door blew in towards her. The figure outside was wearing an oversized anorak, the large hood of which was half-covering the face.

'Nora, I heard the car. Are you all right?'

Once the hood was pulled down, she recognized Mrs Darcy, whom she had not seen since the funeral. Mrs Darcy followed her inside as she closed the door.

'Why didn't you call in first?' she asked.

'I'm just here for a few minutes,' Nora said.

'Get into the car and come on up to the house. You can't stay here.'

Once more she noted the hectoring tone, as though she were a child, unable to make proper decisions. She had tried since the funeral to ignore this tone, or tolerate it. She had tried to understand that it was shorthand for kindness.

Just now, she would have relished taking her few possessions from the house, putting them in the car and driving out of Cush. But it could not be done, she would have to accept Mrs Darcy's hospitality.

Mrs Darcy would not get into the car with her, insisting that she was too wet. She would walk back to her house, while Nora drove, she said.

'I'll be a few more minutes. I'll follow you up,' Nora said.

Mrs Darcy looked at her, puzzled. Nora had tried to sound casual, but she had succeeded instead in sounding secretive.

'I just want to collect a few things to bring home,' she said.

Her visitor's eyes lit on the books and photographs and the mirror resting against the wall, then she swiftly took in everything else in the room. And Nora felt that Mrs Darcy understood immediately what she was doing.

'Don't be long now,' she said. 'I'll have the tea ready for you.'

When Mrs Darcy had left, Nora closed the door and went back into the house.

It was done. In her all-embracing glance around the room, Mrs

Darcy had made it seem real. Nora would leave this house and never come back. She would never walk these lanes again and she would let herself feel no regret. It was over. She took up the few things she had collected and put them in the boot of the car.

Mrs Darcy's kitchen was warm. She put fresh scones on a plate with melting butter and poured the tea.

'We were wondering how you were getting on but Bill Parle told us the night he went in that your house was full of people. Maybe we should have gone in all the same, but we thought we'd leave it until after Christmas when you might like the company more.'

'There have been a lot of visitors,' Nora said. 'But you know you're welcome any time.'

'Well, there are a lot of people who are very fond of you,' Mrs Darcy said.

She took off her apron and sat down.

'And we were all worried about you, that you wouldn't come down here any more. Carmel Redmond, you know, was away when it happened and she was shocked.'

'I know. She wrote to me,' Nora said, 'and then she called in.'

'So she told us,' Mrs Darcy said, 'and Lily was here that day and she said that we should be looking out for you. And I used to wait for that day when you'd all come down and do up the house. For me, it was the beginning of the fine weather. My heart would lift when I'd see you coming.'

'I remember one year,' Nora said, 'it was raining so hard you took pity on us and made us all come up here for our tea.'

'And you know,' Mrs Darcy said, 'your children have the best manners. They are so well reared. Aine used to love coming to see us. All of them did, but she was the one we knew best. And Maurice used to come on a Sunday if there was a match on the wireless.'

Nora looked out at the rain. It was tempting now to mislead Mrs Darcy, to tell her that they were going to keep coming down here, but she could not do that. And she felt that Mrs Darcy understood her silence, had been watching for some clue, something said or left unsaid, to confirm her impression that Nora was going to sell the house.

'Now, what we decided,' Mrs Darcy said, 'was that next year we'd do up the house for you. I was looking at it just now, and it could do with some patching on the galvanize, and we'll be getting that done on the barn here anyway, and so they might as well go down to you. And we'll take turns to do the rest of it. I have a key, and we could have surprised you, but Lily said that I was to ask you, and I was going to do that after Christmas. She said it was your house, and we shouldn't be intruding.'

Nora knew that she should tell her now, but there was something too effusive and warm in Mrs Darcy's tone that stopped her.

'But I thought it would be nice for you,' Mrs Darcy went on, 'to come down and have it all done. So don't say anything now, but let me know if you don't want us to do it. And I'll hold on to the key unless you want it back.'

'No. Of course not, Mrs Darcy. I'd like you to hold on to the key.'

Maybe, she thought as she drove towards Blackwater, maybe Mrs Darcy had presumed all along that she was going to sell the house, and realized that cleaning it up would increase its value; or maybe Mrs Darcy had presumed nothing, maybe Nora herself was watching everyone too closely to see what they thought of her. But she knew she had behaved strangely in closing the gates when she had parked the car in front of the house, in seeming almost furtive when Mrs Darcy called, and in not instantly accepting or turning down her offer to help with the house.

She sighed. It had been awkward and difficult, and now it was finished. She would write to Mrs Darcy and Lily Devereux and Carmel Redmond. Often in the past, when she made a decision like this, she changed her mind the next morning, but this time it was not like that, she would not change her mind.

On the road back to Enniscorthy, she began to calculate. She did not know how much the house was worth. She would think of a figure and send it to Jack Lacey in a sealed envelope – she did not want to negotiate with May Lacey – and if he offered less than she asked for, she would accept it as long as it was reasonable. She did not want to have to advertise the house in the newspaper.

The car was taxed and insured until Christmas. She had planned to give it up then, but if she sold the house, she thought, she would keep the car or buy a newer model. The house money would also pay for the black marble gravestone for Maurice that she wanted, and she would be able to rent a caravan in Curracloe for a week or two next summer. With what she had left she could use for household expenses and buy some new clothes for herself and the girls. And then keep something for an emergency.

The house, she smiled to herself, would become like the two and sixpence a man had given Conor a few summers earlier. She could not remember which summer it was, but it was before his father was sick and it was before he really understood the value of money. Conor had given the two and sixpence to Maurice to mind for him and then all summer, every time they went to Blackwater, he drew on this money, confidently demanding a fresh instalment from his father. When they told him it was all gone, he had refused to believe them.

She wrote to May Lacey, enclosing a letter for Jack. Within a short time, she had a letter from him agreeing to the price she had suggested. She replied with the name of a solicitor in the town who would draw up the contract of sale.

She waited for the right moment to tell the boys about selling the house in Cush, and when she began, she was shocked at how concerned they both seemed, how attentive, as though by listening carefully they might hear something that would have a serious effect on their future. As she spoke to them about how useful the money would be, she learned that they already knew that she had planned to sell the car, although she had not told them this. They did not smile, or even appear relieved, when she said that they were going to keep the car.

'Will we still be able to go to the university?' Conor asked.

'Of course,' she said. 'What made you think about that?'

'Who will pay?'

'I have other money saved up for that.'

She did not want to say that maybe their Uncle Jim and Aunt Margaret would pay. They were Maurice's brother and sister who had not married and lived together in the old family house in the town. The boys remained absolutely still; they watched her intently. She went out to the kitchen and turned on the kettle and when she came back into the room, they had not moved.

'We'll be able to go on holidays to different places,' she said. 'We'll be able to get a caravan in Curracloe or Rosslare. We've never stayed in a caravan.'

'Would we be able to stay in Curracloe the same time as the Mitchells?' Conor asked.

'If we like. We could find out when they're going and go at the same time.'

'Would it be for one week or two weeks?' Conor asked.

'Or longer if we liked,' she said.

'Are we going to b-buy a c-caravan?' Donal asked.

'No, we'll rent one. Buying one would be too much responsibility.'

'Who's going to b-buy the house?' Donal asked.

'It's very private now. If I tell you, you can't tell anyone, but I think that May Lacey's son is going to buy it, you know, the one in England.'

'Is that why she came here?'

'I suppose it is, yes.'

She made tea and the boys pretended to watch the television. She had, she knew, unsettled them. Conor had become all red-faced and Donal was staring at the floor as if awaiting punishment. She picked up a newspaper and tried to read. She knew it was important to stay in the room, not to leave them, despite an urge to go upstairs and do anything, empty out cupboards, wash her face, clean the windows. Eventually, she felt she would have to say something.

'We could go to Dublin next week.'

They looked up.

'Why?' Donal asked.

'For a day out, you could take a day off school,' she said.

'I have d-double Science on Wednesday,' Donal said. 'I hate it, but I c-can't miss it, and I have F-french with Madame D-duffy on Monday.'

'We could go on Thursday.'

'In the car?'

'No, we could go on the train. And we could see Fiona, that's her half-day.'

'Do we have to go?' Conor asked.

'No. We'll only go if we like,' she said.

'What will we tell the school?'

'I'll send in a note saying that you have to go to the doctor.'

'I d-don't need a note if it's j-just one day,' Donal said.

'We'll go then. We'll have a nice day out. I'll write to Fiona.'

She had said it to break the silence and to let them know that there would always be outings, things to look forward to. But it made no difference to them. The news that she was selling the house in Cush seemed to bring home something that they had been managing not to think about. In the days that followed, however, they brightened up again, as though nothing had been said.

For the trip to Dublin she laid their good clothes out for them the night before and made them polish their shoes and leave them on the landing. When she tried to make them go to bed early, they protested that there was something they wanted to watch on the television, and she allowed them to stay up late. Even then, they did not want to go to bed, and when she insisted, they went back and forth to the bathroom and they kept turning on and off the light in their room.

Finally, she went upstairs and found them fast asleep, the bedroom door wide open, their beds tossed. She tried to make them more comfortable, but when Conor began to wake she withdrew, quietly closing the door.

In the morning, they were up and dressed before she was. They brought her tea, which was too strong, and toast. When she got up, she managed to throw the tea down the sink in the bathroom without them noticing.

It was cold. They would drive to the station, she told them, and leave the car in the Railway Square. It would be handy when they came home that night, she said. They both nodded gravely. They already had their coats on.

The town was almost empty as she drove to the station. It was half-dark and some lights in houses were still on.

'Which side of the train will we sit on?' Conor asked when they got to the station.

They were twenty minutes early. She had bought the tickets, but Conor refused to sit with her and Donal in the heated waiting room, he wanted to cross over the iron bridge and wave to them from the other side; he wanted to walk down to the signal box. Again and again, he came back to ask when the train would arrive until a man told him to watch the signal arm between the platform and the tunnel, and when it dropped, it would mean that the train was coming.

'But we know it's coming,' Conor said impatiently.

'It'll drop when the train is in the tunnel,' the man said.

'If you were in the tunnel and the train came, you'd be mince-meat,' Conor said.

'Begoboman, you'd be found in little bits all right. And, you know something, all the cups and saucers rattle in the houses when the train goes under,' the man said.

'They don't rattle in our house.'

'That's because the train doesn't go under your house.'

'How do you know?' Conor said.

'Oh, I know your mammy well.'

Nora recognized the man, as she did so many others in the town; she thought that he worked in Donoghue's garage, but she was not sure. Something in his manner irritated her. She hoped that he did not intend to travel to Dublin with them.

Just before the train came, and the boys had once more gone down to the signal box, the man turned to her.

'I'd say they miss their daddy all the same,' he said.

He searched her face for a response and narrowed his eyes with curiosity. She felt that she needed to say something quickly and sharply to prevent him from speaking again and, more than any-thing, to prevent him from sitting with them on the journey.

'That's the last thing they need to hear at the moment, thank you,' she said.

'Oh, now, I didn't mean to . . .'

She moved away from him as the train came and the boys ran excitedly down the platform towards her. She could feel her face reddening, but they noticed nothing as they argued over which were the best seats on the train.

Once the train started, they wanted everything: to view the toilets, to stand in the precarious space between the carriages where the ground could be seen as they sped along, to go to the restaurant and buy lemonade. By the time the train stopped in Ferns, they had done all of these things, and by the time it reached Camolin, they had fallen asleep.

Nora did not sleep; she glanced at the newspaper she had bought in the station, and put it down, and watched the two boys slumped back in their seats sleeping. She would love to have known just then what they were dreaming of. In these months, she realized, some-thing had changed in the clear, easy connection between her and them, and perhaps, for them, between each other. She felt that she would never be sure about them again.

Conor woke and looked at her and went back to sleep with his head resting on his folded arms on the table. She reached out and touched his hair, let her hands run through it, tossing it and straight-ening it again. Donal was watching her, his calm gaze suggesting to her that he understood everything that was happening, that there was nothing he did not fathom.

'Conor's fast asleep,' she said and smiled.

'Where are we?' he asked.

'We're nearly at Arklow.'

By Wicklow, Conor had woken and gone to the toilet again.

'What would happen if you flushed the toilet in a station?' he asked.

'It would all go on to the tracks,' she said.

'And when the train is moving, where does it go?'

'We'll ask the ticket collector,' she said.

'I b-bet you wouldn't ask him,' Donal said.

'What harm would it do to the tracks in a station?' Conor asked.

'It would be all s-smelly,' Donal said.

The morning was windless, the clouds on the horizon were grey and the sea beyond Wicklow the colour of steel.

'When will the tunnels start?' Conor asked.

'It's a while now,' she said.

'After the next station?'

'Yes, after Greystones.'

'Will that be long?'

'Read your comic,' she suggested.

'The tracks are too bumpy.'

At the first tunnel, the boys covered their ears against the rushing noise, vying with each other in mock fright. The next tunnel was much longer. Conor wanted Nora to cover her ears as well, and she did it to please him, because she knew how little sleep he had had, and how irritable he could be, and how easy it would be to upset him. Donal was already bored covering his ears, but he moved close to the window when the train came out of the tunnel and there was a sheer drop into the rough waters below. Conor now had moved beside her, making her move so he could be at the window too.

'We could fall over,' he said.

'No, no, the train has to stay on the tracks. It's not like a car,' she said.

He kept his nose up against the window, fascinated by the danger. Donal, also, did not move from the window even when the train came into Dún Laoghaire station.

'Is that the end?' Conor asked.

'We're nearly there,' she said.

'Where are we going to go first? Are we going to see Fiona first?'

'We're going to go to Henry Street.'

'Yippee!' Conor shouted. He was trying to stand on the seat, but she made him sit down.

'And we're going to have our dinner in Woolworth's,' she said.

'In the self-service?'

'Yes, so we don't have to wait.'

'Can I have orange with my dinner and no milk?' Conor asked.

'Yes,' she said. 'You can have whatever you like.'

They got off at Amiens Street and walked through the damp and dilapidated station. They moved slowly along Talbot Street, stopping to look into shop windows. She forced herself to relax, there was nothing to do, they could waste time wherever they wanted. She gave them ten shillings each to spend, but as soon as she did, she felt she had made a mistake, it was too much. They examined the money and looked at her suspiciously.

'Do we have to b-buy something?' Donal asked.

'Maybe we'll get some books,' she said.

'Can we get comics or an annual?' Conor asked.

'It's too early for annuals,' Donal said.

As they approached O'Connell Street, they wanted to see where Nelson's Pillar had been.

'I remember it,' Conor said.

'You c-couldn't. You're too young,' Donal told him.

'I do. It was tall and Nelson was on top of it and they blew him into smithereens.'

They crossed O'Connell Street, alert to the several lanes of traffic, cautiously waiting for the lights to change. Nora was aware as they walked into Henry Street that they must seem like country people. The boys managed to take everything in and, at the same time, keep everything at a distance. They watched this world of strangers and strange buildings out of the sides of their eyes.

Conor had become impatient to go into a shop, any shop, to buy something.

'Would you like to look at shoes?' she asked, figuring that when he said no, he would be pleased that he was the one who was deciding where they would go.

'Shoes?' He wrinkled his face in disgust. 'Is that what we came to Dublin for?'

'So where do you want to go?' she asked.

'I want to go up and down an escalator.'

'Do you want to do that too?' she asked Donal.

'I s-suppose s-so,' he said glumly.

In Arnott's in Henry Street, Conor wanted Nora and Donal to watch him going up the escalator and then wait for him and watch him coming down. He insisted that they not come with him and not move. He made them promise. Donal was bored.

The first time, Conor kept looking back at them, and they waited while he disappeared at the top and then reappeared on the escalator coming down. He beamed at them. The second time, he grew brave and took some of the steps two by two, all the while holding on to the rail. The next time, he wanted Donal to come with him, but insisted that Nora still wait below. She explained to him that this would have to be the last go, that maybe they could return here in the afternoon, but three times up and down the escalator was enough.

When they came down, she saw that Donal was animated as well. They explained to her that they had found a lift further over and they wanted to go up and down in that.

'One more and that's it,' she said.

She moved away and began to look at umbrellas, noticing fold-up ones, small enough to put into your handbag, which she had never seen before. She thought that she would buy one in case it rained. As she waited for the cashier, she watched out for the boys, but they did not appear. When she had paid, she walked back to their meeting point, and then to the place near a side door to which the lift descended.

They were not there. She waited between the two points, looking out all the time for them. She thought of going on the lift herself, but realized that this would only add to the confusion. If she stayed here, she thought, she would be bound to see them.

When they found her, they pretended it was nothing, that the lift had merely stopped at every floor. When she told them that she had thought they were lost, they gave each other a look as though something had happened to them in the lift that they did not want her to know about.

By three o'clock, they had seen all the Dublin they wanted to see. They had been to Moore Street and bought a bag of peaches, they had had their dinner in the self-service in Woolworth's and had been to Eason's where they bought comics and books. The boys were tired now as they sat in Bewley's waiting for Fiona. Nora believed that the only thing keeping Conor awake was the idea that you could take as many buns as you liked from the two-tiered plate.

'You have to pay for them,' Nora said.

'How do they know how many you've taken?'

'Most people are honest,' she said.

When Fiona arrived the boys became excited and bright again, both wanting to talk at the same time. To Nora, Fiona appeared thin and pale as she sat opposite her.

'Do you want to hear a D-dublin accent?' Donal asked her.

'We were in Moore Street,' Nora said.

'Get the ripe peaches,' Donal said in a singsong voice without a stammer.

'Look at my "buke",' Conor added.

'Very funny,' Fiona said. 'I'm sorry I'm late, the buses all come in twos and threes and then you have to wait for ages for the next one.'

'I want to go upstairs on a double-decker bus,' Conor said.

'Conor, let Fiona talk for one second and then you can talk,' Nora said.

'Are you having a nice day out?' Fiona asked.

Fiona's smile was shy, but her tone was adult and confident. She had changed in these few months.

'Yes, but we're all tired now and it's nice to be sitting here.'

Neither of them seemed to know what to say next. Nora realized that her answer to the question had been too formal, as though she were talking to a stranger. Fiona ordered coffee.

'Did you buy anything?' she asked.

'I didn't really have time,' Nora said. 'I got a paperback, that's all.'

Nora noticed how briskly and efficiently Fiona had ordered the coffee, and how she looked around the café, her eyes sharp, almost critical. As she began to talk to her brothers, however, she became almost girlish again.

'Have you heard from Aine?' Nora asked her.

'She wrote me a short letter. I think she was worried that the nuns read letters and she's right, they do. So she didn't say too much. Just that she likes the Irish teacher and got good marks in French for a composition.'

'We can go and see her in a week.'

'She mentioned that.'

'We're selling the house,' Conor said to Fiona suddenly in a loud voice.

'And are you going to live on the side of the road?' she asked, laughing.

'No, we're going to rent a caravan in Curracloe,' he said.

Fiona looked at Nora.

'I'm thinking of selling the house in Cush,' Nora said.

'I wondered about that,' Fiona replied.

'I didn't decide until recently.'

'So you are going to sell it?'

'Yes, I am.'

Nora was surprised to see that while Fiona was trying to smile, there were tears in her eyes. She had not cried at Maurice's funeral, just remained silent, staying close to her sister and her aunts, but Nora could sense what she felt all the more because she did nothing to show it. Nora did not know what she should say to her now.

She sipped her coffee. The boys did not move or speak.

'Does Aine know?' Fiona asked.

'I didn't have the heart to tell her in a letter. I'll tell her when we see her.'

'And you've definitely decided?'

Nora did not reply.

'I was hoping to go there in the summer,' Fiona said.

'I thought you were going to England in the summer.'

'I am, at the end of June, but I finish at the end of May. I'd thought about spending the month of June in Cush.'

'I'm sorry,' Nora said.

'He loved that house, didn't he?'

'Your father?'

Fiona lowered her head.

Nora brought Conor with her to find the toilets. When she came back she ordered another coffee.

'Who are you selling the house to?' Fiona asked.

'Jack Lacey, May Lacey's son, who's in England.'

'May Lacey came to the house,' Conor interrupted.

Donal nudged him and put his finger to his lips.

'The money will come in very handy just now,' Nora said.

'In two years' time, I'll be earning a salary,' Fiona said.

'We need the money now,' Nora said.

'Are you not going to get a pension?' Fiona asked. 'Has that not come through?'

Nora thought that maybe she should not have said that she needed the money.

'It means we won't have to sell the car,' Nora said and tried to indicate to Fiona that maybe they should not worry the boys with any more talk about money.

'We had lovely summers there,' Fiona said.

'I know.'

'It's sad to think of losing it.'

'We'll go other places on holiday.'

'I thought we'd always have that house,' Fiona said.

They said nothing for a few moments. Nora wanted to go, take the boys back to Henry Street.

'When are you going to sell it?' Fiona resumed.

'As soon as the contract is ready.'

'Aine will be upset.'

Nora stopped herself saying that she couldn't bear to go there any more. She would not be able to say that in front of the boys; it would sound too emotional, it would give too much away.

She stood up to go.

'How do you pay here? I can't remember.'

'You have to get the waitress to fill out a docket,' Fiona said.

'And you have to tell her how many b-buns you've had,' Donal said.

When they walked out to Westmoreland Street, Nora wanted to say something else to Fiona but she could not think what. Fiona seemed downcast as she stood on the street. For a moment, Nora felt impatient with her. She was starting her life, she could live where she liked, do what she liked. She did not have to get the train back to the town where everybody knew about her and all the years ahead were mapped out for her.

'We're going to walk around to Henry Street by the Ha'penny Bridge,' Nora said.

'Make sure you don't miss the train,' Fiona said.

'How are you getting back to the college?' Nora asked.

'I was going to go to Grafton Street first.'

'Will you not come to the station with us?' Nora asked.

'No, I'll go,' Fiona said. 'I have to get something before I go back and I won't be in the city centre again for a while.'

As they looked at one another, Nora felt Fiona was hostile, and forced herself to remember how upset she must be, and how lonely she might be too. She smiled as she said that they would have to go and in return Fiona smiled at her and at the boys. As soon as Nora walked away, however, she felt helpless and regretted not having said something kind or special or consoling to Fiona before they left her; maybe even something as simple as asking her when she was coming down next, or emphasizing how much they looked forward to seeing her soon. She wished she had a phone in the house so she could keep in more regular touch with her. She thought that she might write Fiona a note in the morning thanking her for coming to meet them.

In Talbot Street, on the way to the station, Conor spent the rest of his money on Lego, but could not decide which colour bricks to choose. Although Nora was tired, she listened, paid attention and offered suggestions as Donal stood apart from them. She smiled at the cashier as Conor changed his mind at the cash register and went back to exchange one box of Lego for another.

It was dark now and becoming cold. They sat on broken plastic seats in the small café of the station. When Nora reached into her shopping bag to find her purse, she discovered that the peaches that had seemed so fresh and firm just a few hours before had become all soggy. The paper bag had split open. She dumped them in a rubbish bin, knowing that there was no point in trying to take them any further, they would only rot more in the train.

The boys had not realized that it would be dark for the trip home, and as the train began the journey south, the window was covered in condensation. They opened the Lego and Conor played with it while Donal read. After a while, Conor moved over to her side of the table and fell asleep against her. She noticed as she looked across at Donal how oddly adult he seemed as he turned a page of his book.

'We're going to school t-tomorrow, aren't we?' he asked.

'Oh, yes, I think you should,' she said.

He nodded and looked back at his book.

'When is F-fiona coming d-down next?' he asked.

Her words with Fiona in the café, she knew, would work quietly on his mind. She wondered if there was one thing she could say that would stop him worrying and brooding over this.

'You know, Fiona will love the caravan,' she said.

'She d-didn't s-sound like that,' he said.

'Donal, we have to start a new life,' she said.

He considered her statement for a moment, as though he had a complex piece of homework in front of him. And then he shrugged his shoulders and went back to reading his book.

Nora gently moved Conor aside while she took off her coat in the overheated train. He woke for a second, but did not even open his eyes. She made a note that she must ask about caravans in Curracloe.

In her mind, she stood in the house in Cush again, and she tried to picture the children on a summer's day, taking their togs and towels from the line and going down to the strand, or herself and Maurice walking home along the lanes at dusk trying to keep the swarms of midges at bay, and coming into the house to the sound of children playing cards. It was all over and would not come back. The house lay empty. She pictured the small rooms in the darkness, how miserable they would be. Inhospitable. She imagined the sound of rain on the galvanized roof, the doors and windows rattling in the wind, the bare bedframes, the insects lurking in the dark crevices, and the relentless sea.

As the train made its way towards Enniscorthy, she felt that the house at Cush was more desolate now than it ever had been.

When Conor woke, he looked around him and smiled at her sleepily. He stretched and lay against her.

'Are we nearly home?' he asked.

'Not long now,' she said.

'When we stay in Curracloe,' he asked, 'are we going to put the caravan near the Winning Post or are we going to the caravan park up the hill?'

'Oh, near the Winning Post,' she said.

She knew she had answered too quickly. Donal and Conor earnestly considered what she had said. Then Conor glanced at Donal, watching for his reaction.

'Is that d-definite?' Donal asked. As the train slowed down, she managed to laugh for the first time all day.

'Definite? Of course it's definite.'

When the train shuddered to a stop, they gathered up their belongings quickly. As they made their way to the door, they met the ticket collector.

'Ask him now about the t-toilets,' Donal whispered as he nudged her.

'I'll tell him that you're the one who wants to know,' she said.

'Would this sausage like to come to Rosslare with us?' the inspector asked.

'Oh, no, he has to go to school tomorrow,' Nora said.

'I'm not a sausage,' Conor said.

The inspector laughed.

As she drove out of the Railway Square she remembered something, and she found herself telling the boys what had come into her mind.

'It was when we were married first, and it must have been during the summer holidays, and didn't we drive to the station one morning to find that we had missed the train by one second. It was gone and, God, we were very disappointed. But the man in charge that morning was not the usual station master, he was a young fellow, and he was taught in school by your daddy, and he told us to get back into the car and drive to Ferns and he would have the train held for us there. It was only six or seven miles away, and that's how we caught the train that morning and that's how we got to Dublin.'

'Did you d-drive or d-did he d-drive?' Donal asked.

'Daddy drove.'

'He must have driven queer fast,' Conor said.

'Was he a better d-driver than you?' Donal asked.

She smiled as she answered him.

'He was a good driver. Do you not remember?'

'I remember once he d-drove over a rat,' Donal said.

The streets of the town were empty and there were no other cars. The two boys seemed alert now, ready to talk more, ask more questions. When they got home, she thought, she would light the fire, and they would tire quickly after the long day.

'But why didn't you just d-drive to D-dublin that d-day and forget the t-train?' Donal asked.

'I don't know, Donal,' she said. 'I'll have to think about that.'

'Can we go to Dublin some day in the car?' Conor asked. 'And then we can stop where we like.'

'Of course we can,' she said as she pulled up in front of the house.

'I'd like to do that,' he said.

Soon she had the fire lit, and the boys were in their pyjamas and ready for bed. They had become quiet and she knew that they would fall asleep as soon as the light in their room was turned off. She wondered if anyone had called that evening, and she pictured someone approaching the house in darkness, and knocking on the front door and getting no answer, and standing there and waiting a while before walking away.

She made herself a cup of tea and came and sat in the armchair beside the fire. She turned on the radio but they were reading sports results and she turned it off. On going upstairs, she found that the boys were sound asleep and she stood watching them before closing the door and leaving them to the night. Downstairs, she wondered if there might be something interesting on the television. She went over and turned it on and waited for the picture to appear. How would she fill these hours? Just then she would have given anything to be back on the train, back walking the streets of Dublin. When the television came on it was an American comedy. She watched it for a few moments but the canned laughter irritated her and she turned it off. The house was silent now.

She thought of the book she had bought in Dublin. She could not remember what had made her buy it. She went out to the kitchen and searched for it in her bag. As soon as she opened the book she put it down again. She closed her eyes. In future, she hoped, fewer people would call. In future, once the boys went to bed, she might have the house to herself more often. She would learn how to spend these hours. In the peace of these winter evenings, she would work out how she was going to live.

Chapter Two

Her Aunt Josie came to visit without warning on a Saturday in late January. Nora had the fire lighting in the back room and the boys were there, engrossed in a television programme while she was in the kitchen washing up dishes. When she heard the knock she thought she should take her apron off and check herself in the mirror before she answered, but instead she dried her hands casually on the apron and went quickly along the short hall to the front door. She almost knew as she peered through the frosted glass that it was Josie; it was as though there were something about her aunt's waiting presence at the top of the steps, something sharp, imposing, impatient, that could make itself felt even through wood and glass.

'I was down in the town, Nora,' Josie said as soon as she opened the door. 'And John dropped me up. He has business now to attend to, but he'll collect me later. And I wanted to see how you were.'

Nora saw John, Josie's son, reversing away from the house. She held the door while her aunt walked into the hall.

'Are the boys here?'

'They're watching television, Josie.'

'Are they well?'

Nora realized that she could not take her aunt into the front room and turn on the electric fire there. The room was too cold. But she knew also that if Josie came into the back room, she would insist on talking, she could not be quiet, and the boys would have to turn off the television or sit up close to the set trying to hear it. She could not remember what programme they were watching or when it would be over. The boys seldom sat together like this now; she wished that she had fully appreciated the calm of the house and the peace, the contentment, in the time before Josie's knock had come.

'Well, you have the room grand and warm, I'll say that for you,' Josie said.

As she greeted the boys, they stood up warily. 'Oh, taller every time I see them, oh, look at them now, little men. Donal is as tall as I am.'

Nora saw both Donal and Conor glancing in her direction, and she almost asked Josie not to talk too much until the programme they had been watching was over.

'And the girls?' Josie asked. 'How are they?'

'Oh, very well,' Nora said quietly.

'Fiona isn't home for the weekend?'

'No, she decided to stay in Dublin.'

'And Aine?'

'She's settling in fine, Josie.'

'Bunclody is a very good school. I'm glad she's there.'

Nora put a few blocks of wood on the fire.

'I brought you some books,' Josie said, putting the carrier bag she had been holding on to the floor. 'I don't know what you'll think of them, some novels, and the rest are what you might call theology, although they are not as dry as they sound. The book at the top is by Thomas Merton, I mentioned him to you already, just after the funeral, and then there's Teilhard de Chardin. I spoke to Maurice about him in the hospital. But anyway, see what you think of them.'

Nora looked over at Donal and Conor. They were staring at the television set. She was almost ready to suggest that they turn the sound up.

'But it's good that everyone is so well,' Josie said. 'Aine must be studying hard. It's very tough nowadays, there's a lot of competition.'

Nora nodded politely.

'That programme will be over soon,' she said. 'The boys hardly watch any television, but they like this programme.'

Donal and Conor did not take their eyes from the television set.

'Oh, when they were staying with me, they were great readers, the two of them. We kept the television for the news. None of those rotten American programmes,' Josie said. 'You wouldn't know what they'd be saying on those American programmes.'

When Donal turned to speak, Nora noticed that his stammer seemed more pronounced. He was not able to get the first word out; she hadn't seen him having to make such an effort before and then failing, stammering before he even spoke. His younger brother, she saw, was moving one of his arms towards him as though to offer Donal some assistance. She was trying to guess what he wanted to say and felt for a moment like filling in for him to help him, to stop the blocked, staccato sound he was making, his brow furrowed in effort. Instead, she looked away, hoping that he might relax and be able to utter whatever it was. Eventually, however, when it was clear that he could not manage, he abandoned his effort and, close to tears, he turned back to watch the television.

Nora found herself wondering if there was somewhere she could go, if there was a town, or a part of Dublin, with a house like this one, a modest semi-detached house on a road lined with trees, where no one could visit them and they could be alone there, all three of them. And then she found her mind moving towards the next thought – that the possibility of such a place, such a house, would include the idea that what had happened could be erased, that the burden that was on her now could be lifted, that the past could be restored and could make its way effortlessly into a painless present.

'Don't you agree with me, Nora?' Josie was saying, staring at her intently.

'God, I don't know, Josie,' she said, standing up then, wondering if the subject had changed and deciding it was best now to offer her aunt tea and a sandwich, or some cake.

'Don't go to any trouble now, just a cup in my hand,' Josie said.

Nora almost smiled to herself in relief as she stood in the kitchen. She knew the boys would not look away from the television unless addressed directly and emphatically by Josie and she knew by the silence coming from the room that Josie was still contemplating the question she could best ask them to gain their full attention. As she boiled the kettle and prepared a tray with cups and saucers, Nora listened but heard only the muffled voices coming from the television. So far, she thought, the boys were winning.

When the programme finished, and the boys stood up to leave the room, she had never seen them so strange, not merely shy but awkward, almost bad-mannered. Donal's face was still flushed; he could not meet her eyes.

Josie began to talk then about the work she was planning to do on her garden, the large vegetable patch she was going to create beyond the haggard, and then spoke about her neighbours. Once the boys were out of the room and the television turned off, Josie asked her about Christmas.

'Well, it's great Christmas is over,' Josie said. 'I always say that for the whole month of January. And you can feel the days getting longer.'

'We had a quiet Christmas,' Nora said. 'And I was glad it was over too.'

'But it must have been nice having the girls home?'

'Yes, it was nice. But we all had our own thoughts, and it was hard to know what to say sometimes. We did our best, all of us.'

As soon as she had admired the cardigan that Nora was wearing, Josie began to talk about clothes and fashion, which was not, Nora thought, a subject that normally interested her.

'Well, there's a shop in Wexford called Fitzgerald's,' she said, 'and I noticed it when I was passing and the problem I had was that I had two hours to fill in before John was finished whatever business he was doing. So I went in, and there was a very friendly assistant all ready to help. And I began to fit on costumes and then she got all the accessories. You should have seen the prices! Oh, she had me rigged out ten times over and went off to get more things that might suit me better. I was only filling in time. And I got a good hour out of it. She was full of this colour and that shade and this cut and that new fashion and what suited me and didn't suit me. And then when I was back in my own clothes and ready to depart, didn't she let out a roar at me, that I was after wasting her time. And she followed me to the door and said to me that I was not to think of coming into her shop again.'

Nora almost had a pain in her side laughing. Josie remained serious, with just a glint in her eye.

'So I won't be going into Fitzgerald's to buy my spring outfit,' she said sadly and shook her head. 'The cheek of that woman! A rip of a one.'

Josie rummaged in her handbag and produced a large envelope.

'Now, I was cleaning out a bit of the old house, Nora, which is something I hardly ever do, or I start doing it and then I stop so the place becomes so bad that I think I'll be divorced from my late husband for untidiness. A divorced widow. In any case, I came across these. I must have always had them, and I thought I'd show you them.'

Inside the envelope was an old sepia-coloured folder with black and white photographs in one pocket and negatives in the other; the spine between the two pockets was badly torn. When Nora pulled the photographs out, she recognized her father instantly and then saw that the child on his lap was herself; the next photograph had her father and her mother standing together and posing proudly, they must have been in their twenties, she thought; they were wearing good clothes. The rest of the photographs showed either or both of her parents, and in some of them she, as a baby, was also in the picture.

'I never knew these existed,' she said. 'I've never seen them before.'

'I think I took them,' Josie said, 'but I can't be sure. I know I had a camera, I was the only one who had a camera then, and I must have had them developed and then forgotten about them.'

'He was very handsome, wasn't he?'

'Your father?'

'Yes.'

'Oh, he was. I remember us all telling her that if she didn't marry him someone else would, and soon.'

'And you think my father and mother never saw these photographs either?' she asked.

'Unless these are copies,' Josie said. 'I just don't know. It's strange that I don't remember. They could have been taken by someone else, but I don't know why I would have had them.'

'It's funny how little they knew then,' Nora said. 'How little any of us knew then. About anything. I was with him when he died.'

'You were all with him.'

'No, we weren't. It was just me. I was fourteen.'

'Your mother always said that you were all around the bed when he died. Nora, that's what she always said.'

'I know she said that, but she made it up. It wasn't true. She used to say it even in front of me. But I was on my own with him and I waited for a minute or two before I ran down the stairs. I waited for a minute or two, just to spare them all, or spare myself. I sat with him quietly after he died. And then, when I told her, my mother ran out into the street screaming, I never knew why she did that, and nearly the whole town came in while he was still warm in the bed.'

'They must have said the Rosary or something.'

'Oh, the Rosary. I hope never to hear another Rosary.'

'Nora!'

'It's true. God knows it's true. I might as well say it.'

'They are very comforting sometimes, the old prayers.'

'Well, they don't comfort me, Josie. Or not the Rosary anyway.'

Josie took the photographs again and began to look at them.

'You were always your father's favourite, even after the others were born.'

She handed Nora the photograph of her on her mother's knee. Nora could see her mother posing for the camera sitting stiffly as though the baby on her knee did not quite belong to her.

'I don't think she knew what to do with you,' Josie said. 'You knew what you wanted from day one.'

'It was easier for the other two,' Nora said.

Josie began to laugh.

'Do you remember what she said about you? It was my own fault for asking her which of her two sons-in-law she liked best and she said that the more she thought about it the more she came to the view that she liked both her sons-in-law and both her other daughters better than Nora. I hadn't even asked her about you. I don't know what you had done on her at the time.'

'I don't either. But I'm sure I had done something. Or maybe not. Maybe I hadn't.'

Josie laughed again.

'You bit the nose off me when I told you.'

'I suppose I believed it was funny too. But maybe I did only when I thought about it afterwards.'

'Anyway, I found these photographs and I'm sure Pat Crane could make copies of them from the negatives for the others if they wanted them.'

'They'll mind of course that they're not in them.'

'I think they'd appreciate having a new photograph of your mother when she was a young woman. I don't think there were many taken of her at that time. They'd enjoy seeing what she was like when she was young.'

Nora understood the implications of the remark, and the suggestion that she would not. She looked at Josie and smiled.

'Yes, indeed.'

The boys came into the room and said goodnight well before Josie left. Later, Nora went upstairs to look; they were asleep. Having locked the doors and switched off all the lights downstairs, she went to her bedroom and prepared for the night. In bed, she stayed awake for some time reading the opening of the book by Thomas Merton that her aunt had given her. When she found that she was not concentrating, she turned out the light and lay in the dark for a while before slowly falling asleep.

When she woke she did not know what time it was, but she thought that it must be the middle of the night. One of the boys had screamed. The sound was so loud and piercing that she believed someone must have broken into the house; she wondered if she should open the window of her bedroom and shout out to the neighbours to see if she could wake someone and ask them to call the Guards.

When the scream came again, she knew it was Donal. The fact that Conor had not also screamed frightened her more and made her wonder again if she should call out for help rather than go straight into their room. As she opened her bedroom door and stood out on the landing, she could hear Donal shouting out some words and then screaming again. He was having a nightmare. She opened the door of the boys' room and turned on the light. When Donal saw her now he sat up in the bed and began to scream louder, almost as though it were his mother he was afraid of. When she moved towards him he recoiled and then put his hands out as if to push her away.

'Donal, it's a dream, it's just a dream,' she said.

Now he was crying rather than screaming and digging his nails into his upper arms in distress.

'Darling, it's just a dream. Everyone has bad dreams.'

She turned and looked at Conor. He was watching her calmly.

'Are you all right?' she asked him.

He nodded.

'Maybe we'll go downstairs and get him a glass of milk. Would you like a glass of milk, Donal?'

He was rocking back and forth, sobbing, and did not reply.

'You're all right,' she said. 'Really, you're all right.'

'He isn't all right,' Conor said quietly.

'What's wrong with him?' she asked.

Conor did not reply.

'Conor, do you know what's wrong with him?'

'He moans in his sleep every night.'

'But not like tonight.'

Conor shrugged.

'Donal, what was the dream about?'

Donal was still rocking back and forth but he was silent now.

'Will you tell me if I get a glass of milk? Would you like a biscuit?'

He shook his head.

She went downstairs and fetched two glasses of milk. In the kitchen, she saw that it was a quarter to four. It was pitch-dark outside. As she went back upstairs and came into the bedroom, she noticed that the boys were looking at each other but they looked away when she appeared.

'What is it?' she asked. 'Was it just a bad dream?'

Donal nodded.

'Do you remember what it was about?'

He began to cry again.

'Would you like me to leave the light on? And I can leave the door open. Would that be good?'

He nodded.

'What was he saying when he was shouting?' she asked Conor.

She could see that Conor was weighing up how he should respond.

'I don't know,' he said.

'Was it Josie's visit?' she asked Donal. 'Did that upset you? Do you not like Josie?'

She looked from one to the other.

'Do you not?' she asked again.

Neither of them replied. Conor seemed ready to curl up under the blankets. He had not touched the milk. Donal drank slowly and avoided her gaze.

'Will we talk about it again in the morning?'

Donal nodded.

'We might go to eleven o'clock Mass so we can have a good sleep in the morning,' she said.

Once more, she noticed them glancing at each other.

'Is there something wrong?' she asked.

Donal stared past her as though there were something on the landing that had caught his attention. She looked behind her but saw nothing.

'I'll definitely leave my bedroom door open as well. Would that be better?'

Donal nodded again.

'Do you think you might go back to sleep?' she asked.

Donal finished the milk and put the glass on the floor.

'And call me if you start having bad dreams again.'

He tried to smile in agreement.

'Why don't I turn the bedroom light off and leave the door open and leave on the light on the landing?'

'OK,' he whispered.

'Nightmares never come back once you wake up from them,' she said as she moved slowly out of the room. 'I think you'll be all right now.'

In the morning, as she made their breakfast, it was clear that Donal would not tell her what the dream was about, even if he could remember, and she decided not to mention it unless he or Conor did, not to dwell on what had happened in the night in case it might increase Donal's anxiety. She would go to Dr Cudigan and ask him if anything could be done for a stammer, but she would not take Donal with her. She believed that paying attention to it would merely serve to make it worse. Maybe it would go of its own accord. She had heard nothing from the school about it and wondered if it were not something that happened only at home. The idea that it would stay with him for his whole life, or even all of his teenage years, frightened her so deeply that she tried not to think about it.

As she sat with the boys having breakfast, and then as she walked across the Back Road with them to the cathedral, and all through Mass, the image returned to her of them looking up when Josie first came into the room the previous evening. Something in their gaze, especially in Conor's but also in Donal's, had appeared uneasy, almost scared. At the time she had thought this was because their television programme was about to be disturbed. But then, when Donal had woken from his nightmare, and she had mentioned Josie, they had both remained silent. Later, if the chance came, she thought, she would mention Josie again and see what happened, but then she also thought that it was best to leave things alone for the moment, hope that Donal would have no more bad dreams, and hope too that the boys would settle in the house, become slowly used to the idea that their father was dead but that life would go on, and things would change and maybe some things change for the better.

Despite the fact that neither of them mentioned Josie, their response to her lingered in the air as the week went on until Nora began to wonder if Josie had come that Saturday to test the water in some way, to see how the boys might react to her, or to see if they had said anything to Nora about her. She went over Josie's visit in her mind, how she was not able to stop talking when she arrived as though she were nervous about something. And the more Nora thought about it the odder it seemed. The boys had been with Josie for the two months as Maurice was dying, but they had not seen her since the funeral. Surely, when she came into the room, they should have been friendlier and there should have been more references to their time with her in the conversation, jokes even, or mention of things they did? Josie was as distant from them as they from her, as though she were a stranger, or worse, Nora thought.

On Friday Fiona came for the weekend. The following day Nora told Fiona and the boys that she was going to Wexford to do some shopping and would be back by teatime. Fiona looked up from her book but did not ask any questions. The boys, Nora thought, were too young still to imagine that their mother could possibly invent where she was going.

She drove towards Bunclody and then turned away from the river to Josie's house. She could be unlucky, she thought, as Josie could easily have gone out or have company, but she felt it was better to come like this, unannounced, and do so today before she had time to think too much about what might have happened when the boys stayed with Josie in the months before Maurice died.

Deliberately, she did not plan what she would say, or even how she would begin. She simply drove towards Josie's, believing that she would know what to do as soon as she saw her aunt. Josie had built her own house to the side of the old farmhouse when John had married and when she had retired from her job as a teacher. She was proud of its design, how it looked as though it were part of the original house, with windows the same shape and similar slates on the roof. She had made summer quarters, a living room upstairs with views of the mountains and a small bedroom and a bathroom beside it. Below, she had another bedroom with a bathroom attached, and then a cosy sitting room with an open fireplace, and a small kitchen off it. The doorways and the bathrooms, she loved telling her visitors, were designed for a wheelchair, but she still had not decided what floor she would live on when she was incapacitated. She would laugh then at the very idea of being incapacitated. She spent her days gardening, reading, listening to the radio and talking on the telephone.

Nora tried to remember how it had happened that the boys had spent two months with her, whether Nora had asked or Josie had offered. She thought back to that time, but certain images were so filled with detail, certain hours so filled with pure, unforgettable moments, that the remaining time seemed as though it had been watched through glass covered with rainwater. Walking with Maurice into the lobby of the hospital in the knowledge that he might not come out of there alive. The moment when he had said he would like to go one more time to look at the sky and that she was to wait for him in the lobby, let him do it alone. And then the watching as he began to cry when he reached the door. All of that was too raw and new for other things such as the arrangements she had made for the boys to stay with Josie to be fully clear to her now.

She should remember what happened, she knew that. It was not as though she was not there and alert when these arrangements were made. But whatever they were, she was sure that they had seemed natural at the time, an obvious solution. She was grateful to Josie for taking the boys in, and relieved that they were safe and away from Maurice as he came home eventually and began to decline in ways that his two sons should not have had to witness.

He had not died at home, of course. She had to move him finally to Brownswood, the old TB hospital outside the town now used for general patients, when the pain grew too great and his faculties failed and she could not nurse him any more. Even though he was on a stretcher and his eyes were closed and he had not spoken a clear sentence for days, she knew that he was aware that he was leaving the house for the last time. She held his hand, but every time he made to grip hers his hand would jerk out of control as though it were a claw. At least the boys had not been there for that.

She drove up the long rutted lane to Josie's, opening and closing the two iron gates along the way, trying to avoid stepping in the patches of mud and muck, noting the bareness of the ditches on each side and some bright red flowers whose name she did not know. The sky was darkening, with clouds hovering low over the Blackstairs Mountains. She found herself shivering as she stood on the gravel path. John's car, she noticed, was not there. She did not know if it was best to knock on the door of the old farmhouse first or walk around and knock on Josie's kitchen door, which was the only entrance to her part of the house. Since there was no sign of life from the farmhouse, she walked around, her shoes sinking in the grass. It must have rained here recently, more than it did in the town, she thought. When she looked in the window, she saw an armchair with a small table beside it with a pair of glasses on an open newspaper, and another table with a vase of bright lilies mixed in with the red flowers she had seen growing in the ditch. Through another window she saw an unmade double bed, and random books on the floor that looked as though they had fallen from the bed. Josie must be enjoying her retirement, she thought and smiled.

She rapped on the kitchen door but there was no answer. It was the stillness that struck her now, the silence broken only by the cawing of crows in the distance and then the faint sound of a tractor that at first seemed as though it were approaching but then seemed to be moving away. She looked around her at the larch and birch trees that almost masked the galvanized sheds in the haggard. There was a pathway leading across the grass to what she knew had once been an orchard. She remembered years before an unexpected harvest of pears and apples, which had come in such abundance only because no one had been tending to the trees, no one had been pruning them, or so Josie had told her, and then after their huge yield the trees had died, or some of them did, and the others yielded no more fruit except some crab-apples that no one wanted. It was easier, or less trouble, Josie had told her, to buy apples in the supermarket and no one liked the hard pears that had grown here even when they were left to soften.

Josie had decided in any case to devote her attention to a new garden she had made beyond the orchard to the side of the haggard. John dug it out for her and she had bought books and manuals on how to grow flowers and vegetables. In her old age, as she enjoyed explaining, she had gradually seen a good reason to live on a farm and had understood for the first time the point not only of manure but of the soil itself and, indeed, the seasons. Nora could almost hear her voice saying all of this, as she ducked under the branches of trees and avoided thorny brambles to see if she would find her aunt in the garden.

She stepped over the stile towards the vegetable garden. Josie was growing something that required lines of wire and bamboo cane. Nora was not sure if these were raspberry bushes. To the side, there were neat ridges where potatoes had been planted. Beyond them were the flower beds but there were no flowers now. It looked as though a great deal of work went on here and she wondered how Josie's back withstood the strain. Just then, as she turned, she saw her aunt and realized that Josie had been quietly observing her for some time.

'Nora, your shoes will be ruined,' Josie said. She had a small garden fork and some stalks in her hand. She was wearing garden gloves that seemed too big for her.

'I didn't see you there.'

'I thought I'd leave you for a moment to look at all my hard work.'

In Josie's tone, there was an edge of challenge as though her territory had been invaded. She must wonder, Nora thought, why she had visited and yet she spoke as though they had been in mid-conversation.

'I think I've done enough now for the day,' Josie said. 'I often start early, I'm getting everything ready so I can start sowing a few annuals when the weather gets better. And then I go and read the paper and have my breakfast and then come up again to look at what I did. By this time of the day, I've finished. I just came up now to admire my own handiwork and tidy the place.'

As she moved towards Nora, she seemed preoccupied by something. Her walk was slow and deliberate, her lips pursed.

'Wait until you're old, Nora,' she said, 'and then you'll know. It's the mixture of being content with even the smallest thing and then feeling a great dissatisfaction with everything. I don't know what it is. I'm not even tired a lot of the time, and all the same I'm half-exhausted if I even stand up.'

She leaned on her as she made her way over the stile and pulled her gloves off as they walked through the orchard.

'Now, we'll go upstairs,' she said when they got to the house. 'It's tidier and I have a new tea-making apparatus up there and a little fridge on the landing and everything. I'll just wash my hands and my face and I'll be with you in no time.'

Nora had forgotten how high the ceilings were in the rooms upstairs. The room was filled with a heavy watery grey light that hit against the grey carpet, the walls painted white, the rich blue lamp-shades, the blue cushions on the sofa, the blue curtains, the patterned rug and the long full bookcase, and gave the room a sort of opulence that no one coming up the lane or looking at the house from the outside or walking through the dead orchard could expect.

As she stood at the window and looked out at the day, it occurred to her for the first time how much her two sons would have disturbed the life of these rooms, which had been prepared with such care. Even the very untidiness was part of Josie's life, a life that seemed designed not to be disturbed. It had been, she thought then, a reasonable idea to leave them with her aunt rather than her sisters. She did not take them to stay with Catherine in Kilkenny, although Catherine had offered, as Catherine had her own children to mind. And Una, her youngest sister, moved into the house and looked after Aine, and Fiona if she came for the weekend. Una could not have taken care of the two boys as well, nor could Maurice's sister, Margaret, even though she doted on them. Nor could Nora have left them to be looked after by neighbours or cousins. Josie, on the other hand, had space and time and she lived close enough to the town; the boys knew her and John and John's wife; the farm-house and even Josie's extension were familiar. It had seemed reasonable then. But, as Nora watched from the window and then turned and took in the space that Josie had created for her retire-ment, the idea that she had left the boys here for so long somehow did not seem reasonable now.

Josie had combed her hair and put on a cashmere sweater. She pushed in a small trolley with a teapot and two cups and saucers and a bowl of sugar and a jug of milk.

'We'll let the tea settle,' she said and then went to the window.

'It's nice here on a fine day and the heating system works so it's warm now in the winter as well. I was worried about the heating. I thought it would dry the air, but it works –'

'Josie, I was going to ask you about the boys,' Nora interrupted her.

'Are they well?' Josie asked, moving towards the trolley.

'I never asked you what it was like having them here.'

'What it was like for me?' she asked.

Nora did not reply.

'I offered to do it, Nora, and I meant the offer.'

'What was it like for them?' Nora asked quietly.

'Nora, are you blaming me for something?' Josie asked.

'No, I'm asking, that's all.'

'Well, sit down then and stop looking at me like that.'

Nora sat on the sofa and Josie on the armchair beside her.

'Donal came home with this terrible stammer.'

'Yes, he got that here, Nora. It began here.'

'And Conor. I don't know what it is about him. And Donal had a nightmare on Saturday night. It was the worst thing.'

Josie began to pour the tea, having moved the trolley closer to her.

'Put the milk and sugar in yourself. I can never judge it.'

'What happened to them here?' Nora asked.

Josie put a lump of sugar in her tea and then some milk. She took a sip and put the cup down on the trolley.

'I suppose they noticed the silence,' Josie said.

'The silence? Is that all?'

'Yes. They're from the town. And maybe I should have arranged for them to play with some of the local boys, but they didn't want that. So they stayed here. And it was silent. And they thought you might come and you never did. Sometimes even if a car began to make its way up the lane, or pulled in on the road, the two of them would stop what they were doing and sit up. And then time went by. I don't know what you were thinking of leaving them here all that time and never once coming to see them.'

'Maurice was dying.'

'Conor wet the bed most nights. I don't know what you were thinking of leaving them here all that time,' Josie repeated.

'I had no choice.'

'There we are then. Did you think they would come home unchanged?'

'I don't know what I thought. I wanted to come and ask you.'

'Well, you've asked me, Nora.'

They both remained silent for some moments. A few times Nora began to say something but then stopped.

'I was looking after Maurice,' she finally said.

'Whatever way you want to put it is fine with me. When Conor began to get upset, I tried to talk to him and reassure him, but I didn't know when you would be coming. I never knew what Donal was thinking. He's the one you have to watch, or maybe you have to watch both of them. I phoned that guest-house you were staying in and you never phoned back.'

'Things changed every day.'

'I phoned and you never phoned back.'

'Everyone was enquiring.'

'Was I just everyone?'

'I never knew how long . . .'

'And the boys didn't either. So we all did the best we could. By the end, they became better. By the end, Conor only wet the bed sometimes.'

'I didn't know about the bed. I'm grateful to you for what you did.'

'Go home to them now.'

'I will, Josie.'

She did not finish her tea, but stood up. She waited for a moment in case Josie stood up too, but Josie did not. Her aunt was sitting forward in the armchair, staring at the floor, her shoulders hunched.

'Maybe we'll see you soon,' Nora said.

'I'll drop in again some day when I'm in the town.'

Nora made her way down the stairs and around the house to the car. It was still the afternoon. When she looked at her watch she saw that her visit had not lasted even half an hour. There was still time to go to Wexford, if she wanted, and do some shopping before she went home.

Chapter Three

Jim, her brother-in-law, sat in an easy chair on the other side of the fireplace. He waited until the boys went into the front room before pulling the sheets of paper from his inside pocket and handing them to her.

'Do you still want to use those prayers?' he asked.

'I do,' Nora said.

'We were hoping you might have changed your mind.'

Margaret, her sister-in-law, smiled.

'Jim doesn't like them,' she said to Nora, almost confidentially, as though Jim were not in the room. 'For your mother's and for ours, God knows, we just had the simple prayers on the memory cards.'

'It would cost more as well,' Jim said.

'Well, it would be a small thing for Maurice,' Nora said. 'And it would be something I'd like.'

'We don't know those prayers at all,' Margaret said.

Nora looked at the sheet Jim had handed her and began to read: '"Too young to die, they say. Too young? No, rather he is blessed in being so young thus to be made swiftly an immortal. He has escaped the tremulous hands of age." It says something. He has been made swiftly an immortal.'

'Why don't you print that yourself?' Margaret suggested. 'And we'll do the other plain one ourselves. We have old relations out the country, the crowd up in Kiltealy, and the Ryans in Cork, and they would think it was too strange, Nora. They'd all like a simple memory card to remember Maurice by.'

'Would they not think we had fallen out if we do separate memory cards?' Nora asked.

'They know how close we all are, Nora, especially now.'

'That might be the best solution,' Jim said.

It was clear to Nora then that he and Margaret had discussed this in detail before they arrived. She was pleased at the compromise and glad that she had not given in to them when they wanted simple plain memory cards with the same old prayers as everyone had.

The silence was soon broken by a knock that came to the door. One of the boys answered, and all three adults listened closely as they heard a woman's voice in the hallway. Nora quietly put the sheets of paper away; she could not tell who it was. She walked across the room and opened the door.

'Oh, Mrs Whelan, come in,' she said. 'It's lovely to see you.'

Maurice was dead six months now and the visitors had eased off; some nights no one came and she was relieved about that. She did not know Mrs Whelan well, and did not think that Maurice had taught any of her sons in school. She wondered if they might have gone to the Vocational School, and was not sure if they were still in the town.

'I won't stay,' Mrs Whelan said. Having greeted Margaret and Jim, she finally agreed to take a chair, although she would not remove her coat or her scarf.

'Just I have a message for you, so I won't delay, and no, I won't have a cup of tea or anything. I'll just give you the message. I work for the Gibneys now, I don't know if you know that. Anyway, Peggy Gibney asked me to tell you that she would love to see you, and so would William, any day after dinner. She's always there, but if you said the day then she would certainly be there.'

Nora noticed Margaret and Jim eyeing Mrs Whelan carefully; they could tell that this invitation was not casual. Even though she had been in school with Peggy Gibney, she had not seen her for years. And, before she married, Nora had worked with William in the office of the flour mill the family owned when his father ran the firm. Now William was the owner of everything, not only the mill but also the largest wholesale business in the town. He and Peggy did not send out invitations for no reason, she knew. Having moved into his father's old house and inherited everything, he had become remote, or so she had heard.

'Whatever day would suit them, Mrs Whelan,' she said, 'that day is fine with me.'

'Will we say Wednesday then? At three? Or half three?'

'Wednesday will be fine.'

Mrs Whelan refused tea again, and insisted that she would not stay. In the hall, alone with Nora, she began to whisper.

'They'd like you to come back to the office. But maybe don't mention that when you see them. Let them tell you themselves.'

'Is there a job vacant?' Nora asked.

'Let them tell you all that,' Mrs Whelan whispered.

When she returned to the back room, Nora knew that Margaret and Jim were searching her face for a sign of what had been said in the hall. When Nora sat down, neither of them spoke for a moment as they waited for her to tell them. She put more coal on the fire as a way of lifting the tension.

'The Gibneys are doing very well, I believe,' Margaret said. 'They are branching out into all sorts of things besides the mill. All the farmers go there to the farm providers and then you often see queues of vans at the cash-and-carry. And the wholesale does a great trade. The sons are very go-ahead.'

'They are a force to be reckoned with all right,' Jim said.

Soon, Donal and Conor came into the room to say goodnight, and Jim and Margaret stood up, saying it was time they went home. Nora led them out into the hall.

'So we'll do the two separate memory cards then,' Jim said. 'With maybe the same photograph.'

Nora nodded and said nothing.

She opened the front door. As Jim passed her he handed her an envelope almost surreptitiously.

'Just to tide you over,' he said. 'Say nothing about it.'

'I can't take money from you. You've paid for everything.'

'Just to tide you over for the moment,' he said, and she understood by his tone that her returning to work in Gibney's after an absence of twenty-one years would not only meet with his approval, but somehow fulfil his expectations. Before he walked down the steps he looked at her knowingly and she wondered, since he knew everyone in the town, if he had had a hand in arranging Mrs Whelan's visit.

When they had left, she sat back in her chair and thought about Gibney's. She remembered, after her father died, the nuns, Sister Catherine especially, coming to the house and asking her mother if there was nothing that could be done, nothing at all, if enough money just for three years' more schooling for Nora could not be found, and then she could even get a university scholarship, but she would certainly get a well-paid job in the civil service. She knew that her mother had tried, and in trying had managed to fall out with both sides of the family. She knew that her mother had no money, and so, since it was known how clever Nora was, she could be found a job in Gibney's instead of staying at school. She began there when she was fourteen and a half; once she was fifteen, she took shorthand and typing classes in the evening so that she could improve her chances of promotion. In the first few years, when she was paid she handed over her entire wage packet to her mother, whose small shop was badly stocked, who sold cigarettes in ones, and who augmented her income by singing in the cathedral at weddings when people had enough money to pay her. In those years, her mother, herself and her two sisters lived on almost nothing until Catherine and Una too found jobs in offices in the town.

For eleven years, then, Nora had worked five and a half days a week in Gibney's, barely tolerating her mother at home and at work operating with an efficiency that was still remembered. In the years when she was married and had children she had never dreamed that she would have to go back; the job there seemed like the distant past. She had only one friend from that time, and she, too, had married well; she and her husband had moved away. Both Nora and her friend viewed the office in Gibney's as a place where they had spent years working merely because the right chances did not come to match their intelligence, an intelligence that, as married women, they had cultivated with care.

She thought of the freedom that marriage to Maurice had given her, the freedom, once the children were in school, or a young child was sleeping, to walk into this room at any time of the day and take down a book and read; the freedom to go into the front room at any time and look out of the window at the street and Vinegar Hill across the valley or the clouds in the sky, letting her mind be idle,

50

going back to the kitchen, or to attend to the children when they came home from school, but as part of a life of ease that included duty. The day belonged to her, even if others could call on her, take up her time, distract her. Never once, in the twenty-one years she had run this household, had she felt a moment of boredom or frustration. Now her day was to be taken from her. Her only hope was that the Gibneys, when they met her, would not, in fact, have a job for her. Returning to work in that office belonged to a memory of being caged. She knew, though, that she would not be able to turn the Gibneys down if they offered her something. Her years of freedom had come to an end; it was as simple as that.

She looked again at the prayers she had chosen for Maurice's memory card. The words lifted her for a moment from the consideration of how she was going to make a living, of how much she had lost, but when she looked again at the prayers tears filled her eyes and she was glad that Jim and Margaret were not here and that the boys had gone to bed as she read the opening words: 'We give them back to Thee, O God, who gave them to us.'

That was, she thought, close to what had happened. She had given Maurice back; there was almost nothing more to be said. She ran her eyes down the second prayer again. 'People sometimes talk in their foolishness of such a one cut off in the prime of life. He is not cut off. Rather he is, if one could vary the metaphor, hurried into the prime, the fullness of life. He is lifted out of this life of ours, which is but a waiting till death shall find us. He is taken out of this. He has escaped, this man of whom they say to us that he is stricken in the midst of years. Too young to die, they say. Too young? No, rather he is blessed in being so young thus to be made swiftly an immortal. He has escaped the tremulous hands of age.'

The words, she thought, seemed to be too certain. Wherever Maurice was at this moment, he would long for the comfort of this house and for her, as much as she longed for the past year of her life to be wiped away and for him to return to them.

On Wednesday morning she went downtown and had her hair done, talking to Bernie in the hairdresser's about a new system of dyeing hair she had read about, wondering if it was time that she did something about the grey.

'I wouldn't like it blue,' she said.

'I know what you mean,' Bernie replied.

'And if it was too black then it would look dyed. And I was never blonde, everyone in the town knows I was never blonde. Is there a good brown, so that it might not look dyed?'

'I could try this one.' Bernie showed her a package with a photograph of a woman with curly brown hair that looked natural.

'Maybe just start off with a small bit?' she said.

'The instructions say to use the whole thing. I've used it before. It's very popular. You would be surprised who has it.'

'Well, try it so,' Nora said.

Once the dye had been applied, Bernie put a nylon net on her head and left her to flick through some magazines. When she saw that she would not be home in time to cook a proper dinner for the boys, she regretted having come here at all and knew that she would have to go soon. She signalled to Bernie, who was now busy with two women who had come in together and appeared to need to consult each other about each clip of the scissors.

'I'll be right with you,' Bernie said.

When she came over to remove the net, Bernie told her not to worry, or look too closely, as the real change would come only once the drier and a brush and comb were used. Nora was aware that the two women Bernie had been looking after were studying her closely. Nora wondered if she should not have consulted other women before getting her hair dyed for the first time, but she couldn't think of anyone she could have asked. Both of her sisters, she presumed, dyed their hair, but she had never heard them talking about it. Slowly, as she watched Bernie working with the hair-drier, she realized that she was being given the hairstyle of a much younger woman, and that the women watching it all happen knew that and were taking it in with considerable satisfaction.

The more Bernie worked, the more her hair seemed to look like a wig. She knew that the dye would take time to wash out, but, in the mirror, she could see how pleased Bernie was with her own work. There would be no point in complaining.

'Is it not a bit young for me?' she asked.

'I think you look great,' Bernie replied. 'This cut is very fashionable at the moment.'

'I've never had a fashionable cut before,' she said.

When it was finished, she knew that anyone who saw her on the way home would think that she had lost her mind, or that she was trying to look like a young woman rather than someone who was recently widowed.

'It'll take a few days to get used to,' Bernie said. 'But no one has grey hair any more.'

'Does the dye not look very unnatural?'

'In a few days it will lose that look and people will think that you've had it all your life. You look very worried but I promise you that by the weekend you'll be delighted with it.'

'You can't wash it out, can you?'

'No, but it will fade, and I guarantee that you'll be back here in a month for the same again. I've never known anyone to go back to the grey. But maybe the next time we'll think of putting some highlights in. They're all the rage now as well.'

'Highlights? Oh, I don't think so.'

Outside, she lifted her head high and hoped that all the women in Court Street and John Street would be busy cooking and that none of them would be standing at the door. She prayed that she would meet no one she knew. In her mind she went through the worst possible encounters, the people who would most deplore the idea that, with her husband six months in the grave, she had dyed her hair a colour it had never been before. She thought of Jim, and knew that she would have to face him and Margaret within a week. They would not know what to think.

As she saw Mrs Hogan from John Street walking towards her, Nora could not tell whether Mrs Hogan simply did not recognize her, or if she wanted to get by her without making any comment. Just as Mrs Hogan approached her, she seemed almost to jump. Her face quivered and then she stopped.

'Well, that will take some getting used to,' she said.

Nora tried to smile.

'Was it Bernie?' Mrs Hogan asked.

Nora nodded.

'I heard she got some new packets in all right. God, I must go to her myself.'

If Mrs Hogan, in her apron and a pair of very worn-looking shoes, felt that she had the right to comment on Nora's hair, then there was, Nora felt, no reason why she could not comment in reply.

'Well, you know where she is,' she said drily, looking at Mrs Hogan's hair, clearly suggesting that it could benefit from some treatment. It took Mrs Hogan a moment to take in the possibility that she was being insulted.

The encounter made Nora feel brave. She would stop for nobody else, but she knew that what had happened was a mistake. She wondered if she had ever done anything like this before in her life, acted on a whim without any thought for the consequences. Before she was married, she remembered, as she came back from work one day at dinnertime, she found a stall of old books outside Warren's Auctioneers at the bottom of Castle Hill. As she perused the books she found a volume of poems by Browning, one of whose poems she had loved in school. She was flicking through the pages when she was joined by old Mrs Carty from Bohreen Hill. They both checked the price of the book, which was written in pencil on the inside page. It was far too high, and, in any case, she had no money. They both walked away and moved together along Friary Place and up Friary Hill. As they parted at the top of the hill, Mrs Carty handed her the book from under her coat.

'No one will miss that,' she said. 'But don't tell anyone where you got it.'

Walking home with her new hair dye reminded her of walking into her mother's house with that volume of Browning's poems. It was the same feeling of guilt, the same feeling that someone would follow her and find her out.

Quickly, when she arrived home, she boiled some potatoes and opened a tin of peas and put three lamb chops on the pan. When the boys arrived, the potatoes were not ready. She waited upstairs, calling down to let them know that their dinner would be a bit late. She sat in front of the mirror at the dressing table and tried to work out if there was anything she could do to her hair to make it look more normal. She wished she had told Bernie not to use the lacquer, which was sticky and had a sweet smell.

As soon as the boys saw her they both became quiet. Donal looked away while Conor moved towards her. He reached up and touched her hair.

'It's all hard,' he said. 'Where did you get it?'

'I had my hair done this morning,' she said. 'Do you like it?'

'What's under there?'

'Under what?'

'Under what you have on your head.'

'What I have on my head is my hair.'

'Are you going to go out with that?' he asked.

Donal glanced at her again and looked away.

Nora was not sure what she should wear to the Gibneys'. If she dressed up too much then it might look as though she did not need a job and that she was coming to their house as an equal, merely on a social visit. But she could not wear old clothes either. The problem of what to wear would never go away, she realized. If she went back to the office there, she would be seen by everyone as a friend of William and Peggy Gibney's. There were still people there whom she had known all those years before but had not kept in touch with. She was sure that they would resent her or feel strange about her, were she to appear back working with them.

Once she decided that she would drive across the town and park the car in the Railway Square so that no one could comment on her hair, however, she no longer felt afraid. She looked at her clothes hanging in the wardrobe and selected a grey suit and a dark blue blouse. She would wear her best shoes. She did not know what the Gibneys intended to say to her, or whether they would offer her work. They could, she thought, hardly discuss rates of pay with her over afternoon tea. Whatever they had in mind, she believed now that it was important not to arrive at their large house like someone in need.

The door was answered by Mrs Whelan, who led Nora into a big sitting room on the right-hand side of the hall. It was filled with darkly upholstered furniture and old pictures. Even though it was still the afternoon, the room was filled with shadows; the long window did not let in much light.

Peggy Gibney rose from her chair. As the cardigan she was wearing around her shoulders slipped, Mrs Whelan moved hastily to put it back in place. Peggy Gibney did not acknowledge this, but behaved as though it were a normal part of the service offered to her as a woman in a grand room. She motioned to Nora to take an armchair opposite her own and then turned to Mrs Whelan.

'Maggie, will you phone across to the office and tell Mr Gibney that Mrs Webster has arrived?'

Nora remembered that, years before, when Peggy found herself pregnant, she was not married to William, and William's parents had not approved of her. One day, while Nora sat quietly in the outer office, she heard old Mr Gibney telling William that Peggy could go to England and have the baby and find a home for it there. She had supposed as William walked out of the office that he was going to find Peggy to tell her. But instead he had married Peggy and Peggy had had the baby in a nursing home in the town, and slowly William's parents had got used to her and grown close to the child. Now Peggy Gibney sat in this house, talking to Nora as though there had never been any doubt about her station in the world.

Peggy's voice had none of the old careless intonations of the town. Instead, she spoke in a way that was considered, almost pre-occupied.

'Oh, well,' she said, as though Nora or someone else had raised the subject, 'with all the taxes now, and the cost of living, I don't know how a lot of people manage.'

When Nora asked her about her brother and her sisters, she realized that she had made a mistake.

'They are fine, Nora, fine,' she said in an accent that became slightly grand. 'We all live our own lives.'

Nora took this to mean that they were not invited into Peggy's sitting room. When she asked about Peggy's children, however, she brightened up immediately.

'You know, William wanted each one of them to have a qualification before they came home to work in the firm so that they'd have an expertise.'

She pronounced the word 'expertise' with deliberation.

'So, William Junior is a fully fledged accountant and Thomas is an efficiency expert and Elizabeth did a commercial course in one of the best colleges in Dublin. So they can all stand on their own feet.'

'Is that right, Peggy?' Nora asked.

She thought of old Mrs Lewis in the Mill Park Road whose only topic of conversation was her children and their careers, and how she would end each time by saying that she planned to make Christina, her youngest, into a typewriter. Nora found it difficult in the sombre air of Peggy's sitting room not to laugh. She had to concentrate fiercely to keep a straight face.

'There are a lot of changes in the town, they tell me,' Peggy said. 'I don't get out much myself, and, you know, we go to Rosslare when we can. It's very peaceful down there, but no matter where I am I always find that I have too much to do.'

Nora tried to think who had told her that Peggy had a full-time maid working in the house, as well as Mrs Whelan.

'But I can't get William to take a proper holiday. Oh, he'd worry too much about this and that. He drives up and down to Rosslare all right but I don't call that a holiday.'

When William came into the room he seemed smaller than Nora remembered. He was wearing a three-piece suit. As he shook Nora's hand, she wondered if he still lived with the memory of how his father had treated him from the time he took him out of school aged sixteen, how badly he had paid him over the years and how he had referred to him in front of anyone who would listen as 'the fool'. But William's father was long dead now, and the firm had passed to him, so perhaps, she thought, all of that had been erased from everyone's memory except her own.

'It was very good of you to visit,' he said, sitting down as Mrs Whelan came in with tea and biscuits.

'Thoughtful, thoughtful,' he added, as though his mind was now on some other, graver subject.

Nora looked at him evenly and did not reply. She was not going to thank him for anything.

'My father always said you were the best and you never made a mistake, you and Greta Wickham. He used to say if only Nora and Greta were here now, we wouldn't be in this mess, even when there was no mess at all.'

'Oh, he talked very warmly about you,' Peggy interjected, 'and William Junior and Thomas had nothing but good words to say about Maurice Webster when he was teaching them. I remember one day Thomas had a temperature and we all wanted him to stay in bed and he wouldn't, oh, no he wouldn't, because he had a double Commerce class with Mr Webster that he could not miss. You know they wanted Thomas to stay in Dublin when he qualified. Oh, he got offers with very good prospects! We told him he should consider them. But he preferred to come home. That's the way it was. It was the same with William. With Elizabeth, you'd never know. She might go anywhere. She's the one to watch.'

There was something in Peggy Gibney's loquaciousness, in the way she felt free to talk about herself and her family, that Nora found almost deliberately created to undermine her, a way of establishing that Peggy had become someone who had a high opinion of herself and she expected others to feel the same. William, Nora supposed, must employ a hundred people, perhaps more. She understood that it might have been difficult for Peggy Gibney to remain ordinary, but she saw no reason why she should sit opposite her and offer her anything except silence.

With William it was different. He seemed to mumble and had a nervous way of repeating words and then stopping as if in search of another word.

'We'd always have an opening, Nora,' he began, 'an opening . . .'

Nora looked at him and smiled.

'Some of the girls in the office can barely spell,' Peggy interjected again, 'and can hardly count and yet when it comes to giving cheek and taking sick days . . .'

'Well now,' William said. 'Well now.'

Nora watched William closely, looking for any indication that he found Peggy as irritating as she did, but he appeared too distanced and fidgety to notice his wife at all.

'And the cut of some of them! Elizabeth says –'

'Thomas,' William interrupted, 'thinks the world of Miss Kavanagh, and she is the office manager, and perhaps if I can get you and Thomas briefly to go over the details, the details, he knows more than I do.'

He stopped for a moment and looked at Nora, as though unsure what he might say now.

'God knows,' he went on, his eyes on the carpet, 'I'm just the manager of the company, the head of the company. But he could introduce you to Miss Kavanagh, and then you could, if you know what I mean, start whenever you wanted. You could start whenever you wanted.'

'Is that Francie Kavanagh?' Nora asked.

'I suppose it is,' William said, 'although it might be a while since anyone called her that.'

'Oh, of course,' Peggy said. 'You would have known her in the old days. Thomas gives a glowing account of her. And have you two kept in touch?'

'Pardon?' Nora asked sharply.

'I mean have you and Miss Kavanagh stayed friends?'

The question implied that Peggy had not had time herself over the years to bother knowing such things, or to bother staying friends with anyone. Nonetheless, Nora wondered how much she knew, if she was aware, for example, of a Thursday twenty-five years or more earlier – surely it had been talked about – a half-day in Gibney's, when Nora and Greta Wickham had decided to cycle to Ballyconnigar and how Francie Kavanagh had asked to come with them, and how they had ridden their bicycles fast to get ahead of her and then had gone to Morriscastle instead of Ballyconnigar. And how they had almost laughed openly rather than apologized when they learned that Francie had got a puncture near The Ballagh on the way home and had got drenched in the rain that came after nightfall and then, having sheltered under a tree, did not get back until the early hours of the morning. She had never spoken to them again.

William and Peggy were watching her. She had not answered their question about Francie Kavanagh and it was too late to do so now. In all the years, then, she thought, when she was married and having children, Francie was still in Gibney's and had become the office manager, just as Peggy Gibney, lifting her teacup in a leisurely manner now, had stayed in this house and gone to Rosslare in the summer, and become falsely grand, modelling herself on her mother-in-law or on one of the other merchants' wives in the town. Nora felt as far away from both of these women as silence was from sound.

William stood up, and a change came into the room. Somehow, he and Peggy managed to suggest that, since the pleasantries were over, Nora was dismissed. When she stood to go, Peggy remained seated; it was clear that she did not feel it was part of her function to show people out of the house. William shook Nora's hand.

'Will you come and see Thomas on Monday at two? Ask for him in the outer office, yes the outer office,' he said and then made his way distractedly out of the room. Nora could hear him closing the front door behind him. Then Mrs Whelan, who had been hovering in the doorway, led Nora into the hallway.

'She'll be delighted you came over,' she whispered. 'You know, she doesn't see too many people.'

'Is that right?' Nora asked. She was aware again of her dyed hair as Mrs Whelan examined it with an almost shameless curiosity.

Chapter Four

She told no one about the arrangement that she had made with Thomas Gibney or about the first encounter she was going to have with Francie Kavanagh in more than twenty years. She would tell Jim and Margaret soon, she thought, but was grateful to them when they came to the house next for not asking her how her visit to Gibneys' had gone. When her sister Una asked her about it, she merely said that she had not made up her mind yet.

'I heard in the golf club that you are going back to work in the office there,' Una said.

'The golf club is a great place for information,' Nora replied. 'I'd join it myself if I could play, or if I was nosy enough.'

When her other sister, Catherine, wrote to her to say that she should come with the boys to stay with her and her family and that any weekend would suit, Nora replied that she would come the following Friday once the boys had finished school and stay until Sunday. Before Maurice became sick he had always enjoyed going to the farmhouse where they lived outside Kilkenny on a Saturday night and talking to Catherine's husband about crops and prices and arguing about politics with him, and hearing all the news about their neighbours. The two couples often went out to a lounge bar, leaving the children to be minded by Fiona or Aine. The boys also seemed to enjoy the change as they were sleeping in strange rooms in a much larger house than they were used to.

It was true, Nora thought, what her mother had said; they all, including her sisters, preferred Maurice to her and listened more to what he said. When the four of them went out for a drink, the two men talked to each other, but Catherine liked to listen to the men, or ask them questions, or raise topics that she knew would interest them. Nora had never minded; she only half-listened because she did not have such strong opinions about what was happening in the country as Maurice did. Also Catherine and her husband, Mark, were religious in the same way that Maurice was. They believed in miracles and the power of prayer, but they also liked the way the church was modernizing. None of them had ever asked Nora what she thought about this; she was not sure herself, but she knew that she did not think what they thought and that she was in favour of much more modernization than they were. She did not take things for granted the way they did. About other things too she had her own thoughts, but was happy to stay outside the conversation. She wondered now that Maurice was dead if this would change, if she would have to start saying more.

By the time the boys came home from school she had packed what things they would need into the car. She made an agreement with them that Donal could sit in the front passenger seat as far as Kiltealy and then they would switch and Conor could sit in the front for the rest of the journey.

In the old days, as they passed a particular farm entrance beyond the Milehouse, Maurice would become tense, absorbed in his own thoughts no matter what was being said in the car. They had never discussed this. It was not something he had ever wanted to talk about. She knew about it because she heard Margaret and one of the cousins discussing it at her mother-in-law's wake. This was the farm from which, at the end of the last century, Maurice's grand-father had been evicted. When he and his wife and their children had arrived in the town, Maurice's grandfather had nothing except a bad reputation with the police for his politics, and some books and clothes in an old bag. Nora always wondered at how seriously Maurice took this event, or at least how strangely preoccupied he became any time they drove by this place, as though mentioning it would be a desecration of some solemn piece of past suffering.

Somewhere beyond Tullow, she knew, there was a house where her own mother had been a servant, and where the man of the house, or his brother, or his son, had come too close to her every day and sometimes at night. Her Aunt Josie had told her all the details, and how the priest had to be called in the end and how the priest approached the manager of Cullen's department store in

Enniscorthy with a special request to help him save the virtue of a servant girl in some remote farmhouse beyond Tullow. Nora remembered that the idea of her mother's virtue and the priest and the remote house beyond Tullow, and the owner and his brother and his son, had seemed to her unlikely enough to be funny. When Josie had insisted that it was true, Nora had found herself laughing even more until Josie warned her never to tell anyone else the story, but, if she did, then not to tell them that she laughed at it. People would not think well of her, Josie said, if they knew she thought such things were funny.

The road was narrow and Nora drove with care. These old stories, she thought, would die out soon. Soon no one would even remember or care about an eviction long ago. Maurice's grandfather and grandmother were buried in an unmarked grave in the cemetery; no one would ever know who they were or had been. And she supposed that neither of her sisters knew about the house beyond Tullow and her mother there and those men. They were likely not even aware that their mother had worked as a servant in the time between leaving her father's house and coming to work in Cullen's in Enniscorthy.

Beyond Kiltealy, when Conor was in the front seat, he told her stories about school and classmates and teachers. He seemed to be looking forward to spending time with his cousins and seeing the farm.

'Is Auntie Catherine's house haunted?' he asked.

'No, Conor, it's just an old house and bigger than ours but it's not haunted.'

'But a lot of people died in it?'

'I don't know.'

'But how would a house get haunted?' Conor asked.

'You know, I think that's all rubbish about haunted houses.'

'Phelans' on the Back Road is haunted. Joe Devereux saw a man outside it one night and he had no face. He was lighting a cigarette but he had no face.'

'But I'd say that was just the shadows,' she said. 'If Joe had a flash-light he would have seen the man's face perfectly.'

'That's why we all used to walk on the other side of the road on the way home from the Presentation,' Conor continued.

'Well, at least you don't have to go there any more.'

'Everyone knows th-th-there's a ghost there,' Donal said from the back seat.

'Well, I never heard of it,' she replied.

Although the boys said nothing for a while, she knew as she drove through Borris that it was still on their minds.

'I think all that stuff about ghosts is nonsense,' she said.

'But there must have been plenty of people who died in Auntie Catherine's house. I mean in the rooms upstairs,' Conor continued.

'But there are no such things as ghosts,' she said.

'What about the Holy G-ghost?' Donal asked.

'Donal, you know that's different.'

'I wouldn't go upstairs in Auntie Catherine's house on my own, all the same,' Conor said. 'Even during the day I wouldn't go up there.'

By the time they arrived they had been silent for some time. She had tried to change the subject, but felt that she failed to stop them thinking about ghosts and haunted houses. These narrow roads, she thought, and the sheer isolation of places along them, the lanes leading for miles to lonely farmhouses that could be seen from nowhere, the untidy ditches and the trees that overhung the road, all of this lent itself to the idea of ghosts and sounds in the night. When Catherine first got married, Nora remembered, she talked about a house owned by a cousin of Mark's, an old place covered in ivy, where the furniture could move or a door open for no reason. Catherine and Mark spoke about it in detail, without any doubt that it was true. Nora wondered if it had something to do with a will, or old money, or a fight, or someone being put out of the house who had a right to be there. In any case, she hoped that neither of them would mention this to the boys over the weekend.

One of the things about Catherine was that she hardly ever sat down. Their mother, Nora remembered, was the same, always bustling about. Nora and Una called it 'foostering'. It was worse because their mother disapproved of women sitting down when there was still work to do. All her married life Nora had made sure that she stayed sitting down for as long as possible each evening once the washing-up after tea had been completed; she tried to make sure that nothing would cause her to stand up again and spend time in the kitchen except perhaps the boiling of a kettle to make a cup of tea for her and for Maurice, or the preparing of a hot water bottle in the winter.

As soon as she carried her bag to the room she had been allocated, the same room where she and Maurice had always stayed, she felt an overwhelming urge not to leave again, to send down word that she was not well and needed to rest. The expression on Catherine's face when she saw her hair had not helped; the fact that she had not spoken immediately meant that she was saving it up for later, and she would, Nora was sure, have a great deal to say.

Mark's farm was large; Nora did not know how many acres he had because Catherine had told no one on her side of the family. This meant that he had more land than Catherine wanted to admit. If the farm had been small, then Catherine would have enjoyed complaining about that. All her life she had bought clothes on sale and she did not change this when she married. But if it was anything other than clothes now, especially if it was something for the house, she spent real money. The phrase of Mark's that Nora and Maurice had enjoyed most was 'a thing is only dear the day you buy it'. Such a concept was entirely foreign to both of them.

This meant that there were two brand-new cars in the drive, and there was always new furniture, or new things for the kitchen, bought in Brown Thomas or Switzer's in Dublin. Nora was sure that Catherine had her hair done in Dublin, or somewhere special in Kilkenny that catered to rich farmers' wives. The idea of letting Bernie Prendergast in Enniscorthy dye your hair was something that would appal Catherine.

If Maurice were with her, she thought, then the focus of attention would be on him, and he would manage with ease and slow charm. As she walked down the well-carpeted stairs, taking in the expensive new wallpaper and the newly framed prints that she knew had belonged to Mark's mother, she realized that while it might seem as though she were the focus of attention, in fact she was an object of pity. Catherine and Mark would be glad to have her and the boys this weekend, and they would be kind and hospitable, but they would also be glad when she was gone and they had done their duty. Once she began working in Gibney's, she thought, she would use that as an excuse not to come here for a while again.

Donal and Conor always took time to get used to the farm. There were things they liked. If there was any reason to go to the orchard with their cousins, they would agree as long as no one wanted them to go near any nettles. And there was a manual pump that brought spring water to the house that had to be pulled back and forth, and they both enjoyed playing with this. But if anything involved putting on boots and old clothes and going near farm animals, or going into the milking parlour or up to the haggard where there was cow dung, they would respond suspiciously. They would watch and wait, checking if they might be allowed to sit with the adults instead and listen to the conversation.

Catherine, Nora discovered when she came into the kitchen, had bought a new washing machine; it had been delivered from Dublin the previous day and Catherine had the manual on the kitchen table in front of her.

'There's a drier as well,' she said, 'but we haven't even unpacked that. I thought I'd concentrate on getting the washing machine to work first. I should have asked the man who came to do the plumbing. I thought once he was finished it would work straight away. There's a friend of mine, Dilly Halpin, and she has one, and when I rang her she told me she nearly had to get a university degree before she could follow the instructions.'

She made space for Nora at the table as Donal and Conor and two of their cousins looked on.

'It would be just my luck now if there's something wrong with it, and it has to go all the way back. The thing is I can't even get it to start.'

She pointed to a number of diagrams.

'You see, it has a lot of different ways of washing, for sheets and tablecloths, and then for shirts and blouses, and then for more delicate fabrics. They're in German and French as well as English, the instructions, but maybe it's a problem with the translation and it might be clearer in some other language.'

Nora wondered if Catherine and her family had already had their tea. It was after six now and Catherine agreed that the children could watch cartoons on the television and whatever children's programmes were on afterwards. But there was no mention of tea nor of food. Nora knew that the boys would be hungry soon and wondered if Catherine believed that they had eaten before they set out. What was strange, she noticed, was that Catherine did not give her any opportunity to mention food, instead she spoke to her as though she were not really there.

Once she noticed this, she found that she could notice nothing else. Catherine was not talking to herself, she was fully aware that her sister was in the room, but she had created an atmosphere in which Nora could have nothing to say. If she had done this deliberately, Nora felt, then it would not work, it could be easily broken. But it seemed to come naturally to Catherine. It was something Nora had been aware of before, but now, with her sister, it was more intense. It was solid, as the outer wall of a vault is solid, built to withstand rather than support. Nora felt herself sitting in some airless space with her sister as Catherine chattered about her washing machine and her drier and then went to the phone in the hall and called Dilly Halpin, who agreed to come over and see if she could assist Catherine in setting up the new machine.

'Don't mention to Dilly I told you this,' Catherine said, 'but I went to Dublin with her last week and we stayed with her sister and brother-in-law, who's a barrister. Oh, it's a fabulous house, Nora, in Malahide, and they have their own boat. It was all modern, I have never seen anything like it. His family are very big in the building trade, and they get a lot of the contracts, but he does very well in his own right. And Dilly's other sister, who's very nice, is married to Mr Justice Murphy of the High Court. They're very high up in Fianna Fáil. One of the other sisters is married to a Delahunt and they are fabulously wealthy, or so Dilly told me.'

Nora had never heard her sister say the word 'fabulously' before or discuss families in this way.

'Well, the thing is, they took us to the Intercontinental Hotel to have our dinner in the evening. Con and Fergus, who are Dilly's two brothers-in-law, and her two sisters, just the six of us. I have never seen food like it, and the wine. I wouldn't tell you what the bill was, but I can read upside down and I nearly had a heart attack. I haven't even told Mark. He wouldn't spend that sort of money, you know. At least not on a dinner. And the restaurant was full. There were all sorts of people there. Dilly came in with me the next day and we bought the washing machine and the drier. I wanted the same one she had.'

Conor appeared and waited until Catherine finished talking.

'What time are we getting our tea?' he asked. 'The others have all had their tea. So when are we getting ours?'

Catherine looked at him as though she had not quite heard him. Conor stood his ground and, having got no response from his aunt, he looked at Nora.

'Are you not watching the television?' Catherine asked.

'We didn't have our tea,' he repeated.

'Did you not?' Catherine asked and looked at Nora, puzzled.

Nora felt as though she were being accused of something.

'We set out as soon as they came home from school. I thought we would have our tea here.'

'Oh, I'm so sorry. Now Dilly will be here before long and Mark will be here too, but I don't know exactly what time he'll be home.'

Catherine seemed distracted. Nora was about to say that a sandwich or beans on toast would be enough for them, but she decided to say nothing. She looked into the distance as though this was not her problem. She was almost angry. Conor stayed there, watching both his mother and his aunt.

'I am so sorry,' Catherine said. 'I should have thought of this before.'

Catherine suddenly became polite and busy, and so ready to make sure that their every need was met, that it occurred to Nora that something of how she felt, even though she had not spoken, had been transmitted to her sister. Catherine went to a large fridge in the pantry.

'I have hamburgers,' she said, 'and I could fry some potatoes. Would they like that? And would you like a steak, Nora, or I could do a couple of chops? And why don't the boys have their tea in the television room?'

'Whatever is easy,' Nora said.

When Dilly Halpin arrived, Nora took over the cooking as the other two women studied the instruction manual for the washing machine. She ignored them as they began to manipulate the various knobs and concentrated fully on the task in hand. It would suit Catherine, she saw, were she to offer to have her tea in the room where the children were. She was determined to make no such offer and waited to cook her own food until she had served Donal and Conor and made sure they had everything they needed.

Once the washing machine had been got going, and Dilly Halpin had reassured Catherine that the drier was simple, that it was merely a question of turning it on and off, Dilly sat down at the kitchen table as Catherine moved about. When Nora offered to make them tea, they accepted. Once the chops were cooked she brought them over to the table with brown bread and butter. She poured the tea when it was ready. She did not know if it was her presence that made the conversation awkward, almost stilted. It seemed to Nora that Catherine and Dilly were performing lines for her benefit rather than actually talking to each other. They discussed an auction they had both attended, an auction of the contents of a large house outside Thomastown.

'You know, I bid for a pair of fire irons,' Dilly said, 'they were eighteenth century, but I didn't get them. There was a dealer from Dublin bidding against me. I gave him the dirtiest looks but it was no use. You did better, Catherine, with that lovely rug. Where are you going to put it?'

'I'm going to surprise Mark,' Catherine said, 'and put it in the bedroom. I'll have to get help, because some of it will have to go under the bed. I hope he notices, that's all I have to say.'

'And the auction went on so long that I needed to go to the bathroom,' Dilly said, 'and I decided I would go into the big house, so I took down the notice that said "No Entry. House Strictly Private" and I marched in and wasn't I on my way up the stairs looking for a bathroom when I was caught by this old Protestant woman, someone's maiden aunt by the look of her. I said that I just had to go to the bathroom and I couldn't find any other convenience and she told me that I could go anywhere I liked between Thomastown and Inistioge, but I was to come down those stairs right now. And she began to move towards me, the old battle-axe. I was in such a rage that when I was driving out of the estate and I saw a field full of sheep, I got out of the car and I opened the gate.'

'You did quite right,' Catherine said.

'I did, and I hope they are still looking for those sheep. The rudeness of that woman! They think they still own the country!'

'You don't know what it's like around here,' Catherine said to Nora.

'That woman is lucky I didn't buy the fire irons and have them with me. I don't know what I would have done with them.'

As Dilly grew in indignation, and was joined by Catherine, Nora began to laugh.

'It's just the thought of the fire irons,' she said.

She stood up from the table, still laughing. She saw that Catherine's face had become red and she seemed to be clenching her jaw. Nora checked that the boys and their cousins were still watching television and then went to the bathroom and stayed there until she was sure that she would not need to laugh again. When she felt that she could genuinely control herself, she went back to find that Dilly Halpin had left. Catherine became busy around the kitchen, and, even when Mark came in, Nora was aware that Catherine was barely speaking to her. This made Nora decide to be all the friendlier and more animated with Mark. As she did this, she could see how irritated Catherine was.

'Nora, it's all right for you,' she said. 'But we have to live here and even though I meet the Protestants from the big houses in the ICA or the golf club, and even though they know Mark in the IFA and knew his father and mother before him, they would see you coming in Kilkenny on the main street and they wouldn't even look at you. I don't know what we went to that auction for.'

'What auction?' Mark asked.

'Catherine's friend Dilly attacked a Protestant woman with a pair of fire irons,' Nora said.

'She did not!'

'She seemed very nice, Catherine,' Nora said. 'But I honestly thought she was joking. I mean between the fire irons and the sheep it was hard to keep a straight face.'

'What sheep?' Mark asked.

They went to bed early. Nora was glad to be away from them and from the talk of auctions and big houses and new washing machines. It was clear to her that there was nothing she could have spoken to Catherine and Dilly about, nothing that would have interested her or them. When she asked herself what she was interested in, she had to conclude that she was interested in nothing at all. What mattered to her now could be shared with no one. Jim and Margaret had been with her when Maurice died, and that meant that all three of them could talk easily when Jim and Margaret came to the house because, while they did not refer to those days in the hospital, what they went through then underlay every word they said. It was there with them in the same way as the air was in the room, it was so present that no one ever commented on it. For them now conversation was a way of managing things. But for Catherine and Dilly and Mark conversation was normal. She wondered if she would ever again be able to have a normal conversation and what topics she might be able to discuss with ease and interest.

At the moment the only topic she could discuss was herself. And everyone, she felt, had heard enough about her. They believed it was time that she stop brooding and think of other things. But there were no other things. There was only what had happened. It was as though she lived under water and had given up on the struggle to swim towards air. It would be too much. Being released into the world of others seemed impossible; it was something she did not even want. How could she explain this to anyone who sought to know how she was or asked if she was getting over what happened?

She woke early in the morning, dreading the day ahead. She wondered if the boys felt like this too. Did Fiona and Aine also dread the day ahead when they woke? Jim and Margaret? Perhaps, she thought, they had found other things to preoccupy them. She, too, could find other things to think about – money, for example, or her children, or the job in Gibney's. Finding things to think about was not the problem for her; the problem for her was that she was on her own now and that she had no idea how to live. She would have to learn, but it was a mistake to try to do so in someone else's house. It was a mistake to lie here in a strange bed when her own bed at home was strange too. The strangeness of home, however, did not require a bright response from her. It would be a long time, she thought, before she would leave her own house for a night again.

Downstairs, she found that Catherine and a local woman who came to help her with the housework had decided to do a full clean-out of the kitchen and the pantry before they installed the drier beside the washing machine in the pantry. Every single piece of delph and crockery had been removed from shelves to be dusted and Catherine was in the process of cleaning out drawers and sorting each object, some for discarding and others to be put back. Conor and one of his cousins were helping while Donal sat apart. As soon as Donal saw her, he shrugged as if to say that all this had nothing to do with him.

'Make yourself a cup of tea, Nora,' Catherine said, 'and if you can find bread and the toaster . . . God, it'll be a relief to get this done. But at least I have plenty of help.'

'I'm going out for a walk,' she said.

Catherine turned and looked puzzled.

'It's very showery now. I don't think it's a good day for walking and we'll be going into Kilkenny later, I have to get detergent for this machine. You know, I'm nearly sorry I bought it. It's just that Dilly says it halves the work.'

'I'll find an umbrella,' Nora said.

'The umbrellas are in the stand by the front door,' Catherine said. 'Will you mind the front door if you're using it? It gets very stiff in this damp weather.'

This was what no one had told her about. She could not have ordinary feelings, ordinary desires. Catherine saw this, she thought, and she had no idea how to deal with it, and this made things worse. As Nora walked down the drive towards the road she felt a rage that she could not control. But she would have to control it, she knew. It made no sense to think that she would not come back here again, to feel a rage against her sister that up to now she had directed solely at the doctor who controlled the ward where Maurice lay in the last days of his life; a rage that caused her to write letters to him in her mind, letters she imagined herself signing and posting, letters that were abusive or coldly factual, letters threatening him that she would let people know wherever he went what he had done when her husband was dying, that he had refused to deal with the pain that caused Maurice to moan. She had sought out the doctor several times, having asked the nurses over and over if they could do anything. All of the nurses had come back with her to the bed and nodded and agreed with her that something would have to be done. But the doctor – the very thought of him made her walk faster and become even more indifferent to the clouds that were gathering overhead – had not come with her to the bed, but had told her that her husband was very sick, that his heart was weak, and so he did not want to prescribe anything to alleviate pain that might affect his heart.

And so Nora and Jim and Margaret had sat by his bed with the screen pulled around it so that the other patients and their visitors could not see. But they could hear. And when Father Quaid from the Manse and Sister Thomas from the St John of God Convent had both visited, they had heard too. Nora and Margaret held Maurice's hands and spoke to him and tried to soothe and console him and they promised him that he would be all right, but they knew that he would not be without pain again until he died.

Death, however, would not come. And Maurice was in such pain that catching his hand when he reached out was almost dangerous because he would clutch so tight. He was more alive then than he had ever been before, she thought, because of his needs and his panic and his fear and the pain that seemed to be burning in him until he was like an animal bellowing and then he could be heard not only in the corridor but even in the reception area of the hospital too.

Working in such a small hospital, a hospital that would soon be closed down, she thought, was clearly not what that doctor had planned when he was studying medicine. He seemed to be the only doctor there, on call day and night, which meant that he could seldom be found. Being stationed in a rural hospital with no surgical wards or private rooms, no heart specialists or professors guiding students through wards, must have been a humiliation. He knew nothing about pain or death, and she remembered him now speaking to her as though she were wasting the time of a very busy man. She felt a profound and active hatred for him and the feeling was like a strange sort of pleasure as she walked along and the rain started.

When the rain became heavy, Catherine came in the car to fetch her. Donal was in the front seat and got out to let her sit there. As he held the car door open, he grinned at her as though they were in a conspiracy together. It was the first time she had seen him smiling in months and as they drove back to the house in silence it was the only thing she thought about.

Catherine led her back in the house like a child who had not listened to advice from people who knew better.

'Your shoes are destroyed,' Catherine said.

'They'll dry out.'

Nora changed her clothes and then found a novel that she had packed. Tiptoeing down the stairs, she went into the sitting room instead of the kitchen. The room was filled with paintings and china and vases and lamps that Mark had inherited. The furniture, too, she knew, had been in his family for generations, and had been recently reupholstered by someone in Dublin. Since they rarely used this room, she presumed that the idea of her being here now in her casual clothes, sitting in an armchair reading a book, would irritate Catherine, still working in the kitchen. Nora found a stool and put her stockinged feet up. She wished that she was further into the book so that she could become engrossed in it. Eventually, she put the book down, lay her head back and closed her eyes. She pictured Donal's face as he held the car door open for her and wondered what Catherine might have said to him as they set out to find her. Whatever she had said, or, even more likely, her impatient silence or exasperated tone, had amused Donal, and that thought amused Nora now.

Nora knew that Catherine would phone Una, even though, having inherited strange residual elements of their mother's frugality, she disliked spending money on trunk calls, especially ones that were likely to go on for some time, as this one would. Catherine would have to recount how rude Nora had been to her friend Dilly Halpin, actually laughing at her openly, and also how she had gone like a madwoman for a walk in the rain and had to be rescued, and then, once back in the house, how she had put her feet up on the stool that had been so recently upholstered. Una, she imagined, would listen sympathetically.

By one o'clock, the kitchen had been put back in order. Catherine loved her kitchen, Nora saw, and seemed happy standing by the Aga or setting the table or talking to anyone who came in and out, including two men who worked for Mark. She had that morning's *Irish Independent* spread out on the kitchen table and at intervals read an item in the newspaper, though never for long. Nora sat opposite her and tried to take an interest in what Catherine's children were saying when they appeared. She discovered from Conor that Donal had found a chess set and was teaching one of his cousins how to play.

Catherine moved between the pantry and the kitchen as she began to prepare the dinner. Nora wondered if she should offer to help, but instead began, absent-mindedly, to read the newspaper. Since Maurice had gone to hospital, she had stopped getting any newspaper at all, but now she thought that she might start getting *The Irish Times*. It was a Protestant newspaper, but it had longer articles, she thought, and they were better written than the articles in the other newspapers. There was something more serious about *The Irish Times*; she would hide it from Jim and Margaret when they came, knowing that they favoured the *Irish Press* and would think, in any case, that she was wasting money.

The atmosphere in the room changed when Mark came in. As soon as he took his cap off, he gave the impression that this was what he had been looking forward to all morning, not only the food, but the company. He had an easy way about him that Nora appreciated now. She wondered if it came from being brought up in this house, knowing always that he would inherit the farm, but she thought it was more than that, he had good manners that would have been apparent anywhere. In similar circumstances Maurice would always be preoccupied with something, some journal, an item on the news, or a book, and there would often be complaints about the noise the children made, although these complaints would be offered in good humour and taken seriously by no one, least of all the children themselves.

Slowly, Nora saw, Catherine changed in Mark's presence. She was interested in everything he said; she asked him intelligent questions. She did not move around as much or seem to want to do two things at the same time. As the children set the table, Nora became also glad she was here, glad to be away from her thoughts. This was almost the first time, she realized, that the full weight of what had happened had lifted from her. It had lifted merely by her listening to Mark and Catherine having a casual conversation; it was as if she had been able to breathe out whatever air was in her lungs, and sit without thinking, without feeling anything. She did not know that this could occur, and she wondered how long it would last.

In the afternoon, Catherine wanted to drive into Kilkenny, but Nora was adamant that she would not go with her.

'I'd like a book and a nice chair and a room with no one else in it,' she said.

'You sound very wise to me,' Mark said. 'Trying to get parking in Kilkenny on a Saturday is a bad business.'

'There are things we need,' Catherine said, 'and we won't be long and maybe the children will go to bed early this evening and then we can sit down and relax.'

Nora saw that Donal, who was listening, was alarmed by this. Like her, he wanted to go nowhere. But more than that, he did not want to be grouped with the rest of the children and sent to bed early. He had a way, when under pressure, of keeping his eyes cast down, raising them to take a fearful look at each person, then lowering them again.

'Donal will stay here with me,' Nora said.

Still, Donal did not look up at her. Whatever the prospect of having to go to Kilkenny with his aunt and his cousins and then face an early bedtime had done to him, it would take him a while to recover. Soon, it was agreed that one of his cousins would remain to play chess with him, and the others, including Conor, would go to Kilkenny.

'You know, wild horses wouldn't drag me into Kilkenny,' Mark said to Nora. 'I go in twice a year to see an accountant, but I would nearly pay him to move out this way so I would never have to go in at all. I don't mind Thomastown or Callan, but there's something about Kilkenny. Too many shops. Too many shoppers. Too many people you half-know. This one here, however, can't get enough of it.'

He nodded in the direction of Catherine, who was putting on lipstick.

'And when it's not Kilkenny, it's Dublin. I don't mind Dublin so much, especially on a Thursday, although I hear it's not as safe as it used to be.'

'Trying to get you to buy clothes,' Catherine said, 'will be the end of me.'

Mark soon put his cap back on and put on his boots in the hall. Farm work, Nora thought, must be a constant relief. She smiled to herself at the thought. Catherine had emptied the contents of her handbag on to the kitchen table and seemed to be looking for something. When it was found, and the handbag had been refilled, she stood looking around the kitchen. It struck Nora that she would be expected to do the washing-up while they were all away; she decided that she was not going to stand by Catherine's sink at any point during this visit.

'I think I'll light a fire in the sitting room,' she said. 'I'm feeling a bit cold.'

While the house had central heating, Nora knew that it was seldom used. The kitchen was kept warm by the Aga cooker.

'We haven't lit a fire in that room since Christmas,' Catherine said, 'and even then it was only for a few hours. I don't know what state the chimney is in.'

Nora nodded, waiting for her to say that she could, nonetheless, try to light the fire there. When she did not, Nora decided that she would look for another book in the old bookcase at the top of the stairs, one with an opening more interesting than the one she had been reading before dinner, and she would spend the afternoon in bed. She might even sleep. She liked the idea of relaxing like this on a Saturday afternoon while her sister went trailing all over Kilkenny, leading the children from shop to shop.

When they came back it was dark. Nora had slept for a while and was now in the sitting room, having found a two-bar electric fire and turned it on.

'Oh, it's very stuffy in here,' Catherine said.

'I think you mean it's warm,' Nora replied. 'The rest of the house is freezing. I don't know how you manage.'

'The central heating eats oil,' Catherine said. 'It's an old system. We should really get it replaced.'

Nora was enjoying the novel and wished now that her sister would leave her in peace until it was bedtime. It struck her that Catherine would like to feel that she had somehow helped to look after Nora. This visit was one way of doing that. And since she wished to look after her, Nora thought, then Catherine could do all the cooking and cleaning and washing-up and leave her alone to read. She thought of the phone call between Catherine and Una, how Catherine could add the sink full of dirty dishes and the two-bar electric fire blazing to her list of what she had to put up with all weekend.

That night, when the house was quiet and the children had gone to bed, Mark asked Nora if she had made any plans, and she told them that she was going back to work in Gibney's. She had told no one, she said, not even Jim and Margaret, nor Fiona and Aine, nor the boys.

'I'll tell them nearer the time.'

From the way Catherine looked at her, Nora knew that Una had already told Catherine what she had heard in the golf club.

'They'll be lucky to get you,' Catherine said.

'There wasn't anything else,' Nora replied. 'I have no qualifications except typing and shorthand and I've forgotten both. I suppose people feel sorry for me, but no one except the Gibneys feels sorry enough for me to offer me a job.'

'Couldn't you get by on the widow's pension and the money you have saved?' Catherine asked.

'We saved nothing. We had nothing except the house in Cush and I sold that and put some of the money away for an emergency and I've been living on the rest. The widow's pension is six pounds a week.'

'It's what?' Mark asked.

'There might be another pension, a contributory pension because of the stamps I have from the years I worked in Gibney's before I was married, but it's means-tested and the man from social welfare thinks I must have money saved. But I don't, and when he believes me I might get that as well.'

'And what are the Gibneys offering?' Catherine asked.

Nora smiled.

'Do you remember the night Billy Considine asked Mark how many acres he had?'

'I remember it well,' Mark said and laughed. 'He didn't get any good of me that night and I suppose you're not telling us either. He was trying to make out that the farmers were living off the fat of the land while the teachers were the only ones who did any work.'

'You really have no money?' Catherine asked.

'No, but I'm going to work, and Jim and Margaret are paying for Aine at school, and Fiona will be qualified the year after next. So I'll be able to keep going, the boys and myself.'

'Have you thought about Donal?' Catherine asked. 'He hasn't spoken a word since he came here, and Aunt Josie is worried about his speech.'

'He has developed a stammer,' Nora said. 'And he's very conscious of it. But I leave him alone about it. I hope it might just be a temporary thing.'

'I wonder if he shouldn't see a speech therapist?' Catherine asked.

'You know when he talks to his Aunt Margaret he doesn't stammer at all. He just chats away to her. He's used to her, so that's what makes me think he'll grow out of it.'

'Margaret always loved him,' Catherine said. 'Do you remember the first summer in Cush when she drove down every night to see him? Even when he was asleep she'd sit beside the cot doing nothing else except looking at him.'

Nora felt herself becoming sad at the memory of that time. When she caught Mark's eye, she saw that he was watching her with sympathy. She wished she had not let them ask her any questions about her life.

'Are you sure you're going to be able for Gibney's?' Catherine asked. 'I mean, is it not a bit soon?'

'I don't have any choice. And that old bag Francie Kavanagh runs the office.'

'Francie Kavanagh? We used to call her the Sacred Heart,' Catherine said. 'I don't know why.'

'And you should see Peggy Gibney. She's grander than your friend Dilly. Almost too grand to move.'

'Is Dilly grand?' Mark asked.

'She is, Mark,' Nora said, and looked at Catherine.

'She remarked on her way out that you looked very well,' Catherine said. 'It must be your new hair.'

'I was waiting for you to mention it.'

'There's a marvellous woman in Kilkenny,' Catherine said. 'We all swear by her. The next time I'd really like you to see her, if only to talk through what the options are.'

'It's a fiver an hour,' Mark said.

'No, it's not, Mark,' Catherine said. 'Really, you should see her.'

'I suppose I should,' Nora said and smiled.

Chapter Five

When they arrived home it was almost dark and the house was cold. She lit a fire quickly in the back room and made sure to give no instructions to Donal and Conor. They had, she felt, been under enough pressure all weekend; now they were home they could do whatever they liked. They had beans on toast and Conor watched television while Donal roamed the house uneasily.

On the way home, she had stopped in Kiltealy to let the boys switch places and, on seeing a shop open, had bought the *Sunday Press*. When she was checking the television listings for Conor she noticed that there was a film after the nine o'clock news. It was *Gaslight* with Ingrid Bergman and Charles Boyer. When Donal came into the room, she pointed it out to him.

'It's one of the best films I have ever seen,' she said.

It was before she was married, she remembered, and there was a temporary picture house in the Abbey Square and she had gone with Greta Wickham. Maurice seldom came with her to the pictures in the years when they were going out together, and, once they were married, he lost all interest in them. He was too busy with Fianna Fáil and writing articles and correcting homework. And he liked being alone for an evening, knowing that later they would be together. It was something that never left him, a pure pleasure in the idea that they were married, that they did not have to separate and each go home, as they did in the years before they were married.

'What's the film?' Conor asked when he heard about it.

'It's about a woman in a house,' she said.

'Is that all?'

'Maybe something h-happens to h-her in the h-house,' Donal said.

Conor looked at Nora.

'Are there robbers?'

'You'd have to see it to know how good it is. And if I explained it to you, it would give it all away and then it would be no use.'

'Can we watch it?'

'It's on very late.'

'Are you going to watch it?'

'Yes I am, I suppose.'

'Then we can watch the beginning, and then we can decide.'

'You won't get up in the morning.'

'It's Donal that doesn't like getting up.'

'I h-hate getting up,' Donal said.

When the nine o'clock news was coming to an end, she noticed that the two boys had not moved. She could not remember watching a film with them before and she became almost flattered that they trusted her opinion about *Gaslight*.

When the film had started, however, she saw that Conor was disappointed, and probably Donal as well.

'Is it just about these people?' Conor asked.

At the first break for advertisements, she decided to tell the story of the film as best she could and then let them decide if they wanted to see the rest of it.

'The man is trying to get the house from her, trying to have her committed to a mental hospital so he can find her aunt's jewels. That is what he is doing in the attic, looking for the jewels.'

'Why doesn't he just kill her?' Conor asked. 'Stick a knife in her or shoot her? Or tie her up?'

'Then he might be caught. He wants to live in this house without her. But he doesn't want to go to jail.'

The two boys took this in quietly as the film resumed. After a few minutes, in a scene where Ingrid Bergman became frightened and perplexed as the gaslight flickered when she was alone in the house, Conor moved towards Nora and sat at her feet.

There was something in the film that she had not remembered. Before, it had seemed like a thriller or a sort of horror film. But now there was something else. Ingrid Bergman seemed so oddly alone and vulnerable in the film; every time the camera was on her face it captured some deep inner turmoil or uncertainty as much as any fright or horror. She was jittery and oddly estranged from things. Her glances were all nervous, her smiles had a worried edge. There was a sense of a damaged inner life. Both Donal and Conor had now become transfixed by the film, and when the next break came Donal moved beside her armchair as well.

As the man made the woman believe that she had forgotten things and mislaid objects, the boys watched intently. The man's plotting against her, his lies, and the maid's cheekiness to her, all added to something, something uneasy and withdrawn. Nora wondered if she had ever seen Ingrid Bergman playing a part in a comedy. It was clear to her now that, if a knock came to their front door, then all three of them would know not to answer it.

And when, in the film, the gaslight flickered again and the woman became even more frightened, all three of them watched with hushed worry. It struck Nora that the boys had only ever before seen adventure films, or episodes of *Tolka Row*, which Conor thought especially funny because of the Dublin accents. They had never seen a film like this and it hit something in them that was raw and open, as though they were in a house with a woman who, despite her best efforts, was jittery and worried too, who kept silent about everything that was on her mind. The more the film went on, the more impossible the idea seemed that Ingrid Bergman had come from a large and happy family, but maybe Nora was imagining this, she thought, reading too much into the performance. Maybe Ingrid Bergman was just a great actress. Whatever it was, she evoked something hidden and strange, as Maurice's absence, his body in a grave, must seem hidden and strange to the boys. She wondered if it might have been better if she had not mentioned the film, and if they had not spent a Sunday evening watching it.

When it was over, they went to bed. She sat up alone in the film's afterglow, feeling the echoes of what she had been watching in the house where she had lived with Maurice for more than twenty years. Every room, every sound, every piece of space, was filled not only with what had been lost, but with the years themselves, and the days. Now, in the silence, she could feel it and know it; for the boys it came as confusion. In the film, somehow it had been obvious, but whatever it was had served to unsettle them even more. She wondered how many other old films would come back to her with new and darker meanings. She sat there imagining Ingrid Bergman as unprotected and innocent, and then she turned off the lights and went upstairs to bed, hoping that she would sleep until the morning.

The following Sunday was her last day of freedom before she began work in the office in Gibney's. When Fiona came home on Saturday she told her; when she told the boys they seemed already to know. She was sure that she had not told anyone in front of them, having given Jim and Margaret the news one night when the boys had long gone to bed. On Sunday Aine came home from school for the afternoon, collected by a neighbour's family whose daughter was also at school in Bunclody. Nora would drive both girls back in time for study in the evening.

Margaret always read the newspapers carefully and looked at the advertisements for jobs. Nora used to joke with Maurice that if there was a vacancy for the assistant to the assistant librarian in West Mayo, Margaret would know about it and would remember the deadline for applications and the qualifications required. Thus when it was announced that there would be grants for students to go to university whose families lived below a certain income, Margaret mentioned this to Nora, saying that she was sure it would apply to Aine. The only problem, Margaret said, was that Aine had given up Latin and she would need Latin to go to University College Dublin, where Maurice had gone when he won a university scholarship. Nora did not know that Aine had given up Latin. Aine must have told her aunt about it, but not her.

On Sunday Aine told Nora that Margaret had written to her, offering to pay for Latin grinds over the holidays, and suggesting that she take merely the pass paper so that she could concentrate on her other subjects. Nora was not sure if she should object that Margaret had not consulted her first, or indeed at all. She seemed to have taken over the entire question of Aine's education. But she concluded that it was best not to think too much about it. She told Aine that she agreed with Margaret that she should take grinds in Latin.

For a few hours that afternoon she watched the boys transformed by the presence of their sisters. Conor followed the two girls from room to room and when he found himself expelled from their bedroom he came downstairs to know how much longer it would be before Fiona had to catch the train to Dublin and Aine return to school. He then went and sat at the top of the stairs until they relented and let him back into their bedroom.

Donal had bought film for his camera; he made them all pose for photographs. Even though the flash of his camera worked only sometimes, he did not become despondent. He kept the camera around his neck on a strap and seemed more alert and involved than usual.

As the afternoon went on, Nora realized that she was not needed. She smiled to herself at the thought that if she slipped out of the house and went for a walk none of them would notice. It was only when Una came and the girls were downstairs that they began to focus on her.

'Well, it's great that you had your hair done before you start work,' Aine said.

'I meant to say it's lovely,' Fiona said. 'But I got such a shock –'

'Girls, when you get to our age,' Una interrupted, 'then you'll know all about hair.'

'Are you going to work in the office full-time?' Aine asked.

Nora nodded.

'And what are the boys going to do when you're working?'

'I'll be home by six.'

'But they'll be home by half three or four.'

'They can do their homework.'

'We'll clean the house,' Conor said.

'Well, you needn't clean our room,' Aine replied.

'We will, we'll turn it upside down and find all the letters from your boyfriends.'

'Mammy, he is not to go into our room,' Aine said.

'Conor is the soul of discretion,' Nora replied.

'What is the soul of discretion?' Conor asked.

'It means you are a nosy little squirt,' Fiona said.

'But, seriously,' Aine asked, 'would it not be better if they went to someone's house and waited there?'

'I'm g-going nowhere,' Donal said.

'And Donal will look after Conor if there's a problem,' Nora said. 'And I'll be home for dinner in the middle of the day.'

'Who's going to make the dinner?'

'I'll have it ready from the night before and Donal will put on the potatoes as soon as he comes in.'

She felt that she was being cross-examined and wondered if she could change the subject. All five of them seemed oddly suspicious of her now, as though her going to work in Gibney's were something she was doing in order to avoid her real duties. None of her children knew how little money she had, and she was not sure how much Catherine had told Una. Since the car was still there and the house appeared untouched by poverty, none of them had any sense of how precarious things were, despite her selling the house in Cush, and how, if she did not start working at some point, the car would have to be sold and she would have to consider moving to a smaller house.

'Why don't you move to Dublin and get a job there?' Aine asked.

'What sort of job?'

'I don't know. In an office.'

'I don't want to go to Dublin,' Conor said. 'I hate Dublin people.'

'What's wrong with them?' Una asked.

'They're like Mrs Butler in *Tolka Row*,' Conor said, 'or Mrs Feeney, or Jack Nolan, or Peggy Nolan. All talk.'

'We could leave you behind here then to make sure you don't miss an episode,' Fiona said.

'Is that woman, the Sacred Heart, still running the office in Gibney's?' Una asked. 'What's her name?'

'She's called Francie Kavanagh,' Nora said.

'Do you remember Breda Dobbs?' Una asked. 'Well, her daughter worked in that office. Oh, God, maybe I shouldn't tell this story.

86

Conor, if you repeat this story I will personally bite both of your ears off.'

'Your secrets are safe with Conor,' Fiona said.

'I won't say anything,' Conor said.

'Well, Breda's daughter hated the Sacred Heart and she was there for years before she married. And on the last day she took her revenge.'

Una stopped.

'What did she do?' Fiona asked.

'I'm not sure I should have started this story,' Una said.

'Go on,' Fiona said.

'Well, they all knew that one of the Sacred Heart's things is that she doesn't take a dinner break. She works right through the day without eating. I suppose this makes her very cranky by four o'clock. And up to this time she used to hang her coat up in the corridor where all the other coats were hanging. Breda's daughter hated her so much that she spent a week collecting dog shit and then she filled both pockets of the Sacred Heart's coat with what she had collected sometime in the morning, and then at four she asked the Heart, or whatever her name is, if she could leave fifteen minutes early since it was her last day and the Heart told her that she most certainly could not and she was to go back to her desk forthwith. The Sacred Heart was working late that evening so none of them ever got to see what happened. Maybe she didn't notice until she was on her way home and she put her hands into her pockets.'

'Were they big pockets?' Conor asked.

'So now she hangs her coat in her own office,' Una went on, 'but the funny thing is that she wore that same coat to work the next morning as though nothing had happened. It's an old brown coat and she may still have it for all I know.'

'Yuck,' Fiona said.

'I'd say that Dobbs girl had no luck for doing that,' Nora said.

'Oh, she married one of the Gethings of Oulart, he's a very nice fellow, and they have a new bungalow. He has his own business. I've played golf with her a few times and you couldn't meet a nicer girl. She'd had enough, that's all.'

'It would have been worse if it was cow shit,' Conor said.

'Or b-bullshit,' Donal said.

On the way to Bunclody, Aine, in the front passenger seat, asked her if she knew that Una was going out with someone in the golf club. Aine's friend in the back seat confirmed that her mother, who was in the golf club, had also heard the news.

'Una?' Nora asked.

'Yes, that's why she is in such good humour. We asked her when she came upstairs but she just blushed and said that there was always too much talk about people in the golf club.'

Nora calculated that, since she was forty-six, Una was forty, or would be soon. She and Catherine had decided some years before that Una would never marry, but would remain working in the offices of Roche's Maltings and living in the house where she had lived with their mother until her death.

'So you don't know who the lucky man is?' Nora asked.

'No, but we told her that if she didn't tell us soon we were going to spread a rumour that it was Larry Kearney. She was raging, but still she didn't tell us.'

Larry Kearney was, she knew, a drunk in the town who often sat on the ground outside the public houses he was barred from entering. Years before, when Catherine and Una had gone to a golfing hotel in County Cavan with Rose Lacey and Lily Devereux, they had to have their tea one evening with a Dublin couple who were very snobbish and had spoken of their posh golf club in Dublin. They boasted about themselves until Lily Devereux said in a grand voice to the Dublin husband that he was the spitting image of a man in Enniscorthy, one of the best golfers in County Wexford, and his name was Larry Kearney and she wondered if they were related in any way. Catherine had to run out of the restaurant howling with laughter, closely followed by Una.

'What are you laughing at?' Aine asked her as they passed through Clohamon.

'Has Larry Kearney joined the golf club?' she asked.

'No, don't be silly.'

*

Later, Donal and Conor came with her to the train Fiona would take back to Dublin. As the boys were standing on the metal bridge, Nora noticed that Fiona seemed sad.

'Are you all right?' she asked.

'I hate going back,' Fiona said.

'Is there something wrong?'

'The nuns, the dorm, the whole Training College. Everything really.'

'But you have friends there?'

'Yes, and we all hate it.'

'You'll be in London in the summer and then it's just one more year and then you can come home.'

'Home?'

'Well, where else would you go?'

'I might stay in Dublin and do a degree at night.'

'Fiona, it's very hard for me here. I just don't know if I'll have enough money.'

'Do you not have the pension? And the money from the house in Cush? And are you not starting in Gibney's?'

'Gibney's are paying twelve pounds a week.'

'Is that all?'

'He was very brusque about it, the son Thomas. He more or less said that I could take it or leave it. His father and mother were all smarmy. But he's the money man. That's how business works, not that I know anything about business.'

'I suppose I could look for a job down here,' Fiona said quietly.

'We'll wait and see anyway,' Nora said.

Fiona nodded and then Conor announced that the train was coming.

'I'm sorry about the house in Cush,' Nora said.

'Oh, I've forgotten about that already,' Fiona said. 'I was upset that day, hearing the news, but I'm OK about it now.'

She picked up her small suitcase.

As they drove back home, Donal said that he had checked the *Sunday Press* and there was another film on the television that night.

'What's it called?' she asked.

He was silent, she knew, because whatever the name of the film was he could not say it.

'Hold your breath and take it slowly,' she said.

'L-lost Horizon,' he said.

'I'm not sure what that is but we can look at the beginning anyway.'

'The one last week was queer frightening,' Conor said.

'Did you like it though?' she asked.

'I told the class about it in school and Mr Dunne said I shouldn't have been up so late.'

'Why did you tell them?'

'We all have to tell a story. It was my turn on Friday.'

'Is th-that in Irish or in English?' Donal asked.

'In English, stupid.'

'Don't call your brother stupid,' Nora said.

'Sure how would you say "Gaslight" in Irish?' Conor asked.

As soon as she read the description of the film in the newspaper, Nora recognized what it was. She remembered the name 'Shangri-La' and was sure that she and Maurice had once laughed at a house in Dublin with that name on the gates. They had wondered if the owners had ventured out into the world only to discover their real age. As she remembered the film, it seemed a fantasy, harmless compared to *Gaslight*, and when the boys asked if they could watch it she agreed, saying that they could go to bed if they got bored.

But as soon as the film began there was something sharp and strange about it. First, it was the music; and then the plane crash itself was frightening, almost hard to watch it was so realistic. When the first break for advertisements came, the boys asked her to tell them the story.

'It's like Tír na nÓg,' she said. 'It's Shangri-La and people don't get old there. Some of them could be a hundred or two hundred but they look young.'

'As old as Mrs Franklin?' Conor asked.

'Yes, and older. She would look like a young girl once she entered Shangri-La. But it's just a film.'

Slowly, however, as the film went on, she saw that no matter what they watched, it would remind them of their circumstances more than anything that had been said all day in the house. She did not know whether it was right or wrong for her to sit like this with them in a silence broken by the dramatic music and the soft voices coming from the television. She could not recall the name of the actor playing the lead part; she did not think she had seen him in anything else. He was a type, reliable, strong, romantic, filled with openness and curiosity.

During the scene where the Lama began to weaken and it was clear that he would die, Conor moved close to Nora until she gave him a cushion and he sat on the floor near her. Donal kept away. He seemed to her even more involved with this film than with *Gaslight*. When the break came, he watched the advertisements and did not even look over when Conor asked questions that she tried to answer.

She knew what was coming in the film; she had not remembered it until now – the three characters leaving, walking over the high mountains in the hope of being rescued and taken back to England. And then the woman's face wizened as soon as they moved out of the sacred space of Shangri-La. And then her death, and the hero's brother jumping to his own death in horror, followed by the rescue and the return to England.

It was the last part of the film that caused Donal to become restless on his chair. The hero wanted to go back, wanted to leave the world and everything familiar and walk until he found it again, the place away from the world where no one could ever locate him and where he would not miss his home but live instead in the paradise where he would not grow old. The message in this was so obvious that Nora did not have to wonder what the boys were thinking about, they were thinking that this was what their father had done. She was thinking it too, and it registered the same for all of them, she thought, so that when it was over there was no need to mention it. They turned the television off and she set about preparing dinner for the next day while the boys went to bed.

The following morning as she walked across the town to go to work for the first time, she felt that she was being closely observed.

She had been up early and had spent some time choosing the clothes that she would wear. She had to make sure that they were not too glamorous, but not shabby or dowdy either. It was not cold enough to wear one of her two woollen coats, so she found a red raincoat that she had bought before Maurice became sick and that she had never worn. It was too bright and might have looked better on a younger woman but it was the only coat she had that was not too heavy on a morning like this.

Now, as she reached Court Street, she knew it was a mistake. She passed women on their way to work in St John's Hospital and men on their way to work in Roche's Maltings. All of them looked at her with her dyed hair and her red coat. She hoped to meet no one she knew well, no one who would stop and talk and ask her questions. She slipped down Friary Hill and along Friary Place to avoid meeting anyone. She crossed Slaney Place and got to the bridge with relief. She was almost there now. Once she arrived at the office building, she was to ask the receptionist for Miss Kavanagh. There was no point, she thought, in trying to be warm and friendly with Francie Kavanagh. They had never liked each other, and they would not like each other now. All she could hope for was that the news that she had been offered the job by William Gibney himself in the presence of his wife, Peggy, and that Maurice had taught the Gibney boys in school might make Francie Kavanagh have some manners.

When the receptionist asked for her name, she found herself speaking too grandly, causing the woman to glance up at her. That tone, she thought, would be no use here. She concentrated now on becoming quiet and mild, but also efficient and in full control of herself. She had no idea what work she would be doing. Thomas Gibney had said that that would be something for Miss Kavanagh to decide, but no matter what she was given to do, it would be new for her and take time to learn. She waited at the reception as some office workers passed her in the narrow corridor. Most of them were women and much younger than she was. A few of them looked like schoolgirls.

Eventually, Miss Kavanagh was alerted by the receptionist to Nora's presence.

'Oh, you picked the worst morning of the whole year,' she

shouted through the half-open window between the receptionist's office and the corridor. 'I don't know what we're going to do. Who said you were to come today?'

'Mr Thomas Gibney said that I was to begin this morning,' Nora said.

'Oh, Mr Thomas Gibney, wait until I get him!' Miss Kavanagh said and rummaged through the drawers of a filing cabinet.

After a while Miss Kavanagh disappeared and when she did not appear again Nora tried to catch the receptionist's attention, but the receptionist did not look up. Nora wondered if she should raise her voice and demand that someone attend to her, but she did not think so.

As she stood waiting, the door was pushed open by a young woman who seemed different to all of the others who had come in before her. Her hair was beautifully cut and her clothes looked expensive. Even her glasses were special.

'Are you Mrs Webster?' she asked.

'Oh, I know who you are,' Nora said. 'You don't look like any of the others coming to work. You're Elizabeth.'

'Lord above, I hope I don't look like any of the others!'

'You're a Gibney, I would know that,' Nora said.

'Well, I would do anything I could not to look like one, but here I am. No one else would have me, so I'm back in Enniscorthy living at home and working in the office. The two things I said I would never do.'

'I knew your grandmother, on your father's side,' Nora said, 'and you are the image of her.'

'I remember her all right,' Elizabeth said. 'She took to the bed in the house over there and never got up. She might well be still there for all I know.'

Nora hesitated for a moment, wondering if she should ask Elizabeth to help her locate Miss Kavanagh.

'Are you waiting for somebody?' Elizabeth asked.

'Yes, Miss Kavanagh.'

'Can she not be found? She's normally buzzing about.'

'She appeared and then disappeared.'

'Yes, she often goes into the accounts department around now and shouts for a while. The best thing is if you come in with me and then we'll steal by her.'

Nora followed Elizabeth through a door into a large and busy office and then into a smaller room that had a window with views of the mountains in the distance and the yard below where many lorries and cars were parked. There were two desks in the room and some filing cabinets.

'The only thing I have managed to achieve since my return,' Elizabeth said, 'is the removal of Elsa Doyle from this office to the office next door, complete with her pinafore and her squint. She started listening to my phone conversations and discussing them with me.'

'Elsa Doyle?' Nora asked. 'Is that Davy Doyle's daughter?'

'That's who she is,' Elizabeth said. 'As nosy as her father, but without his cunning. I told them at home that I was going to go back to Dublin and make my living on the streets if she was not removed from my office. Mind you, it was her office before I arrived. Would you like her desk?'

'Which desk?'

Elizabeth pointed at the desk nearer the door.

'Why don't you claim it before anyone can stop you? I'll say my father said, and no one will contradict me.'

Nora sat down at the desk while Elizabeth went outside and came back carrying a tray with tea and biscuits.

'I keep my own biscuits. I have a secret hiding place for them. And be careful, Francie-Pants Kavanagh is looking for you. She's on the warpath. She asked if I saw you. I neither confirmed nor denied.'

'Should I not go and find her?'

'Have your tea first.'

Soon, someone came to say that Miss Kavanagh was waiting in her office for Mrs Webster and that she had instructions to accompany Mrs Webster there immediately. Miss Kavanagh's office was at the very end of the larger office; from a window she had a full view of everything that happened.

'Did Mr William Senior or Mr Thomas tell you what you are to do here?' Miss Kavanagh asked, looking up for one moment and then flicking through some papers on her desk.

'No, they didn't.'

'Well, they didn't tell me either and they have both gone to Dublin so we will have to work it out ourselves.'

Nora did not respond.

'That Elizabeth Gibney is the laziest girl in Ireland,' Miss Kavanagh said, 'and the most unpleasant. Boss's daughter, or no boss's daughter, it's all the same to me. I treat everyone the same. And she put poor Elsa Doyle out of her office. Elsa is very obliging.'

Suddenly, she looked up.

'Now, there's something I always do with everyone who starts here.'

She took out a folder.

'It's a long tot,' she said, as she handed Nora a grubby sheet of paper with six figures on each line going down one side of the page and half one side of the overleaf.

'If you could tot that up for me, like a good woman,' she said, looking at Nora directly and handing her a pen.

Nora began to tot. It was one of the things she had been good at when she worked at Gibney's before, one of the things that old Mr Gibney, who could not add himself without making mistakes, used always to ask her to do. She ignored Miss Kavanagh, who continued to stare at her while she worked at adding the figures. When she had added up the figures in the first column of numbers, she wrote down the result.

'Don't write the figures down on that piece of paper! I want to use it again. Use this!'

Miss Kavanagh handed her a scrap of paper, thus causing her to lose her concentration. She decided it was better to start again, to make sure that she had everything right. When she had done the first two columns and was halfway through the third, Miss Kavanagh interrupted her again.

'Did Mr William Senior or Mr Thomas say that you were to share the office with that Elizabeth?'

Nora looked up at Miss Kavanagh and held her stare for a moment.

'Well?' Miss Kavanagh asked.

Nora looked down and began to tot up the third column of figures from the beginning. She tried not to think of Miss Kavanagh sitting opposite her and instead directed all her concentration at adding the figures. It was almost a battle between them now and she was ready, if Miss Kavanagh spoke once more, to ask her as politely as she could not to interrupt her. But, in thinking about this, she lost where she had been and was not sure now how much she had carried over from the third column to the fourth. She stopped for a second and, in stopping, lost her concentration completely.

'Hurry now,' Miss Kavanagh said. 'I haven't got all day.'

Nora decided that she would, once more, have to start from the beginning. She added the figures in the first column again as quickly as she could, but the result was not the same as the figure she had written down after her first attempt. She would have one more try, and this time would go very slowly and deliberately. If, a year ago, this scene had appeared before her, it would have been in a bad dream. The idea of totting numbers, being overseen by Francie Kavanagh, would have been unimaginable. It belonged to no future she had ever envisaged for herself. Once more, these thoughts interfered with her concentration and she had to stop. She looked out into the larger office.

'There's no one out there of any interest to you now,' Miss Kavanagh said. 'Head down and look at the figures.'

There was nothing else she could do. She wondered for a second if all the years of being away from work, the years spent cooking and cleaning the house and looking after the children and then being with Maurice when he was sick had affected her ability to keep her mind on the same single thing. If that was the case she would have to try harder, just add the numbers up and think of nothing else. It could not be impossible. No matter what came into her mind, she was to stop it. Just these figures. She started again at the beginning and moved with confidence and efficiency, letting nothing interfere with getting the correct result at the bottom and carrying the right number into the next column, and then presenting the final figure to Francie Kavanagh silently, with only a small hint of arrogance and contempt.

Miss Kavanagh looked at the final figure and then opened the top drawer of her desk and removed an adding machine. She walked out into the outer office and shouted.

'Someone come quickly. You! Miss Lambert. In here now!'

A girl came into the office without looking directly at either Miss Kavanagh or Nora.

'Now, I want you to check these figures on the adding machine. Oh, and don't let Mrs Webster see the result until I do. Bring it straight to me. I'll be down in accounts. And hurry now! Mrs Webster has already taken all day.'

The girl took the piece of paper from Miss Kavanagh and walked out of the room.

When it came to dinnertime, Nora had wasted the whole morning waiting for Miss Kavanagh or being taunted by her. Once she was out of the office and crossing the bridge, it could have been twenty-five years earlier; the feeling of pure freedom was the same. When she left Gibney's at dinnertime or in the evening, she had always tried to pretend that she was never going back, that her time there had come to an end. Now, as she crossed the bottom of Castle Hill on her way home, it was not hard to have that feeling again; it was almost necessary. She would feel it again at half past five when she had finished for the day.

Chapter Six

After much negotiation it was agreed that she would spend the mornings in Elizabeth's office working on orders and invoices and then after dinner she would sit in the larger office and deal with the salaries, bonuses and expenses of all the commercial travellers in the company. Miss Kavanagh explained to her that this was the most difficult job of all, as every traveller was paid at a different rate, but she could check back through the records to find the details. They had all been negotiated, Miss Kavanagh said, many years ago with the older travellers, and then more recently with the younger ones by Mr Thomas Gibney. None of them knew what the others were paid, and none of them needed to know this, Miss Kavanagh said, but each of them was filled with suspicion and resentment.

'If it was me,' she said, 'I would give them only their bonuses with no pay at all, and then we'd see results, and then their manners would improve. And if any of them come to you personally when they find out that you are the one in charge of their salaries, don't even look up at them. Say a small prayer and then send them to me. And if they waylay you and find you when I am not here, tell them that you are under instructions from Miss Kavanagh not to speak to them under any circumstances.'

Nora was distracted for a moment by the brown coat hanging from a hook in Miss Kavanagh's office. She wondered if it was the same one that Una had told her about.

'Mrs Webster,' Miss Kavanagh asked, 'am I to take it that you have understood me?'

'I have understood you perfectly,' Nora said coldly.

Of the dozen commercial travellers, some had company cars; some did not. Some had a mileage allowance that was higher than others, and some of them also had an agreement that if they sold over a certain figure in a given year then their mileage allowance or their bonus, or in some cases both, would increase. There was a full drawer of a filing cabinet with invoices from the commercial travellers, a few of which contained detailed agreements about rates of pay. There was also a drawer with letters of complaint or claim from the commercial travellers and these, when Nora looked at them, gave her the clearest indication of the agreements between the company and the travellers.

When she told Elizabeth about the complexities of dealing with the money to be paid to these men, she laughed.

'My father, Old William, says it's the only way to keep the travellers on their toes.'

Slowly, Nora realized that Miss Kavanagh, despite her claims to the contrary, did not understand the system. A girl called Marian Brickley had dealt with the matter for many years and had left to get married. Since then, there had been chaos. All Miss Kavanagh did was threaten anyone who complained with expulsion from her office. As each new girl had been assigned the task of sorting out the mess, the mess had become even worse until a number of the travellers had gone to see Mr William Gibney Senior, who had instructed his son Thomas to deal with the matter. Thomas had decided that Nora would be the best person to handle the commercial travellers and the payments due to them and also handle Miss Kavanagh herself, who suffered from a great personal antipathy to the commercial travellers and seemed to feel that a day without a noisy confrontation with at least one of them was a day misspent.

Nora found a pile of folders in the stationery cupboard at the end of the long office. Without consulting anyone, she took them to her desk, wrote the name of each traveller on the outside of a folder and began to compile notes on the agreement each one had with Gibney's. When she encountered any of the travellers themselves, with Miss Kavanagh not paying attention, she asked them for a detailed account of the arrangement they had made with the company as well as a sheet of paper outlining how much money they thought they were owed and for what. Most of the travellers were waiting a long time to be paid bonuses or allowances. Since she was new, they began to watch her, some anxious, others more determined and ready to wait for her near the door as she arrived in the morning, or as she left.

One of them told her that she had to write the amount each was owed on a single sheet of paper, just the amount, and then write 'Urgent Payment' and pass this to Miss Kavanagh. When she looked at the files she found copies of these single sheets, so she believed that this was true. But she was also told that payments would only be made once a month on a day that had never been fixed, and that the person who decided the date of payment was Miss Kavanagh.

If travellers approached Miss Kavanagh while Nora was close by, she always began in the same way, as she came to the door of her office to greet them.

'Mrs Webster and I myself are up to our eyes in work as you can see.' She would then retreat, shouting, 'You'll have to come back another time, like a good man!' before closing the door on them.

Nora, as she prepared the folders, developed a shorthand for the travellers. VB meant Very Bald; SB was Skin-and-Bone; SM stood for Smiler; J stood for Jockey. BT meant Bad Teeth; DF meant Dandruff. Soon, she had names for all of them, names she shared only with Donal and Conor, who remembered each name as she invented them. She swore them to secrecy.

Miss Kavanagh fought with everyone, except Mr William Gibney Senior and his two sons. When they appeared, Miss Kavanagh became meek, but after smiling and bowing to them, she would, once they had departed, summon to her office one of the lowliest bookkeepers or typists and start screaming, or she would wander out into the large office and stand behind a girl and shout: 'What are you doing now? What are you doing now this minute to justify your presence in this building?'

Miss Kavanagh and Elizabeth Gibney ignored each other.

'She is unusual,' Elizabeth said to Nora, 'because her bite is actually worse than her bark. I suppose they told you that the woman before you left to get married?'

Nora nodded.

'One day the poor woman was driven so demented that she took out the contents of one of the filing cabinets and threw them up in the air, using language about Miss Francie-Pants that was not edifying. She followed this with her views on my father and my brothers and me and then ran screaming out into the street. Her people, who live in Ballindaggin, were summoned to take her home. Thomas and myself had to stay here late that night trying to refill the filing cabinet with the paper before my father, Old William, got to find out about it all. He won't hear a word against Francie-Pants. He doesn't know that I have nothing to do with the old battle-axe. I got a deal with Little William and Thomas only because I threatened them. I promised to seek revenge in ways as yet unimagined unless I was given my own office and unless Francie-Pants was told that I was off limits.'

Nora enjoyed the mornings with Elizabeth, even when she saw how much of Elizabeth's day was actually spent planning her weekend or discussing on the phone the weekend just past. She found that she could work easily in the office with her. Elizabeth talked to her only when no one whom she phoned was available. She had one phone with a direct line out and another that was an office extension. Often, she went over the same events in her personal life with several friends in succession. Nora learned that there was a man in Dublin called Roger who was steady, dependable and well placed. He wanted to see Elizabeth every weekend.

Elizabeth spent some weeks avoiding calls from him, letting calls on her direct line ring out if she thought it was Roger. She would then phone one of her friends, tell them about the call from Roger and ask for advice about how she might best avoid Roger in Dublin on Saturday night while making sure, in a later conversation with Roger, that he might, were she to come to Dublin, be available to escort her to some dinner or dance.

'I like him. I don't know what he reminds me of,' she said to Nora. 'Maybe a nice car that you're used to, one that never breaks down. Or a winter coat that you never wear but are glad you have. And he's mad about me and that helps. But I'd love a big romance! I mean someone a bit wilder. I'd love an international rugby player, say. Mike Gibson now, or Willie John McBride. Roger took me to one of the rugby dinners and they were all there. I didn't listen to a word Roger said all evening. If he had told me that God Almighty was a woman and she was living in Bellefield with her husband, I would have nodded. I wish William or Thomas played rugby and could introduce me properly to members of the team. I'd love to go to a match in Lansdowne Road knowing that I'd be meeting up with the players in Jury's or the Gresham when they were all washed and dressed up, and they would know who I was.'

Every Friday at four Elizabeth Gibney left the office and drove to Dublin. She shared a room in a flat in Herbert Street and went out with her friends on Friday and Saturday nights and on a Sunday night she drove back to Enniscorthy. On Saturday afternoons she went shopping in Grafton Street. Some weekends, she saw Roger; on other weekends she did not tell him that she was coming to Dublin and then on Monday she would recount to Nora how close she had come to bumping into him, the narrow escapes she had had at various tennis club hops and rugby dances. During the week she tried to recover from the weekend, and lamented the fact that she could not go out in the town, since everyone recognized her as one of the Gibneys. Therefore, if she went out during the week, it was to Wexford or Rosslare and usually in the company of her brothers and their friends. She made such outings sound like duty. Her real life during the week was spent on the telephone to her friends in Dublin. It almost amused Nora to see that she did not know the names of any of the girls or women in the outer office, other than Elsa Doyle, whom she had removed from her office. If one of them came in while she was on the phone, she would ask her caller to wait a moment and then icily outstare the intruder until she had left the room and Elizabeth could resume her discussion of the weekend.

One Monday Elizabeth did not come into work until almost eleven o'clock. Nora discovered that she could do her morning's work in less than two hours without the distraction offered by the boss's daughter, and she could manage the bonuses for the commercial travellers once she had unravelled the details, if she did not have Miss Kavanagh to deal with as well. She liked the peace, enjoyed having the office to herself.

When Elizabeth arrived, she seemed greatly excited.

'Did anyone call?'

'No,' Nora replied.

'On either of the phones?'

'No one called.'

She went over and checked the phones.

'Are you sure?'

'Yes.'

'What is a town clerk?' Elizabeth asked. 'When I enquired from my mother she said it was someone who ran a town. Is that right?'

'Yes,' Nora said. 'It's a good job. A lot of town clerks go on to become county managers.'

'I met one last night.'

'The town clerk of where?'

'That's the problem. I don't remember. His name was, or is, Ray, that's all I know. And someone introduced me as his fiancée, so maybe he has a fiancée, and she was at home watching television last night, or maybe I look like someone's fiancée.'

'Was he nice?'

'At four o'clock in the morning he asked me to marry him, or else he nearly did. That was nice.'

'And what did you say?'

Elizabeth checked the phones again.

'I met him with your sister and her fiancé in Rosslare Golf Club. There was some do on and I went to it. Thomas was with me for a while. I went with him and his girlfriend, but then I got talking to your sister, who was very nice and, since dry Thomas and Dishwater his girlfriend were leaving, she made her fiancé offer me a lift home once we had some drinks in the Talbot, but of course I didn't take the lift in the end. I was driven home by my Town Clerk. Maybe he's Town Clerk of Wexford.'

'That would be a very good job,' Nora said. 'And we can easily check.'

'If he doesn't phone, can you phone your sister and get the full details on him?'

Nora hesitated. She had seen Una regularly, but had not been told that she had a boyfriend, let alone a fiancé. Nora did not want to phone her now on behalf of Elizabeth, which might suggest that she was prying into her life.

'I'm sure he'll phone. I think Town Clerks might be very busy on a Monday morning,' Nora said.

'Or he might be calling his actual fiancée,' Elizabeth said.

'And Una was in good form?'

'Oh, yes, they're a lovely couple. Someone said that last night in Rosslare, and it's true.'

Chapter Seven

Once the summer came, Fiona went to London, where she had got work in a hotel in Earl's Court, and wrote to say that she was enjoying life. The clothes shops, her letter said, were the best in the world and the Saturday markets were like a dream. London was better than she had ever imagined. Aine wrote too from the Kerry Gaeltacht to say that she had met a man who remembered her father and her Uncle Jim when they were learning Irish nearly forty years before. There was even a woman, she said, who had taken a shine to Uncle Jim all those years ago, but, as the woman put it, he was too slow, and so she had married someone else.

The boys went to the tennis club most days. Conor was always waiting for her when she came in; she could see him watching out from the window as she approached the house. She knew that he was too young to be at home on his own and she tried to make sure that he went to friends' houses until Aine came home in August from the Gaeltacht when she could look after him, or at least be there if he came home during the day.

On Saturdays and Sundays, if the weather was fine, Nora drove with the boys to Curracloe or Bentley, and once ventured south to Rosslare Strand. It was hard to imagine that just over a year earlier they had been in the house in Cush as though nothing would change. She was worried that, on the strand in Curracloe, the boys would look north and think of the narrower, stonier strand at the foot of the cliffs that they had known all of their lives. But instead they were most concerned about where Nora would put the beach rug down, finding the right place among the dunes that was sheltered enough. Conor wanted to stay close to her; she was unsure whether she could lie down and read a book or the day's newspaper or whether she should not try to see instead what he wanted to talk about, or what he wanted to do. Donal brought a book about photography that his Aunt Margaret had given him and was content as long as it was agreed that he would not have to go into the sea and they would be back in town by six o'clock when he usually wanted to go to the tennis club.

It was strange, she thought, that she had never before put a single thought into whether they were happy or not, or tried to guess what they were thinking. She had looked after them until the time came when that was difficult. Maurice had wanted her with him when he was in hospital in Dublin after his first heart attack; she could not have denied him that. She could not have left him alone in the hospital. She remembered his eyes watching out for her as she arrived every day, the sense of panic giving way to relief, and then her worry each night as she left him. She knew how lonely he would be. He must have known how serious it was. But she was not sure; he seemed to believe he was being moved home because he was recovering. He must have known, though, that she would not have spent all that time with him in Dublin if he had not been dying.

She noticed then that Conor was watching her.

'Are you going for a swim?' he asked her.

'In a while. Why don't you go down and check if it's warm enough?'

'And if it's not warm enough?'

'We'll still go in. But at least we'll know.'

This was, she thought, a time that she would come to treasure in the future. In a year or two, Donal would not come with them. Perhaps he only came now because he guessed how much she wanted him to. He had a way of reading her mind or sizing up a situation that Conor did not have yet, might never develop. Donal would have known, or almost known, that she was just thinking about Maurice. Conor, on the other hand, would be completely unaware of everything except what was happening now in front of him, or what was coming next. Being with Donal sometimes made her afraid, but being with Conor could make her even more afraid, afraid for his innocence, his sweet loyalty, his open need to be taken care of.

*

When Fiona returned from London, Nora invited Jim and Margaret and Una to come and have tea. Una told her that she would drop in early when she had finished work but she could not stay for tea. She did not give any explanation.

Once Una arrived, Fiona carried down all the new clothes she had bought in London. Nora had noticed a large suitcase when she met her at the railway station but Fiona mentioned nothing of her purchases. She had bought Nora a very discreet pair of earrings, a blouse for Aine and books for the boys. Now, however, once Una was in the house, it was clear that she had bought a number of colourful dresses and skirts and blouses, many of the dresses and blouses low-topped and made of light fabric. Una encouraged her to go out of the room each time and come in wearing something new from London. She commented on each thing, saying that Fiona was developing a very fashionable look, especially when she wore the hooped earrings she had bought and a scarf on her head. Aine joined in, suggesting various combinations and accessories, and standing up at times to fix her sister's hair. There was one russet-coloured dress in a light cotton fabric that both Una and Aine admired; they suggested that Fiona wear it with the earrings and a russet-coloured scarf around her head with no stockings and light sandals.

'If you wore that to Mass, then the whole town would look at you, that is all I have to say,' Una said.

'It would be very nice for Sundays –' Aine said.

'You are not going to Mass in this town dressed like that,' Nora interrupted.

The three others turned and stared at her as though she were an intruder in the room.

'Well, it wouldn't work unless it was a hot day,' Una said. 'I mean, the material is very light. But the look is wonderful –'

Nora interrupted again.

'It might be wonderful in London, or in a magazine, but not down here.'

All three of them glanced at her and then each other. It was obvious that they had recently been talking about her, or they had written to each other about her. During the time when Maurice was sick and the boys were staying with Josie, Una had lived in this house with Aine and they had sometimes seen Fiona. What was strange now was that this was the first time Nora had been in the room with just the three of them since Maurice's illness. It was like being in a room with people who knew each other in ways that she did not, who had a language in common, but perhaps more importantly who could understand each other's silence.

It struck her in that second that Fiona and Aine knew more than she did about Una's romance, that she had told them who her fiancé was and what her plans were. Even though there were twenty years between Una and the girls, their time together had bonded them. They had spoken about clothes and their lives with ease as though they were sisters. They had excluded Nora, as they did now; or perhaps, she thought, she had excluded them. She felt many years older. The bond between them was in the open, a bond that had arisen so naturally that Nora felt that none of them even realized it existed. It must have come into being because of Maurice's absence as much as her own, and it must have been a way of masking the pain the girls felt. Nora crossed the room without looking at them and went to the kitchen.

When Jim and Margaret came and the boys appeared, it was easier. Margaret had no interest in clothes and was merely glad that Fiona had arrived safely home. Once Una left and Margaret went into the front room to talk to Donal, Aine and Jim talked about various places on the Dingle peninsula, the families whom Aine had met in Ballyferriter and Dún Chaoin and how Jim might have known members of the earlier generation. Nora noticed a light coming into his eyes when the name of a place or a person was mentioned. Jim was in his mid-sixties now; he was fifteen years older than Maurice. He was working in the same job as always. He had been a messenger in the War of Independence and was interned in the Civil War. Those years of excitement, followed by summers spent on the Dingle peninsula, must, she imagined, be for him like things from the distant past. He was the most conservative man she knew. He had been thus since she had met him.

Margaret, because she worked for the County Council, earned more money than Jim and had even fewer needs. Paying for Aine's school and giving pocket money to Fiona and the boys pleased her, gave her a stake in how they lived and what they planned to do in the future. It amused Nora, as they sat down to eat, to watch Fiona describing the cultural sights of London with her aunt and uncle rather than Saturday stalls and cheap clothes shops. Fiona had been to a Shakespeare play in which some of the actors had been in the audience and had jumped up at the most unexpected moments.

'How d-did you know they were actors?' Donal asked.

'That's exactly what I was going to ask,' Margaret said.

'They were in costume and they knew their lines,' Fiona said. 'But it was a big shock when they stood up.'

'Well, I hope that doesn't catch on,' Margaret said. 'Then you would never know where you were. The man beside you could be the Bull McCabe.'

'No, I think it's just done in London and it's new,' Fiona said.

There was a discussion about Aine's Latin grinds, with Margaret insisting that she take more grinds at both Christmas and Easter so she could be sure of getting through. Then the subject changed to cameras and the best way for Donal to buy film and have it developed.

'You could take over the communion and confirmation photo business from Pat Crane and Sean Carty,' Jim said. 'Put an ad in the *Echo* saying that you intend to undercut them by half.'

'Or you could add colour,' Fiona said.

'I d-don't like colour,' Donal said solemnly.

'No, he only likes black and white,' Margaret said.

No one had asked Nora about Gibney's or made the smallest reference to it. No one referred to Jim's job either, or to Margaret's. Everything was focused on the four children, on their future. Every word they said was taken up by their aunt and uncle and considered and commented on. Conor's complaint about his tennis racquet, his remarking that one of his friends had a better one, was treated with seriousness and sympathy. Whether it was safe for Fiona and her friends to hitchhike to Dublin was debated and then the price of weekend return train tickets versus day returns and then the price of the bus journey.

By the time the evening was over Nora felt that she knew more details about the lives of her children than she had found out in months. Jim and Margaret had ensured that there was no silence and that everything discussed seemed natural and of immediate interest to one of the children. The fact that Donal and Conor were alone in the house when she was at work, when they were not in the tennis club, was never mentioned, however, nor the fact that Miss Kavanagh was beginning to treat her with the same level of shrill contempt as she treated the most despised members of the female office staff. It had been an ordinary evening, the first in a long time, and Nora was almost grateful for it as she went to bed.

In work the following Monday Elizabeth was busy avoiding calls from Roger and then frantically waiting for them. Twice or three times she spoke to Ray and when she put the phone down she discussed with Nora the chances of someone telling Roger about Ray, or of meeting Ray at some rugby dance or in some golf club bar while she was accompanied by Roger.

'The thing is, I like both of them,' she said. 'Roger is so dependable and he is a member of every club under the sun and he's very well spoken. But I'd be bored to death down here without Ray. I don't know if you can imagine an evening spent with Old William, Little William and Thomas going over business strategy. They drone on even while we are eating. No wonder my mother never leaves the house, it's the result of the shame of being so bored. I don't know what the three of them are talking about at the moment, but they have plans afoot. They talk for hours and hours and write out lists and figures. You'd think they were running the country.'

As Elizabeth's romantic life became richer and more complicated, she spent more and more time on the phone discussing its implications with her friends. Soon, the set of invoices for which she was responsible piled up. Nora spotted her one Friday morning stuffing envelopes with invoices that she did not note in the ledger. Even though Elizabeth did not speak to Miss Kavanagh or work directly for her, each week the ledger with the list of invoices sent out had to be brought to Miss Kavanagh's office to be checked by her with punctilious care. Despite her time on the phone, Elizabeth normally made no mistakes in her work. Nonetheless, there were often queries, but since Miss Kavanagh was not allowed to speak to Elizabeth, then she often spoke to Nora in a tone of barely controlled rage, asking her to pass on what she had said to Miss Gibney. She sometimes sent in one of the office girls with instructions to stand in front of Miss Gibney until she put the phone down and then get some details about invoices that Miss Kavanagh needed.

When Miss Kavanagh discovered that the invoices had gone out without any entries in the ledger, she approached Thomas Gibney and, Nora discovered, suggested that it was Nora as well as Elizabeth who had neglected to enter the invoice details. When Thomas came to Miss Kavanagh's office one afternoon, they called Nora in and closed the door.

'This is a very dangerous situation,' Thomas said. 'We have no record of the invoices and if they are not paid, we'll have no way of telling. This has never happened before.'

Miss Kavanagh stood beside him with a look of great sorrow on her face. Nora said nothing, looking from one of them to the other.

'Mrs Webster, I understand that the system has been explained to you several times,' Thomas said. 'It's not very complicated.'

Still, Nora did not reply.

'No invoices can be sent out unless the details are lodged in the ledger,' Thomas continued. 'What has happened is inexcusable and will potentially mean a financial loss for the company.'

'Have you finished, Mr Gibney?' Nora asked.

'What do you mean?' Thomas asked.

'I want to know if you have finished speaking. And when you have finished, then perhaps you will ask Miss Kavanagh if this has anything, anything at all, to do with me, and she will tell you –'

As Miss Kavanagh made to interrupt her, she left the office, closing the door behind her. Soon, she saw Thomas going from Miss Kavanagh's office to the office occupied by his sister. He seemed determined. Nora kept her head down as she heard shouting. She was aware that everyone in the large office was listening. Miss Kavanagh closed the door to her own office and did not come out for the rest of the afternoon.

The following week Miss Kavanagh began to harass Elizabeth Gibney, having, as far as Nora could make out, got agreement from Thomas that she could do so. To Nora herself, she behaved coldly and appeared unsure how to proceed. In the morning, she would wait for Elizabeth to arrive and then announce that she wished to see in the ledger all the entries for the previous day; invoices waiting to be sent out were to be left in a box outside her office so that she could check them.

On the third morning, when she had come in four times, finding Elizabeth on the phone each time, she closed the door of the office and found a chair and sat opposite Elizabeth, listening with an air of impatience to the conversation. As Elizabeth continued to make arrangements for the weekend, Miss Kavanagh reached over and grabbed the ledger from her desk. She turned it towards her and began to go through the entries.

'Excuse me,' Elizabeth said into the phone, 'I will have to ring off and call you later. I have a person sitting opposite me who looks like something the cat brought home, but with less manners.'

She put down the receiver.

'Now, Miss Kavanagh,' Elizabeth said, 'if you ever come into my office again and as much as touch anything on my desk, I will find a nice big cage for you and I will lock you into it, and that would be the best place for you.'

'Miss Gibney, I am not here to take abuse from you.'

'Maybe that is what you are here for.'

'I will speak to your father about you.'

'Hold on, Miss Francie. I'll get him for you now.'

She lifted the receiver and dialled an extension number and asked to be put through to her father.

'Is that Old William? Hi, Dad. I have the Kavanagh woman here and she wants to see you. And can you, when you see her, tell her to keep her claws off my things and her dirty feet out of my office?

And can you put Thomas back in the kennel? Yes, I'll send her up right now.'

Nora could not stop herself congratulating Elizabeth for standing up to Miss Kavanagh, although she knew it was easy for her as it would have been impossible for anybody else. They were both laughing as Miss Kavanagh returned to fetch the ledger. For one second, Miss Kavanagh caught Nora's eye. The look was both wounded and threatening.

One Saturday night in October, with Jim and Margaret visiting, Nora turned on the nine o'clock news. As soon as the bulletin began, there was film of a riot and baton charge with the newsreader stating that this had happened that very afternoon in Derry. Nora found herself calling to Donal, who was in the other room, to come and look. Soon, they were joined by Conor, who was in his pyjamas. The two boys stood watching as the camera seemed to sway and people on the television screamed and ran from something.

'Is this a film?' Conor asked.

'No, it's the news. It's Derry.'

The newsreader explained that a march in Derry had turned into a riot as the police had beaten the crowd with batons. Then there was more footage with a scene where a number of policemen lifted their batons against men who had their hands on their heads to protect themselves. One of the men batoned, the newsreader said, was Gerry Fitt, who was a member of parliament. The camera showed two or three of the marchers who had fallen to the ground, and then it followed some of the demonstrators who were running with the police in hot pursuit. The camera then focused on a woman who was screaming.

When the news was over, Conor went back upstairs. Donal asked what the riot had been about.

'It's about civil rights,' Jim said.

'Catholics marching for civil rights,' Margaret added.

'D-derry is in N-northern Ireland,' Donal said. 'It's a different c-colour on the map.'

'Yes, but it's all the same country,' Margaret said.

Nora noticed how alert Jim had become. When Donal left the room she turned down the sound of the television, presuming that he wanted to comment. If anything like this had happened while Maurice was alive, Maurice and Jim would normally have talked for a long time about every aspect of it. When Jim said nothing, she asked him what he thought.

'That's one scrap I wouldn't like to be in,' he said. 'There will be no easy way out of that one.'

The following day Nora spoke to a number of people after Mass who had also seen the baton charge on television; she bought some Sunday newspapers so she could read about the events. Later, she went for a walk, but met no one she knew, so she could not talk to anyone about Derry.

In work on Monday she presumed that everyone would be discussing the news, but it seemed to be business as usual. Elizabeth had been in Dublin for the weekend and had not even seen the riots on television. When Nora told her about it, she nodded vaguely. She made some phone calls while Nora worked.

In the afternoon, as Nora worked on files with one of the young bookkeepers, Miss Kavanagh came and stood watching over them.

'What are the two of you doing, in the name of God?' she asked.

Nora decided to ignore her.

'Mrs Webster, look at me when I speak to you!' Miss Kavanagh shouted.

Nora stood up from her desk.

'Can I see you privately in your office, Miss Kavanagh?' she asked.

'I am busy, Mrs Webster.'

'I need to see you in your office.'

She followed as Miss Kavanagh turned reluctantly and went into her office.

'Miss Kavanagh, I am going home now,' she said.

'It's not nearly half past five.'

'Miss Kavanagh, when I am working, you will kindly control your temper and keep your voice down.'

'I am employed here to make this office run smoothly and I don't need back answers from you, Mrs Webster, or anyone like you.'

'I am employed here to do my work, Miss Kavanagh, and your screeching is not helpful.'

'Go home then, Mrs. Plenty of quiet at home! Off with you now! If you see Mr Thomas, you can tell him that I sent you home.'

Nora walked across the town. If she met anyone she knew, she tried to greet them as she normally did. By the time she was approaching the house, she was filled with energy and wondered if she should not drive back across the town and confront Miss Kavanagh once more. As she walked up the steps to the front door, her thoughts of what she might say to Miss Kavanagh and indeed to Thomas Gibney were interrupted by the sound of crying. When she opened the door with her key, the crying stopped and there was silence.

'Who's here?' she shouted. 'Anyone home?'

Donal came out of the back room, looking guilty. He was followed by Conor, who had clearly been crying.

'What happened? What's wrong?'

Neither of them spoke.

'Conor, are you all right?'

'We were n-not expecting you h-home so early,' Donal said.

'Donal, why is Conor crying?'

'I'm not crying now.'

'But you were crying. I could hear you at the door.'

'He t-tried to open my c-camera,' Donal said.

Slowly, it emerged that they had some sort of dispute every day in the time between coming home from school and her return. Neither of them seemed to think there was anything strange about it. Donal's tone was challenging, Conor's almost ashamed. Neither of them wanted her to become involved. Having listened to both of them, she waited until Conor was out of the room.

'He's younger than you, there's no one else to look after him.'

Donal did not reply.

'I want you to promise that you won't make him cry any more. And keep your camera safe and then he won't be able to touch it. Will you promise me that?'

He nodded and then sat staring into the distance.

That night she could not sleep. She wondered if there was any-where they could go after school, or if there was someone who could come to the house to look after them for the two hours between the end of the schoolday and her arrival home. The fol-lowing year, she hoped, Fiona would be teaching in the town and would be home in the late afternoon. Between now and then, she would have to talk to Donal regularly and watch Conor carefully. She remembered how much Donal had resented Conor when he was a baby and people paid him attention. Or if Conor got a new toy, even something Donal had outgrown, he would manipulate things so that he would have control of the toy and decide when Conor could have it and when he could not. Conor always let him do this as though it were natural. But it was not natural now, nor indeed was it natural that the two of them were alone in the house together.

She pictured the house, how strangely filled with absence it must be. She was aware now that the changes in their lives had come to seem normal to them. They did not have her way of watching every scene, every moment, for signs of what was miss-ing or what might have been. The death of their father had entered into a part of them that, as far as she could see, they were not aware of. They could not see how uneasy they were, and maybe no one but she could see it, yet it was something that would not leave them now, she thought, would not leave them for years. She should not have been surprised to have found them fighting with each other when she came home early. She would have to do what she could to lessen their suspicion of each other and of everyone around them.

She fell asleep in the hour before dawn and then woke with a start, realizing that she had not heard the alarm clock. It was twenty to nine. She got up quickly and found that the boys were still asleep. If she moved fast, she thought, she would be able to get them their breakfast. But she would be late for work, even if she drove across the town, which she had never done before.

She was glad that no one noticed her late arrival. Elizabeth came in half an hour after she did, full of the events of the night before, which had taken place in the Pike Grill of the Talbot Hotel and then in Kelly's Hotel in Rosslare.

'Your sister told me a marvellous story. I don't know why I thought it was so funny. She was in Paddy McKenna's in Slaney Street on Saturday getting groceries when the new woman who does her hair at Wheeler's, Tara or Lara or something, came in and said that she'd heard that she had a beautiful engagement ring and asked to see it. And when Una turned to show her the ring, Tara or Lara began to scream about how glorious it was only to discover, when she actually looked, that Una wasn't wearing it that day. She had had to bring it back to the jeweller's as it was too tight. And Tara or Lara had gushed for Ireland with the whole shop listening. Seemingly, it didn't take a feather out of her. She carried on talking as though nothing at all had happened.'

Nora wanted to say that she did not know that her sister was engaged but then she stopped herself.

'And Una's fiancé was there last night too?' she asked.

'Oh, Seamus is great. Old William says that he is the only man in the bank he can talk to. You know, I heard that every town he has been in he has done a strong line, and that when he gets transferred he drops her unceremoniously. But this is the first time he has got engaged. They really are made for each other, aren't they? I wish I could say the same about myself and Roger, or even about myself and Ray. I wish I could have half of Ray and half of Roger. But it would be just my luck to get the half of Roger that is even duller than the other half and the half of Ray that is never happy until he is on his way to the next place.'

Nora wondered what bank Seamus worked in, and if she would know him to see.

As she came back to work in the afternoon she met one of the lorry drivers, whose name she did not know. He was a big man with a ruddy face and sandy hair. She noticed the aura of pure freedom and self-confidence he exuded, which was lacking among the office workers and the commercial travellers.

'God, that was a terrible thing on Saturday,' he said. 'It's the sort of thing your bossman, Mr Webster, God rest him, would have got very fired up about.'

'He would indeed,' she said.

'Mr Webster,' the man continued, 'used to make us cross out the word "London" in Londonderry on every atlas. I think I still have one at home.'

'I'm sure we have one too.'

'Baton charges, if you don't mind. Against a peaceful demonstration.'

'I saw the baton charges on television all right,' she said.

'The last time I saw a baton charge,' the lorry driver said, 'was the night Bill Haley and the Comets played in the Royal in Dublin. We were all waiting outside to meet Bill Haley in person, and the men in blue decided it was a riot and they ran after us with batons. But the baton charge on Saturday was serious. They were marching for civil rights. They were on their own streets. I am telling you now that is a disgrace.'

The lorry driver was in such a state about the riots that she only managed to get away from him when she saw Miss Kavanagh coming, followed by the three commercial travellers who had been in her office the previous day insisting that they had not been paid the proper bonus. She was summoned by Miss Kavanagh to come with them into her office.

'Now, these gentlemen came to Mr William Gibney Junior in a delegation, and Mr Gibney has sent them to me. They want to see what all of the travellers are paid, every bonus, and every detail of every arrangement made. I don't know who they think they represent, but as I told Mr Gibney, we don't have that information to hand. It's a private matter between this company and each commercial traveller.'

'Well,' the traveller whom Nora knew as WLD, shorthand for Walk-Like-a-Duck, said, 'we thought, in that case, that we would ask to see our own details, just the three of us, so we can compare them.'

The other two nodded in agreement.

'No, you see,' Miss Kavanagh said, 'we don't have information like that set out in any format. Do we, Mrs Webster?'

Nora wondered later how she might have responded to this had she not been so tired.

'Well, we do, in fact,' she said. 'I have a folder for each of the travellers and on the first page of each folder I have noted every detail of their arrangements and this means that I can work out the bonuses very quickly and without mistakes.'

'Can we see each of our folders then?' one of the men asked.

'If you come back tomorrow,' Miss Kavanagh said.

'We will see them now and come back tomorrow as well.'

Nora remembered that she had written only initials on the folders and she hoped, were the travellers to see their folders, she would not have to tell them what BT, SB and WLD stood for.

'I'll get them myself if you tell us what filing cabinet they are in,' Walk-Like-a-Duck said.

'You will touch nothing here,' Miss Kavanagh said.

'You told us that you didn't have the information. Now it turns out that you do. We are not moving until we see our folders.'

'Well, you can look now for one minute,' Miss Kavanagh said. 'But we don't have all day to waste.'

She nodded to Nora, who went outside and searched through the cabinet until she found the file on each of the travellers. They cleared space on Miss Kavanagh's desk without consulting her and opened the three files. On a page stapled to the opening page Nora had set out in very clear, large handwriting what each of the men was due. One of the men started to make notes.

'Wait until the others hear about this,' he said.

When they had gone, Miss Kavanagh did not move. Nora returned the files to the cabinet. She felt desperately tired now as if she could easily fall asleep at her desk. When she looked at her watch she saw that it was only two thirty. She did not know how she was going to get through the afternoon.

'What are you doing now?' Miss Kavanagh's voice behind her was very quiet and composed.

Nora realized that there was no work on her desk.

'What are you doing now?' Miss Kavanagh repeated, the voice even quieter.

'Well, I was about to check what bonus claims have come in today.'

'I didn't ask you what you are about to do. That's a question any idler can answer. I asked you what you are doing now.'

'Miss Kavanagh, what do you think I am doing? I am talking to you.'

Miss Kavanagh walked down the long office and found a young woman who had just started to work there. She led her back to her own office.

'Mrs Webster, could you bring in all the files you have made on the commercial travellers?' she shouted.

Nora went to the filing cabinet and took out the files and carried them into the office.

'On the desk! Put them on the desk!' Miss Kavanagh shouted.

'Here are some scissors,' she said to the new girl. 'I want every one of those files cut up into pieces and put into the wastepaper basket. I have specific instructions from Mr William Gibney Senior that no files like this are needed or desirable. He knows what each commercial traveller is due. If we had wanted Mrs Webster to make files we would have asked her to.'

She turned to Nora.

'And what, Mrs Webster, were you talking to that lorry driver about outside this building? What further mischief were you planning?'

'The topic of our discussion is none of your business, Miss Kavanagh,' Nora said.

'There she is, late for work, parking her car any old way, and spending the morning gossiping with Miss Gibney, the laziest girl in Ireland, and then gossiping with a lorry driver! She won't last long here, you know. Do you understand that, Mrs Webster?'

'I have no further interest in listening to you, Miss Kavanagh,' Nora said. 'And can I suggest that you keep your views on Miss Gibney and perhaps most other matters to yourself?'

Miss Kavanagh took up one of the folders and tried to tear it in two. When the paper proved too tough, she grabbed the scissors from the girl and began to cut the folder up.

'You are not down in your house in Ballyconnigar now, Mrs Webster, or sitting in the lounge of Etchingham's pub. You are not Lady Muck any more. You are here, working for me. And I run this office in the way that I am told by Mr William Gibney Senior and it is one of the unspoken rules that no one who works here consorts with the lorry drivers unless it is a part of their daily task. You think you can do what you like, with your daughter here and your daughter there, and that sister of yours out in the golf club, a most unpleasant article if ever there was one. And your husband indeed, oh, he was a great man –'

'Don't speak about my husband!'

Nora took up the scissors. Later, she could not think why she had done this. She walked out of Miss Kavanagh's office with the scissors in her hand, found her coat and left as though nothing special had happened. Once she was in the car, she checked the time. It was not yet three o'clock. The boys would not even be home.

Chapter Eight

As she turned the car, she decided that she would go to Ballyconnigar now. The day was fine and the strand at Keatings' would be empty. She would walk, and maybe the walking would give her an idea what she might do. No matter what happened she would not go back to Gibney's again. She wondered if she could sell the house in Enniscorthy and rent a smaller house, or move to Dublin. It might be easier to find a proper job in Dublin. Aine would be there next year and maybe Fiona could find a teaching job there, and she could find a school for the boys. As she thought about this, the image of leaving Jim and Margaret, and her sister Una, came to her, and from that she was reminded of what Miss Kavanagh had said about Una in the golf club, 'a most unpleasant article if ever there was one', and she laughed. There was something about the phrase, as there was indeed about Miss Kavanagh knowing that she and Maurice went to Etchingham's pub in Blackwater some nights in the summer, that made it clear that Francie Kavanagh had been watching her closely.

She remembered the day years ago when Greta had told her that Francie was coming with them to Ballyconnigar and that there was nothing they could do about it. Both she and Greta were determined that they would not be seen with Francie Kavanagh. Even her clothes then, and the look of her bicycle itself, suggested an old house out in the countryside that did not have running water, a house where upstairs was called 'the loft'. Her voice, her accent, phrases she used, made them wish to keep away from her. But she wanted to join them that day.

They used all their energy on their lighter bicycles to get ahead of her, out of sight, and then went to Morriscastle. Nora imagined her arriving in Ballyconnigar expecting to find herself and Greta. She must have had some dream of changing herself, becoming like a girl from the town. Greta and herself, Nora thought, were very innocent then, but they had ambitions. Greta's rule that they would speak only to men who knew syntax and they would ignore anyone who used bad grammar began as a joke, but slowly it became serious for them. They both married educated men and they both learned to drive, and once they had children, they both stayed near the sea in the summer for as long as they could. In trying to join them that day, Francie Kavanagh had maybe also wanted some of what they wanted, little as it seemed at the time. And they had laughed the following day when they heard about her puncture and the rain. They had certainly not apologized to her. And now she ran the office and moved around all day like a madwoman. As she turned at Finchogue, Nora wondered if there was a normal job available, a job she could do without a madwoman who hated her in control of her. But in any interview now, or in any discussion with a prospective employer, she would have to explain why, on a bright October afternoon, she had walked out of Gibney's with a pair of scissors in her hand.

She stopped in Blackwater and bought a packet of ten Carroll's cigarettes and a box of matches. She had not smoked for years and promised herself that she would not smoke all of these cigarettes either, just two or three before throwing the packet away. When she inhaled, she felt dizzy and that made her remember how tired she was. She threw the cigarette out of the window and then put her head back and fell asleep. When she woke, she spotted a woman standing on the bridge looking over at her car. As the woman approached, she started the engine.

She was tempted to drive to Cush and visit the house and see if Jack Lacey had done any work on it. But she was sure that her car would be noticed. She toyed for a moment with the idea of driving home and writing the Gibneys a sharp letter of resignation. She began to compose it in her mind. But then the energy to do that left her and she decided to drive towards the sea at Keatings'.

She had not expected to find a haze over the water. She sat in the car in front of Keatings' house and looked down in the direction of

Rosslare, taking in the heavy, milky light that lay over the strand going towards Curracloe and Raven Point. When she got out of the car, she felt how unusually close and humid it was, as if there were thunder coming. She put on a pair of flat shoes that she kept in the car. There were no other cars in the car park. She walked carefully on the stony stretch between the grass and the river and crossed the small wooden bridge and made her way south.

In all the years, she thought, she had never come here even as late in the season as October; she imagined now how strange it would be in December and January, how storm-swept and wintry and how biting the cold.

There was hardly any colour. The world in front of her had been washed down. If she moved nearer to the shore, she could look at the small stones that made a rattling sound when the waves broke over them. She saw how exact the colour of each stone was and it allowed her to forget Francie Kavanagh and the Gibneys and to stop worrying about what she would do.

She could barely see ahead of her as she walked. It might have been easy to imagine that this was a place that belonged more to Maurice than to her. It was the world filled with absences. There was merely the hushed sound of the water and stray cries of sea-birds flying close to the surface of the calm sea. She could make out the sun as it glowed through the curtain of haze. It was unlikely that Maurice was anywhere except buried in the graveyard where she had left him. But nonetheless the idea lingered that if he, or his spirit, were anywhere in the world, then he would be here.

She thought it almost natural that if his spirit were on this stretch of strand he would have his own concerns. The details of her life – her job at Gibney's, or what might happen in the future with Fiona and Aine, Donal and Conor – these would be matters that would seem as vague to him as the far distance did now to her, things that would pass as his life had passed. What had happened in the days before his death, the blockage in his system that caused him to cry out so his voice could be heard through the hospital, that would be with him now, more than anything else.

It came to her again, his death. She pictured those who were there – Jim and Margaret, Sister Thomas, who had said special prayers, and old Father Quaid. For the last two days Nora herself had stayed by his bedside. But he was already far away from them, so far that they might have been like shadows, people already lost to him. Maybe he could only imagine them all as vague presences, the ones he had loved, but love hardly mattered then just as the haze here now meant that the line between things hardly mattered.

As she reached Ballyvaloo, and the luminous grey-whiteness was moved down the strand by the mild wind towards Curracloe, she saw that there was a single nun walking back towards the lane that led to the retreat house of the Sisters of St John of God. Wearing a full black habit, she walked slowly and with difficulty. Nora thought that she must be one of the retired nuns who often came here on holiday or on retreat.

When she was closer she saw that the nun was Sister Thomas. Nora was surprised she was in Ballyvaloo; she had not known that she ever spent time away from her own convent and the town. She moved towards her and when she reached her, Sister Thomas greeted her and put out her hands and took both of Nora's hands and held them.

Suddenly, Nora felt cold and began to shiver. She could hear a wind blowing, almost whistling, in the distance, but when she looked out at the sea and down the strand it all seemed calm. There was no sign of the haze lifting.

'You shouldn't be here on your own,' Sister Thomas said. 'I was in Blackwater this morning to see a friend. And just a while ago she saw you fast asleep in the car and then driving towards the strand and she phoned me in the convent because she was worried and wanted to know what she should do. So I walked down here in case I would find you.'

'Who saw me?'

'I thought I would come down to the shoreline to see if you were here,' Sister Thomas said quietly. 'I don't often leave the retreat house. Today it's more like heaven than earth down here.'

'I saw her all right. Someone who can't mind her own business.'

'That is one way of putting it. Someone who is looking out for you.'

Sister Thomas released Nora's hands.

'I was not surprised to see you down here,' she said. 'It was meant to happen, us meeting like this. This is how the Lord works.'

'Don't tell me about how the Lord works! Don't tell me that again!'

'When Maurice was dying I asked the Lord to make it easy for him and for you. I have no needs of my own and I had not asked him for anything in a long time. But I asked him for that and he denied me what I asked. There must have been a reason for saying no, and the reason is hidden from us. But I know that he is watching over you, and maybe that is why we met so I could tell you that.'

'He has not been watching over me! No one has been watching over me!'

'I knew when I woke today and said my prayers this morning that I was to see you.'

Nora was silent.

'So turn back now before the fog comes down so hard that you won't be able to drive home,' Sister Thomas said. 'Go home and the boys will be home soon. The boys will be home from school waiting for you.'

'I can't work in Gibney's any more. Miss Kavanagh shouts at me. She said things today that made it impossible for me to stay.'

'It will be all right. It is a small town and it will guard you. Go back to it now. And stop grieving, Nora. The time for that is over. Do you hear me?'

'I felt as I walked along here –'.

'We all feel that on days like this,' Sister Thomas interrupted. 'And even on other days. It is why we come here. Those who have passed on have it for shelter on their way elsewhere. It is nice to be among them on a day like this.'

'Among them? What do you mean?'

'We walk among them sometimes, the ones who have left us. They are filled with something that none of us knows yet. It is a mystery.'

She held Nora's two hands again, and then turned and walked slowly, as though in pain, back towards the dunes and the lane leading to the retreat house. Nora waited to see if she would look back, but she did not, so Nora stood for a while without moving, looking out at the sea still covered in haze. And then she began to make her way along the strand towards where she had left the car. Miss Kavanagh's large scissors were on the front passenger seat beside the packet of cigarettes. She put the cigarettes in the glove compartment, but took the scissors out of the car and left them down on the gravel for someone else to find.

Chapter Nine

Nora said nothing to anyone about what had happened at Gibney's, not even that she was considering selling the house and moving to Dublin with the boys. She smiled at the thought of them seeing a 'For Sale' sign on the house, or an advertisement for it in the newspapers. She had sent a note to Miss Kavanagh saying that she was ill; she would not bother sending another note to William or Peggy or Elizabeth saying that she was not coming back. They would have to find out. For them it would hardly matter, although they might not, she thought, want people in the town to know that she had been badly treated in the office. She knew that Conor had told Fiona that she had not been at work, but Fiona had not asked her about it.

One Friday evening at the end of that October, when Fiona and Aine were both home, Una arrived to show them all her engagement ring. Catherine, when Nora had phoned her a few days earlier from the booth on the Back Road, had told her that Una and Seamus had been to stay. She and Mark had liked Seamus. She added that Una had told her how nervous she was about mentioning the engagement to Nora. Una, she said, did not know how Nora would respond, since it was all so soon after Maurice's death. Nora had a visit too from her Aunt Josie, who said that Una was going to marry Seamus in the New Year and her only worry was how Nora would deal with the news.

'Your sisters are afraid of you,' Josie said. 'They always have been. I don't know what it is.'

Nora began to have little patience with her sister and to feel nothing except a dry irritation about her and her fiancé, and a remote amusement at the news she had received from Elizabeth about Una and Seamus in Wexford and Rosslare, cavorting like two people half their age.

'Oh, I heard all about the ring,' she said when Una appeared and showed it to her. 'I believe Tara Reagan loved it, or so she said.'

'I suppose Elizabeth Gibney told you that.'

'The whole town told me,' Nora said.

'Tara Reagan is such a fool.'

'She knows a good ring when she sees it,' Nora said.

Una looked at Fiona and Aine as if to say that she had always expected this to be difficult.

'Anyway, that is great news. Catherine told me and Aunt Josie told me as well. Everyone told me. So I know all about it. Congratulations!'

Una blushed.

'I was going to tell you a few times I saw you and then I thought I'd wait and leave it.'

'Oh, no hurry. As I said, the whole town is talking about it, so I only needed to go out of the door to hear about it.'

Una, she saw, wanted to leave, but had come to the house to win Nora's approval and to do so in the softening presence of Fiona and Aine. She wanted, Nora thought, to be able to phone Catherine and Josie and tell them that she had finally broken the news to her sister and it would all be easy now. Nora felt the weight of them all talking about her, all of them thinking that she might in some way object to her sister getting married or say something stinging to Una about it. She wished now that she felt like saying something helpful, but she could not think what it might be. But she also wished that the three of them might go, the two girls back upstairs or to the other room, and Una to her own house. The longer they stayed expecting something from her, the closer she came to feeling a sort of rage that she knew stemmed from her encounter with Miss Kavanagh and from not sleeping well since she had walked out of the office. But it also came from Una herself, and from Fiona and Aine.

'I hear he's in the bank,' Nora said. 'Is he the manager?'

'Well, no,' Una said.

'I heard that some of the best become managers quite young.'

'It's a lot of responsibility,' Una said.

'And is that why he hasn't been married before now as well?'

Una reached for her handbag and made to stand up.

'I suppose he didn't meet the right woman,' Fiona said. 'Until our Una came along.'

'I see,' Nora said.

She realized that she had gone too far. Once more, she tried to think of something to say to relieve the situation quickly, but she could think of nothing. Aine crossed the room and left.

'But it's great news,' Nora said, 'and I'm really looking forward to meeting him.'

Una tried to smile. Fiona stared at Nora.

'Well, I must be going anyway,' Una said.

She walked out of the room, followed by Fiona.

On Monday night Mrs Whelan called and Donal led her into the back room.

'Now, I have a message for you from Peggy Gibney herself. She said that she would love to see you tomorrow in the afternoon. If three o'clock would suit you, she said, that would be fine, but, if not, then four.'

'Oh, I'm not well enough to go out, Mrs Whelan.'

'And Elizabeth misses you. I was told to tell you that.'

'I'm sure. But I'm not well enough to go out of the house at all.'

'So, what will I say to Mrs Gibney?'

'That I'm not well enough to go out, but it's nice that you called, and that you and I had a cup of tea.'

'Oh, I couldn't, Mrs Webster.'

Nora insisted on making tea. It occurred to her once more that it might not suit the Gibneys to have it known that they had bullied Maurice Webster's widow and run her home. She did not know the name of the young girl who had witnessed the final scene with Miss Kavanagh but she imagined that she would have told everyone in the office. Soon it would reach the few people in the town whose opinion the Gibneys might care about.

As she carried the tray into the room, she made every effort to seem sprightly and in perfect health. She hoped that Mrs Whelan would report to the Gibneys that she did not believe there was anything at all wrong with Mrs Webster.

Two days later, Sister Thomas arrived. She was more frail than she had appeared on the strand at Ballyvaloo.

'I wanted to see you before the boys came home from school,' she said once she was sitting in an armchair in the back room. 'Now, I found out everything. You'd be surprised who comes to the convent. Nothing escapes us. Or maybe some things do, but they are always things we have no interest in. So I heard everything, down to the scissors. She is one of God's children, Frances Kavanagh, and very holy. If people only knew! So I spoke to Peggy Gibney and she may tell you herself what I said. And she assembled all of them, her family and your friend Miss Kavanagh. And, strangely enough, they are all afraid of her. I don't know why because she is very gentle. And she may tell you the whole story. I told her that she could. She has never told anyone, but I think she wants to tell you. And you can go and see her tomorrow.'

'I don't want to go back there.'

'She has a new offer for you, and don't turn it down. And also I have one thing to ask you. Could you be nice to your sister?'

'How do you know about that?'

'She came into our little chapel where you came after Maurice died when you wanted to avoid people. And I saw her and I have always had a soft spot for her, the way she was left alone after your mother died.'

'And what did she say about me?'

'Nothing, or nothing much. But enough. So I have to go now because I am busy. And you have two things to do. See Peggy and look after Una. And maybe say a prayer for all of us too.'

She moved slowly towards the hallway.

'I don't know what to say,' Nora said. 'I don't like people knowing my business.'

'Your mother was the same. I knew her when she sang. She was a wonderful singer, but it was the pride, or the not liking people knowing her business, that made her difficult. And that did her no good. Now, you are more practical. And we should all be grateful for that.'

'You want me to go and see Peggy Gibney tomorrow?'

'I do, Nora, at three or four, or in between.'

'I will then.'

'And you'll invite Una and her fiancé up to the house to meet the boys. A wedding is a very cheerful thing and they might enjoy hearing all about it.'

Nora opened the front door for her, and as she made her way laboriously down the steps, she said: 'All I hope is that things will be simpler in heaven. Say a prayer that things in heaven will be simpler.'

When Mrs Whelan answered the door, she whispered that she had told Peggy Gibney that Nora was too sick to visit.

'Will I tell her you got better?' she asked as she took Nora's coat.

'If you like.'

Peggy Gibney was sitting in exactly the same chair as the last time. There was no book or newspaper nearby. Nora wondered if she sat there all day every day in this shadowy room, with the evergreen trees swaying outside the window, thinking her thoughts, being served tea at intervals by Mrs Whelan.

'Here we are again, Nora, then,' she said, speaking like a doctor to a patient who had come to have her bandages removed or her blood pressure taken.

Nora looked at her coldly.

'There has been war in this house,' Peggy said. 'Elizabeth is developing a very sharp tongue, but of course I blame Thomas. It's one way of blaming my husband without having to say so. William Gibney Senior has enough on his plate, what with all the changes afoot, without being blamed too. And Thomas can take it, of course.'

'Peggy, I have no idea what you are talking about,' Nora said.

Peggy put her finger to her lips, stood up and went stealthily to the door and opened it suddenly.

'Maggie, we need some privacy now,' she said. 'If we want tea later, I will find you in the kitchen.'

She sat back in her chair.

'Nora, you'll have to tell me what you want. And then I'll get it for you.'

'Nothing,' Nora said.

'Sister Thomas said that I was to tell you to get down off your high horse if you were on it.'

'I don't want anything, thank you.'

'All of them say, except Elizabeth that is, that Francie Kavanagh is an invaluable office manager. She knows the company inside out, which is why she doesn't need things written down. And she can be abrasive, or so I'm told, because if she wasn't, nothing would get done. My husband and Thomas think the world of her. In my opinion she is a rip and a tartar, but no one listens to me, so even Elizabeth doesn't know that I agree with her. Now, I said that no one listens to me, but every so often I lay down the law in this house. What I do first is I close the kitchen. They can eat where they like, but they will get nothing here. And then I wait. And then I tell them what I want and I get it. So all you have to do is tell me what you want.'

'I want to work only in the mornings and I will work under Thomas and Elizabeth, but Miss Kavanagh cannot be allowed even to look at me. I think I can do the same amount of work, but I might need some help. I will take a small cut in salary, but not much.'

'Done,' Peggy Gibney said. 'Come over here early on Monday morning and you and Elizabeth can arrive together.'

'What does Sister Thomas have to do with this?'

'That's a long story, Nora, from long ago.'

'Was that when you were going out with William?'

'You were the only one who knew because William said that you overheard the argument he had with his father. And we always appreciated that you told no one. I was to go to England. That was what William's father said. You know that. So I went to the nuns at St John's to ask them where I might go. And Sister Thomas had just arrived at that time. Oh, she was very different from the other nuns. She had worked in England, you know, and seen it all, the Irish girls coming. She worked for Michael Collins, you know. Nuns were great messengers and she was one of his messengers.

Did she never tell you about it? Oh, no, I suppose because you were in Fianna Fáil.'

'Maurice was, and Jim. Jim still is.'

'I suppose because of that she might not have mentioned Michael Collins. Anyway, she came over here and in this very room she threatened William's father. She said she would go to the bishop, whom she had known years before, and they would close all the church accounts with Gibney's. She said that she would ask the bishop as a personal favour to call to the house too, unless the matter was sorted to her satisfaction. William and myself were to marry, she said, which was what we wanted, of course, even though the Gibneys didn't think I was good enough. And that was the end of all our problems. I told Sister Thomas then that if she ever needed anything in return she was to come to me. And she waited all these years. So you can see why I could not refuse her. If it wasn't for her, William Junior would have been in an orphanage or would have been adopted in England, and I don't know where I would be.'

'Michael Collins, that's a good one,' Nora said.

'She told me that several times. Seemingly, he had the nuns eating out of his hand.'

'Well, we all seem to be eating out of her hand now.'

'Come on Monday morning and have coffee with myself and Elizabeth. We often have coffee in the morning. She's very lively these days, Elizabeth. I don't know what is wrong with her. Or maybe it's a good sign.'

It was clear to Nora that she should tell no one what had happened. When she called on Una on Saturday, she merely said that she had moved to half-time in Gibney's because she was finding a full day too hard. She had a sense from Una's response that she had heard about the fight with Francie Kavanagh.

It was arranged that Una and Seamus would take her out for drinks in the golf club one evening the following week.

When she told the boys that she would be working half-time, they took it in the same suspicious way as any news about change. And when she told them that she was going to leave them alone for one evening to go to the golf club with Una, which was the first time they would be alone in the house in the evening, they were more openly suspicious, wanting to know if she was going to join the golf club. When they discovered that she was going merely to the bar, they wanted to know at what time she would be home.

It took them a while to get used to the fact that she did not go back to work each afternoon, and that she was there when they came in from school. Even though they fought sometimes, and Donal clearly bullied Conor, that had become their lives, and a change in the regime made them uneasy, as though they had to start all over again.

Una asked if Nora could collect her and take her to the golf club, as Seamus would be on his half-day and was going to play a round of golf and then have some sandwiches in the clubhouse before meeting them. While Nora thought that Seamus should have driven into the town to collect them, and wondered if this might be an excuse for her to cancel, she decided in the end to agree to everything in case she met Sister Thomas, who would ask her about Gibney's and about Una. It occurred to her that in any other century, Sister Thomas would have been burned as a witch.

In the afternoon before going to the golf club she went to get her hair washed and set. She would wear a woollen dress with a cardigan over it and take her winter coat in case there was a walk from the car park to the clubhouse.

'Seamus is delighted you are coming with us,' Una said when she collected her. 'The Gibneys are among the bank's best customers and he thinks very highly of William Gibney Senior. He says he has a real business brain. The sons are going to make big changes and Seamus is very impressed with them too. Seemingly, the whole place is completely overstaffed. Did you know that? Seamus says that cuts in the wage bill will make things more efficient.'

Seamus was in the clubhouse waiting for them. He ordered drinks.

'It's been a bad day all round,' he said when he came back. 'I hit into the rough on the third hole and it might have been wiser to walk away.'

He was tall and red-faced. His accent, Nora thought, was from the midlands. He spoke to her as though he had always known her. This must be useful, she imagined, for someone who worked in a bank and moved from town to town.

Soon they were joined by two other men, one of whom had a chemist shop in the town. Nora had been in his shop but had never spoken to him before.

'I could have been luckier on the fifth hole,' he said. 'I mean, if I had placed the ball better. I think there was a wind.'

'Oh, I noticed that all right,' the other man said. 'It was not as calm as it looked.'

'I think I got the measure of it after the fifth hole,' the chemist said. 'And then the birdie on the eighth hole was the making of me.'

He looked at Nora and Una as though they had been involved in the game too.

'You know,' he went on, 'I always say that this is the best time of the year for a good round of golf. If it's dry, I mean.'

'And it stayed dry, did it?' Una asked.

'I should have called it a day on the third hole, hail, rain or shine,' Seamus said.

'Christy O'Connor himself would not have been able to edge the ball out of there,' the chemist said.

'But there must be a way of doing it,' Seamus said. 'There was an iron I used to have when I lived in Castlebar and that might have done the trick. It was light, you know, with a terrific swing.'

'Could you replace that?' Una asked.

'I lost it in a game of poker,' Seamus replied. 'And the fellow who won it went on to win the club championship that year and the year after.'

The chemist went to the bar to get a round of drinks.

'I prefer here to Rosslare, do you?' Seamus asked the other man. 'I like a well-designed nine-hole golf course. Some people swear by Rosslare, and they might be right at the weekend when there's a crowd down. But there's nothing like a quiet weekday here.'

'Were there many playing?' Una asked.

'Few enough. There was a ladies' foursome. I don't know who they were. That's what being in a new town does for you. Do you play yourself?' he asked Nora.

'No,' Nora replied.

'Ah, it's a great game. It's not just the exercise, but it's a way of getting to know a town. You can tell a town by its golf club.'

When the chemist came back with the drinks, Una excused herself to go to the bathroom. Nora followed her.

'It would be lovely if you could stick it out a bit longer,' Una said.

'Don't worry about me,' Nora said. 'When Maurice was alive I used to have to listen to them all talking about Fianna Fáil, and it got worse at election time, and it's nice and relaxing because you don't have to pay any attention.'

What she had wanted to say was that this was the sort of conversation that Maurice had despised all of his life, despised almost as much as she did now. For a second it seemed as though Una were going to be offended by her suggesting that she didn't need to pay attention, but then Una smiled as she looked into the mirror.

'I know what you mean,' she said.

Later in the night, a man and a woman who was introduced as his fiancée joined the company. Slowly, Nora realized that this was Elizabeth's Ray. It took Ray a bit longer to figure out who she was.

'She talks a lot about you,' Ray said. 'She says you are the quickest worker of anyone she's ever seen. It might be better if she didn't know I was out tonight. I mean, it might be better if you didn't mention it.'

'Elizabeth and I have plenty of other things to talk about,' Nora said.

'Well, she's not short of talk. I'd say that for her.'

'She's very efficient at work,' Nora said in a tone that she hoped would put an end to this conversation. 'Very much her father's daughter.'

'She's a marvellous girl,' Ray said and took a sip of his pint.

'You know, when I said I was coming here tonight, Elizabeth said that she might look in later if she has the time,' Nora said. 'She has a very busy social life, as you know.'

It was untrue. She had not mentioned anything to Elizabeth, but she wanted to see what would happen now. She was pleased when Ray appeared alarmed and looked around him as though checking where the exits were.

In the morning she was surprised to find Elizabeth at work before she was.

'A little bird who was in the golf club last night,' Elizabeth said, 'told me that you had a long conversation with Ray.'

Nora was sure that none of the Gibneys had been in the golf club. She could not think who else might have told Elizabeth.

'He phoned me himself,' Elizabeth said. 'First thing this morning. He had told me he wanted to have an early night when I was all set to go out. But he said no. And then Seamus phoned him and told him he was terrified of meeting you and he wanted support.'

'Terrified of meeting me? No, he was not!'

'That's what Ray said. He said that your sister had told Seamus that he was not to talk golf to you, that he was to think of something more sensible to discuss as you were highly intelligent. And then Seamus got so nervous that golf is all he talked about and you now think he is a total gobshite.'

'A gobshite?' Nora had never heard Elizabeth use such a word before. 'I'm sure he's very nice,' she said. 'But I'm glad to hear he was terrified. He has a funny way of showing it, mind you.'

Elizabeth did not suspect that Ray had, in fact, been in the golf club with his fiancée, but, as she began the morning's work, Nora saw no reason to tell her.

As Christmas approached, Nora was relieved to hear that Una was going to spend Christmas Day with Catherine and then the days afterwards with Seamus. The idea of having to entertain Una and Seamus in the company of Jim and Margaret was more than she was ready for. She did not know if Jim, during his days as a rebel, had tried to blow up the golf club but she was sure that he had his sights on some of its more prominent members. And Seamus's account of the progress of one of his games of golf would not be entertained with any enthusiasm by Jim.

There was much excitement when Fiona and Aine came home for the holidays; they both had been invited to parties, and went out with their friends to a lounge bar in the town. When Nora protested that Aine was too young for lounge bars and needed, in any case, to study her Latin, Aine responded sharply, wondering if she and Fiona, after their hard term's studying, were to be confined to the back room with Nora and Donal and Conor and the TV set. It left Nora silent. Aine had never spoken to her like this before and she was almost amused. On one of the nights when she heard the girls coming in at four, she was tempted to go downstairs and find out where they had been, but instead decided to go back to sleep and ask them the next day when she came home from work.

On the Sunday before Christmas she invited Jim and Margaret to tea. As soon as they arrived, Margaret went into the front room to talk to Donal, as she usually did, leaving Nora to deal with Jim, who hardly responded to her efforts at making conversation. He brightened up, however, when he saw Fiona and Aine.

Nora could not remember how the conversation about Northern Ireland developed. She knew that Aine was in the debating society in school and had seen her speak once, but she did not think that they had debates about politics.

'There's a girl in school,' Aine said, 'who has a cousin in Newry and she says it's a disgrace. I don't know how we let it happen. I think a society that lets that happen has a lot to answer for.'

'It was funny,' Jim said, 'when I was interned in the Curragh, we didn't like the Limerick fellows first because they wanted to organize a soccer league, but then we saw that they didn't mean any harm. We never got used to the Northerners, though. It was the Northerners who stood out.'

'But that's just prejudice,' Aine said. 'A country like Ireland is too small to be divided.'

When Margaret came into the room she asked what they were talking about.

'Northern Ireland, if you don't mind,' Nora said. 'As if we don't have enough of it on the television.'

'Oh, God,' Margaret said. 'We went there on a bus tour. I don't know what part of the North we were in but the people threw stones at the bus. I was delighted when we got back safely over the border. A crowd of Protestants, I'd say.'

On Christmas Eve, Una dropped off the presents to the house before going to Kilkenny. She had bought Fiona and Aine the same expensive make-up she was wearing herself and the two girls were busy all afternoon trying on the make-up and choosing clothes for Fiona to wear on a date that evening that Nora, as she prepared things for the next day, was not supposed to know about.

When Jim and Margaret arrived with presents for the children, Donal and Conor had to go to Margaret's car to help carry the packages. It took everyone a while to spot that there was nothing for Donal except a Selection Box. Nora noticed that Margaret sounded oddly nervous as she explained.

'Well, it will be a nice surprise for everyone,' she said.

'But what is it, Aunt Margaret?' Fiona asked.

'I know,' Conor said.

'Tell us,' Aine said.

'It's a darkroom,' he said.

Over the previous months, it emerged, Margaret had converted the small storeroom off the corridor between her kitchen and bathroom into a darkroom. When Nora discovered that this involved the installing of cold running water and a sink as well as equipment, she realized that Margaret and Jim had gone to considerable expense. This was what was happening in the front room as Margaret stopped by each time to have a talk with Donal. He had worked on her sympathy enough for her to decide, without consulting Nora, who would have prevented it, to build him a special room where he could develop photographs. Fiona and Aine were as puzzled as she was by what had happened. Later, when the boys had gone to bed, and Fiona had gone out on her date, Aine asked Nora if she had really not known about the darkroom.

'He could grow out of that interest,' Aine said. 'And what would Margaret do with her darkroom then?'

'They talk all the time and he must have told her that was what he wanted,' Nora said.

'No one has a darkroom in their house,' Aine said.

'Well, Donal has one now,' Nora said, 'and it will be a good excuse for leaving his own house. Maybe that's what he needs to do as much as anything else.'

Chapter Ten

After much argument, she had finally been granted a second pension, and both pensions had been increased in the previous year's
budget. She had not been aware at first that the extra money had
been backdated by six months and she was surprised to get cheques
in the post for what she thought were large sums of money. When
she mentioned this to Jim and Margaret, Jim responded by saying
that Charlie Haughey had been a hard-working Minister for Justice
though a terrible Minister for Agriculture, but, if he could keep his
head, he would go down in the books as a great Minister for
Finance.

She remembered years before being in the hallway of Dr Ryan's
house in Delgany with Maurice. It was an engagement party for Dr
Ryan's daughter. Dr Ryan was Minister for Finance then. She was
surprised by the opulence of the house itself, and the fact that wait-
ers and caterers had been hired. All of the guests, except those who
had come from Wexford, wore evening clothes. Dr Ryan exuded a
sort of nobility and she was surprised at how Maurice and Shay
Doyle, who had also come from Enniscorthy with them, seemed
cowed and nervous in his presence. As they stood by the Minister in
all his considered grace in the hallway they became less than themselves. She was surprised too at the ease with which the Minister
dismissed Haughey, saying he was a young pup in too big a hurry,
with no roots in Fianna Fáil.

'He joined us because we were in power,' she remembered Dr
Ryan saying, 'and that is all he wants, power.'

She remembered the silence in the car for the first half-hour as
they drove home, and then, a few days later, the gravity with which
Maurice imparted what the Minister had said to Jim. She noticed
afterwards, when the subject of politics came up with others, including Catherine and Mark, or her Aunt Josie, Maurice never repeated

what he had heard from Dr Ryan, or alluded to it. It was private information and was not to be shared.

Only one other time had she seen Maurice cowed like that. It was a meeting of a Catholic lay group in the town, with Dr Sherwood of St Peter's College in the chair, when some theologian spoke about change in the church. He then insisted that the power of the church itself took precedence and came before all other powers, including law, or politics, or human rights. For members of the church, he said, the church must come first not merely in religious questions but in all questions. This did not mean, he said, that it was the only power and that civil law did not matter, but it was the primary power. Nora nudged Maurice when it came to the time for questions and comments because she knew that he did not agree with what the theologian had said, as she certainly did not. But standing up in public to question a theologian was not something he would do. She never forgot the look on Maurice's face, not only puzzled or powerless, but also intimidated, as he had been by Dr Ryan in the hallway in Delgany.

While Jim spoke warmly of Haughey's prospects, she knew that he actually disapproved of him, as he did of most of the young ministers. She herself liked Haughey, or what she knew of him; she admired his ambition and his interest in changing things. She liked him even more now when she read his latest budget speech and saw that he mentioned widows. Once more he increased the pension, also backdating the increase. If she had known that these increases were going to come, she thought, she might not have sold the house in Cush. Once the latest backdated money arrived, she decided she would put it into the account in the bank where she had put some of the money she got for the house in Cush, but she did not know what she would do with it.

When Jim and Margaret came to visit, she spoke of Haughey again. Jim was not impressed.

'Courting popularity, that's all he is doing now, and I saw a picture of him up on a horse, like a lord.'

'Oh, that was ridiculous all right,' Margaret said.

'Nothing good will come of him,' Jim said.

'Well, he's the only politician I know who has bothered about widows,' Nora said.

'Jim heard about him in Courtown,' Margaret said.

'Drinking champagne,' Jim said, 'and ordering more, with all sorts of Flash Harrys and builders and barristers and fellows on the make. And everyone watching him. Like a big performance it was.'

'I have no problem with him enjoying himself,' Nora said.

If Maurice were here now, he would defend Haughey, she thought. Unlike Jim, he had thought it was wrong that men in their seventies should be in positions of power in a country and he supported change.

Jim tapped the arm of the chair with the index finger of his right hand and whistled under his breath. He was not used to women disagreeing with him, and she smiled at the thought that he might, if he was to continue visiting her house, have to learn to tolerate it.

One evening in March she answered a knock to the door herself and saw a man whom she recognized as the lorry driver in Gibney's who had spoken about the riots in Derry. As she invited him into the front room, she thought for a moment that something had happened to one of the children and went through them in her mind one by one. Donal was down in Margaret's developing photographs, Conor was in the back room. It was unlikely that this man would know Fiona or Aine, or indeed Una or Margaret or Jim. He seemed nervous.

'I don't think I know your name,' she said.

'I'm Mick Sinnott. I knew your father well. We were neighbours in the Ross Road. And the bossman, Mr Webster, God rest him, taught me.'

'You knew my father?'

'It was years ago all right. There wouldn't be many left who knew him. We were in and out of one another's houses. It was that way.'

Suddenly, he was at ease, but she could not think why he had come to the house.

'And what can I do for you?' She tried not to sound too imperious.

'I'll tell you now. The others told me I was not to come up, but

144

it was only when I went home and told my own missus and we discussed it. You see, the whole staff of Gibney's, barring a few, are joining the Irish Transport and General Workers' Union and we are going to do it in secret tomorrow night in Wexford town. If they find out about it, they'll stop it, they'll divide us, make better offers to people who won't be able to say no. The others thought that they would leave you out of this, seeing as you are friends with the family and only part-time and new in the place. But I decided I'd let you know. I have seen you all my life. I remember you getting married and everything. Anyway, the long and short of it is that we are all joining the union. And I know you well enough to be sure that you won't say anything to the daughter when you go to work tomorrow, and if you want to come with us, there will be a lift for you, and if you don't, no one will be any the wiser that I spoke to you.'

'What time are you going?'

'We have to be there at eight.'

'Would someone collect me?'

'They would, they would be delighted to.'

'Are all the office workers joining?' she asked.

'All the ones we asked,' he replied.

She said nothing for a moment.

'Do you need time to think?' he asked.

'No, I was wondering how long we'll be down there for.'

'To be honest, none of us have ever done this before, and all I know is that they want every one of us there. They want no one saying they'll join and then telling the Gibneys that they didn't really mean it.'

'That's fine,' she said. 'I'll get someone to look after the boys.'

'I wasn't suggesting that you would be one of the ones who would say one thing and mean another,' he said.

'I know you weren't.'

'Your father would be proud of us now. He had no time for the bosses of this town. He wasn't a diehard or anything, but he was decent.'

'I was the oldest, so I remember him best,' she said and smiled.

'He would be eighty this year if he were alive. That's hard to imagine, isn't it?'

'It is all right,' he replied.

'So I'll be here tomorrow at half seven waiting.'

'There will be some of them surprised when I tell them that. We tried to do it years ago, just a few of us, and the old fellow threatened to sack us. He said he'd close the place and we had to back down because we had no support. But with this son of his, the efficiency expert, and the idea that no one's job is safe, then I think we have support this time. And there's a great man in Wexford by the name of Howlin, Brendan Corish's right-hand man. I know that's not your party now, but there could be changes coming, that's what they say. Anyway, this man in Wexford will make the Gibneys mind their manners, especially the little pup.'

Nora opened the door for him.

'I'll see you tomorrow, missus,' he said as he went down the steps.

When he had gone, Nora felt light, almost happy for a moment. There was something about Mick Sinnott's tone – how oddly confident he was, and talkative, and how perfect his manners were – that reminded her of years before, years when she was young and went to dances. But it was not just that, it was the idea that she had made a decision for herself, the idea that she had asked no one's advice. It was the first time since she had sold the house in Cush that such a chance had come so easily, and she was glad she had taken it. Perhaps it was not wise; perhaps it made more sense to be grateful to the Gibneys. But it pleased her now to be grateful to no one.

She arranged with Donal and Conor once more that they would not need a babysitter and that Donal would be home from Aunt Margaret's by seven.

She did not know what to wear and thought it was funny that no one, certainly not her sisters, or her daughters, or her aunt, would be able to advise her on how to dress at a meeting of the Irish Transport and General Workers' Union. Dowdy, she thought. Clothes that no one would notice.

As she walked down the stairs wearing a plain skirt and blouse and a warm pullover, she liked the idea of how little the Gibneys could imagine what was happening. She was not sure that being a member of a trade union would make any difference to anyone working in Gibney's, and the family would, in time, get used to it. But the fact that it was done behind their backs would irritate them, maybe even shock them. Peggy Gibney, she thought, would never speak to her again when she heard that she was part of it, and that gave her a strange satisfaction.

She had thought it would be Mick Sinnott himself who would collect her and was surprised when the knock came to the door and it was Walk-Like-a-Duck. And waiting in the back seat of the car was the young bookkeeper who had been told by Miss Kavanagh to cut up the files.

On the journey to Wexford, she was surprised by how much they seemed to dislike the Gibneys, especially Thomas and Elizabeth.

'He follows us everywhere,' Walk-Like-a-Duck complained. 'One day I had to take in orders in Blackwater and Kilmuckridge and then in Riverchapel and then in Gorey. So since it was a nice summer's day I brought Rita and the kids with me and the plan was to leave them in Morriscastle and then call for them at the end of the day and have a dip myself. As we were driving through The Ballagh I noticed a car right behind me and who was in it but Thomas Gibney and he followed me the whole way. He never mentioned it when he saw me, but that's what he spent the day doing.'

'And Elizabeth,' the young bookkeeper said, 'never even looks at us, let alone speaks to us.'

'I find her very nice to work with,' Nora said.

'I don't mind Miss Kavanagh at all,' the bookkeeper said. 'I mean it takes time to get used to her. She knows every detail of what happens in the office, and she never forgets anything. You know, she was going to be an accountant, and then her father died and she had to come home.'

'No,' Nora said, 'she has always been in Gibney's. She was there when I worked there before.'

'Yes, but she got a placement in Dublin when she had been in Gibney's a while, and she spent a year there, but then she had to come home. And her mother is still alive and she has to mind her.'

'I didn't know that,' Nora said.

'My father,' the bookkeeper went on, 'works for the Armstrongs, and he says it's better to work for Protestants. But I don't know. The Armstrongs said that if their crowd joined a union, they'd close up and leave the town. I don't think the Gibneys will do that.'

Nora was sorry that she had not asked Mick Sinnott where the meeting in Wexford was going to be held. She could have driven there herself. She realized that the other two would like to say more about the Gibneys but felt restrained because Nora shared an office with Elizabeth and seemed to be on good terms with the rest of the family. It occurred to her that it was a mistake coming down here like this. Yet it had felt so right in the moment she decided to do it. She liked that Mick Sinnott had wanted to include her; it would have been impossible to say no. But now she wondered if it was not wrong, and if it might not appear wrong to most people. If she needed to join a union, she could have done so at a later stage. It should have been easy to agree that since she was new and only part-time she should wait. She felt as they neared Wexford that their joining a trade union would do them no good at all; it would give them courage, or make them feel bellicose, but it would probably cause nothing but trouble in the end. She wished she could go home now, but she could hardly ask Walk-Like-a-Duck or anyone else to drive her back to Enniscorthy before the meeting began.

The hall on the quay was half-full when they arrived. As soon as she came in, she felt that people were watching her. Working in the room with Elizabeth had isolated her, and she did not even know the names of some of the people who worked in the office. The decision to come here would have taken Maurice two weeks to consider. He would have discussed it with her and then with Jim. Nothing, from the buying of the house to the date each year when they went to Cush, was ever decided quickly or easily. And it was not just Maurice. Most people, she believed, needed time to think before they made decisions. Probably everyone in this hall had weeks to think about whether they wanted to join the union or not. She had made the decision in one second, and now she saw it as an act of pure foolishness. For a moment she wondered how she was going to explain it to Maurice, and thought how puzzled he would be by what she had done. And then as she remembered in a flash that she had no one to whom she would have to explain herself, she felt relief.

After a while, Nora moved closer to the front, sitting with other women who worked in the office so that no one would think she was there as a spy. With a Wexford town accent, a man was explaining that they were living in a time of newfangled ideas, with management training and the arrival in offices and companies of so-called efficiency experts, people who knew next to nothing about business and nothing at all about labour relations. For the bosses, he said, the old ways were changing, but for the trade union movement the same priorities remained, as anyone who was a member of the Irish Transport and General Workers' Union would know. But the union did not just live on its history, he went on, it depended for its reputation on the work it did day in, day out for its members, both in times of industrial peace and in times of crisis.

'There comes a moment in every crisis where only one thing carries the day,' he said. 'There comes a moment in the battle with employers when brute force and ignorance carry the day.'

Nora looked at him and listened. She imagined how interested Maurice would have been in this gathering and in the speech. But then she thought of Elizabeth Gibney, the person she spent most time with now. She imagined what a good imitation Elizabeth would do of this man and how funny she would find the phrase 'brute force and ignorance'.

Everyone around her was listening intently; there was applause when the man had finished and agreement that they would form a line and one by one sign their names and become members of the Irish Transport and General Workers' Union.

The following morning everything was quiet in the office. It was clear from Elizabeth that she knew nothing about what had happened the night before in Wexford. She was in good humour all morning and discussed plans to go with Roger to a rugby weekend in Paris in the autumn.

'It will keep him out of harm's way if I'm there. He gets terrible hangovers, the poor mite. And if we go two days before the match I can do plenty of shopping in all the fab places.'

The next morning Elizabeth arrived late and was wearing dark glasses.

'I suppose you heard the news,' she said. 'No one slept in our house last night. Old William is fit to be tied. He started by blaming Fianna Fáil until Little William told him that the union was affiliated to the Labour Party, at which point he started to blame Thomas for bringing down newfangled ideas from Dublin. Thomas, of course, remained calm, which is always a mistake with Old William. That's why he loves Francie-Pants so much, because she creates hysterics. Thomas told him that he would halve the office staff in the next few years and he slowly started to name all the methods he would use until Old William said that he had heard enough. He threatened to sell the firm and move to Dublin and live in Dartry. He said that the buildings alone and all the assets would make a tidy sum. He has a cousin in Dartry and he thinks it's a haven of peace and quiet. And that might have been it, until Little William, my darling brother, said that we would have to get advice about how to deal with the Bolsheviks. That made me laugh so much that my mother said that she was going to close the kitchen if there was any more trouble. And that made Old William worse. He explained how he could make twice the money if he sold the firm, especially the milling part, and invested the proceeds, and that the only reason he didn't was loyalty to all the people who worked in the firm and loyalty to the town. He said that he literally felt stabbed in the back and then he named the ringleaders. Seemingly, there's a very nasty piece of work called Mick Sinnott who's a lorry driver from the Ross Road. He's a lout. Old William was pale at this stage and said that he didn't care if Mother closed the kitchen. And then Thomas said that he would personally sack this Mick Sinnott in the morning and make an example of him and make phone calls to ensure that no one else would take him on. "I'll grind him into the ground," he said. At that point, Little William said that it was not the end of the world, plenty of companies dealt with trade unions. But all Old William could say was that they were curs, every one of them. He said that he would not deal with any union and that was the end of that. Thomas then wanted to get the keys to Mick Sinnott's lorry and move it before he came to work in the morning, but Little William told him not to be a fool. Later in the night, my mother used a word that we didn't know she knew. She used it to describe all the people of the town.'

Nora thought of interrupting Elizabeth to say that she too had been at the meeting in Wexford and had signed her name with the rest of them. She wondered how Elizabeth would react when she found out, thinking that maybe Elizabeth was taking a light view of the matter. But, later in the morning, when she heard her speaking on the phone to Roger, she realized how Elizabeth really felt.

'They did it behind his back,' she said. 'They went down like rats in the night, and, no, he didn't sleep at all, he kept walking up and down the stairs and coming into my room and into Thomas's room and Little William's room, and wondering how it could have happened, how no one at all warned him or any of us about it. There was no loyalty, he said, and if it wasn't for my brothers he would just close the place, having built it up to twice the size it was when he got it from his father. He kept saying it would be a great moment to sell. This morning my mother said to me that the whole thing has broken his heart. He doesn't want to see the place ever again. He has known some of the staff for forty years and some of them have been with the company even longer. They all stabbed him in the back. My mother has a friend a nun, an old bat called Sister Thomas, and I had to phone her and ask her to come over, that is how bad things are.'

As she was leaving for the day at one o'clock Nora came face to face with Thomas Gibney, who stopped and looked at her. His expression suggested cold rage. She knew that it would not be long before Elizabeth and the rest of the Gibneys discovered that she was among those who had betrayed them.

Chapter Eleven

The town had become easier. In Court Street, or John Street, or on the Back Road, no one stopped her any more to express sympathy, no one stood looking into her eyes waiting for her to reply. If she met someone now and they stopped, it was to discuss other things. Sometimes, as they were ready to part, they would ask her how she was, or how the boys were, and this would be a way of quietly acknowledging what had happened. But even still she became nervous when she saw someone coming towards her ready to remind her of her loss. It was at times intrusive and hurtful.

Sunday Mass was the worst. No matter where she sat in the cathedral, people looked at her with special sympathy, or moved to make space for her, or waited for her outside to talk. When this became too much for her, when every eye she caught seemed destined to upset her, she went back to the small chapel in St John's or went to eight o'clock Mass in the morning when the cathedral was only half-full. She could choose her place and then leave at the end without being waylaid.

One day she was coming out of Barry's in Court Street, having bought a new set of batteries for the transistor radio that she liked to keep by her bed now. She was thinking about Fiona listening to Radio Caroline and Radio Luxembourg at weekends when she saw Jim Mooney, who had been a colleague of Maurice's, coming towards her. He lived on his own or with a brother out in the countryside, as he had done all the years since he came back from the seminary without being ordained. Maurice had never liked him; it had, she thought, something to do with his refusal to join the teachers' union, but she was not sure. Unlike most of those who worked with Maurice, Jim Mooney had not written to her when he died.

'Well, I was just thinking about you,' he said.

'How are you?' she asked. She tried to sound formal.

'I was nearly going to call up to you.'

She said nothing. She did not want him to call.

'I asked them in the staffroom what to do, but none of us was sure.'

She wondered if Maurice had disliked his tone, which was both sharp and insinuating, as much as she did now.

'He's a right little brat, that Donal,' he said. 'He sits at the back of the class with a face on him. One day, when I checked, he didn't even have the textbook open. He was reading some other book. Another day, he gave me a very impertinent back answer. I don't know what we're going to do about him.'

Nora was about to say something but then thought better of it.

'In some families,' he went on, 'the boys get all the brains. But in yours the girls got the brains as well as the young fellow Conor, who I hear is very clever. And I hear that the girls are diligent as well. Diligence is a great help.'

The way he said the word 'diligence', like a word in a sermon he was giving, almost made her smile. She wondered what it was that had caused him to leave Maynooth before his ordination.

'I thought if I met you, I'd say it to you. I'm not the only one with complaints about Donal,' he said.

She tried to think of something to say that would silence him. All she could do, however, was look at him; she was angry at how meek she must seem to him.

'So what subjects does he do with you?'

'He does Science and Latin.'

She nodded.

'But it hardly matters what class he's in. He has a bad way about him. Something lacking in the manners department as well as in the brains department.'

'Well, thank you very much for letting me know,' she said, pronouncing each word carefully. She began to ease past him.

'Good day to you, now,' he said.

No one had ever complained about Donal before. Even when she worried about his stammer and thought that he might be having problems at school, there were no negative notes written at the bottom of his Christmas report card. He had never come at the top of the class, and there were a few years when his marks had been low, but the results he got in the Primary Certificate exam and the County Council Scholarship had been good. He spent most evenings alone in the front room with his schoolbooks. She supposed that he was studying, but she often wondered if he was looking at his photography books. She did not know what she should do now, was unsure if she should mention to Donal that she had met Jim Mooney, or if she should say nothing.

It was a few days later that she saw Donal approaching on the other side of the road, coming home from school. He did not notice her and appeared weighed down by something; he was deep in his own thoughts, the expression on his face drawn.

When Fiona came at the weekend she nearly told her about the encounter with Jim Mooney, but since Fiona was going out on the Saturday night and spent Saturday morning in bed listening to the radio and Saturday afternoon meeting friends downtown, Nora knew it was best not to burden her. Also, she did not want Fiona to say anything about Donal that might worry her further.

Late on Saturday afternoon, almost as an excuse to get out of the house, Nora went to have her hair done, letting Bernie slowly add some copper dye. When she saw it in the mirror she was unsure about it, even more than she had been about the original dye. But at least, she felt, she had spent time worrying about something other than Donal.

That evening, when one of Fiona's friends called, Fiona was not ready. They were going to the dance in White's Barn. Conor came in to listen to the conversation and Donal also looked in to see who it was but then darted out of the room again. When Fiona appeared in her best dress, wearing hooped earrings and make-up, Donal came into the room once more and sat on the sofa sullenly as the two girls admired each other's clothes and talked to Nora for a minute before leaving.

When they had gone, Nora turned to Donal.

'I met Jim Mooney during the week,' she said.

'He's a b-big eejit,' Donal said.

'He says you're not paying enough attention in the class.'

'I hate him. He's a c-cretin.'

'He's a teacher in the school.'

Donal began to stammer badly and then tried to stop himself but he was agitated. 'If his house b-burned d-down, it'd b-be g-great news. Or if he d-drowned.'

'It might be better if you paid attention in the class,' Nora said.

On Thursday when Margaret came to visit, she stopped in the front room to talk to Donal. And then when Margaret joined Nora in the back room she spoke about how funny Donal was, and how clever. Nora resisted the urge to say that she did not find Donal funny and Jim Mooney did not find him clever. Margaret spoke of the hours Donal was spending in the darkroom and the techniques he was using to develop film. Nora did not tell her that he had never once shown her any of the photographs that he developed in the darkroom Margaret had created for him.

Nora tired easily of Margaret's simple good cheer; it made her wish she could take out a book or unfold that day's *Irish Times*. It was a relief when Jim arrived on those evenings and she could go to the kitchen and make tea for them and then ensure that the boys were in bed and the light off in their bedroom.

And when they stood up to go, she felt glad that she would finally have the room to herself. In the hallway, however, as she said good-night to them, she became sharply aware that once she had closed the door on them she would be alone in the house except for the boys, who were asleep, and there was nothing ahead but the night.

Elizabeth never mentioned the union again and gave her no further information about how her father and her brothers, or indeed her mother, were dealing with the new state of affairs. Nora attended one union meeting; it was full of heated discussion over who would be on the committee or hold various positions. She did not attend any more.

Nonetheless, she enjoyed watching Mick Sinnott, who had not been fired, moving around with increasing confidence as the main union representative. And since she had joined the union, she found that everyone who worked in Gibney's spoke to her or smiled at her as they passed. The union made little difference to anyone in the office. Without any protest, the numbers of staff were slowly decreasing. If a girl left to be married she was not replaced but her work divided among others. Thomas became increasingly strict about timekeeping. He watched from the shadows, sending notes to anyone who was late, or who was seen talking, or who made mistakes in their work.

Elizabeth returned to her former good humour and told Nora the story of her weekend plans and her romances as before, but Thomas never spoke to Nora again. He glowered at her when he saw her. She, in turn, walked by him as though he were not there. A few times when he had occasion to come into the office she shared with Elizabeth, however, she enjoyed greeting him warmly, using his first name, as though nothing had happened, but he did not respond. Elizabeth developed the habit of asking Thomas as he came into the room to declare what his business was. If she was speaking loudly to one of her friends on the phone, or telling Nora a long story, they could often see Thomas's shadow lingering outside the frosted-glass panels in the upper part of the door. Nora wondered if he was keeping a file on the two of them as well as on everyone else.

Chapter Twelve

When Nora saw Nancy Brophy walking towards the house, she moved away from the window. She could not think why Nancy would want to call on her. She imagined leaving Nancy to knock and wait and listen, and then knock again before walking down the steps, turning to check the windows for a sign of life. She could feel the sheer relief that would come over her entire spirit if she had the courage to make this happen.

At the first knock, Nora went to the door and opened it and invited Nancy in.

'Now, I hope I'm not disturbing you,' Nancy said, 'and I won't come in, but I wanted to ask you a favour.'

'Well, if there is anything I can do,' Nora said.

'Oh, there is,' Nancy said brightly. 'But don't look so frightened.'

Nora did not know how to respond. Nancy was too cheerful, almost silly as she stood in the hall and grinned at her.

'You know that I do the quiz every year with Phyllis Langdon in the parish halls. It's sponsored by Guinness. She asks the questions and I keep the scores. She has a great voice, doesn't need a microphone or anything, and we work well together because I don't ever make a mistake with the scores.'

Nora could not think why Nancy was telling her all of this as though it were urgent and fascinating news.

'Well, the thing is, I can't do tomorrow night. I have to go to Dublin on the last train today because Bridie, my sister, is in the Bon Secours for an operation. So I thought I'd get a replacement before I'd tell Phyllis, and Betty Farrell said that she heard from someone in Gibney's you're a wizard at the numbers so that's what has me here.'

Nora looked at her gravely.

'Now, don't tell me you can't do it!' Nancy said.

'It would be just for one night?' Nora asked.

'One night,' Nancy said. 'And it would be nice for you to get out among people, to mix a bit.'

'I haven't been out much at all.'

'I know that, Nora.'

By the time Nancy was going, it had been arranged that, unless she heard otherwise, Phyllis Langdon would collect her at seven thirty the following evening. It was only when Nancy was on the front steps that Nora asked her where the quiz was to be held and Nancy told her that it would be in Blackwater.

'I didn't know that they were held so far out of town,' Nora said.

'This year only. It's an experiment,' Nancy said.

As Nora stood at the door watching Nancy disappear, she was tempted to follow her and tell her that she had forgotten she had something else to do, something more pressing than writing down the score at a quiz. She tried to think what that might be, and then decided that it was too late now. As she closed the door, she wished she had asked at the very beginning in which village the quiz would be held. She would have said then that she could not go to Blackwater. It was too near Cush and Ballyconnigar.

She thought of Blackwater in the summer, when people from Dublin or Wexford were staying in the houses around, and it was normal for women to go with their husbands to Etchingham's pub there on a Friday or Saturday night and drink Babycham or brandy and soda, and leave the children in the care of a babysitter or an older child. Often, if it was July and the night was fine, she and Maurice would walk the two miles from Ballyconnigar together and then get a lift home with someone. Or, when August came, and the nights were darker with heavy dew coming early on to the grass of the lane that led from the handball alley to the cliff, she would drive the old Morris Minor and they could relax more knowing that they could leave whenever they liked. Maurice always took pleasure in the company, especially if there were people from Enniscorthy among them, or locals from Blackwater, and gradually then she would come to like the company too, and enjoy watching Maurice in such good humour.

*

She explained to the boys that she was going out. They must promise not to fight with each other, she said, and go to bed at the usual time.

'Maybe we c-can stay up a bit later?' Donal asked.

'I'll let you decide,' Nora said. 'But not too late.'

'Can I decide as well?' Conor asked.

'You can both decide.'

At half past seven Nora was watching from the window as Phyllis Langdon drove up in a red Ford Cortina. Nora was wearing a summer dress and carried a cardigan over her arm in case it grew colder. The boys were in the back room with Fiona, who was also going out.

'I'm going!' she shouted. 'Don't come out now and make a fuss. I'll be back when you're asleep.'

She had met Phyllis Langdon a number of times over the years. Her husband was a vet, and both of them were from Dublin. She noticed how efficiently Phyllis reversed the car, and admired the beautiful rings on Phyllis's fingers as she changed gear and they set off towards Blackwater.

'What's amazing,' Phyllis said, 'is how much they all know about sport and how little they know about anything else. On politics, mind you, they are not too bad, and on geography maybe or even history. But questions about books and music have them all flummoxed. You'd wonder if they went to school at all.'

'And who makes up the questions?' Nora asked.

'Oh, I do all that. I get advice about the sport. We start with easy questions. And they all have quiz books, but I only take a few questions from books just to make them feel that it's worth preparing. Last week in Monageer there was a team and they knew nothing. They didn't even seem embarrassed. If you'd asked them to add two and two, they would have looked as though they were required to explain Einstein.'

'I suppose they joined for the fun of it.'

'Ignorance is bliss,' Phyllis said.

'I'm sure some of them are very nice,' Nora said.

'Oh, nice as you like, and thick as planks.'

They turned right at Finchogue and did not speak again until they were on the other side of The Ballagh. Nora could feel Phyllis's deep seriousness about the task ahead and resolved to make no light remarks about the failure of contestants to answer the questions Phyllis had prepared. She saw now why Nancy Brophy had wanted someone who was good at figures to keep the score.

'By the way,' Phyllis said, 'I have a notebook and some good pens for you. We start with two rounds of two-mark questions that a child could answer. It warms things up and then we go on to two rounds of three-mark questions, then four-mark, and then five rounds of six-mark questions that separate the sheep from the goats. In the first rounds of six only the individual contestant can answer, but in the last rounds of six the whole team can answer.'

'It must take a lot of work, preparing the questions,' Nora said.

'I like to get a variety, and a good team, like the Oylegate team, will spend weeks preparing, reading up on subjects they might not know much about.'

'So it's very educational.'

'For some, and not for others,' Phyllis said severely.

Phyllis had not mentioned Maurice and did not give any hint whether she knew that this was one of Nora's first outings since his death. Nora presumed, however, that Phyllis knew everything, having been alerted by Nancy Brophy, and had decided, out of tact, to say nothing. This meant that she, in turn, did not feel she could say that she knew Blackwater, that she had come here on a bicycle through her teenage years, had met Maurice here in the years before they were married and had spent every summer nearby. She would keep all of this to herself and join with Phyllis in taking the quiz seriously, in making sure that she wrote down the correct scores for each team.

When they arrived, Phyllis said she was surprised that the arrangement was to meet the organizers in Etchingham's pub, that she didn't normally go into pubs, but they would make their way to the hall beside the church as soon as they possibly could. She refused an offer of refreshment for both of them.

'We'll need to keep our wits about us,' she said, 'so we'd like a jug of water and some ice, and two glasses. And we'll have the same on the table in the hall.'

The teams were to be from Blackwater itself and from Kilmuckridge. Nora was busy drawing lines down the centre of the pages of the notebook so she did not see that Tom Darcy from Cush was standing at the bar. Still in his work clothes, he approached their table.

'Nora, what way are you?' he asked.

'Tom, I didn't see you there,' she said. 'Are you in for the quiz?'

'We might stay for the fun,' he said, 'but there again, we might not. Sure we know all the answers, Nora.'

For a moment, Nora was going to introduce Tom to Phyllis, but because of the stiffness she sensed in Phyllis, Nora knew that she did not want to be introduced to a man in his work clothes, with the easy, familiar manner of Tom Darcy.

'How's Mrs Darcy?' Nora asked.

'As right as rain,' he said. 'She'll be delighted when I tell her I met you. Now do I know that woman beside you? I'd like to tell the missus who I met when I was out.'

'Phyllis Langdon, this is Tom Darcy,' Nora said.

Phyllis nodded, but did not offer her hand to Tom.

'Oh, Phyllis Langdon,' he said, 'the woman that asks the questions. She's the terror of Monageer.'

Nora could feel Phyllis beside her recoiling from Tom Darcy, who, in turn, had no intention of returning to the bar until he had ferreted out as much information as possible to take home with him.

'I hear they knew nothing in Monageer,' he said.

It was clear that Tom was addressing himself to Phyllis but she made no reply.

'I heard they were as ignorant as what you might find on the floor of a pigsty and I'm not talking about straw,' he went on.

'And how are they all in Cush?' Nora asked.

'Pulling the devil by the tail, the few that are left,' Tom said. 'I'll tell you one thing now. You are sorely missed. We were just saying that the other day. You were the best of the bathers, you always were.'

'Excuse me now,' Phyllis interrupted, 'but we will have to go up to the hall soon and make sure the contestants know where they are sitting.'

'Sure that crowd from Kilmuckridge wouldn't know their elbow from a hole in the wall,' Tom said. 'Ask them how to spell GAA. That'll put manners on them.'

'Manners?' Phyllis asked pointedly.

'Will you have a drink, the two of you?'

'We will not,' Phyllis said.

Nora watched as Tom walked across to the bar and drew the barman's attention to herself and Phyllis.

'Will you have a Babycham, a sherry or a brandy?' he shouted over.

Nora shook her head and then turned to Phyllis, who was busy checking through the questions. There was a red mark on each of her cheeks that seemed to have emerged during her encounter with Tom Darcy.

The barman came over with a Babycham and a brandy and soda.

'Did we not say that we wanted only water?' Phyllis asked. 'And we don't have time.'

'The customer is the boss here, ma'am,' the barman said. 'And you can bring them up to the hall with you, as long as I get the glasses back.'

'That'll crown you now!' Tom Darcy shouted over.

'Have you known that man for long?' Phyllis asked her.

'I've known him all my life,' she said calmly as she poured the Babycham. 'I'm afraid I can't drink brandy, it has a bad effect on me.'

She smiled to herself at the thought of brandy. When she had married Maurice, she had never had an alcoholic drink. At first, she had tried sherry but didn't like it. One night in this very pub someone had offered her a brandy and then, since she and Maurice had fallen into company, she had had three or four more. By the end of the evening she could not stop laughing. Standing at the bar, with his wife sitting on a barstool, was Frankie Doyle from Enniscorthy. As she looked over at them, she saw that he and his wife thought she was laughing at them. Frankie was small enough to be a jockey, and he might, she thought, have been sensitive about that. And also, he and his wife were alone with each other, they had not been invited to join the larger group who were from Enniscorthy too. In any case, every time she looked up they were watching her, and every time she caught their eye she started laughing again. Nothing could stop her. Since that night neither of them had ever spoken to her. From then on she knew that she could not drink brandy.

'You look as though you are in a world of your own,' Phyllis said.

'I was,' Nora said and smiled.

'We should go now, and I think it would be a mistake to be seen carrying drinks through the village, even though Guinness is the sponsor. This is the last time I will agree to meet in a pub.'

She gulped down the brandy and soda.

The hall, when they arrived, was filling up. Some of the people Nora knew by name, others by sight; and then there were people whom she did not know at all, but their way of standing at the doorway, or close to the wall at the back, or looking around them, had something familiar about it; it was both shy and at ease, both friendly and reserved. It made her feel that she knew them as well as she had ever known anyone here.

As the teams identified themselves, Phyllis grew more authoritative. She stood up regularly to make sure that the space between their table and the seats where the contestants would sit was being kept clear, and then insisted that no one could loiter close to the contestants during the quiz to prompt them.

There were three men and one woman on each team. As Phyllis explained the rules, she produced from her bag a stopwatch that she set to sound after ten seconds. Nora studied the contestants. One of the men she knew from Blackwater was a retired teacher and the woman beside him had been on a committee of the Irish Country-women's Association. The next in line looked to her like a schoolboy, and the last, she supposed, was a farmer. As Phyllis spoke, an atmosphere of solemnity came over the contestants. It was, Nora thought, as though the priest had come out on to the altar or the teacher had arrived in the classroom.

The first questions were so simple they were almost insulting. Phyllis asked them, however, as though they were challenging and would require much jogging of memory. Her voice was like that of a continuity announcer on the radio, and it had, when she pronounced certain words, an English edge to it. Nora saw how easy it was going to be to keep the score, but noticed also that Phyllis kept a supervisory eye on what she was writing down during the second and third rounds as the scores started to vary.

As she came to the four-mark questions, a man produced another brandy and soda for Phyllis and another Babycham for her. She had no idea who had bought these drinks as Tom Darcy had not followed them to the hall.

By the time the six-mark questions began, the Blackwater team was slightly ahead. In a round of sports questions, there were cheers from the body of the hall when some of them pertained to the GAA. This caused Phyllis to demand silence for the next round, questions about classical music.

'How many symphonies did Brahms compose?' Phyllis asked.

Nora watched the man from Kilmuckridge. He bided his time, as though he were trying to remember something he once knew. When Phyllis announced that she was activating the stopwatch, he said, 'Twenty-five.'

Phyllis looked contemptuously around the hall, leaving a silence. Nora looked down at the score sheet.

'As everyone knows,' Phyllis said, 'Brahms wrote four symphonies. Twenty-five indeed!'

There was a hush at the next question.

'How many symphonies did Schumann write?'

It was the turn of the retired schoolteacher from Blackwater.

'I'll guess nine,' he said quietly.

'Wrong,' Phyllis said. 'He wrote four.'

She took them then through Haydn, Mozart, Schubert, Mahler, Sibelius and Bruckner to stunned silence as each name was called out and each contestant failed to guess the correct number of symphonies. When she listed operas and asked them for the name of the composer, both the retired teacher and the young man from the Blackwater team knew the answers. This put Blackwater ahead by fifteen points as she came to the last rounds, when the contestants could consult with each other. When one of them asked for a toilet break, Phyllis agreed. Another brandy and soda and Babycham arrived on the table.

When Nora looked over towards the door, she noticed that a few men had gathered there. They were looking at herself and Phyllis with suspicion and resentment. One of them, a young man with sandy hair and a sunburned face, glanced back at his associates when he saw that Nora was watching him. As he approached her, he appeared personally aggrieved.

'She has a quare big grand voice, that one,' he said, nodding towards Phyllis. 'I hope shc's not thinking of driving through Kilmuckridge tonight because there are a few lads are sore enough at her, and the voice on her. She thinks she's someone, I'll say that for her.'

Nora looked away and did not reply.

'I'll tell you now,' he said to another man, 'she'd get a big fright if someone stuck one of her symphonies up her hole. She wouldn't be asking questions then.'

Phyllis whispered to Nora that they should proceed with the quiz as soon as they could.

'Now, cvcrybody,' she shouted, 'get ready for the last exciting rounds. Mrs Webster will give us the score so far.'

The man continued to hover until Phyllis turned her full attention on him.

'I'm afraid you are in the way,' she said. 'There's no reason for you to stand so close. Could you go back and sit down?'

The man hesitated and then gave her a look of pure contempt before he went back to his friends at the doorway.

One of the Kilmuckridge contestants had obviously prepared for this round of questions, about the Prime Ministers and Presidents of various countries. He was able to give the names of the Prime Ministers of both Norway and Sweden. It was when the team was asked the name of the Prime Minister of the Soviet Union, and they agreed first on Brezhnev and then changed to Podgorny, that the problems arose.

'Which is it?' Phyllis asked.

They consulted for a while until Phyllis set the stopwatch.

'It's Podgorny,' one of them said.

'I'm afraid you are wrong with both of your answers. The Premier of the Soviet Union is Kosygin.'

'You asked the name of the Prime Minister,' one of them said.

'And that is Kosygin.'

'You just said he is the Premier.'

'And that is the same as Prime Minister. And my decision is final, I'm afraid. You can argue all you like. Now, the next question.'

As murmurs came from all around, Phyllis raised her voice.

'I will have no more interruptions,' she said.

Nora concentrated on the score sheet and was afraid to look up. By the end of the round, since the Blackwater team had failed to answer some of the questions, there were only three points between the teams. It was clear to Nora, and she presumed to many in the hall, that if the Soviet Union answer had been allowed, then Kilmuckridge would be ahead. In the last round, which focused on famous battles, each team managed to answer every question correctly. By the time the quiz ended, Nora had the score sheet totted up. Blackwater had won by three points. Phyllis got to her feet and demanded silence again and read out the result in an imperious voice. Before she had even time to sit down, a man emerged from the crowd and moved towards her. He was wearing a cap and a check jacket.

'Where are you from?' he asked Phyllis aggressively.

'What has it to do with you?' she replied.

'You're not even from Enniscorthy,' he said. 'You're a blow-in. And you've no right to push your weight around down here.'

'Maybe it's time you went home,' Phyllis said.

'At least I know where my home is.'

'You robbed us!' another man shouted. 'That's all there is to it.'

Just then, Tom Darcy emerged from the crowd.

'Myself and a friend of mine from just outside Kilmuckridge would like to invite you two ladies for a drink in Etchingham's to thank you for your hard work.'

'We should go with him,' Nora said to Phyllis, and was relieved when she agreed.

'Are you Maurice Webster's wife?' the man with Tom Darcy asked when they arrived in the bar.

For a second, she was unsure if the man knew that Maurice was dead.

'I knew him well,' the man added.

Nora looked across to find that Phyllis, with a full glass of brandy and soda in her hand, was talking animatedly to Tom Darcy.

'You knew him years ago?' she asked.

'It was when he came down with his brother and a few others. We went out fishing. Is that brother still in the land of the living?'

'He is,' Nora said.

'And there was a delicate one that died?'

'That's right.'

'And did Margaret, the sister, ever marry?'

'No, she didn't.'

'She was a nice woman, liked by everybody.'

He sipped his drink and looked at Nora.

'I was sorry to hear about Maurice anyway. Lord, we were all very sorry to hear that down here.'

'Thank you for saying that.'

'You'd never know what way life goes. Some of it makes no sense at all.'

They stood at the counter in silence.

'Would you like a better drink than that?' the man asked her eventually.

Nora looked at her Babycham and hesitated.

'I hear it's awful stuff,' the man said. 'A vodka and a white lemonade would be better for you. That's what my missus and the daughter drink nowadays when they go out.'

He ordered her a vodka and white lemonade and poured it for her when it came. She saw that the group of men who had been standing close to the door of the hall were here now and ordering drinks; the bar was filling up after the quiz and there was a brightness in the atmosphere. Something unusual had occurred that had lifted the evening, given people something to talk about. In their liveliness, the men in the bar looked more like a group coming from a hurling or a football match.

Phyllis stayed talking to Tom Darcy, who would have plenty to tell his wife about when he went home. Soon, they were joined by a number of other men, who spoke to Phyllis as though they knew her. Phyllis joined in the discussion and she nodded at remarks made and looked from one man to another. Because her husband was a vet, Nora thought, then she must be used to the company of farmers and knew when to drop her imperious tone. Or maybe it was the brandy.

None of the men would allow Phyllis or Nora to buy a round of drinks, and each time they bought a round for themselves they included a brandy and soda for Phyllis and a vodka and white lemonade for Nora.

When Nora saw Phyllis signalling towards the door, she spotted that Tim Hegarty and his wife, Philomena, were coming in. Tim was a teacher whom Maurice had been to school with. She knew that he and his wife roamed the countryside at the weekend in search of company but she could not think what they were doing in Blackwater. They had two of their children with them. Nora could tell by the expression on Phyllis's face that she disapproved of them.

Tim was famous for his good looks and his singing voice. His wife sang with him when she was not too drunk, and once, at a concert in the Mercy Convent where Nora had been, the entire family of parents and six or seven children played the von Trapp family in *The Sound of Music*. Everyone said that they could have been professional musicians if only Tim and Philomena could stop drinking.

There was a call for silence from the bar. She could see Tim Hegarty standing alone with his eyes closed. His hair was oiled and he wore a thin bow-tie and a striped white and red jacket. He looked like an American film star. Still without opening his eyes, he put his head back and sang in a soft voice but loud enough so that he could be heard all around:

> Mona Lisa, Mona Lisa, men have named you
> You're so like the lady with the mystic smile

At first Nora thought that someone might have sung that song at her wedding; she tried to think back who it might have been. And then she thought no, it was later than that, it was a time when she was not the focus of attention. It was after Fiona was born, and her happiness might have come from how well Fiona was, how she was learning to walk, or beginning to talk. Then as Tim sang the second verse it dawned on her precisely when it was. She and Maurice had left Fiona with her mother for the day and maybe the night as well so they could go to the wedding of Maurice's cousin Aidan to Tilly O'Neill. The reception was in the Talbot Hotel in Wexford, and Pierce Brophy, Nancy's son, the one who went to England later and made all the money, was the best man. Pierce stood up and sang that song, which must, she thought, have been a hit that year, and everyone was amazed that he knew the words. He sang it slowly, just as Tim was singing it now, and even though it was not the sort of song that Maurice liked, Nora loved it, she loved how slow and sad it was, and how clever the words were when they rhymed. More than anything else, she loved that she had Maurice beside her, she loved how they were out together at a wedding wearing new clothes and that everyone in the party knew that she was married to him.

When the song ended, the crowd in the bar cheered Tim. Only Phyllis seemed less than impressed and looked at Nora, raising her eyes to the ceiling. Nora noticed that she had a full glass of brandy and soda in her hand and saw that someone had also left her another vodka and white lemonade. She could hear Philomena Hegarty tuning her guitar at the far end of the room.

In all this noise and confusion, she felt a sharp longing now to be anywhere but here. Even though she often dreaded the night falling when she was in her own house, at least she was alone and could control what she did. The silence and the solitude were a strange relief; she wondered if things were getting better at home without her noticing. Since she was a girl, she had never been alone in a crowd like this. Maurice would always decide when to leave or how long to stay, but they would have a way of consulting each other. It was something she never thought about; indeed, she was often irritated by the way in which Maurice's mood could change, how anxious he would be to go home one minute, and then how eager he could become, how easily involved with company the next minute, while she waited patiently for the night to be over.

So this was what being alone was like, she thought. It was not the solitude she had been going through, nor the moments when she felt his death like a shock to her system, as though she had been in a car accident, it was this wandering in a sea of people with the anchor lifted, and all of it oddly pointless and confusing. Then there was another hush in the bar, the guitar began a tentative melody, and Tim Hegarty started to sing 'Love Me Tender'. In the way he gave in to the melancholy in the song, the yearning, she felt that he was mocking her, looking into her face and laughing, but soon the song itself took over, he softened and strengthened his voice as the melody dictated and also let the guitar do its work, leaving gaps so that its sound could be fully heard. She joined in the cheers and the applause when it had finished, and she listened with everyone else, surprised, when the Hegartys seemed to ignore the applause and moved into a much faster song. Tim Hegarty imitated the American accent of Elvis Presley:

A very old friend came by today
'Cause he was telling everyone in town
About the love that he just found
And Marie's the name of his latest flame.

There were roars of approval and whistles from the crowd as Philomena strummed more loudly on the guitar and Tim sang. Nora put her head back and closed her eyes, enjoying the luxury in the tone of the song, the urgent sound of it, and she remembered the summer that song came out, or maybe the summer after when it arrived in Cush, and at night someone would bring out a record player to a table in front of Treacys' bus, which had been moored and cemented down to make a summer house. They would use a long lead from one of the houses around that had electricity.

She remembered coming back along the lane from Kavanaghs' house from her nightly walk with Maurice and finding all the children standing around in the twilight as the teenagers danced to Elvis. She could see some boys there, shy, and Fiona maybe dancing and Patricia Treacy and Eddie Breen and some of the Murphys and Carrolls and Mangans. That was not even ten years ago, it might have been six or seven years ago, and if anyone had told her that she would be standing here now listening to this song and all the things that had happened between then and now, she would not have believed them.

Tom Darcy approached her when the song was over. He was holding Phyllis, whose face was flushed, by the hand.

'He says you can sing,' Phyllis said.

'Of course she can sing. That's when we met her first and she was staying at Gallaghers' and there used to be parties.'

'I haven't sung since then,' she said.

'Oh, come on,' Phyllis said. 'What songs do you know?'

'My mother was a singer,' Nora said as though she were talking to people who had known her mother.

'Nora is a great singer,' Tom Darcy said. 'Or she was then.'

'What do you know?' Phyllis asked again.

Nora thought for a moment.

'Brahms's Lullaby, I think I know that.'

'In German?'

'I used to know it in German, but I know it in English.'

Phyllis put her drink on the counter of the bar.

'Now we have to do this properly. I'll write out the last verse in German and we can both sing that. I'll sing the first in German, you sing the first in English and we'll sing the last verse in German and then in English together.'

Phyllis, she could see, was excited.

'Could we not make it more simple?' she asked. 'I haven't sung for years. I haven't sung since just after we were married.'

'Give me a sheet of paper and I'll write out the German words. They're really easy.'

From the opposite corner of the pub, a man was singing 'Boola-vogue' in a shaky voice. Phyllis was now writing furiously in a clear hand, and making Nora watch her as she wrote each word, humming the tune as she went along, while taking sips of the brandy.

By the time the man had finished singing all the verses of 'Boola-vogue', Nora noticed a restlessness in the bar. The singing had offered colour and excitement and now people wanted to go back to drinking quietly and chatting to each other. There was also, she knew, a distrust of showiness down here, a feeling that anyone who would expose themselves by singing out loud in public should be mocked maybe, or gently laughed at later.

But Phyllis was determined. She had the verse written out in German and was ready to move into the centre of the bar where she and Nora could be seen. Nora knew that there were people in the bar who would recognize her and would wonder why she was singing in a pub when Maurice was not even a year dead.

Tom clapped his hands and called for silence and then, as Phyllis and Nora watched him, expecting to be introduced, he shrugged and made his way quickly back to where he had been, leaving them alone with everyone watching them.

When Phyllis in a loud voice announced that she and Mrs Webster were going to sing a duet, there was laughter. This caused Phyllis to put her shoulders back and appear even more combative than during the quiz. Nora was glad that Phyllis was going to start alone, as she had no idea how to pitch her voice. As Phyllis began in a quivering German, it was clear to Nora that her voice had been trained either too much or too little. She could see the unfor-giving faces around them. Any display made them uncomfortable, even a new car or a new combine harvester, or the first pair of slacks on a woman. But bad singing, high-pitched bad singing in a foreign language, would never be forgotten. It would be a cause of comment for years to come. If Phyllis had not made her mark on Blackwater during the quiz then she was certainly doing so now.

Nora concentrated as hard as she could. She was aware that there were people in the pub who knew the melody, or at least had heard it, and therefore she thought that she should make it sound like an ordinary song when she took over from Phyllis for the verse in English. She thought that she should bring her voice down, not allow any high soprano sounds to emerge but still sing loudly enough to be heard.

When the company saw that Phyllis was going to hand over to her, as though this were some sort of rehearsed party piece, she could see that some of the older men were unsettled and embarrassed. This was not what they had come out for this evening. But a group in the corner, which included a number of women, seemed to think it was hilarious.

'Lullaby and goodnight,' she began, surprised herself at how loud her voice was. She looked over at the group in the corner; they were nudging each other and laughing at her. She tried as she went on to soften her voice, to make the melody as close to a real lullaby as she could, a song she might sing to a child. She knew that if she did not get this group on her side by the end of this verse, then they would not be able to control themselves when she and Phyllis sang together in German. As she came to the last line, she kept her eyes on them and them only, but two or three of them were still laughing.

For the next verse she let Phyllis lead and tried to follow her, at first singing with her and then trying gently to move below her, but she gave this up when they hit one disastrous note together, both of them out of tune. As Phyllis looked at her almost in fear, she let Phyllis sing the last line on her own, not daring even to glance over at the corner, keeping her eyes on the floor, praying that this would be over soon.

She knew the last verse in English best; when she heard that Phyllis was slowing down, letting her voice quieten, she felt more confident, she moved closer and tried for the last two lines to let her voice merge with Phyllis's, keeping under still, but letting her voice loosen and become louder as Phyllis's did. She did not dare look in the direction of the corner, but saw that those in front of her were listening carefully as the song came to an end.

The applause came more from a sense of relief than from any pleasure and she vowed never to do this again as long as she lived. She glared at the group in the corner, one of whom was now doing an imitation of a soprano voice gone wildly out of tune, to the delight of all the others.

As the bar got ready to close and last orders were called, Phyllis insisted on buying a drink for Tom Darcy and a number of his friends, and for Nora. Tom tried to stop her from paying, going so far as to take the money from her hand, but in the end she prevailed. Nora watched as she gulped down the glass of brandy and soda that she had on the counter while waiting for another one to be served. She wondered if it would be safe for her to drive home. She could see from Phyllis that it would not take much for her to sing another song, and she thought she might make herself most useful in the next few minutes by doing everything she could to prevent that.

In the car, when they had finally said goodnight to everyone, Nora realized that Phyllis was so drunk that she was almost fully sober. She concentrated hard as she reversed the car and seemed to be driving competently until Nora noticed that she had not turned the headlights on. Once alerted, she appeared unable to remember where the switch for the headlights was. Eventually, she remembered, and Nora thought that if she could hold Phyllis's attention in conversation all the way back to the town, then Phyllis might be more likely to concentrate also on the road ahead and not allow her mind to wander or let herself fall asleep.

By the time they reached the crossroads at Castle Ellis, Phyllis had said a number of times how much she liked Tom Darcy and what a gentleman he was, and how much she liked Etchingham's pub and how after the quiz in Monageer she and Nancy were offered no hospitality. She thought that Dick, her husband, might, once the quiz season was finished, come down to Etchingham's on a Saturday night and said how nice it would be if Nora would come with them. When she was saying this for the third time, Nora realized that she was going to drive across the main Gorey to Wexford road without looking to see if anything was coming. She wondered what she could say to make Phyllis concentrate more on the road, if there was a single topic that might force her to slow down and drive with caution.

When they were safely on the narrow road that led from Castle Ellis through The Ballagh to Finchogue, Nora began Brahms's Lullaby again. She let her own voice go even deeper so that when Phyllis joined in they were doing harmony, but she was leading. They sang the two verses in English.

'You're almost a contralto,' Phyllis said.

'No, I'm a soprano,' Nora said.

'No, no, you're a mezzo now, but it's bordering on contralto. Your voice is much deeper than mine.'

'I was always a soprano. My mother was a soprano.'

'It can happen. Your voice can deepen over time.'

'I haven't sung for years.'

'Well, it was happening while you were silent, and with a bit of practice your voice would be very good, quite unusual.'

'I don't know.'

'They do auditions sometimes for the choir in Wexford. It's a lovely choir. We usually sing a mass.'

'I'm not sure I'd have time.'

'Well, I'll tell them about you and we can see. And maybe you could come to the Gramophone Society? We meet every Thursday in Murphy Flood's. We each make a choice of records.'

Nora did not want to tell her that she did not own any records and that the old record player was used only by the children for pop records. Phyllis started the Lullaby again, this time going more slowly and leaving space for Nora to come in under her voice and then holding the last note of each line as long as Nora could.

They sang until they reached Enniscorthy, and even as they drove through the town Phyllis still hummed the tune. Somehow, the singing had steeled her nerve, calmed her and made her concentrate on the road so that as she navigated the narrow streets, Phyllis, in her driving and her general demeanour, did an imitation of a perfectly sober woman driving her friend home. As she got out of the car, having been driven to her door, Nora thanked Phyllis and said that she, too, hoped that they would meet one another again soon.

Chapter Thirteen

On the first morning, in the caravan she had rented for two weeks in Curracloe, Nora had to wake Donal and Conor and give them notice that they had half an hour to vacate their beds so she could fold them away and fix the table in between the seats. At the other end of the small caravan, where she and Fiona and Aine slept, she set out the breakfast things, and went to the shop for bread, milk and the morning paper. When she came back they were still dozing. No matter what she said, they would not get up until she told them that she would pull the blankets from them and put the table in place while they lay there. Even then they moved with reluctance. Within a few minutes, however, Conor was cheerful, but Donal did not speak as they had breakfast; he found the newspaper and read the latest account of the moon voyage and the astronauts with fierce attention, eating without even looking at the food.

Then he lay back on the cushions and stared at the ceiling. After a while he took his camera out and pointed it at objects, focusing carefully and narrowing his eyes, framing a shot with deliberation, often of the smallest, slightest object. He appeared to be thinking, but she wondered also if he was not just trying to annoy her.

She knew that there were two things that preoccupied him. First, he wondered when they would go to the strand so that he could be left alone in the caravan; he watched in case they were taking a picnic, which meant they would not be back at all during the day. When she suggested that he come with them, he shrugged and said that he might come later. Nora knew that he would spend the morning brooding over his photographic magazines, the ones that came every month, that Aunt Margaret paid for, or he bought out of his pocket money; they would cheer him up for at least a few hours, after which he would return to poring over the large manual on photography that Una had given him.

Also, he was watching the time, since coverage of the moon voyage began at different times each day. As soon as they arrived he had gone to the television room of the Strand Hotel. Immediately, he had taken photographs of the television set itself, using the wide-angled lens he had got for Christmas from Nora, and long-exposure shots that she did not fully understand. She knew how deeply involved he was in this, and how easily he could become irritated by any questions about its purpose.

Nora had watched him explain it with too much eagerness and intensity when Una and Seamus had stopped by on that first evening, his stammer becoming even worse than usual. And she had noticed how puzzled they had seemed.

It was hard for Donal to accept that most people brought cameras on their holidays so that they could take snapshots on the beach. There was a box at home under the bed full of black and white photographs from holidays in the past, from the fields behind the cliff at Cush and from the strand there, all of them in pouches in folders with the negatives on the other side. When Seamus asked Donal why he couldn't just take snaps of them all enjoying themselves, Donal almost winced at the word 'snap' and stammered badly at the beginning as he tried to explain again that he was only interested in the television at the hotel and the images of space that might appear on it. And then he spoke too quickly as he explained how he would frame each shot to capture the surface of the television screen and within that the images of space, and that he would work out a special way of developing these photographs in the darkroom in his Aunt Margaret's when he got home.

'Would you not be better all the same,' Seamus asked, 'to take photographs of people?'

Donal shrugged in a mixture of boredom and open contempt.

'Donal!' Nora said.

'I,' Donal began, but his stammer would not let him go much further. They all became silent as he tried. Then he lifted his head and looked brave and determined.

'I don't take photographs of people any more,' he said calmly.

On the next morning, there was a haze over everything. They

found a place in the sand dunes where they could spread two rugs and lie out under the pale sun. Nora made Donal come with them so that he could help them carry the picnic basket and so that he would know where they were if he needed to find them.

'The water is beautiful,' she said. 'At least it was yesterday.'

'You can see n-nothing,' Donal said. 'Is it like this all d-day? I want to take p-pictures of this.'

'The haze will be gone in an hour or two.'

He went back to the caravan to fetch his camera. They made jokes when he appeared again, Fiona and Aine insisting that he could not take photographs of them until their suntan had improved. Donal walked away without speaking and moved towards the sea.

'He'll get nothing in this light,' Aine said. 'Sure you can see nothing.'

'That's what he wants,' Fiona said. 'Have you not seen the pictures he developed? The big ones? They're almost blank.'

'Where are they?' Nora asked.

'He has them with him in a sort of folder.'

'Well, he didn't show them to me.'

'He didn't show them to anyone,' Fiona said. 'But they all fell out on the floor the other day and I started to help him pick them up. He nearly bit me. I think he's still learning how to develop them but he says it's deliberate.'

Nora watched as Donal moved down the strand towards the shoreline. She smiled to herself as she saw him taking his pullover off and tying it around his waist while still holding the camera like a precious object. As he moved further towards the water, she could no longer make him out clearly.

The sea was rougher than she ever remembered it. She wondered if there was more shelter at Cush and if the waves there broke more gently. Also, the strand there was shorter and there were stones at the edge of the shore. Here there were sand dunes and the long strand, no stones, no shelter, no cliffs made of marl. She looked north towards Keatings' but she could see nothing and was glad of that, and glad, too, that, no matter how great the visibility, Cush could never be seen from here. It was probable, she thought, that on a morning like this there would be no one at all in Cush, people would not venture down the cliff there until the haze had lifted.

The girls had changed into their bathing costumes and slowly she did too.

'Did you not bring a book?' Nora asked Conor.

'I'm fed up reading.'

'I hope you don't think you're going to spend the day sitting there looking up in our faces,' Fiona said.

'And listening to our conversation,' Aine added.

'All about your boyfriends?' Conor asked. 'Mammy, you should have heard them last night, it was all about Adamstown and White's Barn.'

'I hate Adamstown,' Aine said.

'Fiona likes it,' Conor said.

'Shut up, Conor,' Fiona said.

'Conor, maybe someday if it rains we'll go into Wexford and get you some books,' Nora said.

'He has his tennis racquet,' Fiona said.

'Leave him alone,' Nora replied.

Fiona went down on her own to test the water.

'The waves are high,' she said when she came back. 'And they're breaking right in close so you don't have a choice about getting wet.'

Once they had persuaded Conor to change into his togs, all four of them walked down the strand towards the water. Suddenly, from the distance, a foghorn boomed.

'It must be Rosslare,' Nora said. 'I've never heard it this loud before.'

The waves were powerful enough to knock her over. Leaving Conor in the care of his sisters, she tried to swim into one of the waves as it broke, attempting to get beyond it, but it toppled her over so that for a moment she was completely powerless in the water. She moved out before the next one broke and then swam out further again to where it was almost calm, finding a sandbank. She stood and signalled to the others, but they were too busy waiting for the next wave to crash, Conor running back to the shoreline, shouting to his sisters and laughing.

They would have twelve more days, she thought. And if the weather stayed like this then the girls might even forget that they had made her promise to drive them into the town and deposit them home at the first sign of boredom or bad weather. Just before they had bought the house in Cush, before Donal and Conor were born, they had rented Kerr's Hut above the river at Keatings'. It had rained every day. It had rained so much that eventually she had no dry clothes for Fiona and Aine, nothing at all. And there was no electricity in the hut and no heater, just a couple of gas rings for cooking. For a day, maybe more, none of them could go out. She had taught the girls a number of card games and they had played Scrabble, but, when they tired of these games, there was nothing for them to do. They could not go home, because this was their only holiday. How strange and distant those days seemed now, all of them cooped up in a two-room hut with the damp seeping in, and clothes everywhere spread out to dry.

Conor had become excited by the water. She watched him taking the full force of a wave and being dragged back to the shoreline. He had looked for a second as though he were going to cry as he picked himself up and stood there in shock, but then she saw him smile and call to his sisters a warning that an even bigger wave was coming. He moved between them, holding their hands as it broke. Nora watched them from the sandbank, noticing the heavier boom of the foghorn coming from Rosslare. She could feel the chill of mist in the air as the power of the sun seemed to weaken. If it began to rain, and if the rain did not lift, they would all go home and she would forget about the money they had paid for the caravan.

In the days that followed, however, the weather did not change much. Sometimes in the morning the sun burned through the haze more quickly; other times, the day settled into a sort of windless greyness. It was always mild enough to stay on the strand and they never changed the spot they had found in the dunes on the first day. Sometimes Donal came to find them, and walked down along the strand with his camera. All their efforts to encourage him to get into the water, however, failed.

Each day he made his way to the television lounge of the Strand Hotel. There were always a number of people, he said, watching the news of the approach of the astronauts to the moon. Sometimes they brought their children with them, children who wanted to talk and shout so that Kevin O'Kelly's commentary could not be heard. He wished that there was somewhere else he could watch television without interruption; one man from Dublin kept giving him advice about how to focus his camera and how to get the best shots.

'Nothing is ever perfect,' Nora said to him. 'The world is made up of men like that. Just thank him and smile and ignore him.'

Fiona had already done interviews and secured a job in a school in the town on the condition that she pass her final exams. When she phoned the Training College from the call box in the village, she learned that she had done so and was now qualified as a teacher. She arranged for a friend to come to collect her and borrowed money from Nora, promising to give it back when she got her first pay cheque. Although she said that she would come back to stay with them in the caravan before the holiday was over, Nora did not expect to see her.

She was now alone with the other three. Using her library card and the cards of her two brothers, Aine had borrowed a stack of books about history and politics, the sort of books that Maurice might have been interested in. She acquired a cheap fold-up chair from the shop in the village one day and began to carry it and her books to the strand. She came swimming with Nora and Conor and managed to be polite, but, with her sister gone, she was oddly distant. When she was not reading she was mainly silent and Nora did not think she wanted her thoughts interrupted. When they passed the tennis court, Nora asked Aine if she might want to go there even to watch a game, as there were boys and girls her own age there, but she was not interested.

One night Donal got special permission to stay late in the hotel as it was possible that the moon walk would begin and he wanted to be sure that he did not miss it. He had already taken four rolls of film, which he kept in a special bag, and Nora knew that he would spend the rest of the summer in the darkroom developing them. It was agreed that Nora could collect him at two in the morning. Although the caravan park was close enough to the hotel, she did not want him walking back there on his own so late at night.

It took a while, as she waited outside the hotel, ringing the bell at intervals, to alert the night porter, who came to the door with a manager. As they opened the door, they seemed suspicious of her; the manager asked her what she wanted. She explained gently that she had come to collect her son who was in the television room watching the moon landing. The night porter stayed with her in the lobby while his colleague fetched Donal. The manager and the night porter seemed unfriendly, but she presumed that this was because she had disturbed them sleeping.

The next day, when all three were settled in their usual place on the strand, she had gone down to the water on her own, leaving Aine reading and Conor looking through the pages of a comic book he had bought with money his Uncle Jim had given him. The waves were still high. When Conor was with her she had to watch out for him and did not feel relaxed swimming on her own into deeper water. Now, she could swim out beyond the waves where the water was calmer and she could float and look at the sky and try the backstroke, which she had learned years before but never perfected.

She was paying no attention to anything, but as she was turning to change to the breaststroke she saw Aine at the edge of the water waving to her. Where was Conor? she thought. Where had Conor gone? She began to swim towards Aine, who was clearly in some distress. Since there were other people on the strand she could not fathom why Aine was not calling on them to help.

She swam in, gasping.

'It's Donal,' Aine said. 'I don't know what's wrong with him.'

'Did he have an accident?'

'No, but something happened at the hotel.'

Aine explained that they had told Donal at the hotel that, since he was not a resident, then he could not use the television lounge.

'But is that all that's wrong with him?'

'You should see him.'

'I thought someone was drowning.'

'He is kind of hysterical, or he was when I left him.'

Donal was sitting on a rug away from Conor, who watched her cautiously when she arrived. He was rocking back and forth, his hands joined around his knees, the camera on a strap around his neck.

'What happened?'

'The m-manager who was th-there last n-night was waiting for me t-today. He s-said the lounge was only for r-residents and it was not for p-people from the caravan p-park. Until l-last night, he th-thought I was a r-resident.'

'Do you not have enough photographs?' she asked.

'I am g-going to miss the l-landing,' he said and began to sob. 'All the photographs I had were j-just l-leading up to that.'

'Donal, you can't have everything,' she said.

'I d-don't want everything,' he replied.

She took a towel and began to dry herself. If Maurice were alive, she thought, Donal would not have become so obsessive about his camera. He would certainly not have a darkroom at his disposal. She tried to remember what he was like before it all happened. It came to her now how attached he was to Maurice, how he would go over from the primary school to the secondary school and find Maurice's classroom and sit at the back and wait for his father, or draw on the blackboard if he was allowed. He knew Maurice's timetable by heart, what days he finished early and what days he taught a Leaving Cert class and could not be disturbed.

She sighed as she changed out of her wet bathing costume. Her sisters would tell her not to do this, and Josie probably too, and her mother would have sharp words for her, were she alive. But she was sure, despite all of them, that it was the right thing to do. Fiona, she thought, was at home. This meant that Nora could drive Donal into the town and leave him in Fiona's charge. He would hardly be any trouble, since the only things that interested him now were the television and the darkroom. She knew that

Fiona would be annoyed, that she wanted to have the house to herself and invite her friends around. But she felt that she had no choice. She would go first into the village and phone Margaret at work, and Margaret would, she knew, be delighted to make Donal his tea in the evening and watch the moon landing on television with him. But he could not sleep in Margaret's house; there was not room for him. He would have to sleep in his own bed. Nora would make him promise to be tidy and not make a nuisance of himself. She thought of phoning Tom O'Connor next door and asking him to speak to Fiona, let her know that they were coming, but she decided that it would be better just to drive Donal home and deposit him there. She hoped that it would not be too much of a surprise for Fiona, but she could object all she wanted, Nora thought. It would be only until the coverage of the moon landing ended.

In the car, she looked severely at Donal, who was pointing his camera at the windscreen.

'Donal, put the camera back in its case. I am trying to drive, and the last thing I need is you pointing the camera at things.'

'I c-can sit in the b-back.'

'Stay where you are and don't annoy me,' she said.

As soon as she put the key in the front door of the house she could smell stale alcohol. She looked into the front room but there was no sign of any disturbance. In the back room she had to turn on the light as the curtains were still drawn. Clearly, there had been a party. No matter what she did now, she would be playing a role. She imagined that Fiona was upstairs in bed, possibly still asleep. Nora could wake her in indignation and force her to get up so that they could discuss who had been in the house the previous night and until what time. Or she could begin to clean up the mess herself now, all the more to shame Fiona when she finally appeared. As she inspected the room further she locked eyes with the awestruck Donal. There was an ashtray full to the brim beside an empty bottle of vodka. She drew the curtains back and opened the window, hearing as she did a noise coming from the room above, the room Fiona and Aine slept in. Quickly, she made a decision to go, to pretend that she had never seen this.

'Fiona will clear all this up,' she said, 'so you should find a chair and turn on the television before those men are on some other planet. I'm leaving money for food, but you can go down to your Aunt Margaret's for your tea today, and your Auntie Una will be looking in too.'

'And what about F-fiona?' he asked.

'You can tell her what happened at the hotel and explain why you need a television. And tell her I have gone back to Curracloe and if anyone wants me they know where to find me.'

'But how will we g-get in t-touch?'

'I don't know. Ask your spacemen to help send a message.'

They heard another noise from the room above. Fiona was now out of bed.

'What will I say to F-fiona about this?'

He pointed to the mess in the room.

'Tell her that this house had better . . . No, just tell her to make sure there's enough food, and don't get in her way.'

Donal looked at her, puzzled. And then he nodded and smiled. As they heard a door opening upstairs, Nora put a finger to her lips and handed him a key to the house.

'Are you sure you want to stay here?' she whispered.

'Yes,' he replied.

She moved towards him and tossed his hair affectionately as he recoiled from her, smiling.

'If you change your mind . . .'

'I w-won't,' he whispered as she crept silently out, closing the front door behind her without making a sound.

In the days that followed in the caravan all three of them were quiet. Conor began to go to the tennis court and made friends with two boys from Wexford town who were staying in one of the thatched houses near Culleton's Gap. In the evening Nora walked over to collect him. In the morning the air in the caravan was stifling and hot. As soon as she woke, Nora went out to the shower in the caravan park and then walked down to the strand. Some mornings, the haze was dense and, even though she could hear the rush of waves like muted thunder, she could not actually see the water until she was very close to the shore.

In the last few days of the holiday she began to feel guilty about Donal on his own away from them. She went into the village and stood by the phone in the kiosk and thought of phoning Margaret. She put coins in the slot and had half-dialled Margaret's number when she realized that she did not want to hear Margaret wondering if she had been wise to leave Donal on his own. She put the receiver back and pressed button B to retrieve her coins and used them again to phone Una at work. She briskly asked her if she would bring Donal down to the caravan for the last weekend. When she noticed Una's coldness, she pretended that she was running out of coins and had just enough to hear Una say that she would drive Donal to Curracloe on the Saturday.

When Una brought Donal, Nora saw that he would need to start shaving and tried to remember if there was a shaving brush and shaving cream and men's razors somewhere. But then she thought that if she had not thrown them out, she should do so soon with all of Maurice's clothes, which were still in the wardrobe. As soon as they got home, she thought, she should buy Donal brand-new equipment to shave.

She was not surprised when Aine announced that she would be going back to the town with Una. Her exam results would come soon and, if the results were good enough, she would be preparing to go to Dublin to university. She had barely spoken in the past few days and was more involved in her books than ever, going to the strand at a different time to Nora and swimming alone when things were quieter, at six or seven in the evening. Often, she set up her beach chair in a shady spot at the side of the caravan and paid no attention to anyone.

Nora smiled to herself as Una spoke of how sensible and quiet Fiona was and how lucky that Nora could trust her alone in the house. She expressed surprise at Nora's leaving Donal to be cared for by his sister and said that his stammer had seemed worse than ever; she wondered how he would manage with it.

On the last morning, Nora packed some things in the car and left the boys sleeping. As she walked to the strand she felt the wind that had woken her in the night. The haze had all gone. Clouds moved across the sky, blocking the sun, and then the sun would appear again, its heat faint. She swam out, braving the cold morning sea, discovering that the sandbank, which had been there all the days when the waves were high, had now gone, dissolved by force of the tides. She found a depth that pleased her and began to swim an overarm stroke that gave her speed and then made her tired. When her arms were too sore to do any more, she turned on her back and floated, keeping her eyes closed and trying to leave her mind empty. The swimming several times a day had made her strong. She would come back later, before they had finally to give up the keys of the caravan. Conor would come too, she thought, for a last swim, and they would let Donal do whatever he wanted, stay in the caravan if he liked and point his camera at the wall.

Fiona never mentioned the party she had held in the house and Nora did not allude to it either. She had had enough trouble with her own mother, she thought, without making unnecessary trouble with her daughters. When Aine's Leaving Cert results came, they could not have been better and this meant that Aine would be going to University College Dublin. Nora enjoyed it when people whom she met on the street congratulated her. She was tempted to say that the success of her two daughters had very little to do with her, but she thought that people might misunderstand.

In the week of her return to work, they were busy at Gibney's, since some of the office staff were dealing with the farmers and charting the moisture in the wheat and working out the value of each consignment. Nora stayed on a couple of afternoons to make sure that everything on her side was up to date and in order. In the evenings, when it was still bright, she drove to Curracloe for a swim, offering a lift to anyone who would come with her. Conor was in the tennis club and did not want to go to the beach, and Aine and Donal were too wrapped up in the riots going on in Belfast and Derry and did not want to miss the news. Only Fiona came with her. She had been learning about her salary, a cheque coming in on the 10th and 24th of every month that would be higher than Nora's income from Gibney's and her pensions combined. Nora had to be careful not to give any hint that she found this strange; she presumed that she and Fiona would, at some stage, discuss how much money Fiona would contribute to the household expenses.

On the second day as they were driving home, Fiona said, 'I was going to ask you for another loan of money. I'll pay you back as soon as I get paid.'

'Are you short of money?' Nora asked her.

'I wanted to go to London for a week before the summer is over and I start working. A lot of the girls from the Training College went this year again and I'd have somewhere to stay.'

'London? Just on holiday?'

'Yes.'

Nora was about to say that she would like to go to London too, never having been there, but she stopped herself.

'How much would you need?'

'I was thinking about a hundred pounds. I'd pay you back from my pay cheques. The girls all say that the clothes shops and the stalls are even cheaper and better this year. And I'm going to need clothes to go to work in and then, well, I'll be going out a lot at the weekends. I need clothes.'

Nora wondered if this implied some criticism of how Fiona had been provided for up to now, but she said nothing and concentrated on her driving. She thought of a number of things to say, including that she had to get up every morning and go to work to pay for Fiona's upkeep and she had to watch every penny that she spent. The idea that she would get the money back as Fiona received her pay cheques did not interest her. It was the idea of money being spent foolishly, money being spent at all.

She intended to talk to Fiona about the money over the weekend but she could not think what to say. On Saturday morning, as she lay in bed, she concluded that it would be best to refuse if Fiona broached the subject again, but as the day went on her resolve softened. All she wanted, she thought, was not to have to discuss it again, or think about Fiona on a shopping spree in London. Somehow, the idea of having to talk about it, or listen to any arguments about it, made a strange anger rise in her.

That afternoon the weather was cold with a sky that threatened rain. As she sat at the front window reading the newspaper, she noticed Donal approaching the house carrying a large box. She had trained herself not to ask any of the children too many questions. If she came home with a parcel of any kind when she was growing up, her mother would need to know what was in it, or if a letter came for her, her mother would need to know who it was from and what news it contained. Nora had found this constantly irritating, and tried with her own children not to intrude.

Later, when she looked into the back room, she saw Aine and Donal on their knees with a pile of photographs on the floor beside the box she had seen Donal carrying.

'These are photographs Donal took of the riots in Derry and the burnings in Belfast,' Aine said.

Donal was so involved in studying his own work that he did not even look up.

'But how did he take them?' Nora asked.

'From the television,' Aine said.

The photographs were very large. She looked at them for a second and then knelt down closer. It was difficult to work out what was happening in them, although she could see traces of fire and figures running. They were blurred, almost smudged.

'This is where I superimposed,' Donal said, as though he were talking to himself. She noticed that he had not stammered, and was so grateful for this that she decided to be very careful not to criticize.

'You should put the dates on the back of each one,' Aine said, 'even if there are two different dates.'

'I'll get some stickers in Godfrey's,' he said.

Nora tiptoed out of the room to the kitchen. She wondered if Margaret or Jim had seen these photographs and had thought about the cost of the paper and all the time that Donal spent in the darkroom they had made for him.

That evening they watched the nine o'clock news. Even Conor

sat still and seemed sombre as the news showed film from Derry and Belfast. Nora had not watched any news coverage during the week. Now, people in Belfast were running down streets, escaping from burning houses, it was like something she had seen years ago on newsreel from the war or after the war in the Astor Cinema. But this was happening now and it was happening close by.

'Do you think it will start happening down here?' Fiona asked.

'What?' Nora asked.

'The violence, the riots.'

'I hope not,' she said.

'What are those people who have left their houses going to do?' Fiona asked.

'They're going to come over the border,' Aine said.

Donal had his camera out and was pointing it at the television.

Nora invited Jim and Margaret and Una and Seamus to tea the following Sunday to celebrate Fiona finishing her training and Aine's results. The extended family sat down for tea at six, the leaves of the table having been pulled out as though it were Christmas. Seamus sat beside Conor and engaged him in conversation, discussing the rules of soccer. Nora noticed that he hardly spoke to anyone else and concluded that Seamus must be nervous. The girls had made salads and there was cold meat and chutney and fresh brown bread that she had baked herself. Una was the first to raise the subject of what was happening in the North.

'I think it's terrible,' she said. 'Those poor people burned out of their own houses.'

Everyone nodded in agreement and there was silence.

'I think our government is as responsible as the British government,' Aine said. 'I mean, we let it happen.'

'Well, I wouldn't go that far,' Jim said.

'We did nothing all the years,' Aine said.

'It must have been very hard to know what to do,' Margaret said.

'I think that we gave the Protestants signal after signal that they could do what they liked,' Aine said. 'I mean, there is every type of discrimination, including gerrymandering.'

'What's "gerrymandering"?' Conor asked.

'It's a way of drawing electoral boundaries so some people's votes don't matter as much as others,' Aine said.

Conor looked puzzled.

'I remember that Dr Devlin was from Cookstown,' Una said, 'and he told me that a Catholic couldn't get a proper job there. Even if you were a doctor. That's why he came south.'

'They still can't get jobs,' Aine said. 'I think it's time our government made a stand.'

'What could we do?' Una asked.

'What's our army for?' Aine asked. 'Who would stop them marching into Derry? It's just a few miles over the border.'

'Ah now,' Seamus interjected.

'I don't think that would be wise,' Jim said.

'What has wise got to do with it when people are living in fear of their lives?' Aine asked.

'Oh, I think we down here should be very cautious about what we do,' Margaret said.

'While people are being killed?' Aine asked.

'It's a bad business, all right,' Jim said.

'Well, it's funny, isn't it?' Aine asked. 'The Irish Army can go to the Congo and to Cyprus, but it can't go into Derry to help our own people.'

Nora tried to catch Aine's eye and indicate that they might best drop the subject, but Aine would not look at her. She had her eyes fixed on her Uncle Jim.

'Well, I don't know how it will all end,' Una said.

'Ah, it'll end soon enough,' Seamus said.

'Well, I wouldn't be sure about that,' Margaret said. 'It's really dreadful. Jim and myself watched it on the news last night. It was hard to believe that it was happening in our own country.'

Aine seemed about to say something and then stopped. There was silence at the table for a few minutes.

'Fiona is going to London,' Conor said and, looking around, sought approval for his remark.

'Conor!' Fiona said.

Jim and Margaret and Una and Seamus looked at Fiona. It was clear from her response that what Conor had said was true.

'London,' Margaret said softly. 'Are you, Fiona?'

'I was thinking of going again this year, just for a few days before I start teaching,' she said, 'and this little creep must have been listening to one of my conversations.'

'There'll be plenty of Protestants in London,' Conor said. 'They'll burn you out and make you run down the street.'

'They're not r-real P-protestants in London,' Donal said.

'London is very nice,' Margaret said. 'And where will you stay, Fiona? You know, I have it written down somewhere the name of the place where we stayed. It's a hotel where Irish people are very welcome, a small hotel. Or maybe you'll stay in the same place as last year?'

'A lot of girls from the Training College went there for the summer to work in hotels and they have a flat,' Fiona said.

'It would be lovely for a few days,' Una said.

Fiona had won whatever battle they had been fighting about the money. Somehow or other, as the discussion went on about London and places to stay and the need to look after yourself there, Fiona's going to London became a definite plan, and it was agreed on by Jim and Margaret and Una and Seamus that she deserved the trip after all her studying and that she would be glad she had made it once she started teaching.

At the end of the evening, Jim had an envelope with notes in it for Fiona and for Aine, and he gave ten shillings each to the boys. Later, as they cleaned up, Nora told Fiona that she would get the money out of the bank on her way home from work the next day and she would drive her to Rosslare if that was how she was going to travel.

'That would be very nice,' Fiona said and smiled. 'I'll check the times of the ferries.'

Chapter Fourteen

Nora watched from the front window as Phyllis reversed her car, navigating the narrow space with confidence. She was not expecting her, but thought it might seem friendly and welcoming if she opened the front door and stood there waiting for her.

'Now, I won't come in,' Phyllis said. 'I hate people who drop in without warning and I have no intention of barging in anywhere unannounced.'

'You're very welcome,' Nora said.

'All I wanted to say to you is that there's a choir in Wexford, and there might be vacancies. I don't know what they are planning to do, but it would be a marvellous experience and I know the choirmaster and he's very good, or at least he is when he's in good humour, and so I have a place automatically. Now I spoke to Laurie O'Keefe and she says that she is ready to prepare you so that you have a few pieces ready. For an audition.'

Nora nodded. She did not want to say that both Fiona and Aine had gone to Laurie O'Keefe for piano and they had both come home after the first lesson swearing never to return.

'Is she not –?'

'Quite,' Phyllis said. 'She is not for everybody, yours truly included. But if she likes you, she's very good, and she's very fond of you.'

'She doesn't know me.'

'Billy, her husband, does, or so he said, and they both insisted that they would do anything for you. Don't ask me now to go into the details of what they said, but they were full of enthusiasm when I mentioned your name.'

'What would I do?'

'Call over to her and make an arrangement, and just let her hear your voice. And then maybe you could learn two or three pieces for Wexford.'

'Would it take long?'

'Well, knowing Laurie . . .'

Nora wondered if she should make a quick decision and ask Phyllis to tell the O'Keefes that she was desperately busy. As she hesitated, she saw that Phyllis was watching her.

'Don't leave it too long,' Phyllis said. 'I wouldn't like to offend her. She is very talented, you know, or she was. I'd say she finds the town a bit dull.'

Nora remembered a night in the new Assembly Hall of the Presentation Convent when Maurice and herself and Jim had gone to a fund-raising concert for the St Vincent de Paul Society. Laurie O'Keefe was conducting an orchestra. As her style grew more vigorous and expressive, Maurice and Jim began to laugh quietly and she had nudged Maurice in disapproval. Halfway through the concert Jim had to make his way to the toilet, all the while silently shaking with laughter. Nora had given Maurice a fierce look before he had to follow Jim. Neither of them returned to their seats. Afterwards, she remembered, she had found them both standing sheepishly at the back of the hall.

Before Phyllis left, Nora agreed that she would make contact with Laurie O'Keefe, but over the next few days, as she postponed doing so, she wondered why she was so open to unexpected visits from people who seemed to know better than she did how she should live and what she should do. She supposed that Phyllis was trying to help her, but wondered also if it might be a good idea to keep her door closed to all newcomers, spend her time making sure that Donal and Conor were well looked after, and letting memories of Maurice come to her at will throughout the day, and allowing them to linger until they might fade of their own accord.

As she thought about singing, the sound of her mother's singing voice came vividly to her, so proud and confident on high notes. Even when her mother was old, Nora was able to distinguish her voice from the other voices in the choir in the cathedral. And she liked it when people told her that when her mother was young her voice could fill the whole space and people would come to eleven o'clock Mass to hear her.

In that great sleepless time when Maurice was dying and she knew that she was facing a life alone with the children, she remembered half-thinking that her mother was close by, or waiting for her somewhere, or that her mother knew a prayer that would work and change things. She had an image now of her mother as a calm, hovering force there in the hospital room.

It made sense, or at least it made sense in those days in the hospital, that her mother, despite all the coldness between her and Nora, would want to be there, be close to Maurice. Her mother had gone ahead of him by only seven years. In her urge to be as far away as she could from that time in the hospital, Nora had tried to keep her mother out of her mind since then; her mother's dream-presence had not pursued her into the life without Maurice she was living now.

When she was downtown a few days after Phyllis's visit, having walked up Weafer Street to the Back Road, she realized that she was close to the O'Keefes' house. She wondered if it would be best to turn and walk home and go there another time, but she steeled herself, thinking that if she did it now, then it would be over. Laurie O'Keefe, she knew, had lived in France and had been a nun at some point. She was Billy's second wife. The first wife was dead and the children from that marriage were grown up and gone. There was something about his first wife that Nora could not remember; she had been frugal, she was sure of that, and she vaguely remembered hearing that she had always gone to seven o'clock Mass on a Sunday so that no one could see how badly dressed she was, and how poor she looked, despite the fact that her husband had a good business.

She pushed open the gate to the O'Keefes' house, noticing how well tended the garden was, and how shiny all the windows of the old house were and how unusual, almost grand, it looked. Billy was retired now; he had owned an insurance company, or been involved in insurance, and she knew, as she knew so much about people in the town, that he went each evening at the same time for a bottle of Guinness in Hayes's in Court Street, a walking stick in his hand. As she went up the steps to the front door of the house, she remembered something that Maurice had once told her – Billy hated music, and he had the room where Laurie played and gave her lessons soundproofed, and he wore earplugs whenever there was a threat of music in the house. It was the sort of detail Maurice enjoyed.

Billy opened the door to her and immediately asked her in, holding back a Labrador dog by the collar. The hallway was wide and dark, with old pictures on the wall. There was a smell of polish. Billy began to call downstairs for his wife but as there was no reply he shut the dog in the room on the left and walked down the creaking staircase to the basement, motioning to Nora to remain in the hall.

'She never hears me,' he said, and seemed amused at the idea.

Soon, Billy O'Keefe appeared again.

'She says you are to come down,' he said.

He led her down the narrow book-lined staircase and into a small tiled hallway. He opened a door in a bright space that had clearly been added to the back of the old house. Laurie O'Keefe stood up from the piano.

'Now, Billy will make us tea, unless you want coffee,' she said. 'And biscuits, Billy, the nice ones I bought.'

She smiled at him as he closed the door.

'It's only a baby grand,' she said, as though Nora had asked her about the piano, 'and of course I have another one there, just a plain old upright, for the students to bang on.'

There was no other furniture in the room except a few old chairs. There was a rug on the floor and sheet music strewn about. The walls were painted white with prints of abstract paintings hanging at different heights.

'We'll have our tea in here.' Laurie led her into another room, which had two armchairs, a stereo record player and speakers and a case from floor to ceiling full of records.

'No one has any pity for a woman married to a man who is tone-deaf,' Laurie said. 'No one!'

Nora did not know what this meant, or if she was expected to reply.

'You know, there's something we have been meaning to say to you,' Laurie went on. 'I almost wrote you a letter when we sent you the Mass card but then I thought no, I'd say it to you when I saw you.'

They sat down on the armchairs. Nora looked out at the garden for a moment and then back at Laurie.

'We were driving down from Dublin, we'd been away. Oh, cousins and nieces and all that! And then we were driving back into the town and all the traffic was stopped. I don't know how long we had to wait in Blackstoops. We thought that there might have been an accident. It never struck us that it was a funeral. I don't know why. And eventually I pulled down the window and asked someone what it was. Oh, we were shocked when they told us. We knew Maurice was sick. But we were very shocked. And Billy said how good Maurice had been to his boys in school and what a great teacher he was. And we thought then that if we could do anything for you . . .'

'You're very kind,' Nora said.

'And then Phyllis said –'

'I'm not sure my voice is up to much,' Nora interrupted.

'There is no better way to heal yourself than singing in a choir,' Laurie said. 'That is why God made music. You know I had my own troubles. Coming out of a convent at fifty and hardly a friend in the world. And it was the choir that got me started again. That was the one thing I had, my voice, and the piano, although I trained first on the harpsichord. That was my first love.'

Billy came into the room with a tray.

'And this,' Laurie said, pointing to Billy, 'I suppose will be my last.'

'Do you mean me, Laurie?' he asked.

'I do, but you can leave us now. We have things to talk about.'

Billy smiled at Nora and tiptoed out of the room.

'You know I sang for Nadia Boulanger,' Laurie continued, 'and one thing she said was that singing is not something you do, it is something you live. Wasn't that wise?'

Nora nodded, doing nothing to indicate that she did not know who Nadia Boulanger was. She tried to remember the name so she could mention it to Phyllis.

'But I do have to get a feel for your voice before we set to work. Can you read music?'

'Yes, I can,' Nora said. 'Not well, mind you, but I learned years ago at school.'

'It might be best to start with something you know.'

She went into the other room and came back with books of sheet music.

'Drink your tea and look through these and pick a song you are familiar with. I'll go into the other room and play the piano. I can't think what to play, but something that I know from memory and maybe the sound will warm us up. And I don't have a pupil until four so there's plenty of time.'

Nora sipped the tea and put down the cup and rested her head against the back of the chair. The music Laurie was playing was too fast and cluttered, she thought; whoever wrote it had put in too many notes. It was a virtuoso piece, and she sensed that Laurie was showing off and felt almost sorry for her that she would need to do this. It could hardly be what she did for relaxation. If Maurice were alive now, she would delight in telling him what had happened and he would say how right Billy O'Keefe was to have earplugs. Imagine being married to a former nun who played the piano! She could hear Maurice's dry tone and see the look of pure amusement on his face.

She flicked through the books of sheet music; most of them were German songs she had never heard of, and she wondered now if Phyllis had given Laurie the impression that she knew more than she did. When she came to a book of Irish songs, they seemed all too silly and old-fashioned and stage-Irish, songs that no one sang any more. At the bottom of a pile were a few single sheets with some of Moore's Melodies. She looked at 'Believe Me, If All Those Endearing Young Charms', but thought it was too stilted. Then she found 'The Last Rose of Summer'; she began studying the notes and was humming the familiar tune when Laurie returned to the room.

'You found something then?'

'Well, I found this.' She handed her the sheet for 'The Last Rose of Summer'.

'I had an old novice mistress from the Alsace and she used to call me the last rose of summer even if I was on time. Oh, she was an old battle-axe. Close to God, I suppose, but an old battle-axe nonetheless.'

Laurie went back to the other room and sat at the piano. Nora followed her.

'Now this is bad for your voice,' Laurie said. 'We should do exercises to warm it up and not go straight into a song. But there's something about you now that might not be there in a while. I saw it when you came in the door. You have . . .'

'What?'

'You have been close to the other side, haven't you?'

'What do you mean?'

'Don't talk now. Let me hear your voice. Let me go through the melody first.'

She played and then stopped.

'I'll go down into a lower key and see where that takes us.'

Laurie played, concentrating on the music, slowing the melody as she went along.

'I think I have it now. We really shouldn't be doing this, but your voice might never be as good as it is today. Let me play for a while again, and when I signal, you come in.'

She held her hands over the keys but did not touch them. The silence in the room was so intense that Nora presumed it must really be soundproofed. Nora felt uneasy, almost alarmed by the quality of the silence, by the need Laurie appeared to have for high drama.

Laurie gently touched the keys, working the pedals so that a new low sound came from the piano. She played very softly and then she made a sign and Nora, looking at the words of the song, began:

> 'Tis the last rose of summer,
> Left blooming alone

She did not know that her voice could be so deep; and whatever way Laurie was stretching out the notes, she found herself moving much more slowly than she had meant to. She had no trouble with her breathing and no fear now of the higher notes. She felt that the piano was controlling her and pulling her along, and the pace meant that she gave each word its full weight. Because of the gaps Laurie left, she felt that she was singing into silence; she was aware of the silence as much as she was of the notes. A few times she faltered because Laurie was adding flourishes and she was unsure what to do until Laurie lifted her hand and then swiftly lowered it to indicate that she was to end the lines more sharply and let the piano do the grace notes.

When the song was finished Laurie did not speak for a while.

'Why didn't you train your voice?' she asked eventually.

'My mother was a better singer always,' Nora said.

'If we had got you young enough . . .'

'I never liked singing, and then I got married.'

'Did he ever hear you singing?'

'Maurice? Once or twice on holidays. But not for years.'

'And the children?'

'No.'

'You kept it to yourself. You saved it up.'

'I never thought about it.'

'I can train you to sing for an audition, and the choir may need contraltos, they often do, but I can do nothing more for you. You've left it too late, but you don't mind that, do you?'

'No.'

'We can all have plenty of lives, but there are limits. You never can tell what they are. If someone had told me I'd be seventy and living in a town in Ireland with an insurance man! But here I am. And I know when we started a few minutes ago you didn't want ever to come back here, but you do now. I know you do now. And you will, won't you?'

'Yes, I will,' Nora said.

Over the following weeks, she went to Laurie O'Keefe's on Tuesdays at two o'clock, sometimes dreading the thought of it when she woke on the morning of the lesson and dreading it even more as she set out to walk along the Back Road to Weafer Street. She hoped that neither Phyllis nor the O'Keefes had told people that she was learning to sing. And she told no one at work, not even Elizabeth. There would be people in the town, including Jim and Margaret, who would wonder what she was doing taking lessons when she should be looking after her job and her house and minding her children.

For the first hour of the class Laurie would not let her sing; she made her lie on the floor and breathe, or stand and hold a note for as long as she could, or go up and down the scale. She concentrated then on the first line of 'The Last Rose of Summer', and Laurie made her not take in a breath after 'summer' as she had been doing, but carry on to the end of the second line and then make it natural, as though she were speaking or telling a story.

It was a way of spending Tuesday afternoon, she thought sometimes, a way of doing something new, getting out of the house into a hidden world, soundproofed from what was really happening. It was when Laurie propped two small framed abstract paintings on the top of the piano and asked her to look at them, insisted that she do nothing except look at them, that the real change came, not in her voice, but in something else that she could not be sure about.

'You must look at them!' Laurie commanded. 'Look at them as though you will need to remember them.'

'Who did them?'

Laurie smiled but did not reply.

'Is it just a pattern?' Nora asked. 'What do they mean?'

'You must look, that's all.'

One had nothing but lines; the other had squares. The lined one was brown; the other was blue. Some of the lines were raised, as though embossed.

'Don't think, just look,' Laurie said.

She could not be sure about the colours, as both were filled with shadow as much as colour. She looked at the shadows, studied the darker end of each of them, and then let her eye move from right to left, following a line towards brightness, or some beginning.

'What I want you to do now,' Laurie said, 'is sing and only look at the colours and don't think about the words or me or anything else. Make the sound from what you look at.'

When the lesson was over, Nora felt free of Laurie and looked forward to the six days ahead when she would not have to stand at the piano obeying orders. She arranged to meet Phyllis that Saturday in the lounge of Murphy Flood's Hotel, and asked her about Laurie.

'Either she knew everyone, including de Gaulle and Napoleon Bonaparte,' Phyllis said, 'or she knew no one and lived in a convent. I can never work out which. And either it was a silent order in perpetual adoration, or they spent their time singing and chattering.'

'She makes me do all sorts of exercises,' Nora said.

'She is a law unto herself. And she landed on her feet. Billy built her those rooms and bought her the piano,' Phyllis said. 'And she really can play. And one day I heard her speaking in French on the phone, so at least that part is true.'

'Why did you send me to her?'

'Because she asked me to. She says that on the day of the funeral she promised that she would do anything for you if she could. She has a very good heart. I think all ex-nuns have good hearts, it's such a relief for them being out of the convent. Or maybe that's a wrong thing to say.'

'She made me look at these two paintings she has.'

'While you were singing?'

'Yes.'

'She does that for very few people. Has she said yet that singing is not something you do, it is something you live?'

'She has.'

'She told me one day that I could sing all I liked, but it would be no use. I didn't have it, she said.'

'Have what?'

'Something quite essential. But I don't know what it's called.'

At the next lesson Laurie told Nora to look again at the colours in the frame and try to imagine them coming into being.

'Not there at all, and then slowly there, tone by tone. Emerging. Emerging.'

Laurie almost whispered these last words and then she watched Nora sharply as Nora looked at the shadows and the grades of colour.

She went to the piano and played the introduction. Nora had learned to wait until the end of each phrase to breathe, and to follow the tone of the piano, and find a pace from the pace of the playing. Her singing voice now was much deeper than her speaking voice, and this led her towards a greater confidence as she allowed the voice to vibrate darkly on end notes. She knew Laurie was checking regularly to see that she was watching the colours, and she learned to trust Laurie's playing, her tact, her ability to respond.

As she sang, she concentrated hard on one small square of colour. Something stirred within the depths of it; something she could see clearly for a second, and then when she blinked it had gone. When the playing stopped and the song had ended, Laurie did not move. Nora stayed still too.

It was only after a month, when she had had four or five lessons, that she realized that the music was leading her away from Maurice, away from her life with him, and her life with the children. But it was not merely that Maurice had no ear for music, and that music was something they had never shared. It was the intensity of her time here; she was alone with herself in a place where he would never have followed her, even in death.

When Phyllis mentioned the Gramophone Society again, Nora nodded and tried to look serious. Of all the things that happened in the town, it was the weekly event that Maurice and Jim, and by extension Margaret, thought funniest. One of its leading lights was Thomas P. Nolan and it was regularly attended by a man from Glenbrien, M. M. Roycroft, who had an old house, Phyllis said it was Georgian, and a large farm. He lived alone there, it was reported, with two thousand records and several rooms full of books. Calling Thomas P. Nolan 'Tom Piss Nolan' and M. M. Roycroft 'Madman Roycroft' gave Maurice and Jim infinite pleasure. The two men would laugh, and Margaret too, and the two girls, if they were in the room, would look at Nora, relishing the fact that she never found this funny. She knew Thomas P. Nolan and liked how courteous he was, and she had seen M. M. Roycroft a number of times driving a strange old car and had wondered about his life in Glenbrien and if he went to Dublin to buy the books and records, or if he sent away for them.

Phyllis now wanted her to come to the meetings of the society every Thursday in Murphy Flood's Hotel. Each week, she said, one of the members chose the music they listened to.

'So you know everyone's taste, including, of course, their bad taste. And that Dr Radford has the worst taste, big, long, modern, German things that would knock you into the middle of next week. But the best of all is Canon Kehoe, he only plays sopranos. He knows more about sopranos than any priest in the western world.'

'I don't have any records,' Nora said. 'Or none that I have listened to in years.'

'That's all the more reason to come, and they love a new member.'

They were all people that she half-recognized, including a teacher and a man who worked in one of the banks. Canon Kehoe, she saw, was in charge of the turntable and the speakers.

She had never been in this room in the hotel before, or never when it was filled, as it was now, with sofas and easy chairs. She wondered if they were provided specially for the Gramophone Society. Maybe, she thought, they were an example of the power of Canon Kehoe. The music, he informed the members, this week, was the choice of Mr M. M. Roycroft from Glenbrien, who bowed and then handed each of them a slip of paper. He would make no comment, Mr Roycroft said in a tone of some gravity, but rather he would allow it to speak for itself. He began by playing a Schubert piano sonata in its entirety. Nora thought of Maurice and Jim and decided that she agreed with them about the Gramophone Society. She knew how easy it would be to burst out laughing in the middle of all this solemnity. No one whispered or moved. When Mr Roycroft played an orchestral piece next, Nora noticed that Betty

Rogers, who had taught for many years in the Protestant school, began to conduct the music with one hand and then two. Nora thought that she would have to excuse herself. Instead, she closed her eyes. No matter what she did, however, images from work came into her mind, things that had happened, or things she would have to do. When the interval came, she realized that she had not really listened to the music at all.

Phyllis said at the bar, 'It'll be better in the second half, I promise, and that old Betty Rogers spends her time simpering over Mr Roycroft. She would have more luck if she turned her attention to Canon Kehoe, and that's not saying much. But at least he likes sopranos.'

'Is Betty a soprano?'

'No, she can't sing at all.'

'Does she always conduct?'

'When she thinks Maitland Roycroft is watching.'

The second half of the recital was devoted to cello music and all of the pieces were slow and sad and beautiful. Nora had heard none of them before even though the names of the composers were familiar. A few times when she opened her eyes she saw that everyone was listening closely. She looked around at the men in the room, at Mr Roycroft himself, at Canon Kehoe, at Dr Radford, at Thomas P. Nolan, and all of them seemed now not only sad but strangely vulnerable.

When the recital ended, Betty Rogers was the first to speak.

'Casals was, of course, the greatest, don't you think, Mr Roycroft?'

'For Bach, maybe,' he replied.

'My husband thinks Casals is too harsh, don't you, darling?' Mrs Radford said.

'Perhaps it's the recording, but in the Beethoven sonatas he loses the beauty, you know the beauty, and goes for something else.'

'What does our new member think?' Canon Kehoe asked.

'I thought it was all beautiful,' Nora said. 'All of it.'

Slowly, led by Canon Kehoe, they went out to the lobby of the hotel.

'You know, those Casals recordings of Beethoven were done live,'

Dr Radford said in a loud voice, 'and I don't think the recording was done well.'

'But you get the immediacy,' Mr Roycroft said, 'I think that compensates.'

'I agree with you totally,' Thomas P. Nolan interjected. 'You feel you are in the room while it is being played, don't you?'

He looked at all of them, seeking their agreement.

It was just then that Nora saw Jim having a drink with a man from Fianna Fáil. They were listening to the conversation about cellists with open amusement. The expression on Jim's face changed when he spotted Nora. She could not think what to do. She had obviously been at a meeting of the Gramophone Society, the organization that Maurice and Jim had singled out for mockery. She turned to Phyllis and asked her if she had enjoyed the recital.

'I prefer singing,' Phyllis said, 'but that's just me, and next week will be Canon Kehoe so we'll have plenty of that.'

Nora kept close to Phyllis, hoping that she could avoid Jim, who now was giving his companion his full attention.

'But it's a democracy,' Phyllis said. 'Everyone gets their turn. Still, it would amaze you the music that some people like.'

When she told Laurie O'Keefe about the Gramophone Society, Laurie smiled and shook her head.

'Someone told me that there's a woman who conducts, waving her hands about.'

'You can close your eyes,' Nora said.

'I would wring her neck. Imagine conducting when you have not been trained!'

'Well, the music was nice,' Nora said.

When Jim and Margaret next came to visit, Nora waited in case they were going to ask her what she was doing at the Gramophone Society; she wondered if Donal, who tended to tell his Aunt Margaret any news she might be interested in, had already told her. But Jim and Margaret said nothing about it. They talked about the town and the boys and asked about Aine in Dublin, and when Fiona came in they discussed the advantage of bigger schools over smaller ones and the advantage of free education. A few times, when Nora found Jim looking at her, she suspected that he was thinking about seeing her in the lobby of the hotel. But he did not mention it.

The following Thursday she met Phyllis for a drink in the lounge of the hotel before the meeting of the Gramophone Society.

'It's hard to know what to say about the Canon,' Phyllis said. 'He talks about the sopranos as though he knows them.'

In the room, most of the members were already assembled. The Canon handed to everyone a list of the tracks he had chosen.

'We are going to listen first to the two Marias – Maria Caniglia, who I think is the best singer of Verdi there is, and then Maria Callas, who is even better again, if you can be better than the best. And after that we are going to have Joan and Elizabeth and Rosa and Rita. We are in for a feast.'

One day when she was in Cloake's electrical shop in Rafter Street buying a new iron, Nora noticed a stereo record player with a sign on it saying that the price had been reduced.

'Is there something wrong with this?' she asked the assistant.

'No,' he said, 'it's perfect, but there are newer models coming in. All the others like this have been sold and there were no complaints. This was the demonstration model so I can easily set it up for you to hear.'

Nora looked out towards the street and hoped that no one she knew was passing as she said that she would like to hear how it sounded.

'Go through the records,' the assistant said, 'and find something you'd like to listen to while I rig this up. You have to put the speakers far apart, or an equal distance from the turntable.'

She flicked through the records, wondering if it would be best to test the sound with a singer or with orchestral music. In the end she selected a record called *Your Favourite Music* and handed it to the assistant.

'Is there any particular track?' he asked.

'No, if you just let a few of them play.'

Nora stood in the shadows so that no one on the street could see her. It was a movement from Grieg's Piano Concerto and, even though it was not turned up loud, it sounded to her as though the pianist were in the shop with them. She could hear every note clearly, but it was not just that, she could also feel an energy from the playing that made the sound seem urgent and present.

In the budget there had been another increase in the widow's pension, also backdated. She still had money from the other back-dated cheques in the bank. Nonetheless, Jim and Margaret and Una and even Fiona would all think buying this was wasting money. She wondered if she could set up the stereo in her bedroom so that none of them could see it, but then it would be hardly worth it.

When the first track ended, she was going to tell the assistant that she would need time to think about it. Then the next track began, the 'Hymn to the Moon' from Dvořák's *Rusalka*. Sometime in the past she had heard Dvořák's 'Humoresque' in a version for solo violin. This was for a soprano. Canon Kehoe would recognize the name of the singer, she thought, but it meant nothing to her. The voice rose steadily with the music and then soared above it. What she felt now more than anything was a sadness that she had lived her life until now without having heard this. But still she could not make up her mind about buying the stereo. It would be too much fuss, she thought, collecting it in the car and then putting a low table in the back room and trying to get it working. She did not know who she could ask to help who would not think her extravagant. When the track ended, she nodded to the assistant to let him know that this was enough.

'I'll have to think about it,' she said and smiled.

One evening a few weeks later, she arrived early at the hotel for the society meeting and found herself alone in the room with Dr Radford and his wife. Years ago he had lent Maurice a book, she could not think what the book was, but Maurice had mislaid it. They had searched the house thoroughly for it, but in vain. Having asked for it to be returned a number of times Dr Radford had driven up to the house early one Saturday morning and said that he needed to consult the book for something he was writing. Maurice was still in his pyjamas and Nora in her dressing gown. Dr Radford stood tall and imposing in the hallway. He was not leaving, he said, until the book was found. Nora remembered his grand and dismissive tone when she offered him a cup of tea. Maurice rummaged among the bookcases in the front room and invited Dr Radford to look too. Maurice then searched in the large press in the back room where he kept all his papers. When it became clear to Dr Radford that the book would not be found, Maurice led him slowly out of the house and closed the door behind him and remained preoccupied all day.

'Are you busy at the moment?' she asked Dr Radford.

'Oh, the waiting room fills up in the morning and it's full all day,' Mrs Radford said.

Nora wondered if Dr Radford was going to ask her if the book had ever turned up. He could not have forgotten the episode on the Saturday morning years ago.

When the recital was over, Mrs Radford motioned Nora to the side so that she could have a private word with her.

'We've noticed how much you enjoy the music,' she said. 'And you don't make a sound when a record is playing. And we'd love to have you down some evening to Riverside House. You know, we often play records in the evening.'

'Well, I'm not sure,' Nora said. 'You see, I have the boys at home and I don't like being out too many evenings.'

'Well, perhaps you could let us know.'

Nora got a phone call at work from Mrs Radford wondering if she could come in the evening any time the following week. She was so surprised that she found herself agreeing to Monday at eight. That Thursday at the Gramophone Society the Radfords sat close to her and a few times between records Mrs Radford nudged her and made some comment about the music. On the way out, Dr Radford spoke to her.

'You'll have to make sure now that we play records on Monday that you like, and maybe introduce you to a few new things.'

When she told Phyllis what had happened, Phyllis insisted that she should phone them and cancel.

'They are a dreadful pair of bores. He's full of Trinity College and the Church of Ireland. You'd wonder that he has any patients at all.'

'Why did they ask me?'

'They like to impress people.'

'They want to impress me?'

'They've seen that everyone in the Gramophone Society likes you.'

'I didn't know that anyone even noticed me.'

'After all you've been through, everyone thinks you are . . .'

'What?'

'Well, dignified. That would be one thing.'

The house lay between the Mill Park Road and the river. There was a small entrance with a notice saying 'Surgery' and then another larger entrance to an old two-storeyed house with a garden in front of it.

The door was opened by Mrs Radford.

'Now, call me Ali,' she said. 'We'll have no formalities. Trevor is upstairs. There's an old patient of his out near Blackstoops who's very weak and if the phone rings then Trevor will have to go. But I'd better not say who it is or Trevor will kill me. You know, we keep things very confidential here.'

Trevor appeared wearing a red pullover and an open-necked white shirt.

'You know, I think before we do anything,' he said, 'we'll have some Schubert. Don't you think? And perhaps a gin and tonic.'

He led her from the hall into the long room on the right. All around the room in the places where other people might have china cabinets or bookcases the Radfords had records. The record player was on a stand with a large speaker on each side of the fireplace.

'Old Roycroft is proud of his collection,' Dr Radford said, 'and, of course, he does have rarities, but he was flabbergasted when he came into this house and saw the room upstairs where we keep most of the records. I work hard and while other people like golf or going on safari, this is what I like. Music.'

Nora nodded and smiled. It was hard to know what to say in reply. Mrs Radford came with gin and tonics in tall glasses as her husband put a record on the turntable.

'I think this is one of the most frightening and saddest songs. It always sends a chill down my spine. It's the "Erlkönig".'

For an hour or more Dr Radford played German and French songs, some of them fast with thumping piano accompaniment, others slower and more melancholy. With each one he gave an introduction as though he were speaking on the radio. As he took each record from the turntable, his wife dutifully put it back in its sleeve and returned it to its place on the shelf. Mrs Radford also replenished their glasses at intervals.

'Do you like Richard Strauss?' he asked.

'I'm not sure,' Nora said.

'Well, I thought we would listen to a few of his early songs, which are very delicate, and then we would be brave and end with the Four Last Songs. Of course, they weren't always called that. You know, I think he was capable of creating a pitch of intensity better than any of them.'

What Nora sensed as the music played, music that meant nothing to her, that had too many swirling rises and falls and too little melody, was how lonely the Radfords were. Their children had grown up and gone. The Radfords were alone in a place where there were few people like them. In Dublin or London they might be happier. But more than anything, as Dr Radford, animated by the gin, turned the sound up until it was too loud, she wondered what had happened to her that she found herself here in this house with these two people on a night when she could be at home. Why had she joined the Gramophone Society in the first place? If anyone she knew discovered that she had spent an evening with Trevor and Ali Radford, they would think that she had lost her mind.

When the songs were finished and Nora stood up to go, Dr Radford asked her who was her favourite composer.

She hesitated, feeling more than slightly drunk.

'I suppose Beethoven,' she said.

'And any particular period?'

'Something quiet,' she said and looked at him pointedly.

'Oh, I know. The trios we got in that package from McCullough Pigott's,' Mrs Radford said.

'Yes, we haven't played them yet. We keep the new recordings over here.'

When he found the record he showed the sleeve to Nora. It had a photograph of two young men and a woman. The woman was blonde and faintly smiling, with a strength in her face. Nora discerned that the woman was the cellist and in that moment she had a thought that she would give anything to be the young woman on the album sleeve, to be her now with a cello beside her and someone taking her photograph. As Dr Radford put the record on, she thought how easy it might have been to be someone else, that having the boys at home waiting for her, and the bed and the lamp beside her bed, and her work in the morning, were all a sort of accident. They were somehow less solid than the clear notes of the cello that came through the speakers.

Nora concentrated on the low, pleading sound. The energy in the playing was sad, and then it became more than sad, as if there were something there and all three players recognized it and were moving towards it. The melody rose more beautifully, and she was sure that someone had suffered, and moved away from suffering and then come back to it, let it linger and live within them.

When Nora looked up she saw that the Radfords were tired. Mrs Radford began to rake the fire. Nora wanted to be away from them now, to walk home alone, cross the Mill Park Road and go up the lane to John Street and then along John Street towards home. When the first movement ended, she stood up.

'That was beautiful,' she said. 'And they are so young, the players.'

'Why don't you take the record home with you?' Dr Radford said.

He put the record back in its sleeve and handed it to her. She knew that she could not say that she did not have a decent record player, but also she did not want to be the focus of their charity. If she took the record from them it would be harder to refuse their hospitality were it to be offered again.

'But you haven't listened to it yourselves,' she said.

'Yes,' Dr Radford said, 'but we have many other records that we haven't listened to yet, and it would be marvellous if you had it.'

In the hallway, they found her coat, and as he opened the door Dr Radford said: 'Let us know what you think of it when you have listened to it a few times.' Nora smiled and thanked both of them and then walked home, sobered up by the cold night air, with the record under her arm. Even if she could not listen to it, she thought, she could look at the sleeve and try to remember the notes she had heard. Maybe that would be enough for the moment.

Chapter Fifteen

She was afraid to spend money. When the cheque came with the backdated increase, she lodged it carefully in the bank. It made a difference to her that it was there if she needed it but she lived on what she earned from Gibney's, her pension and the money Fiona gave her.

She took an interest in Charlie Haughey, the Minister for Finance who had crafted these budgets. Una and Seamus disapproved of him strongly and Jim and Margaret continued to make clear how suspicious they were of him.

'Well, I think he's a very good Minister for Finance and he deserves a break,' Nora said.

'We heard a story,' Margaret said, 'about late night drinking in Groome's Hotel.'

'But there are always stories about politicians, especially good ones,' Nora said. 'They used to say that de Valera and the wife didn't speak to each other and that Seán Lemass had gambling debts.'

'Yes, but those stories weren't true, Nora,' Margaret said. 'These ones are.'

When Haughey was arrested for gun-running, Mick Sinnott came into her office with the news, followed by Elizabeth. Since he had become head of the union, Mick Sinnott was to be seen much more.

'Thomas says he's in the Bridewell,' Elizabeth said, 'and he's in handcuffs. He was importing arms, if you don't mind.'

She did not, in her excitement, appear to realize that she had spoken to Mick Sinnott, to whom she would not normally speak, as well as to Nora.

'Arms for what?' Nora asked.

'To send to the North,' Mick Sinnott said.

'Oh, he'll have us in a right stew then,' Elizabeth said.

Everyone in the office was talking about the arrest. Elizabeth called out to one of the office girls, asking her to go over to the house and fetch her transistor radio.

'Maybe the rest of them will see sense now,' Mick Sinnott said.

'Excuse me, Mr Sinnott,' Elizabeth said. 'Mrs Webster and myself have work to do.'

'Oh, don't let me interfere with work,' Mick Sinnott said and walked out of their office, leaving the door open.

Elizabeth shut the door.

'Thomas says there might be an election,' she said to Nora, 'and Old William would be delighted to see the end of this government. And the cheek of that Mick Sinnott coming in here. It's a pity someone doesn't arrest him too.'

When Jim and Margaret came to visit, Nora noticed that Jim was in good humour; he moved with a quicker step and seemed almost younger.

'We were very shocked at first,' Margaret said. 'I mean, it's not a good thing for any country to have ministers arrested and on trial.'

'Anyway, the situation is dealt with now,' Jim said. 'You know, some people didn't think Jack Lynch had it in him to sack those ministers. But anyone who ever watched him on the hurling pitch would be in no doubt about him. He's a gentleman until you push him and then he's as tough as nails. He's one man I wouldn't cross.'

'Well, I can't think of anything that he has ever done for anyone,' Nora said. 'If I was in the North and someone came to my house to burn it down, I'd want guns.'

'Well, they can get their own guns,' Jim said. 'We don't want cabinet ministers in our part of the country running guns.'

'Haughey always had time for people who were in trouble,' Nora said.

'He was always hasty,' Jim said. 'He was promoted too early, that was the thing. He needed more time on the backbenches. Too ambitious.'

'Jim never really trusted him,' Margaret said.

'Well, he looked after the widows when he needn't have,' Nora said.

One evening Aunt Josie arrived without warning. She spoke to Fiona, going through the names of teachers she had worked with and her own early career when times were much harder and classes much bigger. When Fiona excused herself, Nora realized that she would not be returning.

The boys came in and spoke to Josie.

'They look much better now,' Josie said when they had gone. 'You have really been marvellous, everyone thinks that.'

'It's hard to know,' Nora said. 'Donal's stammer can be very bad.'

'But he looks happier,' Josie said. 'I remember you and Catherine and Una after your father died, and it took you all much longer. It was a very sad house then, but children bounce back, that's the great thing.'

'I don't think they do. I never did,' Nora said. 'You learn, no matter what age you are, to keep things to yourself. I wonder if I should take Donal to Dublin to a speech therapist.'

'Leave him for the moment. Leave well enough alone.'

Nora sighed.

'I wish I knew what to do with him.'

'What I really came in to tell you,' Josie said, 'is that I have money invested. Not much now, but still. And I got the dividend last week and I thought I'd like to do something nice with the money, and I thought in a few months' time at the end of the summer, when everything has calmed down, it would be lovely to go to Spain with you, and you need a break from all of them.'

'Spain? Oh, I'm not sure.'

'I've spoken to Una and she's ready to look after the boys, and all you have to do is make sure you have the time off in Gibney's.'

'I have been working full days when they're busy but I'm not sure if I will be owed days off as well as my holidays. I'll go to Curracloe or Rosslare with the boys for two weeks no matter what happens.'

'Will you think about it?'

'Well, it's very generous of you.'

'A good holiday and plenty of sunshine, and you were always a great swimmer.'

'I've never been on a plane. I went to Wales with Maurice once, but we went by boat. I don't even have a passport.'

In the morning when she woke, Nora did not think she would go. She would have to make too many arrangements, and she would be concerned about being so far away from the boys, who could still become upset by the smallest thing. Within a week she had a letter from Josie with potential dates. She delayed replying, and eventually, having confirmed at Gibney's that she could have time off rather than extra pay, she was on the verge of writing back to Josie to agree to go to Sitges in Spain for the first two weeks of September. But she held back, thinking that two weeks at home, without having to go to work every day, would be better, and also bearing in mind that this was when the boys would be going back to school.

Over the next fortnight, Josie, Nora learned, contacted Una and Margaret and asked them to talk to her. When Margaret raised the subject, she said nothing, but when Una began to tell her that a holiday would do her good, she wondered if they all should be told to leave her alone.

'It's the sort of thing you see on a television ad,' she said, 'that a holiday in Spain would do you good. I've never seen any evidence of it.'

'You wake in the morning and you know there is sunshine all day,' Una said, 'and the sea is warm and there's someone else to cook for you.'

'What about the flight?'

'I fall asleep on flights,' Una said, 'and I'm sure you will too.'

She wrote to Josie to say that she would like to go, but she tore the letter up. Sometimes at night she thought she would love to go, but in the mornings she felt that it would be too much effort. Only when she realized that her silence was rude, and that Josie would be offended, did she determine that, one way or another, she would write to Josie from work and post the letter on her way home. Even when she began to write the letter, she did not know what she would say. And, when she wrote to accept, she was not sure that she had done the right thing. But the following day she applied for a passport.

A few times when Margaret and Una and even Fiona spoke about how much good the holiday would do her, she became irritated. She knew, however, since Josie had already paid, that she could not cancel now. When the holiday in Curracloe with the boys was over, she went to Dublin one Saturday on her own and bought some light clothes for Spain but found herself, when Una asked her, not admitting that she had bought anything at all. Fiona seemed to realize that she did not want the trip mentioned and said nothing to her about it. When Josie sent her a list of things she must not forget, she came close to replying that she could look after her own arrangements.

Yet she did not mind the confined space of the plane and she enjoyed watching Josie saying prayers as the plane took off and landed and any time there was a bump during the flight. What surprised her most was the heat when they arrived, even though it was night, and the strange fetid smell as though something were rotting. On the bus from the airport, Josie began to sigh and complain, but Nora found it almost soothing and wondered what the morning would be like.

That night, as she listened to Josie snoring in the bed beside her, she believed that she could not sleep because of the heat and the excitement. On the beach in the morning she slept for a while, woken only by Josie, who wanted to talk. Since Josie did not swim, Nora realized that she could get away from her by going into the sea and staying in the warm water for as long as she could. When she returned each time, Josie took up the conversation where she had left off.

On the fifth day as they walked from the beach, Nora in her mind went through each one of the four sleepless nights she had spent so far on their holiday. She listened with irritation as Josie talked about a priest who had not come to the house of someone who was dying but was seen that same day at a football match. Thinking about the nights one by one was Nora's way of concentrating, thus keeping herself from lying down now, here on the busy street, or leaning against the wall of a shop, or curling up on the pavement, not caring that it was still daylight and the shops were still open. For a second, as Josie went on with her story, she could detect in her speaking voice a hint of the same sound she made when she snored, a cross between heavy breathing and bronchial groaning.

Nora thought it was Josie's age that made the snoring so heavy and loud. Even when Nora had switched on the bedside lamp and gently set to turning her, or even firmly waking her, Josie had settled back swiftly into sleep. Nora had lain in the bed beside hers and waited, and each time it had begun again, her snoring rising and falling, sometimes becoming a set of hard, rasping sounds, and continuing even as the dawn light peered in through the slats in the shutters. Nora lay there exhausted, exasperated, realizing after the fourth night that she still had ten days and nights left with her aunt until their fortnight's holiday in Sitges would be over.

As they veered into the shady street where their hotel was situated, Nora saw Carol, their tour guide, entering a shop. She had thought that Carol had gone back to Dublin, and wondered now if maybe she had done so and then returned.

If she had not been so tired, she would have instantly approached Carol. But by the time she thought of this she was already in the bedroom and Josie in the garden. She wondered if it would be wise to tell Carol what was wrong. In a few days, if Josie continued snoring through the night, Nora might have to feign illness in the hope she could get an early flight home. Telling Carol the truth would prevent her from doing that. She sensed that Carol would have a way of making clear to her that it was her own fault that she was a light sleeper, and hardly the travel company's concern that her aunt was a heavy snorer. She knew that an additional single room, even if one was available, would cost much more than Josie had paid.

In the lobby of the hotel, when Josie was in the bar, Nora bumped into Carol.

'Are you all right?' Carol asked her.

Nora did not reply.

'I saw you on the street earlier,' Carol said.

'I can't sleep,' Nora said.

'Is it the heat?'

'No, I like the heat.'

Carol nodded and then waited for her to say something more. Nora looked around her and then whispered.

'My aunt snores all night. It is like being in the room with a fog-horn.'

'Did you say it to her?'

'I tried. I don't think she knows what it sounds like. I haven't slept a wink for four nights. I'm going demented.'

'We don't have single rooms,' Carol said.

'Don't worry then,' Nora replied. 'Not to worry. I'll just lie there all night until we go home.'

'I'm really sorry,' Carol said.

As they stood facing each other, Nora could hear the voice of her aunt and then sudden laughter as Josie approached. She seemed in high good humour.

'Oh, there you are, Carol,' she said. 'Well, I just wanted to say that the room is lovely now, couldn't be better, and I was just saying to a man at the bar that I don't know how we are going to get used to making our own beds and cooking our own meals when we go home. But I won't miss the heat. Oh, I won't miss the heat!'

Nora watched her coldly and saw that Carol was staring at her too. For a second, they caught each other's eye. Josie was wearing a loose navy blue dress that made her seem enormous, her hair was dishevelled and she was sweating profusely. She grinned at the two of them.

'Come and have a gin with us,' she said to Carol. 'Or is vodka your tipple?'

'No, thank you. I really must go.'

'I already have one on the counter for you, Nora,' Josie said. 'Oh, the heat!'

She shuffled towards the bar. Nora nodded at Carol and then fetched the key and went upstairs. She had a cold shower before going downstairs to join her aunt in the bar. Somehow, the possibility of the gin, especially if she put very little tonic in it, and then the food, gave her the courage to continue. But once dinner was over, she thought, she would implore her aunt to leave her the room for a few hours, and she would try to get some sleep before the night's snoring began.

When Mercè had served the dessert and poured more white wine for both women, she motioned to Nora to come with her, pointing towards the door to the lobby. She led her down a narrow creaking staircase to the basement. The ceiling of the corridor they moved along now was low, and the paint on the walls was peeling. The air was cool, with an edge of damp and a smell of mustiness that to Nora was refreshing. They squeezed past a pile of cardboard boxes stacked from floor to ceiling and then Mercè opened a door to the right and switched on a light. It was a room like a prison cell, Nora saw, with a single bed and a tiny window with bars at the top of the back wall. The light bulb was bare. The bed was made and the sheets were starkly white in the sharp light coming from the ceiling. When Mercè crossed the corridor she opened a door into a bathroom. The air was even damper here, and there was a smell of mould. There was an old bath with plastic nozzles attached to the taps and a shower head hanging over the side. There was a toilet and a wash-hand basin. This room, too, had a small window with bars. Mercè looked at her, and put her hands out as if to say that this was not much, but it was hers if she wanted it. She managed to say in English that there would be no extra charge. Nora nodded enthusiastically. Mercè had a set of keys in her pocket and tried a number of them before she found the one that locked the bedroom door. She removed it from the keyring and handed it to Nora and then went with her along the corridor and up the stairs to the lobby.

Nora left Josie at the bar once dinner had ended, carried her suitcase and her toilet things down to the basement, and then came and told her aunt that they had given her a room of her own and that she was tired and was going to bed now. Josie, she saw, was ready to become offended, but she did not give her time. She turned and disappeared. The idea that she could sleep, settle into sleep, filled her with such relief that nothing else could matter now. Once she had made her way back down to her basement quarters, closed the door of her room and undressed, she relished how crisp and clean the sheets were on the narrow bed. She turned off the light and tried to stay awake for as long as she could so that she could enjoy the prospect of solitude and long, uninterrupted sleep.

When she woke she knew that it was morning. There was a faint, insistent light coming from the small window but there was no sound at all. She did not think she had slept as deeply as this since she married Maurice and began to share a bed with him, and certainly not since she was pregnant for the first time. There was once, however, she remembered, when Aine was a baby and had cried throughout each night. No matter how often she was fed, or how many times she was lifted and comforted, she cried. Nora, without any warning, had taken Aine and two days' supplies to her mother's house, leaving Fiona with Maurice, and despite her mother's nervous protestations, had left Aine downstairs with her, and gone upstairs to bed and slept solidly for twelve or fourteen hours. That was the only time in her life, she thought, when she had woken like this, the night's sleep a heavy oblivion, utterly satisfying and complete in its blankness.

She felt alert now, excited at the prospect of the day ahead. She went to the bathroom and showered in cold water. When she checked the time, she found that it was only five o'clock. She put on her bathing costume and then a dress and a pair of sandals and stuffed a towel and some underwear into a bag. She walked quietly, stealthily, out of the hotel, aware that any encounter at all could break the spell of the night.

She walked in the early morning sunlight down a sidestreet towards the beach that lay behind the church and was quieter than the others. She was surprised when she passed a few people in the street, people on their way to work. When the sea came into view, she looked at the pale morning sky above it. She walked towards the esplanade past white-painted buildings with shutters coloured a deep dark blue.

As she came to a café on the corner, the owner was rolling up the metal shutters. He greeted her casually as though he knew her. She would come here after her swim and linger at one of the tables the owner might put outside, and not return to the hotel until just before ten o'clock when Josie would come down for breakfast.

There were large machines on the beach flattening out the sand, making everything smooth and perfect for the day. Men sorted sun umbrellas and arranged beach furniture. There was still a cool breeze, a remnant of the night, coming from the sea, and the water was colder than she had imagined, and the waves higher than they had been in previous days. She dived under a wave as it came towards her and felt a chill as she swam out.

She closed her eyes and swam without making much effort, edging out beyond where the waves broke. She noticed the sun's first heat as she lay back and floated. She felt lazy now and tired as well, and yet the energy that had come to her earlier was there too. She would, she thought, stay in the water for as long as she could; she would use up her energy. She knew that a morning like this would not come to her as easily again, the early light so beautiful and calm, the sea so bracing, and the promise of the long day ahead and the night that would follow when she would be alone once more, undisturbed, allowed to sleep.

For the last few days of the holiday Josie became quieter, and the stories she told were more interesting. Nora loved her bed in the basement, although she preferred using the shower in the bathroom beside the room where Josie slept. She swam a few times a day, liking the way her bathing costume dried quickly in the sun. She and Josie did not mind paying for the deckchairs and the sun umbrellas. And Josie never tired of commenting on anyone who went by. One day they found a market where Nora bought cheap clothes and presents for everyone at home.

She studied the buildings along the streets between the beach and the hotel, wondering about the people who lived in them, what their lives were like, and what hers would be like, were she living here. During those last days she thought about her walk to work in the mornings, the red raincoat she wore, an umbrella at the ready.

All of it seemed remote and alien, as far away from here as it was possible to be.

On the last day she bought Mercè a bottle of expensive perfume to thank her for rescuing her.

It was late when she arrived home. The boys had gone to bed and she was careful not to make a sound that might wake them. Fiona was at a dance and Aine was there alone. She sensed from Aine that something had happened, but then felt, as she quietly unpacked upstairs, that it was nothing more than the newness of where she had been and the strangeness of returning home. But the thought remained that there was something wrong so she went back downstairs and asked Aine if there had been a problem while she was away.

'It's just that Conor has been put into the B-class,' Aine said.

'The B-class? Who put him into the B-class?'

'Brother Herlihy moved himself and two others into the B-class.'

'Which two?'

The two Aine mentioned were, Nora knew, along with Conor, among the very best in the A-class.

'Did he give a reason?'

'No, he just did it.'

In the morning, which was Sunday, she spoke to Conor before he went to Mass. He seemed most concerned that she would not think he had been moved because of anything he had done or failed to do.

'He just moved us,' he said. 'And we don't know anyone in the B-class.'

At Mass she could barely concentrate. When a woman in front of the cathedral afterwards admired her suntan, she barely responded and then felt guilty as she walked home. As the day went on she felt more and more resolute, so early that evening when she rang the bell of the Christian Brothers monastery she was determined that she would have Conor put back into the A-class where he belonged. When the door was finally answered by a young Christian Brother, she asked to speak to Brother Herlihy.

'I am not sure that he's available,' he said.

'I'll wait,' she replied.

He did not invite her into the hallway.

'Tell him that I'm Nora Webster, Maurice Webster's widow, and I need to see him now.'

The young Christian Brother examined her cautiously then invited her in and closed the front door behind her.

As she waited, she noticed more than anything else the silence in the monastery. It was like desolation. She did not know how many Brothers lived here but she guessed ten or fifteen. They all had their own cells, she thought, like prisoners, but there was something almost worse than prison about the place, the bare tiles on the floor, the long stained-glass window in the stairwell, everything polished and stark and unwelcoming, a place where every sound and every movement could be noted and heard.

Brother Herlihy seemed very cheerful when he arrived and led her into a reception room on the right.

'Now, Mrs Webster, what can I do for you?' he asked.

'My son, Conor Webster, has just gone into fifth class. And I was away and when I came back I discovered that he had been moved into the B-class.'

'Ah well, it's not really a B-class.'

'It's not the class he was in before.'

'Yes, we're making some changes, just to try and even things out a bit between the two classes.'

'Well, I'd rather you moved him back into the A-class.'

'I'm afraid that's not possible.'

'Why not?'

'The roll-books are all done, and the names have been sent to the department.'

'That's not a problem. You can easily make a change to that.'

'Mrs Webster, I run the school.'

'Brother Herlihy, I'm sure you run it very well. As you know, my husband was a teacher in the secondary school for many years.'

'Yes, he is very much missed.'

'And you would not have moved Conor if my husband were still teaching.'

'Ah now, Mrs Webster, many considerations went into the decision.'

'None of them interests me, Brother. I am interested only in Conor's education.'

'I'm afraid I can't do anything about it at this late stage.'

'Brother Herlihy, I didn't come down here to ask you to move Conor back into the A-class.'

'Oh?'

'I came down to tell you to do it.'

'As I said, I run the school.'

'I hope you heard what I said.'

'I did, Mrs Webster, but it can't be done.'

He moved to accompany her out of the reception room. In the hall he put his hand on her shoulder.

'How are all the family?'

'That's none of your business, Brother Herlihy.'

'Ah now,' he said and smiled, rubbing his hands together.

'You will be hearing from me,' she said, as he opened the door for her. 'And you will find that when I am crossed I am very formidable.'

At home, she found notepaper and an envelope and wrote a letter:

Dear Brother Herlihy

If, by next Friday, Conor is not moved back to the A-class, please be advised that I will take action against you.

She signed her name and walked back down to the monastery, rang the bell again and handed the letter to the young Christian Brother who had answered the door to her earlier.

Later that evening, she wrote down the names of all the teachers in the Christian Brothers, both primary and secondary, whom she knew. For a few of them, she could remember their home addresses; for the rest, she would write to them at the school.

To each of them she wrote the same letter:

As you may be aware, my son Conor Webster, who is in fifth class in the primary school, has been moved from the A-class to the B-class without

*any notice or any justification. As you also must know, this would not
have happened were his father still alive and teaching in the school. This is
to put you on notice that I will not tolerate what has occurred. If Conor is
not back in the A-class by next Friday, then on Monday morning I will put
a picket on the school. If you travel to work by car, I will stand in front of
your car and prevent it from entering the gates of the school. If you travel
by foot, I will stand in front of you. I will continue the picket until Conor
is returned to the A-class.*

 Yours sincerely
 Nora Webster

She did not have enough envelopes but resolved that she would buy
some on her way home from work and write the addresses on them
at the desk in the Post Office. Since she had fourteen teachers'
names, she wrote her letter out fourteen times.

In the morning when she woke, she felt a new energy and realized that she did not mind going back to work after her holiday. She
chose clothes from the wardrobe that she thought would make her
look most dignified. As she walked to work across the town, the
idea that the letters were in her handbag gave her pleasure. At work
there were several notes on her desk with queries that had arisen
while she was away. She dealt with each one briskly and by ten
thirty had settled down to a pile of invoices that needed to be
entered into a ledger.

'I think you could do my work and your own as well,' Elizabeth
Gibney said, 'if we just left you to it.'

'Some mornings,' Nora replied, 'my mind is clear. Do you find
that?'

'Not on Mondays, I don't,' Elizabeth said.

She posted the letters that afternoon and waited, but nothing
happened. Over the following days as she walked home from work,
she expected to see one of the teachers she had written to, but she
did not. Later in the week she walked downtown as the schoolday
ended, but still she saw no one.

On Saturday morning she went to Jim Sheehan's in Rafter Street
and bought a long, thin, flat piece of wood and some nails and then

she went to Godfrey's in the Market Square and bought a black marker, a large piece of cardboard, white paper and thumbtacks. She tried to think what she would put on the placard and concluded that it would be best not to put anything about A-classes and B-classes and not too much detail. She wondered if 'I WANT JUSTICE' would be best and then thought 'I DEMAND JUSTICE' might be better. She also decided to tell both Donal and Conor not to go to school on Monday and to explain to them as best she could that she was preparing to mount a protest outside the school and it would be a good idea if they were at home studying on their own while this was happening. She was not sure, however, how they would respond to this and wondered if she might try some other approach. She would wait, she thought, until Sunday evening before telling Fiona what she intended to do.

On Sunday evening at about seven a car pulled up outside the door. Two teachers from the secondary school, Val Dempsey and John Kerrigan, both of whom she had written to, got out of the car. For the first time, she felt afraid, as though all the courage of the previous week had dissolved and there was nothing except her pride and the threats she had made. She opened the front door for the two teachers before they had time to knock and ushered them into the front room.

'We're very concerned,' Val Dempsey said, 'about the letter you sent. You know, we had nothing but respect for Maurice.'

They both remained standing and she did not ask them to sit down. Somehow, Val Dempsey's tone had restored her determination.

'I can understand that you're upset,' he continued.

'I'm not upset at all,' she interrupted. 'What made you think that?'

'Well, your letter –'

'My letter simply said that if Conor was not put back in the A-class, I would picket the school. So I have the placard upstairs. Would you like to see it? And don't think I won't stand in front of you tomorrow morning, because I will.'

'That would be ill-advised,' John Kerrigan said.

'I didn't look for anyone's advice. If my husband were alive,

Brother Herlihy would not have picked on Conor in this way.'

'Well, the other parents –'

'I have no interest in the other parents.'

'We wondered if you would call off the picket in the morning,' Val Dempsey said. 'And then we'll see what we can do.'

'You've had three or four days and you have done nothing.'

'Well, there was a lot of talk about it among the teachers.'

'Talk, I'm sure, is wonderful, but tomorrow morning there will be more than talk, and perhaps if you are talking to any of your colleagues tonight you might mention to them that I will curse any teacher who passes my picket. I think you might have heard of the power of a widow's curse.'

'Ah, here now,' John Kerrigan said.

'I will curse anyone who passes me.'

The two men looked at each other and then stared at the ground.

'Maybe we'll go and see Brother Herlihy tonight,' Val Dempsey said.

They stood in silence for a moment and then she opened the door of the room and accompanied them both into the hallway.

'We'll let you know if there's any news,' John Kerrigan said.

She did not smile, but looked at him gravely.

Within an hour Val Dempsey and John Kerrigan returned. It would be harder this time, were Fiona or the boys to ask, to think of an excuse for their visit. She would have to tell them that it was about books and notebooks that Maurice used for teaching and that she was going to donate to the school. Both Fiona and Conor came into the hallway to look as Nora led the two teachers into the front room and closed the door.

'We left one sore Christian Brother down in the monastery,' Val Dempsey said.

'He said he wouldn't be bullied or ordered around,' John Kerrigan said. 'We told him how much you were respected in the town, and all your family. But he still wouldn't budge.'

'Then we had to tell him,' Val Dempsey said, 'that he and the other Brothers would be on their own in the school, because no teacher would pass the picket. He went mad when he heard about the picket. No one had told him what was in your letter.'

'He said a few things that I wouldn't repeat,' John Kerrigan said. 'A bit surprising coming from a Christian Brother.'

She smiled at the sound of this, and at how earnest the two teachers seemed. But she became serious as Val Dempsey spoke.

'So we sat down and informed him that we weren't leaving until it was sorted out. God, he was very red in the face. He said it was his school and he would do what he liked. So we just sat there looking at him.'

'I made clear to him eventually,' John Kerrigan said, 'that he could settle this simply and easily. And he asked how and I told him fair and square that he could put the young fellow back into the other class and no one would think any the worse of him.'

'He told me he wouldn't be threatened, but that if we left it with him he would consider what to do.'

'So we told him no, that we needed a decision now. And he walked up and down the room and eventually he stopped and said that he would do nothing tomorrow, he would not be bullied about tomorrow, but some day during the week he would move the lad back into the A-class. And we told him that would be fine and we decided to get out of there while the going was good.'

'So I hope that's all right with you?' Val Dempsey asked.

'It is better than all right, it is perfect,' she said. 'And I am very grateful to the two of you.'

She was almost going to apologize for invoking the curse, but decided not to. It might make it seem as though she had not meant everything else she had said. She accompanied them to the hall and wished them goodnight, then went into the front room and watched them driving away. She was not sure how to feel. No one would believe her, she thought, if she told them that she had the materials to make a placard upstairs in her bedroom and that she had threatened all the teachers in the Christian Brothers school with a curse.

When Conor came home for dinner on Wednesday he found her in the kitchen.

'I got moved back into the A-class,' he said.

'That's great,' she replied.

'There was a big cheer when I came in. Brother Herlihy called me out of the other class and told me to get my schoolbag, that I was moving. I thought he was going to put me in the C-class.'

'But there isn't a C-class,' Nora said.

'Well, they could invent one,' he said. 'Anyway, he came into the A-class with me and asked me who I was sitting beside last year and so I am back sitting beside Andy Mitchell.'

The next day when he came home from school he sought her out again.

'Did you have anything to do with me being moved back into the A-class?'

'Why do you ask?'

'Because I saw Feargal Dempsey's da up here on Sunday night, and today after a break when Brother Barrett had been in a bad mood all morning Feargal said that we'd have to send Webster's ma down after him.'

'I don't know what he meant,' Nora said.

When Fiona went out with a group of teachers on the following Friday night, she was shown the letter that Nora had written. On Saturday morning Nora was in the front room reading the newspaper when Fiona came in.

'It was your handwriting all right,' she said. 'Otherwise, I wouldn't have believed it.'

'Well, it's all resolved now,' Nora said.

'It might be resolved for you, but some of them think that I had something to do with it.'

'Well, I hope you told them that you didn't.'

'I might be applying for another job in the future and the letter would be on my file.'

'I think it will all be forgotten about.'

'And I hear you cursed all the teachers in the Christian Brothers school.'

'I threatened to curse anyone who passed my picket.'

'Well, I have to live here and work here.'

'Yes, and I had to make sure that Conor was back in the A-class.'

'I think I should have been consulted.'

'You would have told me not to send the letter.'

'I certainly would.'

'I'm lucky that I didn't consult you then, aren't I?'

She remembered that years ago Fiona had a cross nun called Sister Agnes teaching her who became crosser by the day so that Fiona was afraid to go to school. Nora had disguised her handwriting and written a number of anonymous letters to Sister Agnes and her reverend mother threatening the law on them unless the nun quietened down and stopped slapping the girls for no reason. The reverend mother had shown the letters to one of the lay teachers who had shown them to Maurice, saying that they believed they had been written by a woman called Nancy Sheridan whose husband owned a supermarket in the Market Square and who had a daughter in Sister Agnes's class. When Maurice told Nora what had happened in a tone of deep disapproval, Nora said nothing. But Sister Agnes had become quieter and nicer, Fiona soon reported.

She was tempted now to tell Fiona about the letters she wrote to Sister Agnes, but did not think that Fiona would find that funny. She was also going to tell her that she was becoming just like her father and her Uncle Jim, but thought better of that too. It occurred to her that Fiona might have said more had she not wanted the car that evening to go to the dance in White's Barn in Wexford.

The fight with Brother Herlihy had given her strength. She found herself, on waking in the morning, thinking of the day ahead with a sort of ease. She did not wish she could go back to sleep. She began to add up all the money she had saved, and, since it would soon be her turn to present her choice of records to the Gramophone Society, she thought that she should really buy a stereo record player and even some records. She decided to ask Phyllis to come with her to Cloake's so they could choose a record player.

Phyllis brought a number of her own records so she could sample the sound using music with which she was familiar. There were two stereo systems reduced in price. Having listened to a record of Maria Callas singing Verdi, she dismissed both of them. Nora had warned her that she did not want to buy anything that was too expensive, and as Phyllis studied what was on display she said several times that she was keeping the price in mind. There would be no extravagance, she said, but at the same time it would be better not to buy something that you would have to replace in a few years. In the corner she spotted a turntable and two very small speakers, which was only slightly more expensive than the two whose price had been marked down.

'I have a hunch about this one. I think it's the one my sister has and she swears by it. Don't mind the small speakers.'

When the assistant played a record for them on this machine, Nora was not sure she could judge the sound. Phyllis, on the other hand, could talk with certainty about depth of sound, and about bass and treble. Even though this one, she said, was more expensive than the other two whose prices had been reduced, she was certain that it was much better.

Phyllis came home with Nora and helped her to set the system up in the back room. She left the Maria Callas record and another one she had brought, of piano music. They would all see it now, all of her visitors, Nora thought, and they would think her extravagant. She would have to steel herself, no matter what comments they made, not to care. She had wanted this and now she had it.

One Saturday a few weeks later, she went on the train with Fiona and the boys to Dublin. They met Aine in The Country Shop for a late lunch, and then she asked the girls if they would look after their brothers for an hour or so, as she needed to go shopping on her own. She said that she would meet Fiona and the boys at Amiens Street station to catch the train home. Phyllis had given her the names of three record shops. One, she said, was small and would be easy to miss; it was opposite a pub called Doheny & Nesbitt's in Baggot Street. Another was called May's, and it was on Stephen's

Green, near the top of Grafton Street; and the third, which she had heard the Radfords mention, was McCullough Pigott's in Suffolk Street at the bottom of Grafton Street.

She had decided to buy ten records. The excitement she felt was new, like something she had felt after she married when she bought a dress or a coat. Phyllis had advised her against compilations, unless the record contained songs and arias by a single singer whose name she knew. She would be better, Phyllis told her, to buy records that had a full concerto, or a symphony, or a trio or quartet. After recitals at the Gramophone Society she had written down names of composers and names of individual pieces that she liked. But she would never have enough time to search for all of them.

When she found the shop on Baggot Street, she realized that she wanted almost everything. She would have to move fast and make choices. If she bought three or four records here and then three each in the other two shops, that would be enough.

In the background there was choral music playing and she thought it was beautiful. She almost asked the man behind the counter what it was and then decided not to. In the end, although she was sure she was making the wrong choices, she selected two Beethoven symphonies, Brahms's Hungarian Rhapsodies and a record of Maria Callas singing. In May's she thought she would buy more records with singing, maybe even with opera highlights, despite Phyllis's advice, and then in McCullough Pigott's she would buy chamber music.

As she was leaving McCullough Pigott's she noticed a pile of records that had no prices on them. They looked as though they had just been taken from the manufacturer's box. At the top of the pile was the album she had heard at Dr Radford's, which she had taken home and later given back, the Archduke Trio, and it had the photograph on the sleeve that had stayed in her mind, the young woman with the strong, shy smile and blue eyes and blonde hair. She brought the record over to the counter and asked how much it was.

'Oh, they're not priced yet,' the assistant said.

'I don't have long,' Nora said, 'but I'd buy it if it wasn't too dear.'

'A lot of people have come in looking for it,' the assistant said. 'We had to reorder it.'

The excitement of buying the records brought with it, she now saw, an ability to be downcast, easily disappointed.

'The manager has gone now,' the assistant said, 'but he'll be back on Monday.'

'I'm going home on the train today to Wexford,' Nora replied.

She tried to appear both humble and persistent. It was clear what the price range of the record was. She looked through a stack of records and found one that had the same label, EMI His Master's Voice, and she brought it over to the assistant, indicating the price.

'I think the price has gone up,' the assistant said. 'I'm sorry now, I'll have to check.'

It was close to half past five and Nora knew she would soon have to start walking towards Amiens Street station. But she was determined to buy the record.

'I come to Dublin often,' she called towards the assistant, who was going through catalogues, 'and if it is more than the other EMI record then I'll pay the difference the next time I'm here.'

When the assistant looked up, the expression on her face seemed to soften.

'What I'll do is I'll let you have it for one pound, and then the next time you are here, if you could ask me, and I'll reimburse you if it's less, and if it's more, which I think it is, then you can pay me.'

Nora fished a pound note from her purse, thanked the woman and left the shop, making her way quickly to the railway station.

On Sunday morning when the boys were at Mass and Fiona was still in bed, she put the record on and studied the photograph on the sleeve, looked at the men with their dark good looks and then at the young woman between them, who seemed happier the more Nora looked at her. She listened to the first movement over and over, relishing the uncertainty of it, as though someone were making an effort to say something even deeper and more difficult, and hesitating and then giving in to a simpler melody before moving out of it again into strange, sudden, lonely moments that the violin or the cello played with a sadness that she wondered how these young people could know about.

From then into the New Year she played the records whenever she had time, or when she was alone in the back room. For Christmas, the two boys and the two girls and Una gave her three Beethoven symphonies that she did not have, Aine buying them in Dublin. Margaret phoned Phyllis and found out that Nora might prefer something quieter and she bought her the Brahms cello sonatas played by János Starker. This meant that she had enough to choose from for her own first recital at the Gramophone Society.

Jim and Margaret came to the house often on Saturday nights and, when Fiona left for the dance in White's Barn and Conor went to bed, they watched *The Late Late Show* with Nora and Donal. The show featured discussions about Northern Ireland week after week, in between discussions about women's liberation and changes in the Catholic church. Jim developed a great dislike for a number of panellists on the show, but Nora often agreed with the ones who were making the case for change, as she felt that Maurice would have done.

One Saturday night in February, when the argument began to centre on the lack of civil rights in the Republic as much as in Northern Ireland, Jim was so enraged that he seemed on the verge of asking her to turn off the television.

When a break came for advertisements, she went to the kitchen and made tea and was coming into the room with a tray as the programme resumed.

Gay Byrne, the host, had clearly been talking to the audience during the break and the camera was focused on a group of women in the front row. Nora recognized some of them, feminists who were often panellists on the show. As Nora put down the tray on the coffee table, one of them was talking about slum housing conditions in Dublin and the march that day by the Dublin Housing Action Committee, which had ended in a sit-in on O'Connell Bridge.

'What would you say to the ordinary people of Dublin,' Gay Byrne asked, 'who were stuck in traffic for hours because of your sit-in?'

The camera moved to the next woman, whom Nora recognized immediately as Aine. Donal shouted out her name, but it took Jim and Margaret a few seconds more to register that it was her.

'Oh, good God,' Margaret said.

'Turn it up!' Nora shouted.

Aine was in mid-sentence, explaining that if the people of the South cared so much about discrimination against Catholics in the North, maybe they should get their own house in order.

'Instead of running guns,' she went on, 'they might be better to put in proper sewage systems and proper water supplies in the tenements of Dublin.'

She ended by saying that she was proud to be involved in the sit-in and would invite people from the North to come down and see the miserable conditions of working people in Dublin. As she was about to add another sentence, Gay Byrne put his hand up and moved the microphone to somebody else.

'Oh, good God,' Margaret said again. 'Our Aine!'

'I-is sh-she in one of th-those organizations?' Donal asked.

'I'm sure she is studying very hard during the week,' Nora said.

'Sh-she sh-should have t-told us. We m-might have m-missed her,' Donal said.

What was strange now, Nora saw, was Jim. He was almost smiling.

'Instead of running guns, they might be better to put in proper sewage systems,' he said. 'They are my sentiments exactly. I couldn't have put it better myself.'

'She speaks very well,' Margaret said. 'And she must have been nervous. I heard that it is very hard to talk on television.'

'And sitting beside all those feminists,' Nora said. 'I'd say there'll be a lot of talk about her after Mass tomorrow.'

'She'll be on the panel next,' Margaret said. 'But I didn't know that she had any interest in housing. Maybe it's on her course.'

Nora looked at Margaret and poured the tea. It was clear how surprised she was, and that she disapproved, but Nora loved how ready she was to disguise her feelings.

They watched the rest of the programme in case Aine spoke again and saw once, when there was a shot of her side of the audience, that she had her hand up to speak, but the microphone did not go to her.

'There we are now,' Margaret said when the show had ended. 'Wasn't that a good one?'

'Is sh-she a s-socialist?' Donal asked.

'I don't know,' Nora said. 'Maybe she'll tell us when she comes down the next time.'

Chapter Sixteen

Week by week, Laurie began to work with her further on 'The Last Rose of Summer' and suggested adding a German song.

'It should be something that would surprise them in an audition, maybe a Schubert song that will show your voice to its best effect. You know, I was in France when the Germans came and they even took the convent, and we had to move into a farmhouse, but I never stopped admiring Schubert and listening to his music. Now, I think I know a song that will make a difference to you.'

She rummaged through her records.

'Now, I have it. And I'm going to play it. Just this song and I want you to listen, let it sink in, and then we'll look at the words in English and then we'll do the German line by line.'

Laurie pulled the record from its sleeve and put it on the turntable. Nora closed her eyes and listened.

'Follow the piano first. Then we'll do the voice.'

At the beginning, the sound the piano made was direct and open. As soon as the woman's voice, a deep, rich contralto, began, however, it quietened and moved with subtlety, hardly there at all sometimes, but always ready to fill the silence, to come back in with more complexity between the verses.

'Now, let's listen again,' Laurie said. 'This time, the voice.'

What she noticed was a lingering tenderness on notes, a way of approaching the melody gently. The tone was neither sweet nor harsh; it hovered strangely between the two. The voice was sincere, she thought, but the singing was perfect and beautiful.

'This is Schubert's hymn to music,' Laurie said. 'The words were written by his poet friend who lived to be old. Imagine the music we would have if Schubert had lived to be old too! But that is the way of things. The German words are beautiful, and it loses a lot in translation. But this is the first verse in English:

"Thou lovely art, in how many grey hours,
When the wild round of life ensnared me,
Hast thou kindled my heart to warm love
And carried me into a better world."

It's very beautiful how Schubert put these words to music. It was, of course, an act of love. He and the poet were lovers, or so they think.'

'Schubert and another man?' Nora asked.

'Yes, isn't that marvellous? But sad, too, because Schubert died so young but the other man lived on and on. But we have the song to remember them, a song that came from love of music and love for someone else.'

'Who is the singer? She has a beautiful voice.'

'She's Kathleen Ferrier. She was from Lancashire and she died young too.'

Laurie made Nora read the German words, made her try to get the pronunciation right. She showed her how, in German, the verb often came at the end of the phrase. They listened to the recording one more time and for the following week Laurie asked her to learn the first of the two verses in German.

Donal bought some records of his own and played them over and over. She did not want to ban his using her record player, but there were times when all she wanted to do was listen to something herself sitting in the armchair in the back room, only to find that Donal was there already.

Both Donal and Conor took a great interest in Fiona's social life, where she was going and who she was seeing. Her preparations for outings at the weekend, the clothes she wore and the make-up she used, and the arrival of her friends, had a way of filling the house with something new. When Aine came for her first visit after her appearance on *The Late Late Show*, she pretended that it was nothing, and did not seem to want to discuss it. Fiona found a way of including Aine in her new social life, and they went to a lounge bar in the town on the Friday night together.

Close to Easter Fiona met a man named Paul Whitney, who was a solicitor from Gorey, at a dance in Wexford. Nora and Maurice had known his parents, as had Jim and Margaret. He was in his mid-thirties and, when Elizabeth Gibney heard the news, she told Nora that she had heard he could become a District Justice.

'He has a very good practice,' she said, 'which he set up on his own, and people speak very highly of him. A friend of Thomas's used him in an insurance case and he was delighted with the outcome.'

Fiona began to invite Paul Whitney to the house. On Friday and Saturday evenings and often on Sunday too he would come into the back room and talk to all the family while Fiona was getting ready to go out. He had an opinion on everything; he knew a great deal not only about politics but about the church as well, as he handled legal affairs for a number of parishes and was on first-name terms with the bishop.

'He misses Rome,' he told Nora one evening. 'He lived in dread of being made a bishop and being sent back to Ireland. And some of the priests in the diocese are a few kopeks short of a rouble, if you know what I mean. Not the brightest.'

Nora had never heard anyone talking about priests, or indeed bishops, in this way before.

He also knew about music and stereo systems. One evening he promised Nora that he would lend her his box set of Beethoven quartets and she could keep them as long as she liked as he had gone back to listening to Bach.

'Ah, he was the genius of them all,' Paul said. 'If God ever existed in Germany, which I doubt, then he came in the form of Bach.'

With Conor, he spoke of hurling and football, and with Donal, about types of cameras. He was open and friendly; even on Saturdays he came to the house wearing a jacket and tie. Each week the jacket was different, and the tie too. On the subject of Charlie Haughey, he had information that Nora had never heard before.

'If he could stay away from the women,' he said, 'that would be the best thing for him and for all of us. But mark my words, he has a lot of the party behind him and he's the coming man.'

One evening in early summer when Jim and Margaret were there, Paul arrived and began to discuss politics with them. Nora noticed how much at ease he was in the company of older people and could see Jim warming to him. She wondered what he spoke to Fiona about when they were alone.

Nora began to look forward to his visits. A few nights when Donal and Conor were in the other room, and Jim and Margaret not there, Paul sat for a while in the chair opposite hers and told stories and discussed matters of the day with herself and Fiona. Fiona would grow quiet as Paul addressed himself to Nora on the subject of music or religion or politics, matters on which Nora had often something to say as well. He was like Maurice in the way politics interested him, but he knew more, and he was interested in music, of course, which Maurice never was, and also, it emerged, in theatre. He read novels and had opinions on writers. On those nights, when Paul and Fiona eventually left together to go to a lounge bar or a dance, Nora found herself sitting alone almost content. She had enjoyed his company and it was clear, she saw, that he had enjoyed talking to her too.

One day in the Market Square, as she was passing Essie's, she saw a dress in the window that she thought might suit her, and she wondered about the price and if it would fit her. It seemed to be made of a light wool and was red and yellow in colour. She had not worn a dress like this for years. Once she went into the shop, she began to try on other dresses in the same light wool and in colours that she liked even better. She agreed to have three of them sent up to the house on approbation, thinking that she would need to check what they looked like in the light of her own house and to check also if she had the shoes to match them. The price was higher than she had ever paid for a dress before, but she thought that if she waited for the sale these dresses might be gone.

Fiona answered the door when the messenger boy came with the parcel of dresses. Later, she mentioned to Nora that Essie had sent up three dresses that she had thought might be for her, as she had been in Essie's recently looking for a new dress, but these were the wrong size and the wrong look. Nora went into the front room where the parcel lay open and came back and told Fiona that they were, in fact, for her.

'Is it for something special?' Fiona asked.

'No, no,' Nora said. 'I was just passing and saw a dress in the window that I liked and then I went in and tried some on.'

'I see,' Fiona said.

Upstairs, when the others had gone to bed, she tried the three dresses on and with each one walked down the stairs and checked herself in the hall mirror and, having carried down various pairs of shoes to see if they would match the dresses, she walked into the back room as though there were other people there and sat down on the armchair she normally used. She liked one of the dresses that had a belt around the waist and brighter colours than the others. She went into the hallway again and looked at her neck in the mirror and saw that the collar of this dress covered her neck better than the other two. She resolved that she would buy this one, and she would also buy new shoes, something more stylish, with a heel, she thought.

She left the other two dresses back with Essie the next day and paid for the one with the belt and the collar, but she did not think she would wear it until she had to go somewhere. It would be a good dress to have in the wardrobe. On Friday after tea, however, as she was in her bedroom, she decided that she would wear it there and then. Having put it on, she sat at the mirror and brushed her hair and looked through her make-up bag, finding a light mascara and a black eyeliner. When she heard a car, she went to the window to see who it was and, on seeing it was just two of the neighbours, she went downstairs and made herself a cup of tea and put on some music.

Later, in the kitchen, she bumped into Fiona.

'You look great,' Fiona said. 'Are you going out?'

'No,' she said, 'I just thought I'd wear the dress since I bought it.'

A few minutes later she heard Fiona going out. She was sitting in the back room listening to a Mozart piano concerto when Fiona returned.

'I'm going to need the car tonight,' Fiona said.

'Are you going to Wexford?'

'I'm not sure where we're going,' Fiona said.

Nora was about to ask if Paul was having a problem with his car, but there was a sort of briskness in Fiona's tone that made her stop. Later, she heard the car starting and thought it strange that Fiona had not come in to say goodbye.

Over the next few weeks Fiona was moody, going to bed early on the nights when she did not go out. When Aine came for the weekend, Nora asked her if Fiona's relationship with Paul Whitney had come to an end.

'No, not at all,' Aine said. 'I think it's going great.'

'But he hasn't been in the house for weeks.'

'That's the way she wants it, I think.'

'What do you mean?'

'I think she felt that everybody here was getting too friendly with him.'

'Who's "everybody here"?'

'You had better ask her, but she said that there were a few nights when she felt left out of the conversation.'

'We all just talked to him in the normal way.'

'Don't ask me. I wasn't there.'

'There's something you're not telling me.'

Aine looked at her sharply.

'One night she saw that you were dressing up.'

'And so?'

'And so she went and phoned Paul and they met in Bennett's Hotel instead.'

'She thinks I dressed up because he was coming?'

'Don't ask me. Ask her.'

'But is that what she thinks?'

'You'll have to ask her.'

'I have more important things to do.'

With Laurie at the piano, she worked hard on her two songs. Sometimes the work was slow and frustrating as Laurie ensured that she knew what every single German word meant and that her pronunciation was perfect.

Sometimes, she wondered about Laurie, about the stories she told and the familiar way she spoke about people whom she did not know, including indeed people long dead. She liked to live in some realm of her own invention, as far away as possible from the small town where she actually found herself. Sometimes, as they worked, Laurie could create the illusion that much depended on the result of this, that they were in Paris or London, and thus, under Laurie's intense scrutiny, Nora learned the two songs and managed to sing one of them in German as best she could, while Laurie's concentration did not slacken for a single second.

One day Laurie told her that she had persuaded Frank Redmond, the choirmaster in Wexford, that, even though he did not actually need a new mezzo-soprano, he should hear her latest pupil, Nora Webster, with a view to allowing her into the choir. It was agreed that Nora should come to the Loreto Convent on a Saturday afternoon when the piano would be free in the music room.

She had her hair done the day before, with some new colouring added, and wore the dress from Essie's, with a new pair of shoes that she had bought in Mahady Breen's. She had arranged to see Phyllis when it was all over, for a coffee in White's. When she arrived at the convent and met Frank Redmond at the door, she was surprised to be ushered immediately into a recital hall. Besides the pianist, there were two other people to whom she was not introduced. She showed Frank Redmond and the pianist the sheet music she had brought; the pianist said that he could play the first song from memory and would need the sheet music only for the Schubert song. He practised while she went to the bathroom.

She wished she had had time to do the vocal exercises that she always did before Laurie would let her sing. She would have to start cold. There was not even a glass of water on the stage and she felt that her mouth was dry. It was clear that these people had other work to do and they wanted this over with as little fuss as possible. She stood beside the piano and faced out into the hall. She put her hands by her sides first and then, since she felt exposed and uncomfortable, she put her right hand on the piano, only to be told by the pianist that she should not do this. Laurie would never let her sing until she was fully comfortable, but she had no choice now, she could feel the pianist's impatience.

The minute he began she knew that there was something wrong. Instead of playing the opening of the melody, he was playing something more complicated. She could not tell at what point she was meant to come in. The playing went under the melody, as though the pianist were harmonizing with someone else, and then he began a number of trills, before going back to the original melody. It was impossible to know what to do, so she simply began to sing. She had come in at the wrong moment, she knew as soon as she started, but there was nothing she could do now. When it came to 'no flower of her kindred', her breathing failed and she wavered too much on the high note.

When it came to the second verse, the pianist was barely playing and that made it easier, but she was not letting the depth of her voice emerge. Still, she did her best, and with a few phrases, concentrating hard, she found a tone she could work with. She relaxed and sang as Laurie had taught her to, controlling her breathing perfectly now as she came to the end of the song.

The three members of the audience left silence when she finished. She saw Frank Redmond making a sign to the pianist and she turned to him to see if he had the sheet music for 'An die Musik' in place. Instead, he shut the piano. She wondered if this meant that, since his playing for the first song had not gone well, he would allow her to sing the Schubert unaccompanied. She was not sure how she would find the right key.

'Maybe it would be better if we went outside,' Frank Redmond said, coming up to the stage, taking the steps in twos.

As she looked puzzled, he took the sheet music from the piano and handed it to her. She presumed that he was going to take her to a smaller and more intimate room to sing the Schubert where she might be less nervous. He led her off the stage and out of the hall and into the corridor.

'Thank you very much,' he said. 'We're very grateful to you for coming all the way down.'

'I haven't sung the Schubert,' she said.

'Yes,' he replied.

'So, is there another room that has a piano?' she asked.

'That song is one of my favourites,' he said, 'and I'd prefer not to hear it just now. Really, if we need to hear you again, we'll let you know.'

'I got off to a bad start. The accompaniment at the opening was not familiar.'

'Was it not?' he asked.

Suddenly, she saw that he was coming close to mocking her and that she was being dismissed. Even though she knew it was better to say nothing, she could not stop herself.

'I think he was using a different arrangement,' she said with some authority, as if she knew about arrangements.

'Yes, the whole thing sounded like the tune the old cow died on, you are right about that.'

He was being openly insulting.

'Thank you,' she said, when he opened the front door for her.

She parked her car at White's and did some shopping before she met Phyllis.

'Well, not since Janet Baker has anyone sung so beautifully. Is that what he told you?' Phyllis asked.

'What is the tune the old cow died on?' Nora asked.

'I don't know,' Phyllis said.

'I'm sure that it was not melodious in any case,' Nora said.

'Nora, did you not triumph?'

'The pianist played his own personal introduction to "The Last Rose of Summer" and they wouldn't even let me sing the Schubert.'

'Who was the pianist?'

'A little mousy fellow in a suit.'

'That's Lar Furlong. He did that before to someone I know.'

'Well, I hope never to see him again.'

'He is a well-known crank.'

'Is he?'

'Yes, he is. Now let's have coffee and cakes and work out how you are going to break the news to Laurie O'Keefe. You are her big discovery.'

★

248

When she arrived home, Jim and Margaret were there, talking to Fiona in the back room.

'We were just having a discussion about Donal,' Margaret said, 'because I met Felicity Barry, who's a speech therapist, and she's working in a number of schools, including St Peter's College in Wexford, and they have great facilities, including darkrooms to develop photographs and a camera club. And some of the boys get very good results in the Leaving Cert.'

'You mean the boarding school?' Nora asked.

'Well, I would be quite happy to pay the fees, especially if there was going to be a speech therapist.'

'Donal's stammer gets better sometimes,' Nora said.

'And then it gets worse,' Fiona said.

'And has anyone discussed this with him?' Nora asked.

'Oh, yes,' Margaret said, and then noticed Nora's irritation. 'I mean, he was going to talk to you about it,' she said.

'I am not sure that a boarding school would suit him. He's older than his years in some ways and younger than his years in others.'

'Well, being with others his own age might be good for him,' Margaret said.

None of this conversation could be happening, Nora thought, without Donal's direct involvement. He spoke to Margaret a great deal when he went to her house to develop photographs; he also spoke to Fiona. They asked him questions about himself that she never did, but, somehow, she felt that she was closer to him and that he depended on her in ways that no one understood. He had a habit of watching and taking things in that none of the others had, and Nora felt that he had absorbed her own feelings just by being in the house with her. He was fifteen now; in two years he would be going to Dublin to university. Maybe he needed to leave home sooner, to experience other things and be released from having to worry about her, but she did not think so. He liked the freedom she gave him, being treated as an adult in the house. His own interests were deep and private, she knew, and would not adapt easily to an imposed routine and a lack of autonomy and solitude.

The following day, when she spoke to him about it, she realized that it was something he wanted. He wanted a speech therapist; the idea of a camera club was also attractive. She tried to make him imagine what sleeping in a dormitory would be like, or obeying a large number of petty rules and regulations. But since he resisted her efforts to make him think negatively about boarding school, she knew to be careful. She did not want him or any of the others to believe that she depended on him, or wanted two more years of him and Conor together in the room beside hers. If she did not try to prevent something that he wanted, then he might decide more easily not to go. On Monday, she found a phone number for Felicity Barry and called her from the phone box on the Back Road, but there was no reply. She wondered if she should write to her and ask her if she would be willing to see Donal privately. She should have done this long before now.

Gradually, Nora watched the question of Donal and boarding school move out of her grasp. She would like to have known how it had actually started, who had mentioned it first. She did not say that she was against it, but she realized that Margaret was aware of her opposition and had grown silent on the subject, leaving it to Jim to say that he had met Father Doyle, the President of the College, at a meeting of the GAA and asked him if there would be a place for Donal in St Peter's College. Father Doyle said that he would be delighted to have any son of Maurice Webster's in the school. Nora found out later that Donal knew about the encounter with Father Doyle before she did.

When, once more, they went to Curracloe and stayed in a caravan, they were visited on their last evening by Jim and Margaret. Nora watched Donal lingering in the caravan, listening to the conversation. It was late July now and, if he was going to boarding school in early September, it would have to be arranged soon. As they talked, and the light of evening faded, Nora understood that it had already been decided. She had never openly confronted Margaret but felt like doing so now, felt like asking Jim to take Donal and Conor to the Winning Post for ice cream, and when they were gone telling Margaret that she was not to interfere in her children's lives. Margaret would, however, be able to claim innocence with full conviction and also claim that she was offering to pay for Donal's schooling, as she had paid for Aine's, only because it might be for the best. Nora would be put in a position of not wanting Donal to have a better education, and not being gracious in the face of Margaret's generosity.

Before Jim and Margaret left, it was agreed that Jim would write formally to Father Doyle. They made it sound as though it were not clear what his response would be, which Nora knew was not true. The school would accept Donal; Father Doyle had already told Jim. And Donal would leave home and go to boarding school. Nora wondered if there was anything she could have done to stop it, or if there was anything she could do now.

In the morning, when they had packed up and were ready to leave, she asked Donal to come for a walk with her. As they approached the strand, using the boardwalk, which was almost covered over with sand, she could see how uncomfortable Donal was, knowing that they were going to have to discuss something serious.

'Are you sure you want to go to St Peter's?' she asked him when they were on the strand.

'I s-suppose s-so,' he said.

'It's a big move,' she replied.

They walked along by the shore.

'I hate the C-christian B-brothers,' he said.

'Do you?'

'I w-wish I d-didn't have to g-go to any school.'

'It's just two more years. Have you spoken to Aine about UCD?'

He nodded.

'You'd be free to study whatever you liked there.'

'I want to st-study photography.'

'That wouldn't be a problem. There must be very good places.'

They walked further in silence. Donal began to pick up small stones from the shoreline and throw them into the water.

'Is there a particular problem in the Brothers?' she eventually asked.

He shrugged.

'It's all a p-problem.'

'Would boarding school be better?'

She could hear his breathing now and could see that he was upset.

'Would St Peter's be better?'

'D-daddy didn't t-teach there.'

He looked at her, and the look suggested a rawness that she had never seen in him before.

'Has it been bad?'

'The rooms are all the rooms he taught in. I sit in the classroom he came into every day.'

His tone was direct and hard; he did not stammer. She held him as he began to cry.

'And they all l-look at me and f-feel sorry for me. And I c-can't st-study. And I c-can't do anything. And I hate them all.'

She put her arm around him until it seemed to make him uncomfortable, and slowly they made their way back towards the caravan.

As she and Fiona and Conor accompanied Donal to St Peter's at the beginning of September, Nora saw immediately how lonely and isolated he was going to be. All of the boys came here for five years; Donal would be here for just the last two. The entrance hall was filled with boys and their parents; the sense Nora got was of the boys coming home, or at least arriving somewhere familiar. A few priests she saw moved around busily. Only Donal seemed at a loss, and Nora had to find a priest and explain that he was new and a boarder arriving for fourth year and did not know where his dormitory was or where to put his things.

'If you tell him to stand there by that table, I will deal with him in one second,' the priest said. He disappeared before she could ask him if she should wait with Donal, or if she should leave him alone with his suitcase and a bag, and drive home. She was also unsure what the system for visiting was and wished that she had checked this before now so that she could reassure Donal that she would see him soon. In the end, as she noticed other parents leaving, she told Donal that she and Fiona and Conor should follow them and that seemed to make him less uneasy as he stood there. She knew not to embrace him or say anything that would make him sad.

'I'll find out about visiting times,' she said, 'and I'll write and let you know, and you write if you need anything.'

He nodded and looked away from her and Fiona and Conor as if he barely knew them.

In the week after her rejection by the choirmaster in Wexford, she had called on Laurie O'Keefe and given her a detailed account of what had transpired. When Laurie suggested they resume singing lessons, Nora said she would prefer to wait for a while. The night after she had left Donal at St Peter's she decided, however, to call on Laurie just to talk, Laurie's house being the only place where her mind might be captured and held by something other than the thought of Donal alone and friendless, his stammer becoming apparent to teachers and fellow students, thus making him even more isolated than he had been when he was at home, where at least he could walk out of the room or take his camera to his aunt's house and spend time in the darkroom making prints.

Laurie took her downstairs to the music room.

'I dealt with Frank Redmond,' she said. Her tone was stern and dramatic as though she were a Prime Minister declaring war.

'I don't think we'll be hearing from him again.'

'What did you do?' Nora asked.

'I arranged for Billy to drive me to Wexford,' she said. 'When we found Frank Redmond's house, I made Billy stay in the car. Mr Redmond lives in a bungalow on the outskirts of the town. His poor wife answered the door and said he was out in the garden. So I told her that he was to come in from the garden now this minute, that I didn't have all day. When he approached, I asked him directly if he had insulted one of my students. Oh, he hemmed and hawed and made me follow him into the sitting room. It was filled with photographs of all of his children graduating. Six or seven of them, all with their scrolls. I asked him again if he had insulted one of my students. Oh, he began a long explanation of how busy they were that day and what pressure they were under. So I asked him a third time: "Did you insult one of my students?" And he said he was sorry if what he said had been construed like that. So I said to him that he could construe what I was going to say to him any way he liked. Here he was, I said, in his bungalow, all painted white on the outside, with a tiled roof like something in Mexico. Even the windows were the wrong shape. And not a book in the house, and awful ornaments on the mantelpiece. He was, I told him, ignorance personified, and he was in a position to judge nothing, least of all anything beautiful. In France, I said, there is a word for someone like him. And then I walked out. Billy said he never saw me in such a rage.'

'Oh, dear,' Nora said.

'Now, the winter is going to be hard. I can feel it. I always know if the winter is going to be hard. So we should make plans. I would like you to learn a French song. I thought maybe something by Fauré. And then maybe I should pay some attention to your friend Phyllis. She has a nice voice and it was well trained, maybe too well trained, but she is –'

'She is very kind,' Nora interrupted.

'Well, you have seen that side of her. There's a Mahler song I was thinking about too, I'll play it for you if I can find it now. It could work for soprano and mezzo. It's from *Des Knaben Wunderhorn* and I have it somewhere. It might be under Geraint Evans, he's the baritone, and Phyllis could sing his lines and then you come in as the mezzo. It's a sort of military song, but it's all about loss. You know, I think Mahler saw what was coming, the First War and then the Second War. You can hear it in his music sometimes, the mayhem, the evil, and then the terrible loss. Yes, he felt the loss.'

When the first notes began, Nora knew that she had heard the song before. And, when the voice came in, she felt herself once more with Dr Radford and his wife; she could almost taste the gin and tonic and almost smell the mixture of polished wood and smoke from the fire. The song this time, however, seemed different. The music was softer, the melody more plaintive and beautiful. But it was a melody she did not think that she could easily learn to sing; and she wondered if she should say to Laurie that perhaps Frank Redmond had a point when he made clear that he did not want his favourite songs destroyed by people who could not sing them.

'Now, I will give Phyllis a ring,' Laurie said when the song had ended, 'but perhaps you might alert her. And if you could intimate gently that she should not talk out of turn. It's one of her habits.'

Nora smiled.

'I'm sure that she will be delighted to hear from you.'

'And what we'll do is work towards having a small concert here when the spring comes. A few of my other students will perform for an invited audience. We'll ask Dr Radford and his wife and maybe a few people from Wexford if I'm talking to them by that time.'

'Oh, Dr Radford?' Nora asked.

'Don't worry. I know you had a dreadful evening with them. They really mean well. They wanted to make a good impression on you because I had spoken about you. They said that you were very cold to them at the Gramophone Society after that, and you handed back a record you had borrowed and you told them that you hadn't listened to it. But let's invite them to our little concert, and I'll keep them under control.'

On Friday of the following week, when she was leaving work, William Gibney Junior was waiting for her with a note.

'You know we have a new policy of not putting personal calls through to anyone,' he said. 'But they insisted that this is urgent and so I took a message.'

He handed her a piece of paper with Father Doyle's name on it and a Wexford town telephone number. She knew instantly that there must be something wrong with Donal. She thought of going back to her office and phoning from there, but she did not want Elizabeth listening to the conversation so she walked swiftly to the phone box in the Post Office, where she would have some privacy.

She got through immediately to Father Doyle.

'I don't want to worry you too much,' he said, 'but Father Larkin, who's Donal's English teacher, thought I should call you. Donal isn't settling in well at all, you see, and I know he has been trying to get in touch with you. I think Father Larkin phoned you but he was told that you were busy.'

'Is Donal . . . ?'

'Well, he's in bed now for a few days, and he hasn't been eating and he hasn't been able to go into the classroom. We've seen this before. I mean, he might just settle down.'

'Should I come to visit?'

'Father Larkin thought you should.'

'When?'

'Well, we thought tomorrow at the normal time for visits. And you can take him downtown. It might reassure him.'

'Father, I'm very grateful to you and to Father Larkin for letting me know.'

'Well, we'll see how he is tomorrow, Mrs Webster, and we'll say a prayer on our side. It's often just a matter of time. We all went through it at one stage or another.'

'Thank you again, Father. I'll be there tomorrow at two.'

She put the phone down.

Nora decided to say nothing to Fiona or Conor, or indeed Margaret. The next day, when she drove to Wexford, she found Donal waiting in the front hall of the school. He was wearing his school uniform, with its black blazer. He seemed taller and thinner and paler, but also more adult.

'I th-think you n-need p-permission to go out,' he said.

'It's fine,' she said, trying to sound as casual as she could. 'I got permission from Father Doyle yesterday.'

They drove towards the town centre in silence. She could feel that he was close to tears. She did not know whether it was better for him to cry or not to cry. Someone would know that, she thought, but she did not. As they walked along the Main Street, all she could think of was how easy it would be for Donal if he had not come to St Peter's. On Saturday, he could get up at whatever time he chose and have whatever he liked for breakfast. If he wanted, he could ignore her and Fiona and Conor. He could read the newspaper, and then make his way to Margaret's house with his camera and his rolls of film. He could come home whenever he liked. The house was his; everyone was used to his silences, his wry comments, his stammer. And now he would never have all that freedom again, except for holidays. It was as though he had joined the army. What he did at every moment of the day was decided by a set of rules. She wondered if all he had lost, all the casual and easy freedom that he would not regain, was going through his mind too as well as hers. But she was only imagining it; he must be feeling it as real.

They went into White's coffee shop but still they did not speak and he said he did not want anything there. As she sipped a coffee, she had no idea what to do. If she tried to talk as though it were an ordinary day, then that would somehow be an affront to what he was feeling. If she softened her voice and was sympathetic, eventually she would have to deposit him back in the school regardless. Saying nothing was simpler, at least for the moment.

When she asked him if he wanted anything, he shook his head, but he followed her to the fruit shop on the Main Street and agreed that he could do with some oranges and apples and, once she had paid for them, he said he needed some concentrated orange juice and some extra toothpaste. It was still only three o'clock. She was tempted to suggest to him that they drive back up to the school and get whatever clothes and books he had there and explain nothing to anyone, just drive home with him and never mention St Peter's again.

When she asked him if he was hungry, he nodded.

'I c-can't eat the food,' he said. As they walked towards the Talbot Hotel, she determined that she would not offer him a soft way out, that having him return home now, going back to the school he had left, would be a defeat and it could not be seen in any other way. Even offering him a time limit, another week, or month, or until Christmas, would leave too much open. They would have a plate of sandwiches in the lounge of the Talbot Hotel, and he could keep the silence going if he wanted to, but her aim now was to get him back to St Peter's before five o'clock. Maybe in the future, if things did not improve, she would consider taking him home with her, but she needed to give him no idea that this was a possibility. He would be more likely to get used to his new circumstances if he felt that there was no chance of an easy alternative. She was almost angry with him for not speaking, for not telling her about the new routines, or what he disliked most.

As they waited for the food, she thought to break the silence, but stopped herself. When the sandwiches came, they ate them without speaking. Donal barely nodded when she asked him if he wanted more. She could see that he was suffering, that his life at home had been destroyed and he could not have it back, but there was an element of rudeness, even aggression, in what he was doing now. Perhaps he was doing his best not to cry or call on her to help him by taking him home. Perhaps he knew that there was nothing she could say in reply to the list of complaints he could make, or any account of how he felt.

Suddenly, she thought of something.

'I will come down every Saturday,' she said, 'and even if we can't go downtown you can come and sit in the car or I can come into the parlour. And I'll bring supplies for the week, whatever you need. And there's also visiting on Sundays, and I know that Margaret will come and make sure you're all right. So that's Saturday and Sunday. And I think there are a few days when you might be able to come home for the afternoon. And if you just take it week by week you won't know it until it's the Christmas holidays, and then you can go down to the darkroom in Margaret's every day.'

He looked at her seriously and nodded. For a few seconds he seemed to be thinking about what she had said. Then he nodded again. It struck her that he had been waiting to see what she would do, and he had now registered that she had not come down to tell him that he could come home with her if he wanted. Everything that she said implied that he was staying at St Peter's. He glanced at her sharply, as if to make sure that she was not going to offer him release, that she was not about to say that these promised visits were merely one option, and there were other options that they might consider. She tried to seem sympathetic but also to make clear that she had nothing more to add, that he would have to return to St Peter's and make the best of it.

She went to the bathroom and when she came back she noticed a subtle change in him. He seemed less blank, less dark in his mood.

'Do you know what I would like?' she asked. 'I would like a letter from you sometime during the week, or even a photograph you have printed. And if there's anything I can do to improve things, let me know. And if anything gets better, I would like to know too, so I won't worry as much. Do you think you could do that?'

Her speaking about herself, her own needs, her own worry, made him appear even more alert. It occurred to her that he had thought more closely about her over the previous few years than she had about him. She wondered if that could be true. She knew that how she felt affected him, and now, for the first time, how he felt seemed more urgent, more worthy of attention than any of her feelings. All she could do was to let him know and make him believe that she would do everything she promised to do.

When they were sitting in the car, she spoke again.

'Every Saturday without fail,' she said. 'And write and let me know what food you want us to bring. Or anything else you need.'

He nodded and then looked away. She saw that he was going to cry and thought it might be easier for him if she said nothing more, just started the car and drove towards St Peter's. If he needed her to stop along the way, then she would. They did not have to be back until five o'clock, so they still had fifteen minutes. But he did not speak again until she had parked the car in front of the school.

Chapter Seventeen

By the time Conor asked her if he could have a camera for Christmas, she knew he had been looking at Donal's photography magazines. He seemed to understand when she explained to him that it was essential that he leave them back exactly as he found them. She had noticed him changing now that Donal was no longer in the house. He went to bed before she told him to, or got coal from the shed for the fire before he was asked. When Margaret and Jim came to the house, he would sit in the back room for a while and listen to the conversation, although he would never go to their house on his own as Donal did. Instead, he would often go to Una's house, where she would make him banana sandwiches.

Even though his school report had him ahead of everybody else, he was not satisfied. Some evenings, he would ask Fiona to take him through his Irish grammar, Fiona remarking to Nora afterwards that she only had to tell him something once and then he remembered. Because he listened to everything and forgot nothing, Nora had to be careful what she said in front of him. He always worried. If the car did not start immediately, he became concerned that they would need a new car. When they went to collect Aine from the train, Conor would walk up and down the platform worried that the train would not come, or that Aine might have missed it. He knew what time Aine had her lectures and what she thought about different professors, just as he found out everything he could from Fiona about where she went with Paul Whitney. So, too, he knew all about Gibney's and the people who worked there, especially Mick Sinnott, who had come up to him at a hurling match and asked him if he was young Webster and told him that his mother was a great woman. Conor took more interest in the family, Nora joked, than she did, and knew more about everyone than they did themselves.

On her visits to St Peter's, Nora did not mention to Donal how much better he seemed to be. He told her more about his activities in the school and the different teachers and priests than he had ever told her about the Christian Brothers and the teachers there. She was so relieved that he had settled down in the school that she did not mind when she discovered that he told Margaret even more than he ever told her. She worked out a system of nodding in recognition when Margaret mentioned some detail of Donal's life that she did not know. She wondered if Donal did this deliberately or if he was merely responding, when Margaret visited him regularly on Sundays, to her keener questioning about every single aspect of his life and every opinion that he had.

She knew she could not manage things between Donal and Conor when Donal came home for the Christmas holidays. Donal could not stop Conor wanting a camera, although he could undermine him by refusing to share any of his knowledge or by ignoring his brother. Conor had more need for approval from others than Donal, who often seemed oblivious to everyone except himself. And now, if Donal decided not to encourage him, Conor would make every effort to get Donal to change his mind. She smiled to herself one Saturday as she and Conor visited Donal in St Peter's.

'Donal, I'm thinking of getting a camera for Christmas,' Conor said.

'What sort of c-camera?'

Donal was in the front passenger seat and looked behind at his brother.

'I don't know.'

'I'll sell you mine. I was th-thinking of r-replacing it.'

'Is there something wrong with yours?'

'No, it's g-good,' Donal said. 'B-but I w-wanted a b-better one.'

She wondered if she should interrupt and either tell Donal that Conor wanted a brand-new camera, or tell Conor that what Donal had meant to say was that, since he was finding out more and more about photography, then he would need a different camera, but the one he was using now would be perfect for someone starting.

'How much?' Conor asked.

'I'll s-sell it to you for t-two p-pounds.'

'What do you think, Mammy?' Conor asked.

'I think what he really means is that he will sell it to you for one pound ten, but if anything goes wrong with it in the first year, he'll give you the money back.'

'Nothing will g-go wrong with it,' Donal said.

'Will you show me how to make prints if I buy the camera?' Conor asked.

'I'll show you how to d-develop p-pictures in Auntie Margaret's d-darkroom. I've learned a whole lot of new things d-down here.'

'When will you show me?' Conor asked.

'When I am home for C-christmas,' Donal said.

Conor, she knew, would go over every word of this conversation in his mind for days.

When the Christmas holidays came, Fiona went to Dublin to stay with Aine in her bedsit in Raglan Road. Donal took Conor down to Margaret's house every day. This meant that, as she prepared the house for Christmas, Nora was alone most of the time. She could listen to records without having to worry about any of the others. She kept the recording of the Archduke Trio as something special; she did not listen to it every day. But if she was annoyed by anyone at work, she would think about this music and promise herself that she would play it as soon as she came in the door. She would listen to it carefully, never using it, as she did with other records, as background music while she was working in the kitchen.

What she had told no one, because it was too strange, was how much this music had come to stand for. It was her dream-life, a life she might have had if she had been born elsewhere. She allowed herself to live for a time each day in a pure fantasy in which she could have learned the cello as a child and then been photographed as this young woman was, eager and talented and in full possession of her world, with men beside her who depended on her to come in with her deeper, darker sound. It almost made her wince in embarrassment when she thought of her own mornings in

Gibney's working with figures and dockets and invoices, and her own morning walk across the town, and her own return home each day, and how meagre were the things she looked forward to, and how far these were from a recording studio, a concert platform, a name that was known, how far from the spirited authority of this young woman's playing. She wondered if she was alone in having nothing in between the dullness of her own days and the sheer brilliance of this imagined life.

It was agreed that she would not take any more singing lessons until early January. Thus in the time leading to Christmas, Nora had nothing new to worry about and Christmas itself was easier than it had been in the other festive seasons since Maurice died. Her relationship with Jim and Margaret was warm and casual; she even enjoyed the visits that Una and Seamus made, and almost looked forward to seeing Catherine and Mark and their family in Una's house on St Stephen's Day. The idea came into her mind that this might have been what Maurice dreaded most when he was dying, that there would come a time when he would not be missed, that they would all manage without him. He would be the one left out. But she forced herself to believe that he would want them to be happy, or feel a semblance of happiness, and that there was no other way for them to live. Still, she wondered if she should try to mention his name at the table while they were having their Christmas dinner, but then she thought it would make them too sad, or sound too forced.

On a Sunday night at the end of January, with Aine back at university and Donal returned, without any obvious difficulty, to school, Nora was ironing clothes upstairs in her bedroom when Conor shouted up to her to come down and look at the news.

'But what is it?' she asked.

'Just come down and look,' he replied.

'They shot a whole lot of Catholics,' he said when she came downstairs.

'Who?'

'The British.'

Soon, Fiona came in and the three of them sat together watching the reports from Derry.

'I hope Aine is all right,' Fiona said.

'What do you mean?' Nora asked. 'She wasn't planning on going to Derry, or anything?'

'No, but she'll be upset by this.'

The British Army had shot into the crowd at a peaceful demonstration in Derry and had killed more than a dozen people. When the television news finished they turned on the radio; they heard tape of people screaming and then the sound of shots and then there were interviews with witnesses and with politicians. Nora watched Conor weighing up each word, and saw that Fiona too was listening closely to everything that was said.

She found it strange that as she walked to work the following morning only one man stopped her and said how terrible it was what had happened in Derry. Thomas Gibney seemed even more vigilant about the time, and who might be late. When Elizabeth came in, she barely mentioned it, and only when Elizabeth went for morning coffee with her mother did Nora feel free to wander out into the larger office, where a few people huddled around a newspaper spread out on a desk. When Mick Sinnott joined them, he said, 'That's it, then. No more waiting around, the whole lot of us should just go over the border. Take the place back.'

'You'd look well,' one of the girls said. 'They'd shoot you too.'

'We'd all be well armed,' he said. 'And we wouldn't be anywhere we could be easily found.'

'You couldn't even shoot a dead rabbit stuck in a gap,' another of the girls said.

In Slaney Street on her way home Nora saw two women she knew. They stopped when they saw her approach.

'Oh,' one of them said, 'the mother of one of the boys shot was on the radio and she said he was only seventeen and he was shot in the back.'

'All we can do is pray for them,' the other woman said.

'It was very shocking,' Nora said. 'Very shocking.'

'And after all the burnings they have been through,' one woman replied.

'There's evil in those soldiers,' the other said. 'Evil. You can see it in them.'

Some days later there was a national day of mourning, with everything closed. Nora and Fiona stayed at home and watched television with Conor. The coverage of the funerals was slow. Conor sat with them at first in case there was going to be more shooting. But the coffins and the church and the commentary did not interest him. Eventually, he drifted into the other room while Nora and Fiona watched quietly.

'We should really get a phone,' Fiona said. 'I tried to call Aine from the phone box on the Back Road but I just got someone in the flat below.'

'It would be nice to have a phone,' Nora said.

'I'd say Aine went on the march in Dublin,' Fiona said.

'I hope she went with people she knows,' Nora said.

'What do you mean?'

'I don't know what I mean. I just thank God we're living down here, miles from it all.'

'We are all Irish,' Fiona said.

'I know. I feel very sorry for those poor people.'

Later, Conor came back to watch with Nora and Fiona as the television showed a crowd gathered around the British Embassy in Dublin.

'I think they're going to burn it,' Fiona said.

'Are there people in it?' Conor asked.

'I'm sure it's well guarded,' Nora said.

Almost as soon as she spoke, she could see a figure breaking down the door of the embassy and then others following. Conor became excited.

'Is this happening now?' he asked.

'I think so,' Fiona said.

'Are more people going to get shot?'

'No one has guns,' Fiona said. 'Or at least I don't think they have.'

The commentary on the television was sketchy and confused. At times the camera wobbled and the view was broken by hands or heads in the foreground.

'Where is it?' Conor asked.

'It's Merrion Square,' Nora said. 'We had our honeymoon in the Mont Clare Hotel, just on the corner of it.'

'Did you?' Fiona asked.

'That was where you went at the time,' Nora said.

'Well, you're lucky you're not on your honeymoon now,' Conor said.

The following evening Jim and Margaret came to visit and Nora could see that Jim was excited by the fact that the crowd on the march in Dublin had gone on to burn down the British Embassy. When the news came on, they watched the charred remains of the building in silence.

'Every malcontent had a great night out,' Jim said. 'They wouldn't build anything even if you gave them lessons, but they'd be good at burning down.'

'It was very shocking all right,' Nora said.

'What were they meant to do?' Fiona asked. 'Walk by the embassy and thank them?'

'Dublin was a very dangerous place to be last night,' Margaret said.

'It was a fine night for the Special Branch,' Jim said. 'They got a good look at a lot of people, I'd say. They'll bide their time, but I imagine there will be some arrests.'

'Well, I think the protestors were right to burn the embassy down,' Fiona said.

'I suppose it's one way of letting the British know how Irish people feel,' Nora said. 'One boy was only seventeen.'

'Isn't that awful?' Margaret said.

'I think the government will know how to deal with this, and we should leave it to them now,' Jim said.

'How will they deal with it?' Fiona asked.

'We'll use all our ambassadors, and they may take it to the UN. But burning the British Embassy won't help our cause. It will make us look like a crowd of Baloobas.'

'Well, I think the protestors made our position very clear,' Fiona said.

'If I was the mother of one of those boys shot, I would get a gun,' Nora said. 'I would have a gun in the house.'

They were silent when Jack Lynch came on the television and was interviewed. The Irish Prime Minister said he had spoken by telephone to his British counterpart, Edward Heath. When he was finished, Jim was the first to speak.

'He is careful,' he said. 'I'd say he put a lot of thought into what he said, and got plenty of advice.'

'I'd say he gave that Edward Heath a good talking-to,' Margaret said. 'He's a very sour-looking man, that Heath.'

'Well, I hope he didn't let us down,' Nora said. 'If the British Army shot my son, I'd like someone a bit tougher in charge down here.'

'I think there's going to be a lot of trouble,' Fiona said. 'And I don't think Lynch is any help.'

'Well, please God now, none of the trouble will come down here,' Margaret said.

On Friday, Fiona finally spoke to the girl in the bedsit below Aine's, who said that she did not think Aine had been home for the previous few days. Fiona asked her to put a note on Aine's door telling her to phone her Aunt Una. She did not want to worry Margaret and Jim so she did not add their names to the message. Fiona told Nora, and went down to Una's house to let her know that Aine might ring. While she was there, she made a few calls to people in Dublin whom Aine knew. When she could not reach them, she left messages asking them to phone Una's. Nora waited for her to return with news of Aine, and when she did not arrive, asked Conor to come with her to Una's.

'Why are we going there?'

'Una invited us.'

'Why have we been invited?' he asked.

Because of the way he asked questions, it was often difficult to tell Conor a half-truth. Immediately on arrival, he sensed that there was something wrong and that this was not a casual visit. She could see his mind working, going through the possibilities. She could not tell him that they were worried about Aine, and that she had not been in her bedsit since Tuesday, the day before the burning of the embassy. When Nora went to the bathroom, Fiona followed her to say that she had called Aine's number again but the phone was answered by someone from another bedsit who had gone to check and found the note still pinned to Aine's door. She had to meet Paul Whitney, she said, and she would ask his advice about what to do.

'He'd know if there were people arrested at the embassy march,' Fiona said.

'Was Aine on the march?'

'I don't know. Maybe she'll phone tonight.'

When, by ten o'clock, only one person had phoned, who said that she had not seen Aine, Nora and Conor walked back from Una's house. Later, as she heard Fiona coming in, Nora tiptoed downstairs so that Conor would not hear her.

'Paul says that he was thinking of going to Dublin anyway tomorrow, so we can go around to Aine's.'

'Are you sure she was on the march?'

'I know she has been going on marches and this was such a big one, she wouldn't have missed it.'

Nora did not want to spend the day at Una's, waiting for a phone call.

'I'll go too in my own car.'

'There's no need.'

She saw that Fiona was on the point of suggesting that if she really did want to travel, she could do so with them, and then deciding that she would not ask her.

'We'll meet in the Shelbourne Hotel at two o'clock,' Nora said firmly. 'I'll ask Una to go and see Donal at St Peter's. And I'll call around to Aine's as soon as I arrive in Dublin. It's probably nothing. She's probably just staying with someone, and she'll be home then.'

'I'm sure you're right,' Fiona said. 'Which is why I wonder if we all need to go.'

'I can do some shopping,' Nora said.

'What will Conor do?'

'I'll deal with him when I've had a night's sleep.'

In the morning, she found Conor in the kitchen.

'What were you and Fiona whispering about last night?' he asked.

'Oh, I woke when she came in and I went and had a cup of tea with her.'

When Una appeared, Conor became even more suspicious. Nora signalled to Una not to say anything in front of him. No matter what room they went into, however, he followed them, at one stage pretending he was looking for something and then finding a chair near the window in the front room when they were there. Eventually, Nora went upstairs to her bedroom and waited for Una to follow.

'A friend of hers rang, she seemed very nice,' Una whispered, 'and she said that they all usually meet in a pub in Leeson Street on a Saturday night, either Hourican's or Hartigan's.'

She agreed to take Conor and visit Donal, bringing him what supplies he had asked for.

As Nora came out of her bedroom she found Conor hovering on the landing. They had not heard him coming up the stairs.

'Has Aine gone missing?' he asked.

'Who said that?'

'Maybe Aine was one of the ones who burned the embassy,' he said. 'Uncle Jim said that the Special Branch would be after them all. Maybe she's trying to escape.'

'Don't be silly!' Nora said.

'Why are you all whispering then?'

'Because Aine has a new boyfriend, and myself and Fiona are going to Dublin to meet him, but she didn't want you or Donal to know because she didn't want the two of you jeering her and asking her nosy questions when she came home. And she was going to tell you in her own good time.'

'What's his name'

'Declan.'

Conor seemed to think about the name for a moment and then he nodded.

'So you can go to Una's,' Nora said, 'and then go and visit Donal. And then we'll be home later.'

She drove to Dublin sure that, wherever Aine was, she had not been arrested. Had anything happened to her, Nora was certain that they would have been notified. She did not want to spend the day waiting to have all this confirmed, that was all; nor did she want Fiona and Paul taking over the role that she and Maurice would have played. Aine was her responsibility, but Aine was, she thought, like Nora herself. From an early age she had been able to take care of herself.

When she found the house where Aine had her bedsit in Raglan Road, she did not know which bell to ring, so she rang all of them. A sleepy-looking young woman came to the door in a dressing gown.

'Oh, yes, she's Flat 4,' she said. 'Did you get no answer for that bell?'

'Do you mind if I come in and knock on the door of the flat?'

'Are you the woman that's been ringing all the time looking for her?'

She pointed to a payphone in the hall beside the open door into her flat.

'I have been looking for her, yes.'

'Well, I went and checked last night and the note I pinned to the door is still there. You can go and check yourself now, but if you rang her bell and she didn't answer, then she isn't there. All the bells work perfectly.'

Fiona and Paul Whitney were in the lounge of the Shelbourne Hotel when she arrived.

'I phoned a friend of mine who's a guard,' Paul said. 'He's in the Branch a good while and he knows his way around. He says it's a very unsettled time. The thing is there were a lot of the Officials in Merrion Square on Wednesday as well as the Provisionals.'

'The Officials?' Nora asked.

'The Official IRA,' Fiona said.

'Oh dear,' Nora said. 'I'm sure Aine is not in any IRA.'

'There are so many new organizations now, it's hard to keep track of them,' Paul said.

'We're going to go up to Earlsfort Terrace,' Fiona said, 'because Aine often studies there, and then we're going to go to Belfield.'

'If she hasn't turned up by the end of the day,' Paul said, 'it would do no harm to put in a missing person report on her. The Guards would find her quickly enough, I'd say.'

'Let's wait until later,' Nora said.

They arranged to meet at the Shelbourne again at six o'clock.

Nora walked down Grafton Street and looked at the records in McCullough Pigott's, and then drove again to the house in Raglan Road. She rang the bell for Flat 4 and, on getting no reply, she went and sat in the car and waited until it was time to meet Fiona and Paul.

Paul liked the Shelbourne Hotel and appeared to enjoy ordering tea and sandwiches for all three of them in the lounge.

'I'd say,' he said, 'that this is one week in Dublin when people have been moving around a lot and staying in all sorts of places. So, I'd say that's it.'

'Yes, but it is strange,' Fiona said, 'that she has not been back to the house in Raglan Road.'

'When I was a student,' Paul said, 'I went to the Cheltenham Races every year. God, if anyone had come looking for me that week, they would not have found me. And one year a few of us got lucky and we went on from there to Paris.'

'And what about your studies?' Nora asked.

'You could do it all in one month. Certainly, in the law you could,' he replied. 'Even the medical students did nothing much until April.'

'I'm sure Aine is studying very hard,' Nora said, 'and hasn't gone to Cheltenham, not to speak of Paris.'

'The Cheltenham Races are actually in March,' Paul said. 'So she wouldn't have gone there.'

Nora looked at Fiona, who seemed as aware as she that Paul lacked a sense of humour. As he stretched and put his right ankle resting on his left knee, Nora noticed his socks. They were red and woollen and had obviously been carefully chosen. Looking at them made her wonder not only what she was doing with him and Fiona in the hotel, but what she was doing in Dublin. She thought back over everything that had led her here; the more she went over it the more she came to see it as a series of misjudgements, triggered by Aine's appearance on *The Late Late Show* a year earlier, but triggered more intensely by the shootings in Derry and the funerals and the burning of the embassy, and maybe too, she thought, by a lingering unease in the house that they had all become used to, but that any crisis, even one they watched on television, could bring to the fore.

She wanted to say that she was going home now and she was sure that Aine would get in touch with them in her own good time. And even if she really was missing, there was nothing that her being in Dublin could do to help. If they did not hear from Aine soon, they would have to make some decision and she would rather make it on her own, or with Una, than in the company of Paul Whitney or anyone else who could make informal phone calls to members of the Special Branch. As she thought about this, it occurred to her to ask Fiona if she had phoned Una.

'I should do that all right,' Fiona said.

'I'll come with you,' Nora said.

They had to wait for the receptionist to put the call through to Una. When the phone was engaged, they waited by the desk, Nora presuming that the receptionist would redial the number.

'We're going to stay the night in Dublin,' Fiona said.

'Where?'

'Oh, Paul has friends and we're going to stay with them.'

'I think I might drive back home now,' Nora said.

'Are we not going to go to Leeson Street to see if Aine is in one of those bars?'

'There's no need for all of us to do that. You can phone Una and let us know if she's there.'

Fiona turned away. Nora was going to say to Fiona that she had been married to a teacher and that teachers' ways of expressing annoyance were not new to her. Instead, she asked the receptionist to phone the number again. When the call was put through to one of the booths, Nora indicated to Fiona that she should be the one to speak to Una. Once Fiona had closed the glass door, however, she was sorry that she had done this. Clearly, there was some news and she felt that Fiona should convey it to her the second she had it. But Fiona left her waiting outside and ignored her when she rapped her knuckles on the glass. The urge came to her again to walk out, find her car and drive home. She would spend the next day, once she had gone to Mass and made sure that Conor was all right, listening to music. If there was any news about Aine, they could come and find her.

Nonetheless, by the time Fiona came out of the phone booth Nora had decided to steel herself and stand there and listen. She realized that she was desperately worried.

'Marian O'Flaherty phoned Una and said that as far as she knew Aine would be on the Dublin Housing Action Committee protest in O'Connell Street today, and then they would be in a pub called the Bachelor Inn on Bachelor's Walk and that later they might go to one of those bars in Leeson Street.'

'Has Marian seen her?'

'Yes, she thinks she's been at lectures all week.'

'So she's not missing?' Nora asked.

'Will you come with us to that pub on Bachelor's Walk?'

'I'm going home.'

'Well, we should see if Aine is there,' Fiona said.

'There's no need for all of us to do that,' Nora replied.

Fiona and Nora went back to the lounge.

'Paul,' Nora said, standing in front of him, 'we are all so grateful to you for everything you have done. I am going home now to look after Conor so I would really appreciate it if you and Fiona phoned my sister to let her know when you have seen Aine.'

He nodded. He seemed for a second almost afraid of her. She nodded to Fiona and left them.

When Nora arrived at Una's, she learned that Fiona had phoned to say that they had found Aine with a placard in her hand on O'Connell Street Bridge and that she was safe and sound. She had not been to her bedsit because she was staying with a friend whose parents were away.

'I hope it's all for a good cause,' Nora said.

'Well, isn't she a little minx for worrying us so much,' Una said.

When Conor appeared he was smiling. Una, he told her, had made him chips for his tea.

'And what's Declan like?' he asked. 'I bet he's small. And is he a socialist too?'

'He's very nice,' Nora said.

'Who's Declan?' Una asked.

'You remember. I told you this morning. He's Aine's new boy-friend.'

'Oh, yes,' Una said. 'I believe he's very nice.'

Conor studied the two of them.

'I don't think she has a new boyfriend at all,' he said.

One morning in late February, when she was walking to work, Nora noticed Phyllis's car parked in John Street. As she got closer, she saw that Phyllis herself was in the driver's seat reading a newspaper. For a second she thought to tap on the window, but then decided it would be better if she slipped by. The second morning, however, when the car was there again, Phyllis spotted her approaching and pulled down the window.

'I'll tell you the whole story at the Gramophone Society,' she said, 'but I am here keeping guard in case Mossy Delaney, who is painting my house, decides to go to paint someone else's house leaving mine half-done. He knows I'm here, so he'll just have to come with me when he deigns to get out of bed. Oh, the trouble I have had!'

On Thursday evening during the tea break at the Gramophone

Society Phyllis told her that when, on the first day, Mossy had failed to turn up she had driven all around the town, but had failed to find him. And then she had called to his house in John Street to be met with impertinence by his wife. She had then roamed the countryside, asking anyone she saw if they had seen Mossy's van, which was painted green and looked like a wreck. Eventually, she said, she had found him at Deacons' grand house near the road to Bunclody. She had gone into the house unannounced and found him halfway up a ladder painting a wall.

'I shook the ladder and let a roar and frightened the life out of him,' Phyllis said, 'and then was escorted out of the house by Mrs Deacon, but not before I had told Mossy that I meant business. So the only way I can be sure to get the work done is by sitting outside his house every morning. I won't tell you what his wife said to me yesterday. She is someone who is in full command of the vernacular.'

Nora became interested when Phyllis mentioned that Mossy was painting over her wallpaper, using a new type of paint that the wallpaper could absorb. The last time she had the back room of her own house repapered she had sworn that she would never do it again. With Fiona and Aine, she had to strip all the old paper off with a scraper. No matter what they did, the scraper cut into the plasterwork. And then she thought that she had chosen the wrong wallpaper; it was too fussy, with too many flowers in a repeated pattern. She had trained herself to ignore it, but sometimes she found that it held her eye and that she was doing nothing else but looking at it.

Phyllis assured her that, once Mossy finally arrived, he was a perfectionist; she described how he began with large strokes of the brush that looked as though they were going to allow the paint to go everywhere. Mossy explained, Phyllis said, that it was important that the paint be applied thinly and quickly so that it would not soak too heavily into the paper.

Nora was not sure that she wanted to spend money on a painter. Also, the idea of someone disrupting the house, not coming when he was meant to come, and leaving work unfinished for a long time, was not something she could face. She began to study the wallpaper in the back room, however, and wondered if she herself could paint over it, wondering also what the room would look like if it were painted white or cream. Everything else would look shabby, she concluded. The lino was worn and the tiles in the fireplace were chipped and the pelmet over the window was made of some thin piece of wood that looked flimsy. The curtains had never been changed in all the years, and it was becoming increasingly difficult to close them at night without them sagging.

The idea of what she might do with the rooms downstairs kept her awake. She had to remind herself that she was free now, that there was no Maurice who would be cautious about costs, and grumpy about anything that would cause disruption to his routine. She was free. She could make any decision she liked about the house. She felt almost guilty as it occurred to her now that she could do whatever pleased her. It could all be done, anything she wanted, as long as she could afford it. If Jim and Margaret disapproved, or her sisters or daughters came with advice, she could ignore all of them.

She would have to be careful with the boys. They were suspicious of everything, and watched her with nervous attention if she mentioned money. Conor had formed the habit of checking the price of things, and commenting on her purchases. If he were to find her looking at carpets in Dan Bolger's, he would worry; it might be best if a new carpet arrived before he knew that she had bought it.

She wrote a list of things to make the rooms more modern. A new carpet and fireplace in the back room; then the walls to be painted. She might do the painting herself if she could watch Mossy Delaney working in Phyllis's house and maybe find out what paint he was using. Then she would move the dining table from the back room into the front room, and maybe put a new carpet in that room too, and perhaps even paint the walls there. Conor could do his homework at the table in that room or Fiona could use it. And she would move the three-piece suite from the front room into the back room and throw out the two fireside chairs, which were shabby and not very comfortable.

In Dan Bolger's in the Market Square she looked at curtain material and saw a catalogue in which the curtains stretched right across a wall, even though the window needed only half the amount of material to cover it. She wondered if this would work in her back room. If the walls were painted white, she could select some colour for the curtains that would be warm and rich. The living room pictured in the catalogue used lamplight at night rather than a single light in the ceiling overhead. She could take the standard lamp from the front room, where it had hardly ever been used, and put it in the back room. Maybe she would buy more lamps in Dublin – in Arnott's or in Clery's – or in a shop in Wexford.

She began to put prices on things. Some days at work, Nora took out her list and looked at it. The painting would have to come last when all the dust had settled; replacing the fireplace would have to be done at the very beginning.

When she explained to Phyllis that she did not want to use Mossy Delaney, Phyllis told her she was wise.

'Oh, I am sorry I didn't have him up here just to get all the best advice from him. And then start it myself the minute he left. It would have saved a lot of trouble, and it's probably very good exercise.'

Within a few days Phyllis called on her, having received full instructions about paint and brushes from Mossy Delaney. Phyllis had even found out the best way to apply the new type of paint and how to stop it dripping. She did imitation strokes on the wall.

Dan Bolger had noticed Nora in the shop, and came over one day to say that he had known Maurice well when they were trying to set up the Credit Union. He and Jim Farrell always said, he told her, that if it had not been for Maurice it would have taken another year to get things going properly.

'I'm not Fianna Fáil myself, as you probably know,' he said, 'but I always say that if Maurice Webster had run for the Dáil I would have given him a number one vote, and that's the highest compliment you can get from a dyed-in-the-wool Fine Gaeler like myself.'

Nora smiled.

'So if there is anything I can do for you, with wallpaper, or curtain material or carpets,' he said, 'then I will.'

Nora realized that if she spoke to Dan Bolger, she would get a reduction on everything. Somehow, she felt, it would make a difference if she could tell everyone that she had done it all cheaply. She produced her list.

'I'll phone Smyth's now because I don't have that paint but they will have it,' Dan Bolger said. 'And I can do you a good deal on the curtain material and the fireplace and the carpets. And there's only one man can put in a fireplace without making your house look like the entrance to Croke Park on a wet all-Ireland Sunday and that's Mogue Cloney. You won't get much talk out of him, but he'll do the job.'

Once she selected the curtain material and the carpets, Dan Bolger sent a man to take the measurements. When she told him that she wanted the curtains to run the entire length of the wall, he explained that there was a new system for hanging curtains that would not require a large pelmet.

'Can you hang curtains?' she asked him.

'We don't normally do that. We'll fit the carpet all right,' he said. 'But we'll just have the curtains made up for you.'

She left silence and did not move, as though what he had said was causing her anxiety. She could almost feel him wondering how he was going to get out of her house without having to offer to hang the curtains for her. For a second, she wished she knew his name or something about him so she could soften his determination.

'I can't think who would hang curtains,' she finally said.

'Ah well,' he said, 'I wouldn't leave you stuck.'

'Thanks very much,' she said. 'That is really very nice of you.'

Mogue Cloney came one morning at eight thirty with a helper. She explained to Conor that he was going to take out the old fireplace and put in a new one.

'How do you take out a fireplace?' Conor asked.

'A few blows of a hammer against a metal bar will unsettle the cement,' Mogue Cloney said.

'Would it not take bits of the wall with it?' Conor asked.

'Begob, you sound like an old Guard who has stopped me for bald tyres,' Mogue Cloney said as he and his helper laughed.

When she came home, the back room was covered in dust and the old fireplace was lying on the lino in the middle of the room. As soon as Conor arrived, he went with Fiona to inspect everything, as though the two men were working for him.

'Where's the new fireplace?' he asked.

'It's in the van,' Mogue Cloney said.

'Are we sure it will fit?' he asked.

'We are,' Mogue Cloney replied.

Conor looked around the room. He seemed to be checking if everything else was still in place or if Mogue Cloney had done any damage.

When Conor and Fiona went back to school after dinner, Nora thought that she should go out. But she was uncertain if she should not be there to supervise.

'If you give us a good sweeping brush and a good scrubbing brush,' Mogue Cloney said, 'you won't even know we've been here.'

Once the paint was delivered, she went to Wexford one Saturday to buy the exact brushes Mossy Delaney had used in Phyllis's house. When she borrowed a ladder from Una, her sister told her that she should not attempt the painting herself.

'It's just a few days' work,' Nora said.

'I think you have enough to do,' Una said.

She began one day as soon as Fiona and Conor had gone back to school. If she stood on the top rung of the ladder and put the pot of paint resting on the flat top of the ladder, then she could reach the ceiling. The paint was thin and it dripped on her hair, so she had to find a shower-cap to cover her head. She was determined to do this in three or four days and also to have a visible sign of progress by the time Fiona and Conor came home. Each stroke of the brush took work and concentration as she had to balance herself carefully and spread the paint evenly. The ceiling would be the hardest part, she thought; the walls would be much easier.

The work gave her a strange happiness and made her look forward to coming home from Gibney's the next day and doing more. It was only when the weekend came that the pains in the arm and her chest began. She had to ask Fiona to go to see Donal on Saturday as she did not think she could drive; she was in such pain by the afternoon that it was clear she would have to go to the doctor. She wondered as the pain seemed to dart and intensify if she was not having a heart attack.

She winced when Dr Cudigan touched her arm and almost cried out when he pressed a thumb into the soft space beneath her collarbone.

'Have you painted a ceiling before?' he asked.

'No,' she said.

'It's not something anyone should take on lightly,' he said. 'You were straining muscles that you normally don't use at all. I am going to give you a strong painkiller and that will bring the pain down and then the muscles will go back to where they were if you don't strain them any more.'

'I won't be able to do any more painting?'

'You could have done yourself real damage,' he said. 'So you'd be better to leave the painting to painters.'

That evening she looked at the room. Three-quarters of the ceiling was done, and not done very well. She asked Fiona to phone Phyllis to see if she could visit whenever she had time.

The next day when Phyllis came, she inspected the back room.

'Well, there's only one solution,' she said. 'And that is to call in Mossy Delaney. Today is Sunday and it might at least be possible to find him. And if I were you I would play the part of the poor woman who thought you could paint a ceiling. He objects to me most when I am high and mighty, so humility might work with him. But of course money would work too. He leaves every job to begin another, so he can leave one for you if you pay him on the first day. But you have to put the right face on.'

That evening, when she knocked on Mossy Delaney's door, his wife answered and asked her what she wanted.

'I would like to talk to Mr Delaney,' she said quietly.

When Mossy appeared, it was clear that he had been asleep. Nora tried to speak softly so that his wife would not hear. She explained to him what had happened.

'So I should have come to you in the first place. I am in a dreadful situation now. Really stuck. And I can pay you before you start.'

'Is it just one of those small rooms?' he asked. 'It's not the whole house?'

She nodded humbly.

'I'll do that for you in the morning. Do you have the paint?'

'I do.'

'I'll be there at half past eight.'

She nodded again.

'Do you need the missus to walk up home with you? You look very shook.'

'No, I'll be able to get home,' she said. 'But I am very grateful to you.'

Chapter Eighteen

The pills Dr Cudigan prescribed took the pain away, or they masked whatever was still happening in her chest and in her arms. There was still a heaviness and a sense of strain. On the third morning she believed again she was having a heart attack. But then the sharp pain died down once she got up.

She moved carefully and slowly all the more now since she could not sleep. She did not know if the painkillers caused her to lie awake in the night with rushing thoughts and then a blank state of being half-alert, or whether it was the lingering ache in her arms and chest.

Mossy Delaney and a helper finished the painting in a day and a half. When he was done, she told him that she appreciated how obliging he had been.

'The thing is,' he said, 'you'd work for people with plenty of money and they would be just plain ignorant. The money makes them ignorant. I won't name anyone now, but there are ignorant people in this town, and if you want to know them, then go and work for them. There's one woman I could name. All I know is that I will get my reward in heaven for not spilling a can of red paint all over her. I came close to it, mind. And I would have enjoyed the screaming. But I'd always like to help someone out, and you are a brave woman for thinking you could paint a ceiling yourself. God, we got a great laugh when we saw what you had done! Painting a room is like anything else. You have to know how to do it, missus, you have to have the skills. I mean, you wouldn't go to Larry Kearney if you needed the bank manager, now, would you? Or Babby Rourke if you needed the bishop?'

Fiona supervised the men who came to put down the carpet and she and Conor also dealt with the man from Dan Bolger's who came to hang the curtains. There were a few things still missing, such as a new shade to cover the bare bulb that hung from the ceiling in the middle of the room, and the white walls without any pictures seemed strange and bare. During the day, the heavy curtains made the back room seem dark; after work she sat in the newly made room with the smell of fresh paint and dozed and woke again. She knew that she should stay awake so that she could find a rhythm of sleeping, but it was too hard. All night now she longed for the morning, but once she was half an hour at work she felt a desperate tiredness.

She formed the habit in Gibney's of going to the bathroom and sitting in one of the stalls, letting her head rest against the wall and falling asleep for a few minutes, and then washing her face in cold water before returning to her desk. Since Elizabeth had dropped both boyfriends for a new one, and the new one seemed to Nora to be solid and serious, and devoted to Elizabeth, they had a lot to discuss and that helped to keep her awake.

She found that if she had a cup of instant coffee in the morning with three spoonfuls of coffee and as much sugar as she could stomach, then she would be fine for the first hour, or maybe longer. If Elizabeth left the office, she boiled the kettle that Elizabeth kept beside her desk and had another large cup of coffee. It almost made her sick but if she concentrated she did not have the same urge throughout the morning to put her head on her arms at the desk and fall into a deep sleep.

When she went back to Dr Cudigan after seven days, he told her that it would be a mistake to take sleeping pills with the painkillers. He checked her pulse and ran his stethoscope over her chest and back, and said that, as she had strained her muscles quite badly, maybe she should stay with the painkillers for another week or so, and then, if she still could not sleep, he would take her off the painkillers and prescribe sleeping pills.

She was so tired at night that she had to make sure that neither Fiona nor Conor was close by when she went up the stairs, gasping for breath when she was halfway up, and holding the banister so that she would not fall back. Without taking her clothes off, she lay on the bed with the light on, and her sleep then was the same sleep of oblivion as she had slept in that basement bedroom in Sitges. But it lasted sometimes for less than ten minutes. After it, she was fully awake, with thoughts darting. Once she was in her nightdress and in bed with the light off, she did everything she could to make herself sleep. She counted sheep; she lay on one side and then on the other. She refused to let any thought come into her mind. But nothing worked. She would have to go back to Dr Cudigan and insist on sleeping pills or insist that she could stop taking the painkillers.

Lying awake like this in the dark she could be anyone in the past, she thought. She could be either of her grandmothers, whom she had never known. They had both died before she was born and were dust now, a skull and some bones under the ground somewhere. Her mind moved back and forth over them and what she knew about them until it shifted and focused on her mother, whose face came to her now and whose presence seemed close. She could be her mother lying here. It was just a difference of years. She lay still in the dark with her eyes open, breathing and then not hearing her breath. In the half-sleep, her mother came closer. Slowly, the image of her mother laid out after her death appeared to her, as though her mother were lying on this bed in this instant, seeing nothing, hearing nothing. No matter what she did to avoid it, that last time with her mother's body resurfaced in vivid detail.

She had not loved her mother when she was alive. She wondered if Catherine and Una thought about that when their mother died, as all three left her body in the care of the nuns who had come to lay her out in the upstairs bedroom of her house. As Nora sat in the kitchen without speaking to them, she knew that the next time she would see her mother she would be in the stilled, formal pose of death. The room would be darkened. There would be flickering candlelight; her mother would be at rest, no longer there, gone from them. She would lie in repose through the night and for most of the following day.

It struck her what she would do. She had seen it once before when her father died. Her Aunt Josie, and her Aunt Mary, her mother's older sister, had found a chair on each side of the laid-out body and they sat there without speaking until the undertakers came with the coffin. A few times the two women took tea, but mostly they refused. They took hardly any food either. Sometimes they prayed, sometimes they merely looked closely at their dead brother-in-law, a few times they acknowledged the arrival or the departure of someone they knew. They watched and waited, having found a place where no one would disturb them. They did vigil.

Nora knew there was a chair on the other side of the bed from the door in her mother's room, an old armchair that had once been downstairs. Her mother had used it to put clothes on. Her mother, in the old days, would have made sure that all her clothes were in the wardrobe or in the chest of drawers. But in recent years she was too weak. Moving was hard. Her mother did as little as she could. Nora remembered that she suddenly felt a sadness then, something she had not felt before. It had come to her in one second what death meant: her mother would never speak again, never come into a room again. The woman who had given birth to her was not breathing now and would not breathe again. In some way, Nora had not bargained for this, had always felt that there would be time for herself and her mother to meet and talk with ease and warmth, or something like warmth. But they never had, and they never would now.

She waited, without lifting her head, until someone said that the room was ready. She passed the others without speaking. When Catherine asked her a question, she did not listen and did not reply. Whatever Catherine needed to know, she could find out in some other way. Nora was the eldest of the daughters; now she would be the first in the room. She walked up the stairs and nodded to the young nun who was standing in the doorway. The curtains had been drawn and there was a smell of freshly starched linen. She waited for a moment and then passed into the room. It was her mother's chin she noticed first; somehow, in settling her head against the pillow, they had made the chin seem longer than it should have been. It appeared out of place. She wondered if she should say something to the nun, if something could be done about it. But she supposed not. It was too late now, she thought. Maybe it would make no difference.

She found the chair across the room. The clothes that had been on it had been put away somewhere. She hoped that her staying here would not cause her sisters or the neighbours to feel that it was because of remorse or the need to make up to her mother, to show regret for what she might have done, or what she had not done, in the past. She did not feel remorse. Instead, as she looked at her mother's dead face, she felt a closeness to her, a connection that she had in some way always felt, but never acted on, or spoken about.

The face, cleared of suffering and of familiar expression, resembled her mother in old photographs when she had a thin, dark, shy, watchful beauty. That, or traces of it, had returned. Her mother would have liked the idea that her youth, or some part of it, had come back.

Her two sisters came and looked at their dead mother. Catherine knelt and bowed in prayer and blessed herself as she rose to her feet. Nora watched her as she self-consciously stood by the bed in the role of prayerful, sorrowing daughter. She wished that Catherine would go downstairs. When she caught her sister's eye for a moment, she found an expression there that she did not trust and she determined that no matter what happened over the time that followed she would not find herself alone with Catherine; she would stay here in the room all night if she had to. She would not leave the chair. When Maurice arrived to be with her, she told him that she was going to stay the night here in the room. He held her hand for a moment and then said that he would bring the children in the morning, but he would go home now and stay with them. She smiled at him as he left. Her mother had loved Maurice. That was not unusual, Nora thought, as everyone loved Maurice.

Over the next few hours neighbours came. They each knelt down and said a prayer. A few leaned in to touch the dead woman's hands with rosary beads entwined, or her forehead. They nodded at Nora and a few whispered to her, about how peaceful her mother looked, or how she had gone to a better place, or how she would be missed.

When Nora was alone in the room, she could hear voices downstairs and she guessed that people were having tea and sandwiches. The candles had burned down to half their size. Her mother was nothing now except an old woman who had died. There were no features in her face that Nora could make out, just whitened, wrinkled skin and a chin that was still oddly noticeable. Without her eyes open, without her voice speaking, her mother was nobody, there was no life in her.

Eventually, the house became quiet. Una came and offered to stay instead of her, but Nora refused, and she suggested that her two sisters try to get some sleep. She would make sure that there were candles kept burning and that her mother was not alone on her last night in the world. There was silence in the house, broken sometimes by the passing of cars and by the rattling of the windows in the bedroom in the night wind.

Nora wondered if it was the tiredness, or the light from the candles that cast long shadows on the wall, but she would not have been surprised if her mother had moved now or spoken. The talk between them might have been easy.

What was strange as she began to look at her mother again was how little she was sure of. The details of her mother's face had vanished, but there was an expression still, a sense of someone. And then that sense became more exact, more clear the more she watched. She could see other people in her mother's face – the faces of cousins, the Holdens and the Murphys and the Baileys and the Kavanaghs; the faces of Catherine and Una; Nora's own face; the faces of Nora's children, especially Fiona. It was as though her mother in this long night alone became all of them.

All the natural life had gone and instead something else had come, something a long time in the making. It lingered there, and then it faded and something else replaced it. The face exuded an impression more powerful than anything it had ever done in the days and nights when there was breath and voice.

Nora was not sure. She tried to picture her mother as she remembered her best – an old woman in a grey coat of soft wool, a brooch in the lapel of the coat, a scarf. An old woman walking towards her; or a young woman in a photograph. But none of these images was as real as the face in the bed that night. She wondered how she would remember this, but remembering would be nothing compared to this looking, the intensity of this here and now.

The chin ceased to matter, it was a mere detail, and details now were of no consequence. What mattered could not be named or easily seen; if one of the others came into the room they might not see it at all. It was maybe what she and her mother had been waiting for. She wondered if she had kept away so that this encounter with the body of her mother, with her mother's dead image, could matter more, or simply be possible. Her mother's face was both more mask-like and also more individual than it ever had been; Nora would be the only one who would recognize that. None of the others would be able to see it, they were too busy, too close, too involved. It was her distance that made it possible. It was her distance now that allowed her to sleep for a while and then wake with a start in her own room and realize that she had been dreaming, that the night's vigil by her mother's bed was part of a dream. She was in her own house and it was time to get up and wake the others and make breakfast and go to work.

That day, when she went to the cupboard in the office to fetch a file, she fell over. When she came to, Elizabeth was on the phone to Peggy Gibney, who gave orders that if Mrs Webster could walk at all, she was to be taken over to the house. As soon as she was standing up, Elizabeth insisted on guiding Nora out of the office and through the storeroom at the side and across the street to the family house.

'You know, really I'm fine,' Nora said.

'My mother is always the expert on how people are,' Elizabeth said.

Peggy Gibney was sitting in her usual chair. When Elizabeth and Nora appeared, she called for tea.

'Well, I think you are looking very pale,' she said. 'Now, who is your doctor?'

'Dr Cudigan.'

'Oh, we know him well. Now, I am going to phone him and ask him whether it would be better for him to come here, or for you to go to him, or for you to go home and let him call there.'

She went into the hall, followed by Elizabeth. Nora was afraid to close her eyes, afraid that she would fall asleep here in the Gibneys' living room. She thought that if she could go home now she would sleep for the rest of the day. But she knew that if she did, then she would not sleep again that night or she would have more dreams. It would be better to get sleeping pills from Dr Cudigan even if he thought they would not be good for her with the painkillers. She touched her chest and arms and could feel the residual pain in the muscles. It was taking its time to fade.

'Dr Cudigan is out on a call,' Peggy Gibney said when she returned. 'He does the County Home so he might be there. I don't know who it was who answered the phone. I thought of phoning Dr Radford instead. He's our doctor.'

The implication that there was something wrong with Dr Cudigan and that somehow Dr Radford was superior to him woke Nora up.

'Oh, no,' she said. 'You see, I know the Radfords socially, so I would really rather not.'

Peggy Gibney sat back in her chair. The idea that someone working in the office saw her doctor socially seemed to offend her.

'I think the best idea would be if Elizabeth drove you home and then I'll arrange for Dr Cudigan to call as soon as he can. But we'll have tea first. You were pale as a ghost when you came in. And Elizabeth will let Thomas know you have taken ill. I mean, you might be better tomorrow. Thomas always likes to know what's going on. And I wish I knew what was keeping that Child of God Maggie Whelan with the tea.'

When tea came, they sat in silence. Somehow or other, Nora sensed that she had not been grateful enough for being taken into the house rather than being sent home or to the doctor directly.

'Elizabeth, can you spare a few moments now to drive Mrs Webster across the town?' Peggy Gibney asked.

The way she said 'across the town' suggested somewhere quite far away from her own comfortable place of residence.

'My mother,' Elizabeth said as soon as they were in the car, 'is marvellous, isn't she? She could run the country. She's the real power behind the throne.'

Nora nodded. She was too tired to think of anything to say. She wondered about sleeping pills. They were dangerous things to have in a house. She determined that if she had to take them, she would keep the bottle of pills in her wardrobe and throw them out as soon as she was back sleeping normally again.

Once she was in the house, she found that she had forgotten if she had had any further conversation with Elizabeth Gibney in the car. They must have talked about something, she thought, and she must have thanked her for driving her home. Or perhaps she had slept in the car; the journey was blank; she had no idea what route they had taken home.

She went into the back room and sat in her armchair and slept, woken only by an insistent banging at the front door. When she checked the time, she saw that it was only eleven o'clock so it could not be Conor or Fiona. And then she remembered that they had a key anyway. When she went to answer the door she heard a voice calling her name and recognized Dr Cudigan.

'Oh, thank God,' he said. 'I was going to get the Fire Brigade. I got an urgent message from Peggy Gibney. She phoned all over town looking for me. She phoned Sister Thomas in the St John of God, and she found me. There's an old man very sick in there.'

She brought him into the front room and told him that she could not sleep.

'It happens to us all,' he said. 'We all need less sleep as we get older.'

'I have not slept at all,' she said.

'For how long?'

'I told you. It's eight days since I started on those other pills.'

'I could prescribe sleeping pills for you, but I don't like doing it. Have you tried giving up tea and coffee?'

A surge of anger came over her.

'I am really at my wit's end,' she said. She wondered if Dr Cudigan treated his female patients in a different way to his male patients.

'Peggy Gibney led poor Sister Thomas to believe that you were at death's door. I'll have to find her now and tell her that you are in one piece.'

'I can't sleep,' she said.

'I'll give you a prescription for sleeping pills. One pill will knock you out for five or six hours. Don't stay on them for too long, or you'll get used to them, and don't drive when you're taking them, or maybe just slowly around the town, but don't tell anyone I said that. And come over and see me in about a week and we'll check how you are getting on. Don't take a pill until tonight and try and stay awake if you can until then.'

'And should I go on taking the painkillers?'

'Until I see you next week.'

She was almost going to remind him that he had told her that she could not take both.

'You're very good to come up,' she said.

'Sister Thomas told me that they do an exposition of the Blessed Sacrament every day at three o'clock and she goes into the nuns' chapel and she prays for you every day. She's the holiest of them all, I think. And she went out and found me today when Peggy Gibney phoned her.'

'Peggy Gibney,' Nora said and sighed.

'I hear she sits in that house being waited on hand and foot,' Dr Cudigan said. 'Women have it very easy.'

'It was nice of her to phone,' Nora said.

Dr Cudigan gave her the prescription and left.

When Fiona and Conor came in, she did not tell them that she had come home early from work. She drank a cup of coffee in the kitchen and this gave her enough energy so she could talk as though there were nothing wrong. As Fiona was going back to school, she handed her the prescription and asked her if she would get the pills in Kelly's on the way home.

'When did you get the prescription?' Fiona asked her.

'Dr Cudigan sent it over to Gibney's,' she said.

'Are you all right? You started saying something and then you stopped.'

'I'm fine. It's just the pills have me a bit groggy.'

'And what's the prescription for?'

'It's for sleeping pills,' she said. 'I've been having trouble sleeping.'

When they had gone, she went back to her armchair. She could feel her heart racing and she was having difficulty breathing. It occurred to her that putting on some music might soothe her. She stood up and crossed the room and flicked through the records, but none of them was what she wanted, they were too distant and loud and full of their own passions, but when she found the Archduke Trio she looked at the jacket sleeve again and thought that even if the music made no difference she could dream of being young, as the players were, and free. If she listened carefully, she thought, and followed each note of the cello as though she were playing it, the music might distract her and keep her awake.

The notes the cello played caused her to sit up almost involuntarily. The players were moving towards a melody but hinting at it and then resisting. She loved the groaning sound the cello made. A few times, when her mind wandered, she forced it back again, to listen to every note, every suggestion of the melody. She smiled when they played it out bravely before letting in the sadness, the hesitancy.

When the slow movement began, she noticed that she was struggling for breath every few seconds. She closed her eyes and began to shiver. It felt much colder in the room and she wondered if she should light a fire. She decided not to move, to sit and listen, to follow the deep tones of the cello.

It was when the slow movement swung into the faster movement as though it had been going there all along, and the music became almost joyous, that she heard a noise upstairs. She went across the room quietly and opened the door, hardly making a sound. She listened. Something moved upstairs; someone was moving a piece of furniture. No one could be upstairs, she was certain. She had seen Fiona and Conor going out and they could not have returned without her hearing.

A sound came again, louder. She thought that maybe she should go next door and see if the O'Connors were there, and if Tom would come in with her to see what the noise upstairs was. She made sure that the front door was locked. She checked the back door too. There was silence for a while, but it was broken as the noise came again, and louder, of furniture being pulled across the floor. She went quickly up the stairs, calling out.

'Who is it? Who is there?'

Her bedroom door was closed. She usually left it open when she was not inside. She listened again. A sound came. Suddenly, she winced in pain and lifted her hand up to look. She had driven the fingernails in so hard that there was blood on the palm of her hand. When she heard the noise now, it was more like a voice. She opened the door of the bedroom.

'Maurice!' she called out.

He was sitting in the rocking chair by the window, facing her.

'Maurice,' she whispered.

He was wearing the sports coat with green and blue flecks that they had bought in Funge's in Gorey, and grey slacks and a grey shirt and a grey tie. He smiled for a moment as she pushed the door closed with her back. He was like he had been before he got sick.

'Maurice, can you speak? Can you say something?'

He gave her the shy smile he had, curling his lip.

'The music's sad,' he whispered.

'Yes, the music is sad,' she said. 'But not always.'

'Sister Thomas,' he said. His voice was fainter now.

'Yes, she prays for us every day. She found me on the strand in Ballyvaloo.'

He nodded.

'I felt you were there, but not for long. That's the only time.'

'I know.'

His voice was softer than she had ever heard it.

'Your voice,' she said and smiled, 'has changed.'

He looked at her sadly as if to say that there was no adequate reply he could make.

'Maurice, can you stay a while?'

He shifted then and his presence was less complete, his down-turned face more blurred and even the colours on the jacket less vivid to her.

'Are you . . . ?' she began. 'I mean, is there anything . . . ?'

He shrugged and almost smiled.

'No,' he whispered. 'No.'

'Will we be all right? I don't know if we will be all right.'

He did not reply.

'Will Fiona be all right?'

'Yes, she will.'

'And Aine, will she be all right?'

He nodded.

'And Donal?'

'Yes, Donal.'

'And Conor?'

He lowered his head and seemed not to hear her.

'Maurice, will Conor be all right?'

His eyes appeared to have filled with tears.

'Maurice, I need you to answer. Will Conor be all right?'

'Don't ask,' he whispered, his voice hoarse and faltering. 'Don't ask.'

When she edged towards him, he put his hands out, indicating that she should not move closer.

'Did you know . . . ?' she began.

'Yes, yes,' he said.

'It was only when you were sick I knew . . .'

'Yes, yes.'

'And did you ever regret . . . ?'

'Regret?' he asked, his voice louder.

'Us?'

'No, no.'

He smiled again, and then the expression on his face was puzzled.

'Maurice, is there something else?'

'The other one. There is one other,' he said.

'You mean Jim?'

'No.'

'Margaret?'

'No.'

'Who?'

'The other one.'

'There is no other one.'

'There is.'

'Maurice, give me a name. There is no other one.'

He covered his face with his hands. She watched him; he was in pain. Then he looked at her. He seemed ready to smile again, but he did not smile.

'Maurice, stay a while.'

He shook his head.

'Maurice, is it the music? If I play the music, will you come another time?'

'No, not the music.'

'Maurice, tell me about Conor. Is there something . . . ?'

'There is one other.'

'Maurice, there is no one else. Tell me a name.'

He faded again, and she heard a low gasp from him.

'Maurice, will you be there when I come?'

'No one knows,' he said. 'No one.'

She heard the sound then of a car horn beeping on the street. She was lying across the bed with all her clothes on. When she sat up the room was empty. When she crossed the room and touched the rocking chair it rocked gently back and forth on the old springs. She put her hand where he had been sitting but there was no heat from it, nor any sign that anyone had been there.

Downstairs, she found the keys to the house and the keys to the car. She put a coat over her arm and walked out, closing the door behind her. As she started the car, she wondered where she would go, but it hardly mattered. It was only when she found herself veering off the Dublin Road towards Bunclody that she knew that she was going towards her Aunt Josie's. She concentrated hard on the road ahead, forcing herself to stay awake. As she turned away from the river up the steep hill towards Josie's, she wondered what she should say, how she could explain why she was here. There was a gateway on the left with space for a car or a tractor to pull in. She parked the car there and switched off the engine. She put her head back and closed her eyes.

She wondered if she should turn now and drive back into the town, but she felt that she would not be able to concentrate enough on the driving. She would rest here for a while, she thought, hope that Josie or John or John's wife would not pass and see her. She would sleep for a while and then drive somewhere else. She did not know where.

When she woke, John was rapping on the window. She started in fright when she saw him and then pulled down the window of the car.

'I couldn't think who it was for a minute,' he said and smiled. He had left the engine of his tractor running.

'I was having a rest,' she said, although she knew that this would make no sense to him.

'My mother's in the garden,' he said.

'Are you going up to the house?' she asked.

'I am,' he said.

'I'll follow you then.'

Once she was sitting in Josie's kitchen, John put on the kettle and went in search of his mother. Nora moved from being sharply awake, noticing colours in the room and hearing sounds outside, to feeling drowsy and then feeling the desire to sleep, to lie down anywhere and sleep.

When John and Josie came into the room, she could see the look of concern on their faces. John stood at the door for a moment and then withdrew. Josie was wearing her work clothes and began to pull off her gardening gloves.

'Has something happened?'

'Maurice came back. He was in the room upstairs, our bedroom.'

'What?'

'He spoke to me, Josie. He said things.'

As the kettle boiled, Josie moved to turn it off.

'Nora, what is wrong with you?'

'I can't sleep, and then when I sleep . . .'

'Are you on some medication?'

'Yes, I strained my arm and the muscles in my chest. I'm on pain-killers.'

'How long is it since you have slept?'

'More than a week. Sometimes I can fall into the deepest sleep but it never lasts.'

'Have you told the doctor this?'

'Yes, and Fiona is collecting sleeping pills for me on her way home from school.'

Josie filled the teapot with hot water.

'Maurice was in the room and he spoke,' Nora said.

'Did you tell this to anyone else?'

'No, I came out here. I have nowhere else to go.'

'John says that you were fast asleep in the car.'

'I don't know what I'm going to do,' Nora said. 'And he said, Maurice said, when I asked him if Conor would be all right . . . he told me not to ask. What did that mean?'

'You were dreaming, Nora. No one appeared.'

'He was in the room,' Nora said. 'I know what a dream is, but he was in the room. And he said –'

'He was not in the room.'

'He was, he was, he was.' She began to rock back and forth, crying. 'If I could be with him . . .'

'What did you say?'

'If I could be with him, that's what I said.'

Josie and John led her to the bedroom upstairs and gave her a nightdress. Josie came in a minute later with a glass of water.

'Now, this pill is going to put you fast asleep, and when you wake you'll feel groggy for a while, but I'll be here and just call out and don't try and walk. These are the most powerful sleeping pills you can get so we use them carefully. And I need the key to your house.'

Nora handed it to her.

'Now, I am going into the town to settle some things and John will check on you.'

'And Conor . . . ?'

'You don't worry about Conor or anyone. Your job is to sleep.'

When she woke she felt a heaviness in her limbs. She tried to move her arms but they were sore and her chest was sore. She wondered where the painkillers were. She thought she had them in the drawer in the table beside the bed but she was not sure. When she reached for the table, she found nothing. It was not her own room. It was dark and there was a faint sound coming from somewhere but she could not think what it was. And then she remembered Josie and the pill and the feel of the sheets and the big pillow and the soft mattress. She wondered if there was a lamp and reached out in case there was a bedside table further away from the bed but there did not seem to be one.

She called out and Josie came, turning on a lamp that was near the window.

'I came and looked at you earlier,' Josie said, 'and you were fast asleep.'

'What day is it?'

'Friday.'

'What time?'

'Nine o'clock.'

'I have to go. Conor . . . and Donal tomorrow.'

'You are going nowhere. Conor is fine. I told him that you were staying out with us for the weekend and I called in on Margaret and he is going to spend the day there working on his photographs. And Una is going to visit Donal tomorrow and maybe Fiona will go with her. And Una and Seamus will also make sure that Conor is all right and maybe Conor will come out here on Sunday if you are well enough. And I phoned Sister Thomas, you know I often talk to her if I am worried about you, and she'll talk to the Gibneys and tell them that you'll be back as soon as you're better. And I have the sleeping tablets that Dr Cudigan prescribed and the other pills that Fiona was able to find. They are very strong painkillers. You wouldn't give them to a horse. But maybe you needed them. So everything is taken care of. All you have to do is sleep, that's all you have to do. And, in return, when I get sick, you can come out and look after me when the others get fed up of me. That's what we are all for.'

Josie took the dressing gown from the back of the door.

'You must get up now. I am going to run a bath for you and I'll put on music so you don't fall asleep in the bath and it would be best if you leave the bathroom door open. And then we'll have something nice to eat and you can go back to bed and see if you can sleep naturally, and if you can't I'll leave a pill out for you.'

'Please don't put on any music,' Nora said.

'All right, but don't fall asleep in the bath.'

'I won't.'

Nora sat in the room downstairs as Josie made spaghetti with a tomato sauce. She opened a bottle of wine.

'I bought that bottle in Dublin,' she said. 'We'll have a glass or two tonight. They say you shouldn't drink alcohol with sleeping pills, but I often find the opposite is the case.'

'You don't believe me about Maurice,' Nora said.

'No, I don't.'

'It was him all right, everything about him.'

'We barely manage, all of us,' Josie said, 'to see what's there. That's the hardest thing, although no one would tell you that. If we could just look at what's there!'

'You don't believe in anything . . . ?'

'I get through the day, Nora. That's all I do. And I leave everything else to itself.'

'Conor, he said . . .'

'He said nothing, Nora. Conor is perfect now, but he has an eye and ear for trouble so don't trouble him.'

Nora suddenly felt trapped. She wondered where the car keys were and the keys of the house and thought that, if she could find them, as soon as Josie went away, she would leave the house and drive home.

'Oh, and make sure you take the painkillers before you go to sleep,' Josie said. 'Poor Fiona was very worried about you, and she's glad you are out here. Those two girls are a credit to you. And Aine is gone all political. She got that from the Webster side. Our side had none of that. And Fiona showed me the back room and it's beautiful. It will be a lovely room for you.'

'Maurice asked if there was not one other, but I couldn't think of anyone else. I don't know what he meant. But you believe I dreamed it all?'

'I do.'

'But it was real. I mean, he was real.'

'Of course he was. But he is gone. You have to make yourself understand that he is gone and he will not be back.'

The wine made her drowsy again and, as she settled back into the bed, she could not imagine that she would ever return to normal and not want to sleep all the time. She took the sleeping pill and the painkiller before she turned out the lamp.

When she woke again the room was bright and she could hear the sound of a radio and dishes clattering and crows battling around one of the old trees. She looked at the bedside table but there was no clock. She lay back and sighed.

All day she moved between the sitting room and the bedroom. Josie came and went; since it was a fine day she wanted to do some planting in her garden. In the afternoon, John and his wife came but they did not stay long. Josie had brought fresh clothes for her from the house in case she wanted to dress but she stayed in the night-gown and the dressing gown and her bare feet.

As the light began to wane Josie came and sat with her.

'I know this is none of my business,' she said, 'but yesterday when I was looking for clothes for you I was shocked to see that the wardrobe is full of Maurice's clothes. Jackets and trousers and suits and ties and shirts, and even his shoes.'

'I didn't have the heart to throw them out. I just couldn't do it.'

'Nora, he is more than three years dead. You will have to do it soon.'

'That will be the end then, will it?'

'Do the children know his clothes are still there?'

'The children don't snoop in my wardrobe, Josie.'

'Your mother would smile now if she heard you.'

'My mother?'

'An ungrateful child is like a serpent's tooth, that's what she used to say.'

'And that was on a good day,' Nora laughed.

Nora lay on the sofa and slept. When she woke it was dark. She went downstairs and found that Josie was setting the table for four.

'Who is coming?' she asked.

'I asked Catherine to come. She should be here soon.'

'I don't want to see Catherine.'

'Well, what you want or don't want doesn't matter. Do something to your hair and put on fresh clothes because I invited your friend Phyllis as well. You can't sleep all the time.'

When the four of them had finished their main course, another car pulled up outside. Nora went to the window and saw Una.

'It's Una. She's meant to be with Conor,' she said.

'She said she would leave Conor with Fiona so as not to worry him,' Josie said.

She poured more wine when Una joined them at the table.

Nora moved into one of the armchairs and began to doze, comforted by the animated sounds of the voices around her. When she woke, she found that they were talking about her.

'She was a demon,' Catherine said. 'That's all I have to say about her.'

'Was she?' Phyllis asked.

'And then she met Maurice. From the first time she went out with him she was a new person. I mean, she didn't exactly become meek and mild. But she changed.'

'I suppose she was happy,' Una said.

'Maurice was the love of her life,' Catherine said.

'Oh, that's true all right,' Josie interjected.

'She could still be a demon, though,' Una said. 'Do you remember the time she wouldn't speak to my mother? We all lived in the house and she wouldn't speak to her or look at her.'

'Oh, I remember it well,' Josie said. 'Myself and your Aunt Mary, God rest her, were at our wit's end about it.'

'And why wouldn't she speak to her?' Phyllis asked.

'Maurice had a brother who died of TB,' Catherine said. 'He was a lovely boy and it was a very sad thing and I don't know who our mother said it to, but she said to someone when Nora started going out with Maurice that she was afraid that Maurice might have TB as well. Or something anyway about Maurice and TB. And then the person told someone who told Nora. And she got it into her head that our mother was going around the town talking about Maurice and his family and TB and she just stopped talking to her.'

'Nothing would bring her down from her high horse,' Catherine said.

'And then,' Una went on, 'Father Quaid found out. He was very friendly with our mother because she was in the choir and often sang in the cathedral. And he asked her about it and she confirmed it. So he waylaid Nora one day when it was coming up to Christmas and he instructed her to stop all the nonsense and they agreed that she would wish her mother a happy Christmas on Christmas Day and that would be the end of it.'

'We were relieved,' Una said. 'I think the whole town was relieved, or the ones who knew us.'

'And what happened?' Phyllis asked.

'She waited,' Catherine said, 'until my mother was bending over to take the turkey out of the oven and she leaned over and wished her a happy Christmas, but it looked as though she was wishing a happy Christmas to her backside.'

'I remember I nearly burst,' Una said.

Nora began to laugh.

'Look, she's awake,' Phyllis said.

'We were just talking about you,' Catherine said.

'I heard every word,' Nora replied.

Once she went back to work, Nora began to sleep through the night. Slowly, the pains went away. She told no one else what had happened in the bedroom. She supposed that it had been, as Josie said, a dream. But it seemed stronger than a dream. At night, when she turned off the light it comforted her to think that Maurice had recently been in this room, and vividly so. She tried not to whisper to him, but she could not stop herself and this, she felt, made her sleep more easily and got her through the night.

At work, she looked forward to going home and spending time alone in the room she had decorated. She borrowed books from the library and, with the fire lit and the lamps all on in the evening, she read or left her mind empty. She liked it when Fiona went out and she was alone in the house with Conor in the front room doing his homework until he would come in and sit on the sofa in the back room and look through his photographs or read the magazines and manuals that Donal had let him have. Unlike Fiona, who often found the music irritating, Conor barely noticed it. She felt that he associated it with ease or comfort or lack of tension, but sometimes she found that he was studying her, and his look was still worried and unsettled. He would always be like this, she thought; he would become a man who worried about things, who watched the world for signs that something would go wrong.

In Dublin one day, she found there was a sale in May's record shop on Stephen's Green; a large collection of Deutsche Grammophon had been reduced to less than a pound each. She bought as many as she could carry. When she met Aine and Fiona in the National Gallery, they selected prints from the gift shop that she could hang in the back room. When she went home she sent them to be framed. Someone else could hammer in the nail and hang them when they came back, she thought.

Josie arranged that Catherine and Una would come with boxes and empty out the wardrobe where she kept Maurice's clothes. She waited until a weekend when Fiona was gone to Dublin with Paul, and she was sure that Aine was not coming home. She arranged with Margaret that Conor would have his tea with her and stay late. In the early afternoon, she drove to Wexford. She had written to Donal to say that she would be early. She bought him chicken and chips in the chip shop closest to the school and also a few bottles of Miranda lemon, which was his favourite. He preferred, she knew, if she came with Conor or Fiona or Aine, so they would talk and argue among themselves when he wanted to be silent. When he was on his own with her, there was always a strain. He resented it if she gave him advice.

'D-do you know about the p-paradox of f-faith?' he asked her when he was finished eating.

'I'm not sure I do,' she said.

'F-father Moorehouse gave us a sermon on it. J-just a s-small g-group who are d-doing special re-re-religious st-studies.'

'What is it?' she asked.

'In order to b-believe, you have to b-believe,' he said. 'Once you have faith, then you can b-believe more, but you c-can't b-believe until you b-begin to b-believe. That f-first b-belief is a mystery. It is like a g-gift. And then the r-rest is r-rational, or it c-can be.'

'But it can't be proved,' she said. 'You can only sense it.'

'Yes, b-but he says it's not like p-proof. It's n-not adding two and two, but more like adding light to w-water.'

'That sounds very deep.'

'No, it's simple really. It explains things.'

She noticed that he had not stammered on the last sentence.

'You must have s-something first,' he went on. 'I suppose th-that is what he is saying.'

'And if you don't?'

'That is the atheist position.'

She looked down at the roofs of houses and the spires of churches and the calm light over the harbour beyond them. Donal was sixteen, and she thought how less certain everything would seem as the years went on for him, and how important it was for her to say nothing that might cause him to know that, since he did not need to know it yet.

Since she had come early, he made it clear that he understood she had something to do, and he told her that if he had an hour free now, when many of the others were playing hurling or football or walking around the field surreptitiously smoking, he would have the darkroom to himself, and there was a new sort of photographic paper, not glossy, which he wanted to experiment with. She could not work out whether he was dismissing her because he wanted her to go, or whether he was making it easy for her. She sat in the car and watched him through the side mirror walking confidently back into the school.

*

At home, she sat listening to Victoria de los Ángeles singing Schubert and Fauré and then to a recording of Beethoven's Violin Concerto, waiting for Catherine and Una to arrive.

She hoped that when they had finished the work they would leave; they would take Maurice's clothes, she hoped, and not tell her what they were going to do with them. Once they had gone, she would have some hours alone, with the fire lighting and music. She would maybe find a book that had belonged to Maurice and keep it close to her. And she would wait for Conor to come in and then go to bed soon after he did. She would make Catherine and Una tea so that they would not complain about her too much to Josie and to their husbands, but she would not, she decided, give them anything to eat. That might encourage them not to linger once they had finished what they had come to do. She was sure that they were somewhere together now with much to say about her and about Josie and about having their Saturday filled up in this way.

When they came, she met them at the front door and did not invite them into the back room.

'All his things are in that wardrobe beside the window,' she said. 'There's nothing else in that wardrobe.'

They looked at her, expecting her to follow them upstairs, but instead she returned to the back room, adding more logs and briquettes to the fire and changing the Violin Concerto for some calmer piano music and turning the sound down low. What they had come to do was easy; it was a question only of piling everything from the wardrobe into the bags and boxes and taking them downstairs and then to the car. She had not opened the wardrobe since soon after he died, when she had put the rest of his clothes into it. Moths may well have eaten holes in the wool, but the shoes would be as they were, the laces as he had left them, and there might even be chalk from the classroom in the pockets of some of the jackets. She almost felt sorry that she was letting it all go, or that she had not done it gradually herself over time. She wished now that they would do it more quickly. She could hear their feet on the floorboards above. They seemed to be moving around too much.

*

When they had the bags and boxes full and in the hall and had gone back upstairs to check the wardrobe one last time, a knock came at the door. Nora was very surprised to see Laurie O'Keefe. Laurie had never come to the house before. For a second, Nora could not think what to do. Somehow, the world of Laurie would not match in any way with the world Catherine and Una inhabited; they would think Laurie was mad. She was almost going to say to Laurie that this was a very bad time, but she was prevented by Laurie's eagerness and friendliness. Laurie also seemed out of breath. She put her sitting in the back room as Catherine and Una came downstairs and she introduced them. She made tea while she wondered how long Laurie and her sisters might now stay.

'I don't like calling unannounced on anyone,' Laurie said. 'Do you?'

She looked at Catherine and Una and then at Nora.

'I wish Nora would get a phone,' Catherine said.

'Well, there's that,' Laurie said. 'But some people don't like phones.'

'And others can't afford them,' Nora said as she sat down.

'Or they prefer buying records,' Una said.

'Indeed,' Nora said.

'Well, I have good news,' Laurie said when the tea was poured, 'and I wanted to let you know. I know it's a hard day for you, Nora, so I weighed it up and thought good news would not be any harm on a day like today.'

'How did you know about today?' Nora asked.

'I hate mysteries so I'll tell you. Your aunt told Sister Thomas and she told me, and it was she who advised me to come.'

'She's an awful busybody,' Una said.

'That's one way of putting it, all right,' Laurie said. 'Anyway, what happened is that someone died and we don't know who it is but she left some money in her will for a recital of religious music in Wexford or Kilkenny or Carlow. Whoever it is, she must have had a lovely soul to have such a thought, as well as the money of course. So they approached Frank Redmond and, even though I am not speaking to him, he approached me to organize the choir, as he is too busy for that, and it occurred to me that it was all a gift from God.'

She stopped and looked at all three women as though they would understand. Nora saw that Catherine, who was the most religious of them, was watching Laurie intently.

'It is the twenty-fifth anniversary,' Laurie spoke very dramatically, 'of the convent being reopened and the church reconsecrated after the war. The Nazis took it from us and unspeakable things happened there.'

'Laurie was a Sacred Heart nun in France during the war,' Nora said.

'And we had a great reverend mother,' Laurie said. 'She was from a very old family in France. It was 1947 and she said we were going to put on a concert to thank the Lord for the end of the war and to celebrate the reopening of our church and our return to the old building. We had a marvellous choir even then, although we had lost so many men in the war, and women too. She wanted to perform Brahms's German Requiem, she said, as both a thanksgiving and an expiation, and she would play the piano, and she chose the best soprano and baritone to do the lead parts, and then the nuns and the people of the village would be the choir. Oh, the people protested and there were nuns too who wanted to protest, but of course we had sworn a vow of obedience. But it was hard, even for the nuns. The German language had been a nightmare for all of Europe, and it was the one thing that no one wanted to hear, let alone sing in. And on top of that, it's not a Catholic piece, but that was part of her dream too, to reach out to the other side. None of the men would come until Mère Marie-Thérèse went to one of them, the one she knew best. He had a beautiful voice but he had lost his two sons in the war, one of the bodies was never found, and his wife had died and his own heart was very hard. And she asked him to come to the newly consecrated chapel and pray with her. She asked him to pray, that's all she did. She asked him to pray.'

Laurie stopped, as though she had now said enough.

'And what did he do?' Catherine asked.

'He implored her to sing a Catholic requiem in French for the

French dead, but she refused. We will sing to honour God who is all-forgiving, that's what she said, and we will sing in German to show that we come made in God's likeness, and we too can forgive. She went every day to the man's house and prayed with him. She brought two novices with her.'

'And did he agree?' Catherine asked.

'No, he never did, but enough of the others did. She went to see all of them. And then in October 1947 we performed the concert. I always believe that day was the beginning of the peace. When it was hard to forgive, we sang in German and our words went up, they went up. That is where they went.'

A log slipped and sank in the fire and began to burn brightly. No one said anything for a minute.

'And you were in France in those years?' Catherine asked.

'And now, to mark the twenty-five years, I'm going to put together a choir and we'll rehearse the German Requiem in Wexford town and Frank Redmond will organize a small orchestra or two pianos and the two lead singers. And your sister Mrs Webster is the first person I want in my choir.'

'Nora?' Catherine asked.

'Yes, she's my best pupil.'

'Well, I'll tell you something now,' Catherine said, 'if my mother was alive she would be amazed because she was a wonderful singer and she knew Nora was too, but Nora would never sing.'

'We all change, Catherine,' Laurie said.

Catherine looked at her sceptically.

'Now, I must go,' Laurie said. 'I just came over to tell you that.'

When she had gone, Catherine and Una returned with Nora to the back room.

'Is she for real?' Catherine asked.

'Oh, I've heard about her, and she is for real,' Una said. 'She's very well thought of.'

'She has been a very good friend,' Nora said.

'And are you really going to sing in a choir?' Catherine asked.

'I'll do my best,' Nora said.

They carried all the boxes to the car while Nora stood in the hallway keeping the door open for them. When everything was done, Una went upstairs one more time and came down with a small wooden box, which was locked.

'This was at the bottom of the wardrobe,' she said. She shook it but there was no sound.

Nora shuddered. She knew what it was.

'I don't have the key any more,' she said. 'Can one of you help me to open it?'

'It needs to be prised open, but that will ruin the box,' Catherine said.

'That's fine,' Nora said.

Catherine tried using a metal tool she found in the kitchen, but it did not work.

'I need it opened,' Nora said.

'Well, I can't do it.'

'Una,' Nora said, 'would you take it next door to Tom O'Connor? He has every tool under the sun.'

When Una had gone, Catherine went to the bathroom. Nora could see that she was upset by having to handle Maurice's clothes and she understood that her sister did not want to be alone with her. Catherine did not come downstairs again until Una had returned.

'He found it hard enough to open,' she said. 'He had to split the wood.'

Nora put it on the table beside her and went back to the hall where her sisters were.

'Will you be all right now on your own?' Catherine asked.

'Conor will be back soon,' she said.

As they both found their coats, she waited for them.

'I could never have done that myself,' she said.

'If we'd known about it, we would have done it before,' Una said.

She stood at the door then and watched them go, watched Catherine carefully reversing the car, and all of Maurice's clothes, each item bought without any knowledge of what would happen to him, being taken somewhere to be thrown out, or given away. She closed the front door and went into the back room again and emptied the contents of the wooden box.

All of Maurice's letters to her in the years before they married were there. She had kept them in the box, locked away. She remembered how shy his tone was when he wrote to her. The letters were often short, just suggesting a place in the town where they might meet, and a time.

She did not have to look at them; she knew them. He often talked about himself as though he were someone else, saying that he had met a man who had told him how fond he was of a certain girl, or how he had a friend who walked home from seeing his girlfriend and all he thought was how much he would like to see her again soon, or how he would like to go to Ballyconnigar with her and walk along the cliffs at Cush and maybe have a swim with her if the weather was good.

She knelt down and slowly fed the letters into the fire. She thought about how much had happened since they were written and how much they belonged to a time that was over now and would not come back. It was the way things were; it was the way things had worked out.

When Conor came home he noticed the half-burned wooden box in the grate among the logs and the coal and the briquettes. He asked what it was.

'Just something I was clearing out,' she said.

He looked at it suspiciously.

'I am going to be in a choir,' she said.

'In the cathedral?'

'No, in a different choir. In Wexford.'

'I thought that man didn't like you.'

'Well, they have changed their minds.'

'And what are you going to sing?'

'Brahms's German Requiem.'

'Is that a song?'

'It's a series of songs, but for a lot of voices.'

He seemed to think about this, weighing it up, and then he nodded. He smiled at her, satisfied, and then he went upstairs to his room. She sat alone by the fire and thought that she would put on music, something she particularly liked. She hoped that he would sit with her for a while before he went to bed. In the meantime, the house was quiet, the silence broken only by the faint noises from Conor upstairs and the crackling of wood burning slowly in the fire.

COLM TÓIBÍN

BROOKLYN

It is Ireland in the early 1950s and for Eilis Lacey, as for so many young Irish girls, opportunities are scarce. So when her sister arranges for her to emigrate to New York, Eilis knows she must go, leaving behind her family and her home for the first time.

Arriving in a crowded lodging house in Brooklyn, Eilis can only be reminded of what she has sacrificed. She is far from home – and homesick. And just as she takes tentative steps towards friendship, and perhaps something more, Eilis receives news which sends her back to Ireland. There she will be confronted by a terrible dilemma – a devastating choice between duty and one great love.

'With this elating and humane novel about an Irish girl's emigration to America, Colm Tóibín has produced a masterwork' *Sunday Times*

'The most compelling and moving portrait of a young woman I have read in a long time' Zoë Heller, *Guardian*, Books of the Year

'Full of sly fun, lovely comic observation and an almost tangible pleasure in storytelling' *Observer*